Also by Richard Harbroe Wright

Loft Island

Set on the Salcombe (Devon) Estuary in the 1950s, that near-forgotten time between the war and the swinging '60s. Rescued from a flood, Mary (11) comes to live with the father and 13 year old son who saved her, though her parents and brother were drowned. The land they farmed is now an island. Practical and emotional help with their losses comes sometimes from unlikely sources. They are faced with a variety of attitudes from authorities and friends.

The long established friendship between the children develops slowly,, innocently, with neither of them realising. Gradually life becomes stable, only to be ripped apart again.

A continuation of the story will be published in 2020, to be called
The Island and The Town

The Suspects

A light-hearted story with spikes. Faced with little to do over the summer, six mid-teen mates camp illegally. Evicted back to their home town, they soon find they have to return to camp to keep out of the way. A dog, a Dutch recluse, a town gang of adults, parents, maps and a hospital all play their part. There are brambles, nettles, blackthorns, wild swimming, self-sufficiency, fires, friendships and of course the dog. And those truffles…

CHANGE AT TIDE MILLS

Richard Harbroe Wright

Published by Richard Wright
Seaford, Sussex

books@harbroe.org

First edition 2019

ISBN 9781706113409

For Judy, with love and as always copious amounts of thanks for the eradication of mistypes, nonsense sentences and historical inaccuracies.

Thanks also to the Templemans, Seaford and Newhaven Museums and the many others locally who wittingly or unwittingly helped with information or by being themselves: no names, no pack-drill.
Front and back cover artwork is based on photos from Seaford Museum, to whom my further sincere thanks for providing so much information.
If you've not visited them at Seaford's Martello Tower (near Seaford Head) then you need to! Open at weekends – see SeafordMuseum.co.uk

To set the scene -

Setting a story in your own back yard is a daunting prospect. I remember 1963: I was fifteen, it snowed and the snow lay thick, but not thick enough in Hove to stop the bus taking me to school.

At the time I was hardly ever in Newhaven or Seaford, and knew nothing of Tide Mills. I've researched as thoroughly as I could in the interests of authenticity, but residents of my age will know the district of that time far better than I despite my best efforts.

In this story the Tide Mill is still fully operational. The cottages are occupied. The 200 year old original Buckle Inn is still thriving and the present lighthouse-like Buckle B & B doesn't exist. The old pub was demolished in 1963.

Tide Mills exists now, but as ruins. The mill actually stopped work in 1883. The working buildings were demolished in 1900 and the houses at the start of World War II. There's a glossary at the end of the book to answer most other questions.

The Catt family owned Tide Mills in real life. There is absolutely no connection between them and their conduct and the Foxes of the story. One or two other people in the story are real – even the author comes into it – though the majority are not. There will have been pupils in Seaford and Lewes schools with the names Wilson, Decks and Baker, but they are not the people in the story either.

Most buildings and businesses are real, though for privacy reasons I have not identified others – such as the Fox / Galley house in Bishopstone.

So far as I know the Sussex dialect had only just started fading away in the 1960s. It can be tedious to read your way through phonetic dialect spelling so I've used it sparingly; just enough to give a flavour and then only when spoken by the older characters. All the other locals, in the book as in real life, will have heard it and used it from birth, yet it will have started to fade because of the influence of incomers – like the Wilsons. If you're interested, try *Sussex As She Wus Spoke* by Tony Wales, or search the internet for *Sussex dialect*.

A railway line from south London to Lewes is mentioned as being due to close in 1964. The East Grinstead – Lewes line actually closed around 1960 (it's a long story). However a section soon reopened as the very non-fictional Bluebell Railway which now runs between East Grinstead and Sheffield Park, through the centre of rural mid-Sussex. A visit is highly recommended; details are at www.bluebell-railway.com. You might even find the author is your Guard. His cap has the number 268 on the front.

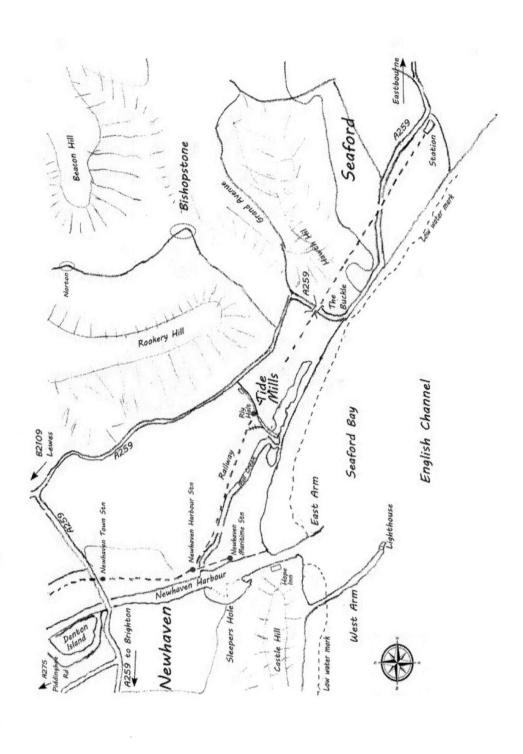

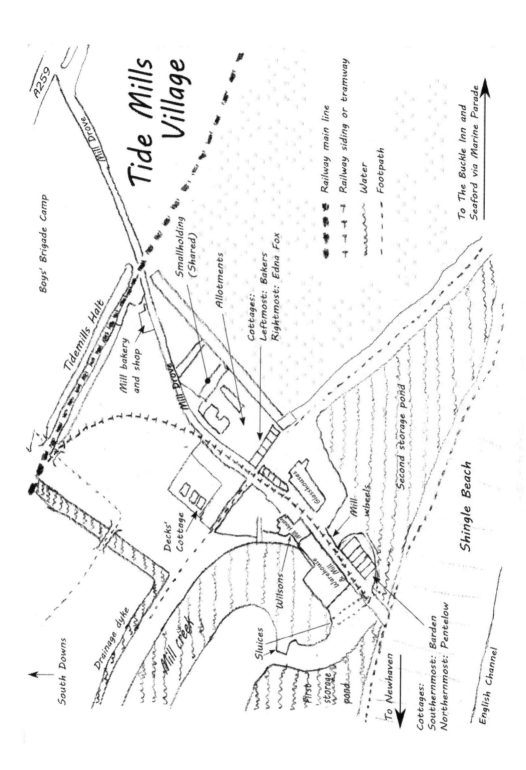

Tide Mills Village

A259

Mill Drove

Boys' Brigade Camp

Tidemills Halt

Mill bakery and shop

Mill Drove

South Downs

Drainage dyke

Mill creek

Decks' Cottage

First storage pond

Sluices

Willsons

Warehouse & Mill

Mill

Glasshouses

Mill-wheels

Second storage pond

Smallholding (Shared)

Allotments

Cottages:
Leftmost: Bakers
Rightmost: Edna Fox

Shingle Beach

To The Buckle Inn and
Seaford via Marine Parade

Railway main line
Railway siding or tramway
Water
Footpath

To Newhaven

Cottages:
Southernmost: Barden
Northernmost: Pentelow

English Channel

Contents

1 – Diverted journey

"Eastbourne! Why Eastbourne?"

It was a dim, wet, soggy morning. Owen, returned from playing football (his team lost), was depressed of spirit, damp of body, muddy of clothing and skin. And cold. Added to this he was still suffering from having had to get up for the early kick-off. London playing fields were much sought after. They were used from early morning to dusk.

He was in his room, his sanctum, slowly changing from his muddy kit and the shout from downstairs interrupted his thoughts.

"Starting for Eastbourne in half an hour. Hurry up."

That was the cause of his exclamation, to which came Max's, his father's, answer: "We told you we were going. Really, Owen, you have a memory like a sieve."

He pursed his lips in annoyance. The game had been lost, he was scarcely out of his kit on the way to a bath and was now being hassled to ready himself for a journey he didn't want to make. It wasn't as if he was a kid, either. He was nearing his fourteenth birthday and quite able to look after himself at home. Experience told him that they wouldn't allow him that freedom, but he thought he'd try.

"I don't want to go. I'm tired after the match. I'll stay here – I'll be ok."

Now his father's voice, firm: "You know you can't do that. Not in London. Not in this part of London, anyway. Come on, get ready please, and quickly."

He *was* old enough: he knew it. But he also knew his father's tone of voice. It allowed no arguments.

His arrival in the hallway twenty five minutes later, hastily bathed and changed, served only to prompt a comment from Max: "About time too. Come on, we'll miss the train."

"Train?"

"Train. How else do we travel to Eastbourne?"

"Car?"

"Still in the garage being worked on. Come on, a train journey will be a change."

Oh for goodness sake. Dirty, slow, trains. Boring. They'd travelled by train to Brighton before now and he knew what to expect. More dirt and depression, with bomb sites added for good measure. Until they reached Gatwick Airport; that at least could be interesting. They might even see one of the new Boeing 727s.

The bus took them to a station he'd only noticed when travelling through on the Victoria to Brighton train. Dad was now being mysterious, not telling him anything about the platform they were going to, so all he could do was follow like a seven year old. Finally they arrived at a quiet, almost remote, and certainly very dirty platform. His mother refused to sit on any of the platform's vacant benches as she said they would be too dirty, so the other two stood too, out of politeness.

Ten minutes later they were rewarded, not by the clatter and whine of an electric train but by a clanking, hissing, chuffing, grubby little steam engine. It appeared slowly from under the road bridge as if it had just got out of bed. Four elderly coaches emerged after it, enveloped in a cloud of steam.

Owen's mood lifted. *This* was different. The family had travelled a few times by train but never behind a steam engine. He watched, now impressed, as the tank engine clanked along the platform and was hardly surprised when both parents made their way down towards it instead of immediately boarding the nearest carriage.

It was a memorable start to a journey. The weather was still overcast. There were still a few piles of the dirty slush that had built up in places after the early months of snow and freezing weather. They were melting, but slowly. It seemed ridiculous to all of them that there should still be snow visible in April. The winter had been exceptionally harsh.

Owen barely noticed. The sound and smells of the engine had brought a smile to his face, and to Max's. Owen met his glance and his smile and knew this was for the benefit of both of them. He grinned back, suddenly happier. He knew his father had been interested in trains ever since he could remember. Max had often tried to involve his son, and lately with increasing success.

Gradually the grime and greyness of south London gave way to parks, scrubland and the countryside proper. He watched the unfamiliar names of the stations they passed through. Upper Warlingham, Woldingham; he was waiting for the next when there was a shriek from the engine, startling him, and they plunged into the darkness of a tunnel. A few seconds later the carriage lights came on. "Bit late," grunted his father.

Oxted - even the names sounded rural, thought Owen. He watched as another line peeled off to the left. More country, more fields. Dormans – which he had to read twice as it seemed at first glance like 'Dormouse' – and at last they puffed into a larger town: "East Grinstead!" shouted a porter.

"This is one of the quietest parts of the line," he was told soon after the train had been whistled away and they rumbled out of the station on to a viaduct. "In fact soon there's a line that branches off to the right, then we're on a single line almost all the way to Lewes."

"We don't go past Gatwick Airport, do we?"

"Not on this line."

Kingscote and East Hoathly stations, a tunnel, more countryside, more signs of piles of melting snow and then they slowed down yet again. There were about five cottages at Horsted Keynes, whose station seemed to have far too many platforms for so small a settlement. After a short wait the signalman gave something to the driver, they heard the whistle again, and the train restarted. Owen was intrigued to see as they left the station that a line went off to their right, as Max had said, losing itself in a wood. On their own line, the trees and bushes seemed to be almost touching the train. There were no rails other than those they were on.

A few stations and a fair amount of time later and they were in a valley with houses on the right and a town ahead. They crawled over some bridges, by some coal yards, and into Lewes station. Ahead of them was the line of green hills that his father just referred to as "The Downs" which even now bore traces of snow.

"We change here for the Eastbourne train," Max said as he led the way over a footbridge, only to be accosted, along with the few other passengers, by a porter who said curtly: "Eastbourne trains are cancelled. You need to go to Seaford and catch a bus."

They looked at each other. Owen knew his father would be annoyed at having his plans disrupted.

"What about our tickets?" he asked when he could get the man's attention.

"What about them?"

"Will they be all right for the bus?"

"Should be, Mate. Just tell the conductor what's happened." Max just continued staring at him until he withered visibly and walked away.

"Come on, darling," said Barbara. "Let's find the Seaford train."

"I'm 'Mate' to my friends at work, but not to a bloke who's meant to be representing a railway." Owen raised his eyebrows at him and Max had to laugh. "I didn't protect Atlantic convoys to be 'Mated' like that. It does looks as if we're Seaford bound, though."

To their disappointment the Seaford train was electric. And dirty. And old. It had a bellows affair in front which Owen recognised as the corridor connector. He'd never seen it just hanging loosely in the centre of the driving cab before. They got on.

"That's where we should be going," said his father, pointing to the left soon after a road bridge where a set of tracks branched off. "That's the main line to Eastbourne. I don't know this line at all. Everything's new to me from now on."

The line of hills that had been drawing nearer were now rising quite steeply, starting only a short way from the left of the train. At the train's other side was a raised bank, and the occasional glint of water told of a river. They slowed, and another station appeared. A board proudly announced "Southease". It was apparently in the middle of nowhere, though a party of young men with heavy rucksacks left the train.

"Walkers," said Max.

"What, here?" asked Owen, "There's nothing to see."

"Oh, they'll be off walking over the hills up there." His mother pointed to a green, rounded buttress of a hill that seemed to go up to the heavens. Owen had to get low down at the window to be able to see how far it reached, but the upper slopes were obscured by the outcrop at the side of the road.

The river was now more visible, meandering in places by the side of the railway. More houses started to appear on their left, and some goods yards to left and right. Their train crawled across a level crossing and Owen had a shock when he finally saw the river on his right. It was now much wider and businesslike. There were a few small boats to be seen but soon afterwards a large, dark building blocked the view. It reminded him of some of the old factories near his home.

"Newhaven Town" boasted the sign. People got off and people got on, but the train stayed.

Then with a rumble and a roar of diesel, an important looking engine passed in the opposite direction, hauling a long line of coaches that seemed about to burst with people. It was as if their train had just wanted to stop and stare at its big relation in astonishment before it left. There was a guard's whistle and they jerked into movement.

The station buildings came to an end and Owen's eyes opened wide, for there, on the river, was a ship. To him, seen so close and on a river so different from his native Thames in central London, it looked immense. Their train passed only a short distance from its towering white and blue sides, making it appear even more important. The dockside was a hive of activity, with people still busily descending the gangways. All too soon the view was blocked by another station building. "Newhaven Harbour", it said. They stopped again. Doors opened; people and cases entered. Almost immediately there was a whistle, the doors slammed and they were on their way again.

More glimpses of the ship were to be had before their line swung to the left and they encountered another level crossing. But Owen was still looking toward the docks and was intrigued to see yet another station on a separate line, this time labelled 'Newhaven Marine.' Three stations in one town, he thought. Must be a big place.

After the excitement of the little river that had become big as if it had suddenly grown up, and a ship that looked too big even to be floated by such an adult river, the mud and rank grass that followed was an anticlimax. Another river seemed to start from nowhere and run parallel with the railway before it too bent away to leave them. Fields of crops surrounded them here; with a road away to the left. But to the right, to the south, beyond a long, low bank of what looked like pebbles, was the sea. It looked as if it would be an uncomfortable walk from towel to water if you swam off the beach there.

Further on, in a grassy field near the road to his left, Owen saw regimented rows of tents with what looked like boys playing football nearby. He was once again interested, wondering what was happening.

And soon the rattly train was slowing again, stopping at what was little more than a bare concrete platform. A dilapidated sign gave the name of "Tidemills Halt". Looking around, Owen saw a large, dingy white building with a grey slate roof to his right. It was surrounded by ancient cottages. Just past its bulk there rose a white windmill. A few people, young and old, were standing looking idly at the train. Owen's eye was attracted to one, a girl who looked to be about his age. There was something elfin about her face and the way she looked sideways at the interruption to the quiet of the afternoon. He felt he wanted to ask her what she was thinking, what life was like at... what was it? Tide Mills. What did they do? Was life interesting there? Where did she go to school? Was she Grammar or Secondary?

One elderly-looking lady boarded the train, glared around and took what was by then the only available seat, across the corridor from them.

4

On noticing for the first time the sign and the buildings Max startled Owen by giving an exclamation. "I never knew there were any tide mills left working!"

The old lady overheard him. "This one's hardly working at all. That's the trouble," she muttered, half to them and half to herself. "All the big mills up country are doing the milling now."

"Why aren't people using yours?" asked Max.

"They say it's too expensive to carry it too and fro. Grain in *and* flour out. But it's still got to get to Horsebridge by road, hasn't it? Stands to reason."

"Why not use the railway?"

She snorted. "'Cos the owner, he wants to shut it down and sell the land, but no one wants to buy it 'cos they'd have to find somewhere for us to go... and we don't want to go anyhow! And they can't make us. 'Sussex wunt be druv!'"

She had a mixture of what Owen was already thinking of as a Sussex accent and an educated voice. It was strange, and he wondered at it.

"Sounds like you want someone to take the mill over who's got a bit more imagination. Shouldn't be difficult. And you could get people in to watch how it works; sightseers and such. And charge them, too."

She glared at him. The train slowed down ready for the next station: Bishopstone.

"And what d'you know about milling?" she almost snarled.

"I run a big mill in London," said Max as if it was the most natural thing in the world, "so quite a bit, really."

She jumped up and Owen thought she was going to explode at Max. But she just said "Huh. Chance'd be a fine thing," and hurriedly left the carriage to stomp back down toward the exit.

"Was it something I said?" he asked to no one in particular.

A face looked round from the seats behind them. "Couldn't help overhearing. You came out of that better than most of us – she's a difficult old girl is Mrs Fox. Family used to own it but her husband died and the family had to sell up. She doesn't get the train to Seaford 'cos she knows she'd be asked for her ticket if she did." This raised a general laugh.

"Nah. Ol' Tide Mills is finished 'less someone taks over who cares about 'er," said another voice.

There was no reply to this, mainly because people were gathering their belongings together before the train arrived at Seaford. But Owen saw Max was looking thoughtful, and Barbara was looking at him with a worried look on her face. The train slowed and at last stopped. They got off.

Seaford station proved to be somewhat scruffy, needing a long drink of paint rather than just a lick. Tickets were shown at the barrier and they were assured by the man in the hat with "Porter" on its badge that they would be accepted on the bus. "But," he continued, "one's just gone and there's not another one for half an hour."

His parents exchanged glances and shrugged. "Is it worth going to Eastbourne? We'd not have much time there with two bus journeys involved."

"How else are we going to look at estate agents, see if we could find anything suitable?"

Owen's ears pricked up, and his jaw dropped.

"WHAT? Are you thinking of moving? You never told me! You never tell me anything!"

They tactfully moved through the ticket office and out onto the street before answering. "It's not really even got that far," Barbara said. "We just said 'what about getting out of London', and the next thing Dad was planning on travelling down to Eastbourne and maybe looking there."

"And now I'm wondering about Tide Mills, and whether we could make a go of that," said Max.

"You're not really?" asked Barbara. "It looks horrible and if it's not being used much it'll be run down. And what d'you think the houses would be like there? Probably no bathrooms, all the toilets would be at the end of the gardens like your mother's used to be…"

"Hang on," his father was laughing now, "let's not jump to conclusions! It's not something to look at now. If we were to go into that we need to start at the beginning and see what the trade down here really is, and see whether the situation's as bad as that woman said. How about looking at some estate agents here, then go and have a look at the town?"

Owen was still smarting from not having been consulted about a possible move. Estate agents and walking round a town seemed really boring. On the other hand he was still wondering what the footballers were doing at the camp, and whether the girl he had seen was still there and what she and her little village were like. He thought he'd try his luck.

"If you're doing that, can I go back to Tide Mills and have a look round?" he asked. "It's only very close, so I'd be ok."

"Don't you want to come and explore, and look for houses just in case?" asked his mother. "We've never seen Seaford."

"I'd prefer to go back to Tide Mills," he said, hopeful in the absence of an instant refusal.

"Well… "

"*Thanks,* Mum," he said, seizing the advantage.

"Just a minute. What are you going to do there?" asked Max.

"Oh you know; look round, explore. Go down to the sea. Whatever. If I get bored I can come back here."

"And how would you find us?"

"I'd be ok."

"Yes, but how would you find us? No, come with us and look for a while. We need a snack, anyway. Then we can find somewhere central and arrange to meet there later, if you really want to go off on your own."

It was a compromise, and more than Owen thought he'd achieve. They found a café nearby and had their snack.

Emerging, they looked around them. The main street which stretched away to their right resembled an airier, cleaner and emptier version of one of the London shopping streets he was used to. Before that there was a crossroads, and they walked to it. More shops and a cafe appeared to the right, and an ancient, comfortable looking church with a clock face sat beyond, looking as if it had settled there centuries ago and decided not to move. Another parade of shops curved round to reveal a road parallel with the main road they'd just left. A pub was on one side and still more shops on the other. Further on was a cinema, to Owen's delight.

They decided to walk down past the church, and his parents noticed a school and looked hopeful.

"It's a junior school," said Owen thankfully.

Another pub... shops, another pub; shops... the road bent round to the left. They walked on, with Owen feeling more and more fed up.

"There's the sea!" exclaimed his mother, looking down a road to the right which had a yet another pub at the end. It was not so much the sea, just that from where they stood there appeared to be no more land. The road went along to a crossroads, then headed gently upwards to end with a wall. And over that, just sky. As one, they crossed over the road, past a more modern church, past houses of all sorts; and still there was no sign of water.

At the top there was another road, and as they reached it the sea appeared as if it had been in hiding, waiting for their inquisitiveness to bring them to it. A pebbly beach was held in by regular, dark wood breakwaters. They crossed to join a concrete promenade and stood at the railings, looking down.

For a day in late April it was quite warm, although an oddly penetrating breeze ensured that nobody overheated. After the rain of that morning the clouds had lightened and a weak sun was still trying to fight its way through them. It was almost inspiring enough to encourage people to sit on the beach. A few fishermen were hunched at the water's edge, but to Owen it seemed far from being a haven of excitement. His thoughts wandered back to the little halt and the settlement – and the girl – that he'd seen on the way at Tide Mills.

Looking along the coast to his left he saw a headland rise up into cliffs. Not that way, then. To the right... and there was a distant sea wall with a lighthouse, and a cliff beyond it. Between him and it was just visible the windmill that had overshadowed the little group of buildings by the old halt.

"I can walk there," he said. "Can I go? I'll see you back at the station."

"Walk where?" asked his father.

"Tide Mills. Look, where that windmill is."

They looked.

"Well, if you must," his mother said. "But you don't know what you might be missing."

"You can tell me later. And who knows what *you* might be missing?"

"Hmph!" said his father.

"What time will you be at the station?" his mother asked. "We want to be on our way by about six o'clock, and we need to eat before we start back."

"Oh... I'll be back about four-thirty. That all right?"

She looked at her watch. "That gives you three hours. All right, but..."

Knowing that the next words were going to be "be careful" he set off at a run, calling a brief "Bye" over his shoulder as he did.

He was glad to be on his own, and running. Running along the promenade where a low wall bounded the road to his right, and the railings on his left protected walkers from a drop to the beach. Over the road were some old looking houses and what looked like a pub – it was called the Viking. Outside it were some people not very much older than him, and they seemed to be holding beer mugs, to his surprise. He sped past them and another pub where there were a few, slightly older people drinking. He stopped for a rest and looked over the edge of the promenade. Would it be quicker to run along the beach? No: all pebbles.

It was a longer journey than he thought. Nothing much to the left, apart from the sea and the wooden groynes down into it. The other side seemed to offer a large recreation ground, and he could see the top of rugby goals. Houses started again past it, and nothing much happened until the road and the promenade separated, the road rising but his way continuing on the flat past some benches.

He paced himself. It would be too far to run all the way; he was a sprinter and middle distance runner, not a mile man.

Further on, the road rejoined the promenade and ran alongside it. There was another pub, old, comfortable in its surroundings but in need of some repairs and a great deal of paint. He saw its name on the water-stained sign with some puzzlement: "Buckle Inn".

Shortly after it, the road and its traffic veered away to the right and eventually under a railway bridge. The mill lay straight ahead. In the distance was the cliff, and the sea wall stretched out from it and ended with its lighthouse. Beyond it, the sky was brighter. There was a small patch of blue, he noticed with hope.

A concrete path led on, parallel with the low bank of shingle beyond which, he thought, were the beach and the sea. To his surprise there were railway tracks set in the concrete, visible at times, though they were so rusty that he knew he had no danger from a train. Despite their obvious age and condition he found himself checking over his shoulder to make sure, and smiled at his doubt.

Low plants hugged the ground up to the shingle. Higher, prickly looking scrub partly obscured his view to the right, but he saw glimpses of a long, wide expanse of water with dark mud between it and the encircling scrub..

It all looked somehow desolate, despite the thinning cloud, the lightening sky. He shivered.

The path swung right to avoid some odd, square masonry piles, then left again to head for a bridge. This was obviously the entrance to Tide Mills. The bridge crossed a channel between the muddy area he had passed and another, similarly muddy lake to its left. Immediately the buildings started. On his right were small cottages and opposite was the great mass of the first of the mill buildings.

Owen crossed the bridge and slowed, looking at the old buildings with interest. A hum of distant machinery reached his ears. It meant, at least, that there was someone about. A door opened in the large building further up, on his left. A man came out and lit a cigarette, inhaled deeply and looked round. He saw Owen and smiled.

"Come to see how the other half live, have you?" It was said without sarcasm, and with a laugh, so he took it as a greeting. He grinned back, but cautiously.

"Just come to see what it's like here."

"Windy. Not busy enough. Apart from that, great."

The breeze had certainly been a feature of his run and walk along the coast.

"Sounds like the mill's working," he offered.

"Yeah… just. At least some farmers still use us."

"My Dad manages a mill."

"Does he? Where?"

"London."

"*London?* And they get trade?"

"Seem to."

"Blimey. There's hope for us yet. You'd better get him to give our guv'nor some hints."

"I'll see if I can get him to come here. I know he looked interested as we came past on the train."

"Did he now? Doesn't want to buy it, does he?"

"*Buy* it?"

"Owner who took it over isn't interested. Hardly ever comes down. Manager makes all the decisions but he's told there's no money." He stopped and looked guilty. "I'm talking too much. Shouldn't have said that."

"But if I can get my Dad down here, you could talk to him."

"Best he talks to the manager. Mr Pentelow. Get him to ask for him over there." He pointed to one of the doors which had a dilapidated sign on it saying 'Report Here'. Owen nodded. He was about to look round when a movement caught his eye. A glance up towards the mill; a girl was hobbling towards them. *The* girl. The girl he had seen from the train. She came to stand by the man, who looked fondly at her.

"My daughter, Ruth" he said.

"Hallo," said Owen, desperately thinking of something else he could add.

"Hallo. I saw you in the train."

Her father looked at her, astonished.

"You've not gone into town today, have you?"

She shook her head, still looking at Owen, but with a smile.

"*He* was in the train. *I* was just looking. *He* was looking at *me*."

She had even more of an elfin face close up, Owen decided. A slightly upturned nose, a wide, attractive smile, and a direct glaze that he found difficult to break away from. The effect was framed by curly, light brown hair.

Owen, disarmed by the ready smile, grinned back.

"I was. It was only Mrs Fox on the platform, and I could see you just watching. So I just watched back."

She laughed. Her father asked how he knew Mrs Fox.

"She heard Dad say something about the mill, and started on at him a bit. When she got off at…er…"

"Bishopstone," sighed the man, "she always does. Must take her just as long to reach the town from there as it does from here. Did she argue much?"

Owen grinned. "She was silenced a bit when Dad said he managed a mill in London."

They both laughed at that. "Takes something to shut her up when she gets going. She lives in the smallest cottage here, cooks on a range, lights the place with paraffin lamps and refuses to move."

Owen wondered what he should say to this and ended up saying nothing.

"Are there many houses here?" he asked, going back to his parents' sudden thoughts about moving from London.

"There's a few. The Manager has one, We and some of the other blokes in the mill live here with families, and Mrs Fox does of course. And there's the Mill House. That's empty 'cos the owner doesn't live here."

He nodded.

"So there'd be some room for your family," said Ruth, smiling even wider.

"Us! At the Mill House! Which one is that?"

"Come along. We'll show you."

There was a shout of "Arthur!" from the mill at Owen's back.

The man looked heavenwards. "Not a moment's peace," he said under his breath. Then, louder, to the shouter: "Coming!"

As he walked away he said over his shoulder: "Take him up and show him the old House, Ruth. If anything will put him off, the state of that will!"

The two of them watched as Ruth's dad returned to the mill. He turned at the door and waved to them.

Owen looked at Ruth. She looked back, her gaze held his as before. "What's your name?"

"Owen," said Owen.

She nodded. "Come on then!"

They passed the mill and, on the right, a larger house than the others. Ruth told him that's where the Manager lived. Further on the roadway narrowed to run between the mill building and a low wall. Owen looked over at the remains of the water.

"It's nearly spent," said Ruth. Owen's eyebrows raised.

"The water. That's what works the mill. It comes in as the tide rises and goes through the sluice near the beach, and fills all that up." She indicated the long, wide lagoon; the water he'd passed and found desolate.

"So where does it go? Under here?" He indicated the bridge.

"Yes. In there are the mill wheels. They power everything."

He nodded. On visits to his dad's mill he had seen their many millstones, all run by electricity, so that part of it was not new.

"So you can run a lot cheaper than Dad's mill," he said.

"Why?"

"His runs on electricity. You get free power."

She nodded. "S'right. And we use the windmill to power hoists and things. Here's the Mill House."

The Mill House was attached to the mill building. From where they stood it looked as if it was actually just an extension to it. But as they walked a little further on and looked back it became obvious that it was a dwelling; a quite large manor house in style. Originally it had been painted white but was now unkempt, with paint and render missing from the walls and paint peeling from window frames. But it still had an air of having been a home.

"And nobody lives in it?" asked Owen.

"Nope. Not for about ten years, they say."

"Ten years? But that's ages! Why did they go?"

She paused. "Mr Fox, the owner, died. Tide Mills was willed away to someone else but they hadn't a clue about it and sold the whole place. Mrs Fox insisted on staying in the village, but had to move from here to her tiny cottage."

"No wonder she's not very happy."

"No – especially as the new owner isn't interested in the mill and won't live in her old house."

Owen was about to comment when a door slammed shut with a crash. He looked round. On the opposite side of the pathway which ran at right angles to the road were two cottages. The nearest of them now had two boys standing uncertainly outside it, staring at Ruth and at Owen, the stranger.

"Those are the Baker kids," Ruth said. "They don't look very happy."

The boys were about 12 and 10, black haired and straight faced.

"Ruth," the elder acknowledged.

"Alan, Eric," said Ruth, more to introduce them to Owen than to tell them their names. "This is Owen. His father runs a mill in London."

Alan nodded. After a pause, so did his brother.

"Been sent to town to get some chops. When's the train?"

Ruth looked at her watch. "Just before 4.00."

"What's the time now?"

"Where's your watch? Half past three. I'm showing Owen around so he can get his father to come and look, and buy the mill."

"*Buy* the mill? Doesn't he know it'll fall down soon?"

"It won't fall down, silly. It just needs more work. Didn't you hear what I said? His Dad's someone who runs a mill in London."

"*London*? They have mills in London?"

"Not many," admitted Owen. "But his does all right. It's big."

"Well, he's not going to want to come down here, then," said Alan. "We're just waiting for the owner to shut it, Dad says."

"All the more reason for Owen's Dad to buy it," said Ruth.

"Just a mo," said Owen. "He hasn't seen it yet, and I don't know if he'd have the money to buy it, just like that."

"See?" said Alan. "It's not going to happen, is it?"

Ruth glared at him. "What's Gran say? Don't count your chickens before they're hatched."

"Don't keep chickens any more," Eric offered.

"You know what I mean. Come on. We'll show him the rest of the Mills as we go to the station. And don't forget it's a request stop. You don't want to get stranded again."

"Shut *up*, Ruth."

Owen smiled.

Undaunted, Ruth led on up the road that Owen was to come to know as Mill Drove.

She paused again. "This used to be a stables, they say. Useless now, of course."

'This' was a squat building on the left just before the footpath, with a cobbled area in front. Owen could imagine a few horses being saddled up in front of it.

"The other side of the road are some more cottages, but not everyone living there works at the mill. Some are empty. We still use the glasshouses, though. Everyone does some work in them and takes what they need.

"And this is Alan and Eric's house. It used to be two but they took over the other one before the new owner took over, and their dad managed to persuade him the rent was for both of them. He says it's the only time he's managed to get one over on anybody!"

Owen grinned again.

"Then there are the railway buildings. I think that's what they were. But the signalman only comes out when there are deliveries, so he doesn't need the cottage any more. That's the one on the left. The others are just stores and a cattle yard, but who used that I don't know."

She stopped for breath. Owen's head was reeling.

"Must be like at school when the teacher bleats on and then says she'll be testing you on all that," joked Eric. Ruth put her tongue out at him.

"Better go and get on the platform," said Alan, "in case it's early. Come on."

Owen hesitated. "What time does it get to Seaford?" he asked, pronouncing it Seefud.

"Tell you're a foreigner!" said Alan. "It's Sea Ford. A ford over the sea."

"Okay, Sea Ford" Owen exaggerated, and was surprised to be told that was better. "What time does it get there, anyway?"

"About five minutes after it's here," Alan answered.

Owen thought. "So if I walk back it'll take about three quarters of an hour, but by train it's five minutes. I think I'd better come with you. I've got to meet my parents at half past four."

"Going to bring them back?" Alan's tone was slightly jeering. Ruth looked at him sharply.

"Depends. They said we're having a meal, then catching the train back. But if I can get him to, I will. But I'll certainly get them to come back sometime soon."

"Mill doesn't work on Sundays. Used to, but there's not enough work for it."

12

Owen nodded. They crossed the line and he was astonished to see just a sign saying 'Beware Trains' and an ordinary gate leading straight onto the track, with another the other side.

"We don't get this in London!" he exclaimed.

"Dad says it's only since the war they put gates on," Ruth told him. "Before that you just crossed."

"Blimey. Any accidents?"

"Foxes. Everything else has to be led."

"Foxes or foxes?" he asked as they walked up the ramp to platform level. It took a few moments to sink in before they laughed.

"She's never been run over," Ruth told him unnecessarily.

A distant two-tone horn from along the coast told of the train's approach.

Owen had a sudden thought. "Just a minute, I've got no ticket."

"Didn't you see the ticket office?" asked Alan.

"No – where is it?"

"Shut up, Alan," said Ruth. "He's joking. There's no ticket office here. We have to pay at Seaford."

"Of course," he said, "that's why Mrs Fox gets off at Bishopstone, so she doesn't have to buy one."

Alan put his hand out when the train was still quite a way off. "In case he's going too fast to stop," he said.

But it did stop. They moved to get on, all except Ruth.

"Aren't you coming?" asked Owen.

"Dad doesn't know where I am," she said. "But I'll see you when you come back with your parents."

Owen felt he should have walked back through the village with her. He still had a lot to ask. Sadly he just said: "Okay… I'll come back. Promise. If I need to, I'll come on my own, another day. Bye."

They were now on the train, and he opened the window to look back and wave until she was almost invisible.

"You're soft on her!" Alan accused.

Owen ignored him.

With a stop at Bishopstone, whose station seemed a bit dilapidated, they reached Seaford in six minutes. Silently, the ticket collector pointed them all to the ticket office where they bought tickets. Owen handed his to the man and thought it must have been the shortest time he'd ever owned anything.

The boys were heading into the town, to one of the butchers. Owen hesitated.

"Come with us," said Alan, "and we'll show you around."

That cheered him up. They walked down toward the church – where Owen and his parents had gone before – but then turned left down a different road. He was intrigued to see it was called Place Lane, and he wondered why it couldn't make up its mind which it was. Not only did it not know whether it was a place or a lane but it also seemed undecided about having a pavement. At the further end of it was a much wider street with trees lining it and shops on either side.

"The butchers' is just up here," said Alan.

For the sake of company Owen went too.

"Good day, lovely day," said the butcher as they entered the shop. "Oh, it's you two. And another one. Friend of yours?"

"He's coming to live at Tide Mills."

"His Dad's going to buy Tide Mills."

Simultaneous answers aren't guaranteed to provide a concise answer but nevertheless the man understood.

"Is he now. And when might this be happening?"

Alan shrugged. "Don't know. Don't think his Dad knows about it yet either."

The butcher tossed his head. "You boys... What do you want, anyway?"

"Chops," said Eric.

"Lamb, Pork, back of the neck? And people who say 'please' get better meat."

"Please," said Eric.

"Sorry," said Alan. "Pork, please, and enough for four."

He nodded, turned and removed what looked like a rack of bones from one of the many occupied hooks at the back of the shop. The only time Owen had seen chops they were on a tray in the shop, or cooked and on his plate. But this was new and he watched in some alarm as the butcher picked up a big saw and cut four times through the bones. Then he reached for a large cleaver and brought it down with amazing accuracy hard on the bony back of the meat. A chop separated.

"And that's why they're called chops," he announced.

When they were all cut he wrapped them in greaseproof paper, weighed them, then wrapped them in newspaper and gave the package to Alan.

"Six and tenpence, please."

"They've gone up sixpence," said Alan.

"Everything's going up, all the time. Anyway, these are a bit heavier than I usually give you."

"Well..."

"I'll see what Mum says when we get back," Alan told him.

"And you tell her I said you need building up with more food at your age," said the butcher. "Get along with you."

They left the shop, Alan still grumbling under his breath.

"I'd better go," said Owen as the church clock appeared as they walked down Place Lane again. "It's getting on for 4.30 now, and if I'm late they definitely won't go back to Tide Mills tonight."

"Do you think they really will?" asked Alan.

"Dad was interested when he passed – he said so. Shouldn't take much to persuade him."

The boy looked impressed. "I'll believe it when I see it, but it'd be good if he did. Take it on, that is."

Owen grinned. "I can only ask. And nag a bit. And think of all the good things, like getting out of London."

"What's it like there?"

"Crowded. Dirty. Dangerous sometimes, Mum says. Boring…"

"Dangerous?" asked Eric. "Why?"

"Oh, I don't know. I think she reads too many crime books."

They turned right at the school and joined the main road at the complicated junction. Owen noticed the bus garage down to the left, opposite the cinema.

"I saw the cinema earlier. Any good? "

"Yeah. We're not backwards, you know. You should take Ruth there. It's the back row they all go for."

"Who?" Owen was sure he knew what was coming, so wasn't surprised when Eric piped up.

"Couples who want a bit of fiddle-de-dee!"

Alan cuffed him.

"You've been listening to that Jack again. You say that in front of Mum and she'll do more than fiddle-de-dee on your bum!"

Eric just grinned. Owen was quite glad it had rebounded on him because he didn't know Alan well enough to punch him for hinting again that he and Ruth might be interested in the back row of the cinema – and after only knowing each other for an hour!

2 – Tide Mills

He had very little time to wait at the station for his parents. In those fifteen minutes more people passed the time of day with him than would have happened in a month back home in London. He felt quite bemused – if pleased – by their friendliness. At last he heard his parents' voices approaching, talking houses, and hoped no decisions had been made. Surely they wouldn't have been, not without him.

"Hallo darling. Bored?" Barbara always assumed that would be what he'd say. He often described school in those terms. Apart from sports, of course.

"No. Mum, it was good. Dad, we've got to go back to Tide Mills. There's a great house there. It needs some work but it's big enough. And the mills themselves could be made to work better, no doubt about that – just like you said."

He was about to carry on when his father held up a hand with a "Whoah!" as if he was a horse. He stopped.

"Just a mo... let's go and have a proper meal and you can tell us all about it. We've not had much luck. There are some really nice houses here but they're too far from the town for me to get the train every day. And they're too expensive. There's nothing for sale down here that's big enough or in the right place..."

"But Dad..."

"Yes, I know. And I know what I said on the train. But think of your mother. She's got to have something to do too. It isn't as if you were still eight and needed to be with her all the time!"

"There's trains to Seaford, Dad."

"I know, but one thing at a time, okay?"

He was leading them back around the corner to the hotel they had seen earlier: The Terminus. Its chief attraction was that it was near; it certainly looked a little run down.

"We don't start serving food until 6.00 pm, sir. There's no call for it before."

"We're calling for it... okay, is there anywhere else where we can get a proper meal, please?"

"Can't rightly say, sir. Cafés should be open."

"Thanks for your help." Owen and Barbara recognised the sarcasm and smiled. The man behind the hotel's reception didn't.

They had a council of war outside.

"If we're late back, Owen won't be in bed until late. Don't forget he's only thirteen."

"*Mum!* I'm fourteen and not a kid. And it's Sunday tomorrow anyway."

"Owen's got us an entry into this mill, Barbara. It's an opportunity that's too good to miss as it's so run down. Think of the potential."

"Yes, but do we really want to live in a remote, run-down place like that? We know nothing about it."

"Mum, unless we go we'll never know anything about it. That's the whole point. You'd be able to see for yourself what it's really like."

"And think what a really nice house it is – according to Owen" said Max, getting into his stride. "And there would be genuine-spirited, local people around us, and a workforce who are there because they've always been there. And I doubt if there'd ever be any Union problems."

"When would we get back? And where would we eat tonight?"

Owen was glad to hear the last question as it concerned the problem his stomach had been telling him about ever since food was mentioned earlier.

"Oh, we can eat in Newhaven when we've done. I saw a hotel there – for the ferries, you know."

"And they'll be open once we're there, after visiting the Mill. Oh, come on Mum, you know it makes sense."

Much to his surprise, Tide Mills won, though qualified with "Do you mind, darling, just for a quick look?" to his mother. She did mind, but knew her husband well enough.

During the wait and on the short train journey, Owen was worried lest his parents think, once they'd seen the place, that he'd been wasting their time. He was almost silent until they drew into the tiny, bare station and the train shuddered to a halt.

"This way," he almost shouted at them, and bounded up towards the gate.

The place looked deserted, despite the sun which was doing its watery best to make the place look cheerful ("Thank goodness," thought Owen). As they came level with the Bakers' cottage, though, the door was flung open and a small cannonball of a boy shot out.

"You did it! You did it!" he shouted, then stopped, embarrassed at the prospect of meeting two strange adults, even if accompanied by someone he just about knew.

"Told you!" Owen accused him.

"Who's this, Owen, and what is it you did?" asked his father.

"Eric Baker. He lives here with his parents and his brother Alan. And what I did was to get you here."

Max nodded, then turned to the boy. "Hallo Eric. I'm Owen's dad, and like he said, he's brought us here. Do you work at the mill?"

Eric's face changed in an instant with the grin that appeared on it. "No, sir. I'm at school. But Dad does. He's there now."

The voices had brought his mother and brother to the door. Alan grinned too.

"You did it!" he said, echoing his brother. "Hallo, sir."

"Hallo, sir," their mother echoed, sounding as if she should have used words different from her son's.

"Hallo Mrs Baker," said Max. "I don't know what your sons have been saying – in fact I'm not sure what mine's been saying either. But I said on the train that Tide Mills looked interesting and I'd like to take a closer look."

She walked over and shook his hand. "And you manage a mill in London, Alan tells me?"

"And Owen must have told him. Yes, I do. So I have an interest, so to speak."

"Well, sir, we're in a right pickle. Owner, he's not interested. Wants to sell and build on the site. We all reckon there's life in the old Mill yet, but it needs money spent on it, that's for certain. But the owner; he won't spend."

"And I haven't got that sort of money either, Mrs Baker, let's get that established. But my employers – that might be a different matter."

Even Owen could detect the look of hope that passed over the woman's face.

"Best if you go and talk to the Manager. Mr Pentelow's in his office, I reckon, though he's about to knock off as it's just about pushing five."

"Thank you. Can one of you tell me which way to go, please?"

"We will!" shouted Eric. "Mum's cooking, so Alan and I will."

Another cottage door opened, further up. A girl appeared: Ruth. Despite the boys' presence Owen smiled. He waved. Ruth waved back and limped towards them.

"Hallo," she said, talking to Owen's parents first. "You must belong to Owen. He said he would get you back here if it was the last thing he did."

"*Ruth*!" Owen exclaimed. His parents laughed.

"He never mentioned you," said his mother. Owen blushed.

"This is Ruth... her father works at the mill too."

"Hallo, Ruth. We've just been sent to talk to Mr Pentelow. You haven't seen him go, I suppose?"

"No, not yet. He's usually late leaving, but it is Saturday. I'll take you."

"*We're* taking him," Eric announced fiercely.

She laughed. "We'll *all* take them," she said echoing Eric's tone.

Like a pair of battleships entering harbour, Barbara and Max Wilson were escorted, by a scurry of four tugboats, through the door clearly marked 'Report here'. Alan rang the bell with some pride. Eric was about to press it again but was stopped by his brother.

Nothing happened.

Eric's hand was hovering over it to make it sound again when footsteps were to be heard. A man appeared, and the first impression Owen had was that this was truly Father Christmas (even if he was too old for things like that.) Along with a full head of long, snowy hair he sported rich sideburns, also white, which merged with as luxuriant a (white) beard as anyone could wish for. Even if his surname had been Claus.

"And how can I help you...? Oh, it's you three is it? 'Allo."

"Hallo, Mr Pentelow, I'm Max Wilson," started Owen's dad, and outlined the reason for the unannounced visit. The others waited with bated breath as if at the end of a few paragraphs of conversation the two would shake hands and it would all be arranged.

All that happened was that Mr Pentelow nodded many times, and when Max had finished he stayed silent.

At last the younger ones started fidgeting and the Manager fixed them with a piecing gaze. "Lovely to see you, and thanks for bringing them, but 'oppit."

With "awww..." from the boys and a grin from Ruth, they 'opped it. With Ruth and Owen.

"Well, will he or won't he?" asked Alan.

"Who? What?"

"Take it over, of course."

There was a shout from the direction of the boys' home.

"Dinner," added Alan. "Well?"

"You can't decide that sort of thing in five minutes," said Owen. "And it's up to Dad's mill and the owner here, not those two."

Alan nodded. Eric looked disappointed. There was another shout, more annoyed this time.

"See yer," they said in unison, and ran back home.

"So what do we do now?" asked Ruth.

"Now, this minute?"

"Well – yes, but I meant how do we get them to make the right choice?"

"Dad'll make the choice," Owen said grimly. "He always does. But he'll take into account everything and say yes or no, and tell us the reasons. At least he does that."

She nodded. "What will you do if you do come here?"

The suddenness of the question caught Owen off guard. "Well, go to school, I suppose. Where do you all go?"

"I'm at the Grammar in Lewes. Eric's still at Primary school and Alan's at Secondary in Seaford. Schools in Newhaven aren't meant to be very good."

"Apart from that, I don't know what I'd do. Not yet. Maybe join a football team. I do judo too. Then see what else there is going..."

"I can't do sport."

"Why?

"My leg."

"What's wrong with it? I saw you're limping."

"Right one's shorter than the left."

If he'd been Alan's age he would immediately have looked. But he stopped himself in time. "Does it stop you doing much?"

"Yes. Most things. It all takes longer and aches, whatever it is."

"Can't anything be done?"

"I've got a built up shoe," she said grimly. "That's all that's ever happened for it. What else can I do? Hang upside down from it so it stretches?"

"I'd still visit you. Even if you looked like a bat."

The look she gave him could have killed at three paces, but then it softened and she had to smile. "Owen Wilson, you nearly got a punch then, but I know you didn't mean it nastily."

"Surely nobody picks on you because of it, do they?"

"Don't they?" she asked, grim once more. "And have you ever tried to catch someone when you can't run properly?"

Silence.

"If I go to your school and anyone starts on you, they'll have me to reckon with."

He said it quietly, but her face had an expression he didn't understand.

"I think you would, too."

"If I say something, I do it."

This time the smile was warm. "You'd have a job to go to my school, though. It's the Girls' Grammar. Are you at a Grammar?"

"Yes. I passed the eleven-plus."

She nodded, as if it was obvious, paused and continued with more important matters.

"We could go to the pictures in Seaford," she said.

"Now?"

Laughter. "No! When you live here."

"*If* I live here."

"You could come and stay..."

He looked astonished. At school, very occasionally, there had been parties where he was invited, and an open invitation to sleep on the floor of a room afterwards. But those were people he'd met years ago, went to school with and knew as well as he knew anybody. But, suddenly, here; here was this girl he'd just met a few hours ago, had liked on sight and wanted to talk to. And now she was inviting him to stay at her house as if they'd known each other for years. Wow.

"I'd like that," he said, simply.

The door opened again and Max's head looked out. "Can you come in, Owen? We're going on a tour of the mill."

"I'd better go," said Ruth.

"No. You come too. Dad?" he shouted just as the head was about to vanish inside again. It re-emerged. "Ruth can come, can't she."

Without meaning to he had used a trick of his father's, that of turning a request for permission into a statement. It worked, because the head just said "Yes," and this time vanished.

"Come on. Please?"

She grinned again. "Looks like I don't have an option!"

"Like I don't when Dad makes his mind up."

"You're not bossy, are you?"

"Certainly not! I just know what I want. Like Dad."

"Sorry," said Max to Ruth when they were all together. "I don't know your name."

"Ruth Decks, Mr Wilson. My Dad works here."

"Is he the chap Mr Pentelow here says is his right hand man?"

"That he is," said the Manager. "And without him the Mill wouldn't run as efficiently as it does. And you can tell him I said so, young Ruth."

She smiled.

Any general description of a mill will annoy the enthusiast and baffle the uninitiated. An enthusiast will know the general layout and the purpose of the different areas. The uninitiated is strongly advised to visit a mill, preferably a water mill because of the similarities to a tide mill, learn, drink in the atmosphere and ask questions. Imagination must be the best guide to the layout of Bishopstone Tide Mills – except for stating the obvious: the mill's main purpose is to turn many sets of two deeply scored stones of about 5ft diameter which grind the grain between them. The real differences were that instead of water from a stream, Tide Mills' wheels were turned by water stored from the incoming tide.

Unusually, everyone who toured the mill that evening knew a lot about mills and milling. It's impossible to be married to, or the son or daughter of, a miller and be ignorant of a mill's basic design and purpose. So the questions fired at Mr Pentelow over that thirty minutes were specific and often quite technical.

At the end of it Max sounded quite hopeful. More questions about staff were asked. That might be a problem, it seemed, although there were always school leavers in June or July – Owen was suddenly hopeful – or summer students. And there were a few who might come back, who had only left because there was no longer enough work for them.

Eventually there were no more questions. The Wilson family members looked at each other; one thoughtful and full of plans and possibilities, one hopeful, and one becoming resigned to another 'what might be'. Barbara was aware that the area was much safer and more healthy than the part of London they lived in. She was not so sure about the remoteness of Tide Mills, even if it did have its own railway station and presumably buses at the nearby main road. Most of all she was aware that they would need to live somewhere and no house had been mentioned yet except by her son, who was scarcely an expert.

"So have I put you off too much?" asked the Manager.

"Not at all, not at all. If my lot were to run it there would be changes, not just in the source of the grains, but in what we did with it afterwards. What other space is there to expand into?"

"Expand! There's a word we've not heard here for years! The grain store is very greatly under-used. Not just because of the level of trade but because grain's brought in when wanted, by road, nowadays. So there's most of that space available."

"Excuse me," said Barbara faintly, "but may we look at the house that Owen's told us about?"

"The House! Yes, of course. It's not been lived in for years, so it'll need a lot done to it. But it has a chance to be a really nice place, just like it always was." Mr Pentelow was enthusiastic. From a cabinet on the wall he collected an old-fashioned key.

They followed him up the roadway, over the millraces, and stopped at the house that Ruth had shown Owen earlier. The lock protested as its key was turned, and the door creaked theatrically as it opened. Inside the hall was dusty and gloomy.

"There's a lot of creeper covering the windows this side," the Manager explained. "Started off as a decorative feature – old Mr Fox loved anything growing – but it's taken over a bit. This is what they used as the office."

He opened a door into another large, dusty room which, oddly, still had a massive desk by the window so that light from the window at its back shone on it despite the creeper.

"It'd make a great living room," said Max.

"When it's completely cleaned, redecorated and those windows are cleared of creeper," said his wife.

They toured the two other storeys of the rest of the house. It was of a good size, oversized for a family of three, really, but all of them could see it was full of scope.

"How much would the Company pay to get this place made habitable?" Barbara asked her husband.

"They don't even know about it yet! It depends on what they think about the whole scheme, but they won't mind investing in something that's going to work. And they'll need to provide a house for whoever's looking after it apart from Mr Pentelow."

Owen had been particularly attracted to a room on the second floor. One of its windows looked over the mill creek towards Newhaven's harbour. The other looked north, over the foothills of the Downs. It was large and well lit as the creeper had not grown on that side of the building, and according to him it had a nice feel to it. There was even an old bed frame, a well built one, in a corner.

"This is mine," he announced to them all. They smiled indulgently and he felt let down. "Well, if we come here, this is the room I want. Please."

His father looked at him, this time taking him more seriously.

"Okay," he said. "If we do, it will be. That all right with you, Barbara?"

His wife nodded. "*If* we come here, yes."

Owen switched his attention to Ruth, who returned his gaze full on.

"What do you think, Ruth?"

"Nice room, except in the gales. Then that west window will rattle. Mine does, no matter what I do to it."

"Can't be that windy, surely?"

She laughed. "Can't it? You're facing west there, and although the mill's in the way, the sou'-westerlies will still catch it. It's usually south-west here. All the time."

"Don't put him off, Ruth!" said Mr Pentelow. "It's not that bad, really, and you get used to the wind. It's worse in Seaford itself, really. Most of the bay faces sou'-west and cops it head on."

"You wanted fresh air, Barbara, just like we all do. It sounds as if we'll get our fair share here."

"*If* we move here," his wife reminded him. He just grinned.

"Anything else you want to see? Else my tea will be on the table by now – yours too, young Ruth, and you'll be in trouble."

Max consulted his watch. "Good heavens – we need to catch a train! We need a meal too. Is there a hotel or something in Newhaven that will serve food to non-residents?"

"Certainly... The Bridge will, or the Railway Hotel if you're going by train."

"When's the next train, please?"

Mr Pentelow's turn to look at his watch. "You've just missed one. If you walk up to the road you can get a bus – about fifteen minutes, I reckon. You'll do that. Ask the conductor for the Bridge Hotel. He'll put you right."

"That's very kind. We'd better let you both get home, and thank you so much for your time."

"You're welcome. But don't say too much about anything that the owner will get to hear about. If he knows a big company is interested he'll up the price."

"True, said Max. "I'll get everyone to keep their mouths shut. And you'd better do the same with everyone here, from those two boys to Mrs Fox. Tell them that if the owner wants too much, it just won't happen, and that'll be that. Their future depends on it."

"And mine," said Mr Pentelow quietly.

"And yours. Maybe ours too. And I'd better say now that assuming it all goes my way, your job here remains essential."

The man nodded, as if there had never been a doubt. "When do we hear anything?"

Max shrugged. "I'll need to get my thoughts on paper, then present the whole idea to the top brass. That'll take a fortnight. After that – who knows? But I'll keep you informed – by phone if necessary. I've got the mill's phone number."

They said their farewells. Owen couldn't help looking back over his shoulder as they walked up to the railway, and once he was sure he saw Ruth looking back.

They caught their bus. They found the Bridge Hotel. They had a meal. They discussed the possibilities.

They caught a train and arrived home in London very late. Owen overslept on Sunday.

School, football, judo, other clubs and general busy-ness almost squashed any anxiety over what was happening over the following two weeks. Owen was dimly aware that Max seemed to be working a lot at home in the evenings, yet despite his presence the two hardly found time to speak. The following Friday his father was late home, threw his briefcase onto a chair and sat down heavily on another.

"Well, that's that. Now it's in the lap of the gods."

Owen, watching television, was distracted; itself an achievement. He knew what it was likely to be about. His mother less TV-centred, looked up.

"Plans for Tide Mills?"

"Yes, and I've discovered a lot about what could happen there, and the likely costs. It will be profitable if it's done properly, that I have discovered."

"So is it going to happen, Dad?"

"That's what's in the lap of the gods – the Directors. If they can see that it will work, and if the finance is available, then it should. But there are one or two 'stick-in-the-muds' amongst them who might dig their heels in."

"In the mud," Owen offered.

"In anything they can. If there's every reason in the world that the scheme will work, they're just as likely to say no on the basis that 'we've never done that sort of thing before.'"

"Will they?" asked Barbara.

He shrugged. "I can work on them. I can say that my son's already chosen his room in the newly refurbished house..."

Owen grinned.

"I can say that there's expertise down there. I can say that there are companies, competitors of ours, who are starting to do what I'm proposing, but that none of them is anywhere near the coastal area between Eastbourne and Brighton. I can say that we are a successful company and that we should grasp a nettle or two. But if they get cold feet..." He shrugged again.

"When are you going down again?" asked Owen.

"Who knows? Maybe next week. Maybe never. Maybe once just to say 'Sorry, we tried'."

"When you go, can I come?"

"It'll be a weekday. You'll be at school. So will Ruth. So no."

That surprisingly observant comment shut Owen up. Bed time came soon after, despite the usual 'can I just' attempts. His thoughts as he lay waiting for sleep to take over were about some untidy old buildings, a stiff south-west breeze blowing around them, and a girl standing, waiting for him, with her skirt being blown by that wind.

Sleep was a long time coming.

On the Monday morning a postcard arrived. It was addressed to Mr O Wilson and showed the old church of Seaford with its clock face, but from the opposite side. He hadn't realised that it also had a roofed lych gate at the start of the path to its main door. Apart from the address on the other side there were three words and a signature: "Any news? Love, Ruth"

It was propped in his room during the day. That night he slept with it on the pillow beside him.

He sent one back the next day, with a picture of Buckingham Palace on it. He wrote: "Not yet, Directors are still thinking. I'll tell you. Love, Owen." Many minutes were spent looking at it before he realised that he didn't know her address. At last common sense took hold and he wrote firmly: "Miss R Decks, Tide Mills..." and then paused. Newhaven? Seaford? He smiled and said 'Sea Ford' firmly to himself, then addressed the card with that town's name and 'Sussex'.

That night he stood in front of the mirror, really looking at himself for the first time in ages. He was aware – perhaps he just thought, or maybe even just hoped – that Ruth really did want them to move to Tide Mills and it might have something to do with him. What did she see in him, if anything? Height – was he a bit taller than he remembered? Long gone were the days when his parents stood him against the edge of a door and marked the increases.

As to the rest: long-ish mid brown hair that had a mind of its own; he made a mental note to keep it tidy or he'd be sent to the barbers again. Face? Was his nose somehow bigger than it had been? Surely not. He wasn't Pinocchio.

It still lifted slightly at the end but perhaps wasn't as 'snub' as it looked in the last photo his parents had taken.

Mouth... was it as wide as Ruth's? It seemed wider than some of the others' at school, but it was the only one he'd got so there was nothing he could do about that. Eyes? He shrugged. Average. Brown.

This was a pointless exercise. Either she wanted the family at the mill or she just wanted to be with him. Or both. How would he know? He couldn't just go and ask her.

Common sense is a wonderful thing. But still he wondered.

It was nearly a month later that the Directors finally made a decision. They decided that... that they would go and look at the place.

"As soon as the cars had disappeared I got on the phone to Pentelow to tell him that although they were quite keen..."

"Didn't they arrange it beforehand? How rude!"

"Oh yes, they did that. I had to stop them talking to the owner and landing themselves with an inflated price if they do go ahead. At least they talked to Pentelow – without involving me, but I'm used to that sort of thing, here and in the Navy. Anyway, I tipped Pentelow the wink that they were interested, and told him that the more he can talk up the space available for extra machinery instead of storage, the better."

He wife's expression was puzzled.

"We need the machinery for mixing flour with ingredients for one thing, and then for packaging the results for people to buy. If they take up my plan, we'll be selling cake mixes that anyone can use – yes, darling, even me – and bread mixes, maybe sauce mixes and so on too. And we'll have tours round the mill and the factory, and a café where people can sample our bread and cakes. And – " he chuckled – "they could even watch them being made. I've just thought of that!"

"And will people really come to see all that?"

"Other mills are already doing it. There's a small watermill somewhere else in Sussex that's just been made to work again, and people go there in droves. Why not us? There aren't many tide mills around the country, and most of those few are closed or are about to close. And that's what would happen to Bishopstone if we don't use it."

"You're serious about this, aren't you?"

"It's just the sort of thing I'd love to get to grips with. And it's well out of London, which was the main reason for going to look for somewhere on the coast in the first place. It's cleaner, more airy, spacious and safe. The house, once they've done it up, will be really nice, I'd say. And..."

"And what am I going to do all day?"

"Seaford and Newhaven are a few minutes away on the train. There are going to be things to do there. If you wanted you could work – *if* you wanted. The improved mill might need someone with beauty and intelligence..."

Barbara looked at him under lowered brows. "Flannel, Max Wilson, and you know it."

"Or of course you could do the sort of voluntary work you did in the war," Max continued.

"Most of that's gone, I imagine."

"It's worth looking. People like the Missions to Seamen need help, and they're bound to have a place in Newhaven. There's all sorts of voluntary organisations – what about the Lifeboat? Surely they need some help with administration?"

"You're trying to sell it to me, aren't you?"

He smiled at her. "I'm just trying to be positive."

"We still don't know what they'll say."

"No," he admitted, "we don't."

Owen had been forced upstairs to finish his homework but shortly after their discussion he returned to switch on the television.

"Before you do, old chap," his father started, and then explained what had happened.

"What do you think they'll say?" he asked.

"Frankly, if they have half the sense they were born with, they'll go for it."

"And have they?" asked Barbara.

"Have they what?"

"Got half the sense they were born with," Owen explained.

He laughed at them both. "If only I knew!"

"But Dad, it's going to take a lot of money to do up, isn't it?"

"Yes. It will. But I think if we handle it properly it will become profitable fairly quickly. Many of the ideas we've been considering for the main mill here in London are just sticking in the mud because the Unions can't see further than the end of their noses. They've got a stranglehold on the staff and almost always lead them into their way of thinking. But if all those ideas go down to Sussex with the Sussex staff who really want the mill to stay in business, we can just get on with it."

"You mean, *you* can get on with it." Barbara was getting a point in again.

"Yes. I need a challenge. And I've just thought – there's no one to do the accounts down there. What do you think about taking that on if I can persuade the Governors?"

"Me? They'd never agree to that!" she said, surprised.

"Why not, Mum? You're always saying how much responsibility it was in the war, having to deal with all that money."

"The Bank of England is different, dear. And I wasn't an accountant, just a secretary."

"Yes, but a senior one."

She smiled at him. "Yes, a senior one. But still not an accountant."

"But you could do it."

"I don't know. I've never tried."

"Well," Max interjected, "You could face a challenge too! If you wanted to."

"What? Learn to be an accountant? That would take ages!"

"I imagine you could do most of it on the job. Oh true, they might have to get someone to do the formal bits, but you could learn."

She wondered at the thought.

"Go on, Mum! You could be doing that while Dad gets dirty doing up our house."

His father smiled. "I doubt if I'll be doing it myself! We'd get people in. People who are used to working on large sites. I might be able to paper a wall, but that's about it."

"And even then the paper fell off," said Barbara.

"I try to forget that," said Max. Owen laughed.

Later that night he wrote a postcard to Ruth: "Directors visited without Dad yesterday. Should decide soon. Love, Owen."

It was a week before Max was called to see his Directors. By this time he had adjusted his proposals a little and explained the changes to them.

"I am really enthusiastic about the business opportunities in Sussex, and would greatly welcome – on a personal as well as a business level – the challenges that developing them would present," he finished.

The men around the board room table exchanged glances with raised eyebrows, most nodding. One, an original founder of the company, looked stony faced. The Managing Director asked if they were agreed and requested a show of hands. All but one was raised. He looked at the Company Secretary who nodded.

"Mr Wilson, we regard this proposal as a viable proposition. It will proceed with our nearly undivided support."

Max carefully avoided looking at the one person who was patently against the idea.

"It will not be as simple as just installing machinery and getting staff," the Managing Director continued. "There are properties there whose condition we cannot allow if we are to put the company name to the development. Although it will be on the face of it unproductive money, the houses and the mill buildings will require a facelift. If we are to introduce sightseers to the mill then there are alterations needed to protect them from working machinery. There is a gift shop to install – somewhere.

"If we are to proceed, and we have determined that we are, we need to ensure that improvements, developments and alterations are made in a logical and timely manner. Since this information and recommendation came from yourself, we would like you to oversee it. That will mean you moving to Sussex, since we would also want you to oversee the plant once it is developed.

"Are you prepared to take on this challenge, and are you prepared to move? I suppose it would mean moving as a family, would it not?"

Max had been listening with increasing hope. At the final question he narrowly avoided shouting 'YES!' and forced his face into a thoughtful pose.

"I would of course need to ask my family, sir. But thank you for your confidence in offering to entrust the overall management of the scheme to me, and its subsequent operation. May I check with you that I would have *carte blanche* to take whatever actions I need in order to ensure that the plant opens as efficiently, and as soon, as possible?"

"We'll consider those details later."

"But with respect, just as the company's good name hangs on what happens with Tide Mills, so does mine as the scheme's Manager. I would need to feel completely confident that I have the appropriate financial tools and the complete authority from the company. It would require me to make my own decisions for the benefit of the company, since you have demonstrated that you have the confidence in me to do so."

This caused a buzz of quiet talk around the table. Max hoped he hadn't gone too far, asked too much.

The Managing Director cleared his throat. Muttering subsided.

"I understand your concern. I believe we need to discuss this and ensure that authority and pecuniary limits for sole action is in place, along with requirements for reporting to the Board. You need to talk to your family. May I suggest that we reconvene at the same time tomorrow? Will that give us enough time?"

That evening there was a family conference in the Wilson household. When a conclusion had been reached Owen was almost hugging himself with delight. Barbara Wilson was still more than a little worried, partly wanting to support her husband and partly anticipating unforeseen problems.

The head of the household was relieved and pleased, and eagerly anticipating being able to start work. There was still the small matter of the purchase of the property to face, and on a more personal note the scope of his authority, but he almost dismissed these.

A letter was written that night. It would be more secret, Owen decided. He added "Keep it quiet, please" to it, remembering that they still had to contact the current owner of the mill.

3 – First meeting

The purchase seemed to drag on forever. Initially the owner was suspicious and quoted a price that would have bought Buckingham Palace. Max's employers were dismissive and made a ridiculously low offer, quoting the publicly obvious desperate state of all the buildings, the low morale of the staff, the lack of recent investment anywhere and the most recent business figures they had obtained.

Offers and counter-offers were exchanged like a rally in a tennis match and after a delay a figure was offered which the Board – and Max – regarded as sensible. A deal was struck. But still no start could be made on the improvements until the last documents were signed and the conveyancing completed. Finally, in mid-September, four months after their first visit, it was all complete.

Max was very late home that night, having had exhaustive and exhausting discussions with the Governors who, to be fair, were now treating him with rather more respect and trust than they seemed to have done at the start. After a lot of discussion and persuasion they had allowed Max most of the authority to act alone that he had requested. The choice of the winner of the initial tender for the works was to be agreed by the Board, however, after hearing recommendations from him.

He made his peace with his wife and, the next morning, with Owen.

Now he could really start work. Building companies were invited down to the village for familiarisation, and were each given specifications of the work on which to tender. Max had already decided that the main priority should be to make the Mill House habitable, not only to demonstrate that his employers were serious, but so that, come the move, he would be able to live in peace with his wife. After Mill House the other domestic properties would be improved, then the major work on the Mill and its associated buildings started. Finally, machinery for the new activities for the Mill would be installed.

He was at Tide Mills regularly during that week, causing much comment locally and a lot of excitement with the staff. Even old Mrs Fox seemed to be happier than usual – if 'slightly less argumentative' can be described as 'happy'. The weekend after the sale had completed the whole family travelled down. Max had decided to surprise them.

Once again they took the old steam train as far as Lewes but this time were heading directly for the Seaford train. Owen's attention was drawn to a poster stuck to a wall: "CLOSURE OF EAST GRINSTEAD-LEWES LINE" it shouted. He read it, causing his parents to look back in some annoyance, then hurried to join them.

"They're closing the line," he said.

"What line?" His father had a sudden vision of the Seaford line's death, and all their plans being wasted.

"The East Grinstead one. The one we've just come down."

"Really? Why?"

"It didn't say."

"What didn't?"

"The poster on the wall over there."

"I didn't notice that. Oh dear, that's a shame. When will it close?"

He thought, trying to recall the wording without success. "Can't remember. We'll have to look on the way back."

"Really hope they'll leave a few steam engines doing something," Max said as they boarded the old Seaford train.

There seemed to be no one about at Tide Mills, not on the platform, not in the village. There was no sound from the mill wheels, though as the tide was by then flowing inwards that wasn't surprising as it was filling the east mill pond for milling later. Owen was sad that there was no welcoming committee, especially from Ruth.

Max seemed to know where he was going, however, and led the way down toward the beach, only turning round when he reached almost the end of the buildings. He went to a door and waited for his puzzled family to catch up.

"Where are they all?" asked Owen. His father just smiled and opened the nearby door. They followed him in. The door shut behind them, making Barbara and Owen jump. Lights came on. There was a roar of approval and applause.

The entire village seemed to be there, all smiles and waving. Mother and son stood and gaped whilst Max was just grinning.

Jack Pentelow came over and gradually the hubbub quietened.

"Not going to say much," he said. "But three loads of thanks. Firstly to young Owen Wilson who was interested enough in Tide Mills to persuade his father to come and look. Secondly to Mr Max Wilson for seeing the possibilities and persuading his Governors to back him. And thirdly to Mrs Barbara Wilson for agreeing to come and live here. It's not a bad place, really."

Barbara smiled. Owen found that Ruth had quietly moved to his side, and smiled too.

Max took the floor. "Thank you, Mr Pentelow – Jack. And thank you for suggesting this get-together and for laying it on. We do really appreciate it. You'll know that the next few months won't be easy, with builders around the place wanting to disturb your – our – lives, but I can promise you that the results and the job security will be worth it. Or my name won't be Max Wilson."

"Nor mine Jack Pentelow. I'm supporting this to the full and suggest that everyone else does the same. It's genuinely our best shot at a secure future. Now, behind Alan and Eric there may be some food still left, if they haven't already scoffed it. So everyone – dig in!"

It was lunch time, everyone was hungry so did as requested. Alan and Eric, unable either to speak or complain through the amount of food in their mouths, were led away by their parents to allow everyone else to eat. Owen noticed that Ruth was being left out, so elbowed in towards the table with her.

Even Mrs Fox gave way to them, and once was seen almost to smile. Ruth and he gravitated to a quieter spot. Ruth sat. Soon the boys were with them, having been told to stay away from the tables until everyone else had some food.

As the family spoke to more and more people, barriers started to crumble. The strict, almost scared politeness and caution in speech that was the norm between employer and employed seemed to change to more normal conversation. It was mainly that the staff could see that here was someone who had come to be on their side and was enthusiastic, someone who had experience and knew the technical side of their working life. From Max's point of view he was delighted that speech was flowing – a barrel of Harvey's beer may have been partly responsible for that – and that genuine grievances and suggestions were being aired. He knew that being granted trust and openness from his prospective staff so quickly was a great advantage as well as a compliment.

After about an hour he realised that if he was to say anything it was going to have to be before some of the employees became too much the worse for wear.

He climbed onto a chair, to Barbara's alarm as she thought wrongly that he too had enjoyed more from the barrel than was good for him, and gave a loud whistle. Conversation stilled.

"I am really sorry to interrupt everyone. If I don't speak now, and have yet another pint of this beer you all refer to just as Harvey's, then I shan't be able to. And if that were to be the case, I guess that one or two others wouldn't be able to listen, either."

Laughter at that, and a sprinkling of applause.

"You know that Tide Mills is going to see changes. I've been able to make as sure as I can that they are changes that will give the company we all now work for a chance of doing really new things, things that stand a chance of taking the market – and I hope the buying public – by storm. But to start with, as I said earlier, we're going to go through an uncomfortable period. It'll be me who will oversee that, so I'm to blame for any inconvenience, not anyone else, because I planned it."

Silence.

"Firstly, I need to be based here. As soon as possible. That way I can make sure that inconvenience for everyone else is controlled and you all have a point of reference. If I'm to be here, I want my family with me, please. You don't know it, but the reason we made the first journey to Sussex was to look for a place here so we could escape London. So it's in the interest of the three of us that we should do so, and if it's going to happen, why not soon?

"So although it looks like preferential treatment the first thing is that the Mill House will be repaired and brought up to standard. I can work from there, use a room as an office, and as soon as possible we'll move in."

He looked round to the other two and was rewarded by a grin and a nod from Owen and a faint smile and loyal nod from Barbara.

"As soon as builders can be released from that they will start bringing your homes up to date. Modern facilities will be installed, including proper plumbing and hot water. Electricity installations will be made safe and we will provide more electric sockets too.

"We'll be doing something else for all the houses, something new. In America they have two panes of glass in the windows to keep out the worst of the weather. It's called double glazing. We'll be one of the first settlements in Great Britain to have it, but only on the south and west, the windows that face the winter gales."

At this there was a murmur. No one could visualise the idea.

"The work required *might* need a family to move temporarily into another house – one that's already been improved – if the work would cause too much disruption. But there will never be any suggestion of the company telling anyone to move permanently. Not whilst I have any say in the matter.

"Now then, only when that's been completed and I know everyone's living in good, dry, comfortable conditions, will work be started on the Mill and its outbuildings. And that will be the subject of another meeting where I'll tell you in detail what we're going to be doing. But I'll say this: we will always be milling grains. Of that there is no doubt.

Mutters of agreement, and relief, were heard.

"Last but not least, I will not be the Manager here. Mr Jack Pentelow will still fulfil that role, and I'm as relived about that as you must be."

A more robust muttering this time, and Jack was patted on the back by one or two.

"My job will be to represent the company, oversee the developments, start off the new products we will be bringing out and, with help from London, publicising them. We'll also be inviting the public here, showing them round and having a potted history of the place and what's happened over the years, and providing a bakery, a café and a shop. It's just another way of making a bit of money. I'm hoping that much of that side of it can be used to make even more improvements to the place and perhaps have more gatherings like this.

"Speaking of meetings, all I suggested to Jack… Mr Pentelow… was just that we have a meeting today. The rest of this has been a surprise, and a welcome one. Where the food and drink came from I haven't a clue, but thank you all for it. Most welcome. If we're milling tonight I suggest those involved might want to hold back on the beer, or at least be very careful. I don't want us to start milling people!"

There was a burst of laughter. Jack Pentelow took the floor.

"Thanks, Mr Wilson. I think we all appreciate your honesty. Now is probably not the best time for questions, but if there's anything either of us can answer we'll be happy to. This won't be the only one of these village meetings, so there will be plenty of opportunity."

To Max's surprise Mrs Fox swayed to her feet. She looked round as if defying anyone to shout her down.

"And what about my cottage?" she asked fiercely. "Am I going to get all prettified as well?"

Max thought swiftly. "Well, as your home is also company property we should spend the money on it. If the Mill House is having to have electricity laid on, and all the other improvements, it's only right that your home should have the chance of the same, don't you think? The offer is there, anyway. And there's obviously no question of any one of us being asked to pay anything towards it."

For once in her life the old woman was silenced. She nodded at Max, then carefully sat down. Owen smiled to himself.

Someone else asked which of the houses was going to be dealt with first.

"One of the empty ones," said Max decisively. "That way it can be made available temporarily to any family who needed to be out of the way of the builders. As to which occupied house will be done first, I think that needs to be left to the builders. They might well need to do them in a certain order. But everyone will have as much notice as possible."

Another question: "What will the Mill be making once it's all done?"

Max smiled. "This is where I have to be cautious. You see, we need to avoid getting any hint of that to our potential competitors. How would it be if Horsebridge was to hear, and then beat us to it? So I'm keeping that under wraps for the moment, if you don't mind, so that anything in conversation can't spread through friends and relations and risk our plans. You'll probably guess as soon as the machinery arrives, but before that I promise I'll level with you."

"Why isn't the main mill in London doing all this, sir?" someone asked.

Max hesitated. This was the uncomfortable question he'd been hoping wouldn't be asked. Jack got to his feet and would have silenced the questioner, but Max had come to a decision.

"You can tell from the pause that the answer is an awkward one for me to give. But I've talked to many of you casually this afternoon, and I can tell that everyone here is as enthusiastic as I am about the future of this village and the mill. I feel that this is the nearest I've experienced to having a crew around me since my time as a Captain in the Royal Navy. And that pleases me more than you can probably realise."

He would have continued, but to his surprise Arthur Decks, Ruth's father, stood. "I do, sir," he said. "Retired Chief Petty Officer here, and today that's just how it feels." He sat again.

Max grinned delightedly. "Thanks, Chief. Good to meet another from the Grey Funnel Line, and I guess that some others are also ex-Navy. So, for this crew only, I'll tell you that the guys at the Mill in London felt it necessary to join a Union some years ago when it was seen as the thing to do. Unfortunately the local Union people, presented with the idea of doing something apart from actually milling, declined on behalf of their members. When we put the proposals directly to the staff it got back to the Union and ruffled their feathers so much that they threatened a strike.

"We've quietly tried since, but the Union won't back down. So we were stuck. So when I met you, people who could actually see for themselves what the future could hold, and decide for themselves, I was pleased as Punch. But if – or when – Union people come down here, just please be sure that they are actually on your side and don't dissuade you from doing what's best for you. For us. For the crew."

He grinned at that.

Jack Pentelow did get up this time. "We've got a saying in Sussex; comes from an old rhyme. 'There ent no place like Sussex, until you goos Above. For Sussex will be Sussex, and Sussex wunt be druv.' No Londoners will get much shrift from us, mark my words."

"That's good to know. Thanks. Any more questions?"

There were none.

"Well, other questions will occur, I'm sure. Never be frightened to ask me, or Mr Pentelow of course. We're human beings, after all."

He climbed down from his chair and conversation, noticeably more animated, restarted. Jack Pentelow came up to him.

"That was good, sir, and I think it did what you wanted, especially that last part. I believe that with this lot, being absolutely honest with them will work wonders."

"I agree. I'd only met a few before tonight but the genuineness of their feelings comes over. If we can run it as a ship's crew – without the urgency needed when you're at sea – then I have every confidence it'll go well. And please – my name's Max, Jack, and unless we're in desperately formal mode that's what I'd prefer."

He smiled. "That'll take me some time to get used to! It's never happened before."

"Well, seems logical to me. I suppose if the Governors come down we'll have to go to Mr Pentelow mode, but as soon as they've bu… gone it'll be back to normal."

He laughed. "I heard the start of that Navy slang. Pity I've got no Navy background or I could be First Mate or something!"

"Mr Mate… yes, has a ring to it, doesn't it."

They laughed and Max went to talk to his wife. Owen was still talking to Ruth and the brothers.

"Are you fairly happy about it all?" Max asked Barbara.

She smiled and paused a moment. "Yes. I've been talking to a lot of them and they are nice, genuine people, just as you said. Even Mrs Fox came and told me she never believed you'd make it happen. I said that you – we – were just glad that the Governors agreed with your proposals and that we were now here."

"What did she say to that?"

"Just that she hoped it would work out and not just go down the pan."

Max laughed. "That's her. I wonder if she'll let her house be improved. Somehow the idea of someone like her with double glazing doesn't seem right."

"Where did you get that idea from?" asked Barbara.

"There was an article in one of the magazines we get at work. I think it was about mills in America and it had more to do with sound insulation than anything else. But they mentioned temperature insulation, and it just seemed

34

the right thing to do here, exposed as it is."

"Yes," she replied with some grimness in her voice, "it will be, won't it?"

"But in the summer it'll be great. Lots of visitors, we can plant flowers, and trees where they'd be sheltered. That'll brighten everything up. There are glasshouses here, and even now there are communal allotments. So we should be okay for growing flowers. And vegetables. "

"Salty ones."

He smiled at her. "Saves on table salt."

That brought a genuine laugh.

"Where's Owen?" she asked.

"Probably with Ruth and those boys. Gone outside, I imagine. You know, this place will be good for him, I think."

"There's certainly enough fresh air coming his way. Maybe too fresh."

"But he can escape to Seaford or Newhaven..."

Owen was indeed outside with the others, sitting on the wall over the sluices. He had asked what they did in the winter. Mainly, it seemed, the answer was a football club in Seaford, Scouts in Seaford ("I'm still a Wolf Cub," Eric complained), the radio at home, or sometimes the cinema in Newhaven or Seaford. Or a book.

To Owen, it sounded familiar, except that even at his advanced age of nearly fourteen he hadn't been allowed a long distance from home in London on his own.

"What's Scouts like?" he asked.

Alan went into a description of learning how to look after yourself, to be healthy, to make things, to camp, to hike over the Downs...

Owen blinked. To be able to walk over the hills at the back of Tide Mills. To have that freedom. To know what to do if things got difficult...

"I wish I was allowed to walk. Properly walk. Long distances. Perhaps they'll let me, down here."

Ruth could see the interest in his eyes and felt more left out than she did at school when she couldn't play any games. She longed to be able to walk for hours over those gentle looking green hills visible in the distance. With Owen, preferably.

"Perhaps I should join," said Owen. "Then I could learn and we could go where we wanted."

"I could take you," Alan offered.

"Thanks, Alan. But there are some things I need to learn for myself. And Ruth can. Wherever there are Scouts, girl Guides are nearby, surely?"

The two younger boys exchanged glances. "We were camping with the Cubs once, and there were Guides in the next field. We weren't exactly welcome... in fact our Scoutmaster was going to send some of us home."

"Not me," Eric piped up. "I was in bed."

Alan just looked uncomfortable. "All we did was poke our heads in one of the tents when the girls had been sent to bed and say goodnight. The screams went right through me!"

Owen laughed, visualising the scene. And the sounds.

"Did they forgive you? Ever?"

"P'raps. One of the girls goes out with one of our older Scouts now," Alan replied. "He went up to the Senior Scouts just after we got back – so maybe they did."

"Worth it, then."

"Not for the rest of us. We got properly shouted at."

"All forgiven now?"

"Well, they let us go to camp this year, so I suppose so. But there weren't any Guides on that site."

"Hard luck."

He shrugged. "It was still good fun. And I suppose we got more done without having to think about the girls all the time."

Owen nodded. Ruth looked non-committal.

"Are you in the Guides, Ruth?" asked Owen.

"No."

"How about joining?"

She shrugged her shoulders. "They wouldn't want me."

"Why on earth not?"

She looked daggers at him. "I couldn't keep up."

It was an uncomfortable answer but he persevered. "Have you ever asked anyone?"

She shook her head. He was about to say more when there was a shout from opposite them. "There's still some food left! We need some gannets! Come on!"

"Wrong time of year for gannets," Eric observed as they made their way towards the door. "And how do we catch one?"

"I think they mean us," his brother told him.

"Oh…"

All four came in and were waved to the tables.

"But if you get ill, you two, I'll give you castor oil all next week." Mrs Baker was at her shrill best.

"Yes, Mum," they chorused as best they could through mouths already full. All four found that they had room left for more, and made suitable inroads.

Max asked Jack if he could have a key to Mill House. "Not if it's the only one," he said. "The builders will need one. But I need a space to work from and it seems that's the best place without being in your way."

"Oh, I can make room," he was told.

"Yes, but if I'm working in there if you're not around when there's a problem it'd look as if I'm taking over. I don't even want to hint at that. No, best if I'm well away, then it's obvious. Is there someone who could just give the room with the desk a bit of a clean? I can use that. Though I'll have to keep coming down to you for the phone."

"We can get an extension installed, surely."

"We'll have to. In fact that's one aspect of the whole thing I haven't thought through. When we've got different departments taking orders and needing to buy stuff, we're going to need quite a few extensions. I'll plan over the weekend and talk to you on Monday."

"You're coming down on Monday?"

"Yes, of course. There'll be builders popping in at any time, I should think. I'll have to commute until the building's ready – or at least until one room is habitable."

Jack blinked, surprised at the speed it looked as if things might be moving.

"Let me talk to my wife. We might be able to do something."

Max raised his eyebrows. Jack grinned.

"I won't say anything more until I know I'm on safe ground."

A laugh. "Touché!" said Max.

Whilst the main party was still enjoying the remainder of the food and the beer barrel Jack took the Wilsons over to the office with his wife.

He didn't beat about the bush. "Max, how do you feel about staying with us when you need to, until the House is ready? I don't want to take you away from your family but if the alternative is commuting each day it makes sense. I know people commute to London from Seaford but – well, it's your decision."

Max paused. Owen didn't like the idea of his father not coming home each night as he had being doing ever since he was born. But he knew that the offer made sense. And it would only be until the house was ready for them to move into. After that they would be seeing even more of each other than they had ever done.

Barbara was half scared this might be an option. How could she look after him if she hardly ever saw him? But she, too, decided that so long as he returned at weekends – or she and Owen travelled to Sussex at the weekends, it would make sense and be more efficient. And cheaper.

"It's a very kind offer," said Max. "But I think I need to talk to Barbara and Owen about it first. It's a big change."

"Of course you should." Maud spoke for the first time. "Decisions like that are family matters. We'll go into the other room and you can talk."

But nothing was decided then

After the following Sunday's football match Owen found himself talking to his father.

"Are you sure you want to leave school and all your friends here, and go and live in a tiny community with only three other people your own age?"

He wasn't expecting a question like that, having just accepted that's exactly what was going to happen.

"Yes." He was able to answer without delay. "I like them. I like the place, And, Dad, I *will* be able to go where I want there, won't I? Not have you or Mum saying that I'm too young, it's too dangerous or something, all the time?"

Max smiled. "Within reason, yes. Sussex, especially there, is so much safer than London. That's one of the reasons your mother and I wanted to move. There's more space there, more freedom for us all."

"So I'll just be able to get on a train – or a bus – and go into Seaford, or Newhaven."

"We'll talk it over with Mum, but I don't see why not, so long as we know where you are."

He nodded. "And can I join the Scouts there, and the football club?"

Max looked surprised. "Scouts… well, yes. I'm sure the football club's all right. We'll find out."

Owen nodded again. Max went back to his Sunday paper, Owen to his book. Then:

"Dad…"

The paper shook a little. A voice behind it said "Ye-es?"

"Can anything be done when someone has one leg shorter than the other?"

The paper lowered. "Well, I think the usual thing is to build up the shoe. But she's had that, hasn't she?"

"Yes. But she can't run like that, and it's very tiring, she says."

He thought.

"If she was a chair, I'd say she should have the other legs shortened too." He gave a sudden laugh.

Owen's face was straight. He looked into his father's eyes, willing him to realise what he'd just said. Max saw the look and the last vestiges of the laugh faded away. He looked back.

"Not funny, Dad."

It was the expression that was always used on him when he'd said something inappropriate. In Owen's case it was usually to prompt a response, a laugh, always without realising how the comment could be taken. This time Max had to re-run the conversation through his mind and think how his comment, intended as a joke, would be taken. At last he gave a wry nod to his son.

"No. It wasn't, was it? I'm sorry. Really."

It was one of the first apologies of that depth that Owen had ever received from either parent. It hinted to him, more than any more obvious conversation could have done, that he might actually be growing up. It seemed that at least Max was taking him more seriously than might have been the case even a few months previously. At the outskirts of his consciousness he couldn't help but wonder whether he would be taken more seriously, more often, once his voice broke.

"But what *can* be done, Dad?"

"I really don't know, old son. I imagine that her parents have looked into it and can't come up with anything. If they can't, how can we? It's not our job, really."

"But her Dad's on your staff."

Max smiled wryly. "Yes, but there's a limit to how far an employer can interfere in private lives, even if they care about their staff."

"But I can ask Ruth, Dad, can't I?"

"You can, but don't give any false hopes."

"It's just such a shame, seeing her hobbling everywhere. And it's so tiring for her. And she can't do sport or anything…"

"I know, I know. I suppose if necessary we can help, but let's find out what might be possible, if anything, eh?"

Owen nodded.

Max spent the week in Sussex, staying with the Pentelows as they had suggested. There were so many comings and goings, even that early in the scheme, that he couldn't afford to return to London each night.

He learnt how everyone in the village relied on each other for items forgotten or run out, and even for just a chat now and again. Maud Pentelow managed to run out of Bisto that first night, and was appalled and embarrassed when Max jumped up and said he'd go and borrow some from their neighbours who had just come to them for sugar.

"I can't have you doing that!" she cried. "You're a guest and you're Jack's boss. It's not right!"

"But how can I get to know people unless I talk to them?"

"But not like that, to borrow something off them!"

He smiled at her. "Best way of doing it. I'm a human. I got liked by my crews in the War by showing I was human, but it never stopped them from obeying orders when I gave them. Probably the reverse, in fact. So I'll nip up to the Decks' and borrow a cup of Bisto, shall I?"

He wouldn't be persuaded, and soon was knocking at their neighbours' door. Mary Decks was shocked to see him in just a jumper – it was raining – and awkwardly told him to come in. She seemed overawed.

"Who is it, duck?" came a voice at the door.

"It's... it's Mr Wilson, Arthur."

"Oh, hallo, sir. Is this a social call?"

"Well, sociable, but not social, if you see what I mean. Maud has run out of Bisto, you see, and she wondered if she might borrow some."

The old sailor grinned. His wife looked scandalised.

"And she sent you up to borrow some? Well, I never..."

Max laughed. "No, I embarrassed her by telling her I'd go. It's only fair. They're going out of their way to make me comfortable and I need a way to show my thanks."

"Well, yes, but..."

"And – well, that's the way I work."

Her expression softened. She smiled then, as did Arthur.

"Ruth okay?" asked Max. "My son will want to know."

"She's upstairs, resting that leg of hers and doing her homework. They get more of it as they get older, it seems. She's at the Lewes Grammar, you know." Unsurprisingly there was a note of pride in her voice.

"Owen gets a fair amount too. Seems a shame, but I suppose it's necessary."

"The school thinks so. He's at a Grammar, is he?"

"Yes. I suppose he'll go to Lewes too. He suffers from homework at the moment so it sounds as if he'll be working at home, just as Ruth does. Tell me, though – does that leg of hers give her much trouble?"

Mary Decks looked at him strangely. "What makes you ask... sir?"

"Oh," Max said airily, "you mentioned she was resting it, so I wondered if it was a real trouble."

"Well, yes it is. And the older she gets the worse it seems to be. She gets tired a lot. But it's a sore point with her and she doesn't like talking about it."

"I suppose not. Difficult. Does she get bullied at school over it? I remember in my school there was a lad with the same thing and he got treated quite badly."

"She doesn't really say. She just talks as little as possible about it. Just puts up with it, I suppose. Anyway look, here's the Bisto and you'd better get back before Maud wonders where you've got to."

Damn, thought Max to himself, and that was such a good introduction to the subject. Perhaps it would be best if Owen asks her after all. The natural tactlessness of youth and all that...

4 – Killicks

Tenders for the start of the works arrived over the next few weeks. There were enough companies interested to keep Max busy for the week after. And they did. He was so busy that he made no phone calls to his family at all. He was reminded about his shortcomings when he appeared at last at home, slightly dishevelled and very tired.

"We've got the people we want," he told Barbara and Owen. "They're not the cheapest but they come best recommended and aren't too expensive. Nice chap, I seem to remember from their visit. Now I have to persuade the Board to use them."

But the Board, when presented with the information, told him to use a different company, Smith and Co., who had submitted the lowest tender. They were insistent and he returned home with his tail between his legs.

At their cottage Ruth was told about the enquiry into her health from Owen via his father, and smiled. No one mentioned her leg.

The employees naturally discussed the upcoming changes and, in their cautious Sussex way, welcomed them. Even Mrs Fox was almost looking forward to having proper heated water, electricity and an indoor toilet, though she said nothing to anyone apart from "I'll believe it when I see it!"

Jack Barden, a young man referred to universally as "Jack the Lad" by other Mill residents, lived at the sea end cottage. At weekends since the announcement about refurbishing the Mill's housing he was to be seen carrying parcels from his house up to the station, where he caught a train to see his mother in Southease, just up the river. He had left the family home at sixteen when life in the little village had become too hot for him but now, four years later, he returned there when he had to, or needed to, or needed something done. Though he was always welcomed by her, if not his stepfather, it was always a welcome tinged with suspicion.

He returned from these laden outward journeys empty handed. His mother's garden shed gradually filled.

Max's return on Monday, muttering near obscenities to Jack Pentelow, brought a sympathetic but alarmed response.

"Truth is, I hoped they wouldn't tender. Not that lot. They have a bad name in the town for reliability and standards. You really need to get the Board to forget them and go to Killicks like I knew you wanted."

"Do you think I haven't tried? It took two hours of arguing just to get their backs up! Killicks it has to be, but how do we get them to agree?"

They both thought in silence.

"I know someone who started off a building with Smiths," said the Manager slowly. "They'd talk to us, and we could write down what they said. And if they know, others will have heard, and we could do the same there."

"Is that fair?" asked Max.

"Well... yes. It's a recommendation, but in reverse if you understand me. And if Smiths are allowed to start work here – well, it's your house they'd be doing first. When they're done with that perhaps you could ask the Board down to have a look at the quality."

"And then get Killicks to do it properly at the Board's expense?"

"What's the expression? No comment?"

Jack just grinned at him, and got a grin back.

Smiths received a call the next day telling them their success. Max made it very clear that it was strictly subject to the quality of the work being acceptable to the building's eventual residents and to the company's Board of Directors. If it failed to pass muster, not only would the contract be null and void but the invoices would have the cost of subsequent rectification deducted from them.

"I hope that is acceptable," he said. "I'll write to summarise what we've said, of course, and look forward to receiving confirmation and agreement by return of post, please. Subject to that, when would you be able to make a start on the Mill House?" he finished.

There was a pause on the other end of the phone.

"So you're expecting us to do the work, then if you're not happy we have to foot the bill for it to be put right. Is that it?"

"I suppose that's it in a nutshell, but I'm sure that you'd want to see the work done to a high standard."

"But it's only for one of the workers at the Mill, surely?"

"Does that matter? Or are you saying you wish to withdraw your tender?"

There was another pause.

"We might need to revise it."

"But it was a tender, not an estimate. If we now have to start the tender process again it will add further delay; a delay the company isn't prepared to accept."

"It doesn't have to be, surely? We could re-tender and you would make sure it's still the lowest."

"And how do I guarantee that, pray?"

"I'm sure you have ways."

"The Board of Directors and I are not fools. If one tender is higher than another we make a judgement about content, trust and attitude, influenced by local opinion." As Max spoke he just wished the Board had observed those standards.

"So having given us the contract, you're now taking it away."

"Not at all. You are saying that despite tendering, you now wish to quote a higher price. That is not observing the contents of the tender, as you'll discover if you read its preamble."

Another silence, then a disgruntled: "I'll have to phone you back."

"Can that be today, please? Other companies who have tendered are waiting for answers."

"I don't know if I can do that. Not all our people are here."

"Then I think it would be a good idea if you did what you have to so as to ensure a decision is made. It is now 9.45 am. I expect an answer by exactly this time tomorrow, otherwise we will contact the next acceptable lowest tender."

"Who is that?"

"I am not prepared to discuss that. The tender process is confidential, as you know."

When he had disconnected the call something made him wonder about the other tenders. Carefully he looked through, comparing not the prices but the names of each company's directors. Yes, there was a match. A managing director of Eastway's, a company with a higher tender amount had the same name as Smiths managing director.

On a whim, he called the second company. As soon as the phone was answered he put the receiver down.

It was the man he had been speaking to.

Max looked up at Jack across the office they were still sharing whilst the Post Office was considering when it would install more phone lines.

"Do you know either of those two?"

"Which two?"

"The two companies I was talking to."

"I wasn't listening. Sorry."

"Smith's and Eastway's."

"Wouldn't touch either of them."

"I think they're the same company."

"What?"

"They have the same managing director and the person who answers the phone is the same man."

"Is that legal?"

"I suppose so.

Max rose to his feet. "I need to write a letter to Smith's so it's all above board. See you later."

"Do you want a tea when we brew up?"

"That would be very nice. Thank you."

He returned to the Mill House with its one clean room. With two pieces of carbon paper to make two copies, he carefully wrote a response to Smiths' tender and summarised what they had said, including his deadline of the following morning for a reply. He was just checking it through when Arthur Decks appeared with a cup of tea.

"Thanks, Chief. That's very welcome. And by the way, I'm sorry if I embarrassed your wife the other day. It wasn't intentional. But as I said, I am a human being and I like talking to other human beings."

"Don't you worry, sir. She's just a bit reserved. She'll come round to it. She doesn't quite know what to do about our Ruth taking up with your boy either. But I told her that they're both young, and they'll find their own level at some point."

"Well, seeing that Owen will be going to the same school, chances are they'll continue friends. Whether anything comes of it is anybody's guess."

"But won't he be going to a private school, sir? There's enough of them in Seaford, after all."

"We've not discussed it, to be honest. He goes to a London Grammar school at the moment, so I doubt if we'll do anything different here."

"But should we stop them seeing each other, sir? They always seem to be together when young Owen is here."

"Why do that? No reason to, is there?"

"I didn't think you'd want your son getting too close to the likes of us."

Max felt astonished and almost offended. "The likes of you? CPO in the Royal Navy and you think you're family's not good enough for my son? Think again, Arthur. Men like you, people like yours are respected by ships' captains everywhere. Be proud. And Ruth's a lovely girl, too. And if they're friends, what the hell?"

"But what if it got serious, sir?"

"Then it gets serious, and if they marry we'll be sort of related. And that would please me a lot."

He found himself being scrutinised by two honest eyes in a way he'd not experienced since being weighed up by his crew as the new Captain of a ship. Then abruptly Arthur stood, facing him, at attention, and gave him the Navy salute. Instinctively he stood too and returned it. Arthur marched himself out.

Max sat again and grinned, then his grin faded as he realised he'd missed another opportunity to ask about Ruth's leg and its treatment.

Five minutes later there was another knock at the door. Jack Pentelow with a man Max recognised as a representative of one of the tendering construction companies.

"Mr Killick, sir, if it's convenient."

"Of course. Come in, and thank you, Jack."

"Thank you, Mr Wilson, and I'm sorry to barge in like this. See you later, Jack."

The man crossed to him and they shook hands.

"You know each other?" asked Max.

"Jack Pentelow? Yes. We play in a team at the Buckle."

"The Buckle – that's the pub at this end of Seaford, isn't it? What team?"

"That's the one. We play in a Toad-in-the-Hole league."

Startled, Max laughed. "I thought that was sausages in batter!"

The man laughed back. "It's a Sussex game. You chuck a big brass toad – a coin – at a lead topped table."

Max still looked startled. "It can't be as easy as it sounds."

"It's not, that's why it's a good game. And it goes well with beer."

"Sounds like I'd better come with Jack when there's next a game on."

"Tonight, then, as it happens. You'd better ask him."

"I will – see if he'll let me come."

"I shouldn't think he could object, really."

"Ah, but I'm a 'vurriner', as I heard Mrs Fox describe me the other day. I wouldn't want to push my nose in."

He laughed. "That woman! She doesn't know which side her bread's buttered."

"Ah, but she's honest – well, except with the rail company. And I appreciate that."

"You've heard about that, have you?"

"I experienced it the first time we came down here. But I thought Jack would have told you about that."

"Well, actually Jack has said nothing about you at all. Even the invitation to tender for work here took a lot of us by surprise."

"Good. Well done, Jack."

"You wanted it that way?"

"I didn't want news of our intentions getting out to anyone before the company I work for had bought Tide Mills. And it wouldn't have been right for him to have told you anything about the work."

"He's been as tight as a du... I mean, he's been almost comically silent about the Mill ever since he met you. We knew something was going on, because people kept coming down. But he refuses to say anything.

"But it's really the tender I wanted to talk about, if I may. I know yesterday was the due day, and I wondered if any decisions had been reached yet."

Max thought. He knew he could work with this large, tough looking man but didn't want to give too much away or run the risk of giving him false hopes.

"It's a bit of a difficult position at the moment," he said cautiously. "Can I just tell you that we are waiting for a decision from another company? You see, Killicks' wasn't the lowest tender and... well, it's a bit awkward."

His visitor nodded, wryly. "And I have to tell you that I can't come down from the price we tendered. That's because it was a tender and not a quotation, of course; but mainly because that was the best realistic price we could be confident with. I know there are some of our competitors who will quote lower, but... well... you must make up your own mind."

"Mr Killick, I hope it's obvious it's not my decision to make alone. Not this one. But this I'll promise to you: I'll do all in my power to get a definite answer to you by this time tomorrow."

"I know it's difficult. And I'm trying so hard not to see the company name on the envelope on your desk, and even harder not to make any comment. So I'd better go. Maybe we'll meet tonight at the Buckle."

Max chuckled, but didn't hide the envelope. "I'll enjoy it. I'll stand you a pint."

"Should be me doing that for you, surely?" Mr Killick said with a smile.

"Best not. It might look like bribery."

They both laughed, shook hands and the visitor left.

Max posted his letters, one to Smith's and the other to his Chairman of Governors.

His head was thick the next morning. Toad-in-the-Hole turned out to be a game that worked best with copious quantities of Harveys bitter and he had apparently made it work quite well. He and Jack were now on Christian name terms, as was Martin Killick; something he almost regretted the next morning.

The phone was ringing when he entered their shared office. With some consternation he discovered the person on the other end was his Managing Director, who was being curt with him about the Smith's business.

"I haven't heard from Smith's yet about the contents of our phone conversation yesterday," Max said with some asperity. "They will have had the letter summarising its contents by now, as I got it delivered last night. You have a copy of it."

"If they are not acceptable or decline, what do you intend to do?"

"The next reliable tender is that from Killicks. Mr Killick visited me yesterday to ask about progress as he knew the closing date had passed. I told him, naturally, that I could give him no answer as the situation was unclear."

"And have Smith's contacted you yet?"

"No; the post has yet to arrive, and of course the telephone line is currently engaged."

"I want to know the situation as soon as something is known. Really, a construction company who doesn't understand how the tender process works... really!"

"I'm sure they do. I'm sure they quoted low believing they could skimp because it was, as they put it, 'only mill staff' who would occupy the houses'."

"Well, it will be."

"And my family. And we would be the first affected."

"Well, let me know what happens."

"Very well. If I have no contact from Smiths by 9.45 this morning I intend to call Killicks and tell them their tender is the preferred one, and they can consider the start of the contract theirs. Once I have their response I will call you immediately."

There was a very long pause. Max wondered if the connection had failed.

"Very well. It is not what the Board or I wanted but if there is no alternative then that is what must be."

"Indeed. It is a nuisance. But from what I am being told Killicks is the better firm by far. In fact Smiths have received a very bad press locally, as I said to you and the Board. Only word of mouth, you understand, but that almost always counts for a lot. And putting in another tender under a different company name – well!"

"Yes. That was an attempt at very sharp practice. I'm glad we saw through that."

Who saw through it? Max asked himself. Then, into the phone: "Indeed. Very well, I will tell you what happens, and that will probably happen within the next hour."

The telephone did not ring again before 9.45. Max gave it another fifteen minutes.

"Jack?"

"Max."

"You keep a diary, don't you?"

"I do."

"Then can you note that we were awaiting a call from a contractor which was due at 9.45 this morning, but no calls whatsoever were received by 10.00?"

"I can. Consider it done."

"And how is your head this morning?"

"Well, if truth be told…" he grinned shamefacedly "…not particularly wonderful."

"Thank goodness. I thought it was just me. Now I need to do something I've wanted to do since yesterday."

"What's that"

"Phone Martin Killick and ask him how *his* head is and tell him he's won the tender."

Jack laughed. "Be careful he doesn't offer you a pint in celebration!"

Max dialled the number.

"Mr Killick, please. Maxwell Wilson from Tide Mills."

Pause.

"Killick."

"Good morning Mr Killick."

"Good morning… er… Mr Wilson."

"I'm telephoning to ask you… how your head is this morning."

Pause, then laughter.

"It's bloody awful, Max! As yours probably is."

"Well, maybe. But I just thought I'd check with you to make sure I'm not coming down with something."

"No, it's definitely to do with Harveys and toads."

"That sounds like a firm of solicitors."

More laughter, then "Ow!"

"Well, while you're holding your head – I take it that was what the 'ow' was about – I suppose I'd better tell you that you have won the tender for the work at Tide Mills."

A pause. Then a sigh.

"I hope that doesn't mean you can't do it," said Max, suddenly worried.

"No. No, not at all. It was a sigh of relief."

"Relief?"

"Yes. We just had a large customer cancel a massive build because someone else has quoted lower than us."

"Can I guess it's one of two companies?"

"You can guess, Max, but I can't confirm. Anyway, when do you want us to start?"

"Today."

"Okay."

"WHAT?" Max was now thoroughly startled.

"Well, we have some spare capacity today. Now, usually that would give me no pleasure at all, but if I can at least start getting plant into the village it'd be useful. As more people become free I can get them there, and we can get to full speed next week, more or less. How does that sound?"

"That sounds absolutely wonderful. I really wasn't expecting to see a start before next month, especially as it's getting on towards the end of the year."

"Which is a good time to do indoor jobs, which is why I want to start as soon as possible."

"And I thought I was going to startle *you!*"

He laughed. "You did, Max. But nicely. And what is better still, I'm glad to be working with you."

"The same here. Now look, I need to confirm the bones of this and include a payment schedule…"

They chatted about the details, then Max sat back with a satisfied smile.

"I couldn't help overhearing," said Jack. "To see your face makes me think it went well."

"You are absolutely spot on," Max told him. "And now I must tell my Board the good news – who knows, I might even persuade them that we are getting the quality of work we want for a lower price than Smiths would have charged."

But before he could lift the receiver again, the phone rang. Jack answered, as agreed.

"Just a moment," he said after listening for a few seconds, "I'll try and find him."

He covered the receiver with his hand. "Smith's," Max was told quietly.

"Tell them I'm on my way back to the office, would you? I'll make appropriate sound effects in a few minutes."

The manager smiled and put the phone on the desk. Unhurriedly Max went to the door, opened and closed it, and walked back.

"It's Smith's," said Jack, acting the part without being asked.

"Oh! Oh dear, they're 45 minutes too late. I told them 9.45. Oh well…" He picked up the receiver and identified himself. This time the man was quite a bit more apologetic.

"I'm really sorry to be later than you wanted, but we had a lot of work to do on the quotation, then your line was engaged…"

Max stopped him. "There is no quotation involved. As we discussed yesterday and as I reinforced in my letter last night, the process was a tender. We chose the lowest, most acceptable tender figure."

"Well, we discussed…"

"Also, I told you on the phone and in writing that I needed your response by 9.45 this morning. I gave you fifteen minutes leeway after that time. No calls were received or made on this line before that point. That indicated to me that Smiths were unable to honour their tender whilst providing the quality of workmanship we expect."

"Now just hold on…"

"I'm afraid you have misunderstood both the tender documents and my letter."

"Not at all. I needed some time to consult with my Managing Director to see what we could do for you. He's now given me an answer."

"Which I can't accept as you have not responded within the deadline I set

48

you yesterday, by phone and in writing."

"But… but our Managing Director will have my guts for garters if I don't get this contract."

"You need to tell him that he was too late getting the information to you. My requirement was very clear. You never even contacted me to ask for more time."

"Well, you will be hearing from my Managing Director…"

"Will I now? Would that be your own Managing Director, or the Managing Director from Eastways?"

Silence.

"Goodbye, Mr Wilson."

Killicks were as good as Martin's word. Equipment and materials started arriving late that afternoon and continued the following morning. Max went to Seaford to get some more keys cut so they could come and go without reference to him. His return saw them working on the kitchen, and looking anxiously at his study, wondering about its being vacated.

Max made appropriate arrangements simply by moving temporarily in with Jack.

"Although," he said, "I don't really know what I can do until we have a timescale. Certainly not a lot without an office, anyway, with due respect to you."

"Why don't you go home and spend some time with the family, Max? Perhaps bring them down at the weekend to see what's happening. There'll be a young lass looking forward to seeing Owen again, I'm thinking, and the Baker boys will be pleased too."

"I might just do that, if Barbara hasn't made different plans. And we could take you two out for a meal; it's about time we fed you!"

"There's no need…"

"Maybe not, but I'd like to. I'll go, then call you about which day we can come, which actually means which day that son of mine doesn't have a football match!"

His arrival in London was met with pleased surprise by Barbara, and a typically more muted, but sincere, welcome from his son when he returned from school. Twice he explained all that had happened and both of his listeners were suitably impressed.

"When can we move in, Dad?" was the inevitable question from one of them.

Max laughed. "Killicks have only just started, and Christmas is coming. You have a term to finish here, and actually we need to make arrangements to get you into a school from January, I suppose."

Although they had been planning a move for ages it struck both Barbara and Owen that this was now actually going to happen. Soon. In practical terms and sooner than they had been imagining.

Barbara just hoped, again, that it would work out and that they – she – would find a way to be happy in the tiny, remote settlement, a community that was different from everything she had ever known. She realised she would have a lot of adjustments to make, not just in what she did but in how she viewed her surroundings.

Owen was ambivalent, despite having been the *agent provocateur* behind the move. He was looking forward to the company at Tide Mills, certainly, and to the freedom which he had been denied in London where his parents deemed it risky. But in London was his football club, his good acquaintances and one or two real friends. There was also the school he was used to and knew like the back of his hand. He weighed up the pluses and minuses constantly. Every time the scales tipped in favour of moving he would think that he'd missed some argument, and would start agonising all over again.

They made the journey to Sussex again that Saturday as Owen had no match that weekend. Once again they used the little steam hauled train to Lewes before joining the elderly electric version to Seaford. This time the weather was more unkind, the sea rougher and everything appeared more workaday and dismal.

Mother and son thought back to parts of London in this weather: was it really so much more depressing? They walked down from the little station, collars up and heads down against the weather. The street was deserted.

"Can we go to the Mill House first, Dad, and see what they've done so far?"

"I suppose so. Then we can leave anything there that we don't want to carry around with us."

The newly lubricated lock opened easily and the smell of new paint welcomed them. The hallway was littered with paint cans, wallpaper tables, tools and a variety of building materials to be used for structural repairs and alterations.

They discovered the kitchen to be uninhabitable, just a cleaned and redecorated shell. The office had just been started.

"Well," said Barbara, "We can't live here yet."

"They've only had three days!" Max exclaimed. "The stuff only started arriving on Tuesday. I think they've done well to get even this far. Look!" he crossed to a window in its west wall and pointed at it. "They've even put a double-glazed window in already."

They crowded round it, the first that any of them had seen. It looked deep, and heavy for its size. But what they noticed most was that although the wind and rain were coming straight at it, hardly a sound could be heard of it. There was no draught to be felt coming in as there would have been through one of their London home's windows.

There was a noise at the door. They swung round. Ruth stood there, dripping from the school mac that she had hurriedly put over her head. Owen felt his face crease into a smile.

"Oh, it's you," said the dripping one, "I'm so glad. I thought we had intruders."

"No," Owen wanted to get in first, "It's only us."

"Hallo Mrs Wilson, Mr Wilson… good to see you again." She stuck there, lost for words.

"Put your mac down with ours, Ruth." Barbara took command. "We're just looking round again and seeing what they've done. And I'm too impatient, thinking it would all be done in just three days!"

"I know they started on Wednesday," Ruth said. "I saw them there when I was going to school."

"They've nearly finished the kitchen," said Owen. "Come and look."

"I hope they haven't," exclaimed his mother. "There's a lot more to be done there. There are cupboards and all sorts of things still to go in, and we want more electrical points, and the sink's got to be put in properly, and..."

"Have you seen the plans, Ruth?" Owen interrupted. "Then you can see what she's asked for. I think she plans to start a restaurant."

"I most certainly do NOT!" his mother smiled. "But things have moved on since these places were equipped, so why shouldn't we build in some convenience?"

"Mum would like that," said Ruth wistfully.

"Well, now's her chance to tell me." Max's turn to interrupt. "Up to a point the company will provide, but this one the Wilsons are part funding too. I need to talk to everyone about what they want, in detail."

"Come and look at this window, Ruth," Owen commanded. "It's magic. See? It's raining cats and dogs and you can't feel it in here."

She looked.

"You'll need that in your room too."

"Because it faces west?"

"Yes."

"Then you need one in yours too."

She flushed. "I don't think..."

"But Dad said that all the cottages were going to get double glazing. Didn't you, Dad? It's not just the Mill House."

"I did, and they will. All windows on the south and west where the weather mainly comes from."

"You're doing that for us?" she asked, astonished.

"The Company is. I said so. Why not? We all deserve a little comfort."

She was silent for a moment, then just said: "Thank you."

"How about upstairs?" Owen asked. "Have they started up there yet? Come on, Ruth; let's go up to my room and see what they've done. Perhaps I've got double glazing already."

He ran upstairs, two at a time as usual. Ruth followed more slowly, her shorter leg obviously giving trouble. Owen realised on the first floor landing and waited.

"Sorry."

"It's okay."

"Should have thought."

"No, s'okay really."

He climbed the next set of stairs more normally, matching his speed to hers. At last they were in his room. She looked round. Nothing had been touched in it yet.

"Still dirty," said Owen.

"Hmm. But I like it. It feels right."

"That's what I felt," he said

"Did you?"

"Yes. That's why I said that it was going to be mine."

She smiled again, then the smile faded. Owen didn't notice. He was busy looking around.

"What can I see from here, then?" he asked of no one in particular. Used to being on his own he would often ask himself a question out loud.

"Rain, I should think. But normally you could see the harbour and the ships, and Castle Hill behind it. There's an old fort up there – they used it in the war, but I think it's going to be built on."

A particularly strong gust of wind made her step back and she trod on Owen's toe. She almost overbalanced and Owen put an arm to her shoulder to steady her.

"Ow," he said.

"Sorry."

"I shouldn't have been in the way."

"*I* shouldn't have overbalanced."

"Does it hurt much?"

"The leg? No. Not at all. It just hurts when I walk a long way, or try and run."

"Can't anything be done to help?"

"It has been. My shoe's been built up."

"No, I mean permanently."

"What – stretching it, you mean? No. We've been through all that with the doctor, and I don't like talking about it."

"But… if that one can't be stretched, how about making the other one shorter?"

He felt awkward making the suggestion in view of her previous comment. Also, this sounded to him like his father's argument which he had reacted against.

"Sorry…" he muttered.

Silence.

"What about from this window?" he asked, trying to restart communications.

"Just the station and the road. The hill is Rookery Hill. They've been talking about building on it on top of the cliff by the road."

He nodded. "There's even a draught through this one. Good thing they'll both be double glazed."

"I'll come up and tell you if I prefer it," she told him.

He smiled. "And I'll come to yours when yours are done."

She laughed quietly. "I've never had a boy in my room before."

"And I've never had a girl in mine. You're the first."

She wasn't sure how to take that, and after considering it in the silence that ensued he blushed.

"I didn't mean…"

She interrupted. "Well, actually I have had boys in my room. Alan and Eric. But they don't count, really."

"And I do?"

He found himself being pierced by her gaze.

"Walked here from Seaford, didn't you?"

He had to grin at that.

"Anyway, I don't think I'd want to be any shorter."

Owen blinked, then realised. He shrugged.

"Just a thought. They're your legs, anyway." He sat on wide mattress support slats on the old bed which creaked mournfully. Ruth joined him, causing more creaking. They grinned at each other.

"Hope that *was* the bed and not you," said Ruth.

"Blinking cheek!" he said, and dug her gently in the ribs. She bent sideways, lost her balance and ended up with her top half lying on the slats. Owen smiled down at her. She was about to hoist herself up when she noticed the edge of a piece of paper. It seemed as if most of it was held under the wood of the slat.

"What's this?"

"What's what?"

"This. Get up and I'll see if I can get it out."

5 – Sovereigns

They stood. Cautiously she gripped the visible edge and pulled, and grittily the remainder of a folded sheet appeared. She opened it.

"It's a letter."

They sat again and read the scribbled writing as best they could.

> *Three weeks back I was rescued from the Annie by the kings men. They suspect nothing. I was sick and put to bed here. Mas Holden had made me hide what I had against the revenue. That I have but think Mas Holden will tak me and use me badly when he wants his money or the Revenue will hold me until I tell. If you see this come find me I pray. Use the coins to pay for my freedom. Isaac Galley the fifteenth May 1914*

"Wow!" said Ruth. "Isaac Galley. What a name! I wonder what happened to him? And what was the Annie? And what's this money, and where is it?"

"It must be in here somewhere," said Owen. "Is there nothing anywhere on the bed? Under it?"

"How? There's nowhere it could be."

"Underneath? Inside it somewhere?"

"Surely they'd have been discovered by now."

"Not if the house was shut up soon after… when was it closed?"

"Dad said it was empty for twenty years. That's only 1944."

"The year before the war ended."

"And this was written in 1914 – thirty years before."

"Someone here must remember him," said Ruth thoughtfully. "I wonder if Dad does. Or Mr Pentelow."

"Or Mrs Fox…"

"You can go and ask her," said Ruth. "She scares me. Always has."

"She's probably lonely, Dad says. Perhaps if she was asked about the past…"

"Huh!"

"Well, if you get no information from your parents or Mr Pentelow I'll go and ask her. Are you sure there's nowhere else you haven't looked?"

She ran her hands along the bottom of the rails and the rest of the slats. Nothing.

Owen knelt on the floor and looked all round. Still nothing. Just about to get to his feet again he noticed something that puzzled him.

"Odd."

"What?"

"There's a gap between the slats and the wood they rest on."

"But they're all screwed down."

"I know. But still… let's try unscrewing one."

"What with?"

"There's bound to be a screwdriver somewhere – the whole house is full of tools at the moment."

He stood, looked down, and brushed off his trousers. Ruth giggled.

"You're going to get into trouble!"

Downstairs again they found a large, bluff man talking to the Wilson parents. Max looked round as they appeared.

"Owen, this is Mr Killick. It's his company doing the alterations and decorating."

Owen found his hand in a grip which threatened to crush it.

"Hallo Owen. And this is your sister?"

"No sir, a friend. She lives here already."

Martin looked disconcerted. "But we thought there was nobody living here…"

"No, not *here*, in Tide Mills," Ruth corrected him.

"Ah, that's all right then. We'll be seeing your family later, I hope. That is if we do a good job here and Owen's Dad keeps us on as his contractor."

"Are you doing my room next?" asked Owen hopefully.

"And which one might that be?"

"Top floor, first on the right."

"Well, we can, but the first thing is to get the windows in and make sure all the rooms have a power socket. When the juice was laid on they just put one in the hallways. That's no good nowadays. I suppose you want a basin in your room, or a complete bathroom in the corner like they do in America?"

Owen's eyes opened wide.

"Yes please…" he started, then saw the laughter in the eyes.

"Okay Owen," said his father, "you can if you pay for it."

It was Owen's turn to smile, though not to forget the idea.

Martin turned back to address Barbara and Max. "We'll be able to make real inroads into it from next Monday," he said. "I was going to get the cleaning gang in first, but as we're doing windows and power, as well as the bathroom, it'd actually be quicker to get them in after that so we can decorate. Another three weeks should see most of it complete. By that time you'll be able to see what's what and have a check on the quality. If you agree it's all right we could have a look at one or two of the smaller cottages and get plans drawn up properly."

"If the treatment you've given this window is anything to go by, I think the quality is good already."

"Thanks. We do our best. I had an inkling you'd be down this weekend so I got our guys to get on with it – so I'll hold my hands up to that!"

There was more talk about the Mill House and they made to walk down to see Jack Pentelow.

"Dad, can we stay here, please? I want to look for something."

His father looked surprised. "Okay, but we're taking the Pentelows out to lunch, remember."

"We'll catch you up," he promised. "We'll come down to the Pentelows afterwards, shall we?"

"Yes, or we'll shout up the stairs at Mill House as we pass if the door's still unlocked."

They parted. Owen was about to run back to the House when he remembered Ruth's leg, so walked instead. In the hallway they found a screwdriver without difficulty and returned to the bedroom. Owen sat on the slats which groaned as they had before. He applied the screwdriver carefully and after a while the two screws holding one end of one of the slats was free.

He handed the tool to Ruth. She undid the screws on the other end of the slat. They lifted it.

Between the two screw holes at each end of where the slat had been was a golden disc. They each grabbed one and the heads bent.

On one side there seemed to be a horse whose hooves were trampling something. Riding the horse was what each of them recognised as Britannia, the same figure from the front of their own pennies, but in a more mobile pose. On the back was the still familiar head of George V with the usual writing around it.

"*Is* that a sovereign?" asked Ruth.

"I think so," Owen said, "But I don't really know. Should we get more out?"

They had unscrewed another ten slats by the time a shout came from below. They now had twenty-two of the coins.

"Now what?" asked Ruth.

"How many more might there be?"

They each counted the remaining slats.

"Five," said Owen, "That's another ten of them."

"That's… that's thirty two altogether," said Ruth. "But what do we do with them now?"

There was another shout from downstairs. Owen called back: "Coming."

"We'll take them down with us and put them in your mac pockets," said Owen. "I'll take one up to London and find a coin collector somehow. I know, there's a goldsmiths near us. He'll know what to do."

Downstairs, with no one in the hall, they were able to balance the coins between Ruth's pockets, making her mac extremely heavy.

The others were outside. Ruth was due to return home, to Owen's regret, although he acknowledged that she had to dispose of the coins safely.

"I'll ask Mum or Dad about Isaac Galley," she promised.

To Owen it seemed inadequate just to say okay and wave to her as he walked away. He felt there should be something else.

Whilst they were having lunch with the Pentelows Owen did some mental arithmetic. By the sound of the note they had found, Isaac must have been quite young if he was in danger of being 'used badly' by Mas Holden. So if the note was written in 1914 and it was now 1963 that would be 49 years ago. If Isaac was, say, mid teens, he would have been born at about the turn of the century. Isaac would be about 63 now, the same age as the year.

Looking at Jack Pentelow he wondered how old the man was. He wished he could quietly ask Ruth whether she'd mind the man being shown the note. But she wasn't there.

During a lull in the conversation he asked outright.

"Excuse me, sir, but have you heard of the name Isaac Galley?"

Jack gave a start. "Good heavens, Owen, where did you get that name from? Haven't heard of him for years."

"Oh... well, I heard it somewhere and it was connected to here, I thought."

"Well now... it's a sad story, really. Yes, old Galley and his son were here. Galley himself worked at the Mills and Isaac was one of the boys I was at school with, though he was a few years older than me. But it's a name you remember, isn't it? So yes, I know the name. And I knew the boy."

"What happened, please sir?"

The man shook his head. "The father was on his own. I don't know what had happened to the mother. He wasn't good with money, we learnt afterwards. Isaac got into bad company and got involved in smuggling, it was said, though nobody knew much about it. Then one day he had to be rescued from a fishing boat that had been forced onshore on a southerly gale. The boat was floated next day by the owner, but he either didn't know or wouldn't say who had been commanding her that day. The owner said he wasn't. We thought someone else had taken her without permission.

"All the others on board were seen scarpering along to Seaford, see, with the wind behind them, and no one could see where they went, let alone follow them.

"Anyway, young Isaac was near drowned, and pretty ill, and spent a couple of months in the Mill House. As he got better the Revenue men talked to him but although they were thorough – so Isaac told me afterwards – they didn't get anything from him even by searching his clothes which were all that were left him.

"They said they would come back when he was better, but one day he came to us and told us he was running away. Someone must have overheard and told the Revenue because we were told they came and arrested him for smuggling.

"You know what it's like. We were all about your age, and even when it's one of your own in trouble you don't just turn up and go to a Court to listen. And we all had school anyway. And we never saw him again. Soon after, the father just upped sticks and left, and we never saw either of them again."

Owen digested this.

"And he's not been seen since."

"Not once."

"But what about the others on the boat? Or the owner? Did they catch them?"

"No. The crowd who ran, they just vanished. And the owner – well, he was a Councillor too, and the Police and Revenue people left him well alone. What he said counted as fact as far as they were concerned."

"His name wasn't Mas Holden, was it?"

"How did you know that?"

"I heard it from the same people. Is Mas a Sussex name?"

"No – Holden's name was James. 'Mas' is just Sussex for Master, or Mister as we'd say now. But Holden was a right bully of a man. If you were around Newhaven somewhere he didn't want you to be, he'd likely thump you, kid or adult. You didn't mess with him."

The waiter visited the table again, so putting a halt to the questions. Owen had got many of the answers he needed, and Mr Pentelow seemed to know nothing more. Owen didn't want to be pushed into revealing the reasons for his questions.

When they returned the adults went into the office. Owen called at Ruth's cottage – with the key to the Mill House – and gave her the news.

"Does that mean the money's his, if he's still alive?" she asked.

"I suppose so," he said after some thought. "But how did he get it?"

She shrugged. "Does it matter? After all he went through? And nobody knows where it came from – there's nobody to ask."

"Perhaps it was this Holden's."

"Well, if it was he doesn't deserve it," she said decisively.

Owen nodded. "So if Isaac is still around, we think it's his. If he's not, we can keep it."

"You mean *you* can keep it. It's going to be *your* house."

"But *we* found it. It belongs to both of us."

"If we can't find Isaac."

"If we can't find Isaac. I can go to the Post Office in central London and see if he's listed in any of the local directories. They've got them all there."

"Do you live near the main part of London, then?"

"No, but we can just get on a tube and get there. Easy. Look, should I tell the parents about this?"

"You can if you want. It's your money."

"No, it's *our* money if we can't find Isaac. So you decide too."

She gave in. "All right, *our* money. I suppose we can if necessary, but let's see how far we can get on our own, shall we?"

By this time they had left her house and were walking towards the Mill House. Two figures bounded out of a cottage and ran up to them.

"We saw you when you went in to the Big House," Eric told them, "but Mum said leave them alone because they want to look at it properly."

Alan nodded. "Can we come and have a look?"

"How d'you know we're going there?" asked Ruth.

"Well, you are, aren't you?"

Owen lifted his eyebrows. How could they get the rest of the coins with the two boys there? Ruth would have to take them round the rest of the house while he undid the screws.

He unlocked the door. "Ruth, could you take them round? I'm going up to what's going to be my room to decide where things are going, and start getting rid of that old bed frame."

She understood the message and started off with the work that had been done so far. Using delaying tactics and making a lot of noise when finally they arrived on the second floor she was glad to see Owen's door opening and the room's owner peering out. He nodded privately to her.

Alan and Eric were suitably impressed.

"What's happening in the attic?" asked Alan.

"The attic? I don't know," Owen told him. "Don't even know how to get into it."

"Through there," Alan told him, pointing to a trapdoor in the hall ceiling that the other two hadn't noticed.

"Have to get a ladder some time and explore," he replied.

"Can we come?" asked Eric.

"I'd need to look first, see what's up there."

"Aww..."

"It's not your house, Eric."

He looked sulky for a moment. "Well, when you've seen, can we?"

Owen laughed. "Once I've had a look, Ruth will too, and you can."

"I like your room," said Alan. Eric nodded.

"Thanks. Not bad, is it?"

Eventually they left. He was able to say quietly to Ruth that he had two more slats to remove, then he'd come downstairs. Alone again he attacked the screws again. The last four, on the last slat, were impossible to turn. Looking at it he noticed that it was flush to its supports. There would be no room for any coins.

He did more mental arithmetic. Thirty sovereigns. Thirty pounds if they were worth a pound each still. But he knew that old coins were often more valuable than that to collectors. A visit to the jewellers was the next step. He distributed the remainder of the coins between his pockets and joined the others downstairs.

As privately as possible he handed the remaining eight coins to Ruth, and whispered "Thirty" to her. Her eyes sparkled.

"Have you still got one?" she whispered back.

His parents had been talking schools to the Pentelows and the Decks who had joined them.

"He's coming to the Grammar in Lewes, surely," said Ruth.

"We don't know that," said her mother. "He might go to one of the posh schools."

"No," said Max, "Not unless we find that the Grammar is useless; and from what you've told me, it's not. But Barbara and I need to see it, with Owen of course. I'll make an appointment on Monday, I think, then we can all come down in the week and look at it."

"Does that mean a day off for me, Dad?" asked Owen.

"Looks like it. Or half a day if we can get back in time."

He looked almost disappointed. But half a day was better than none, and he was pretty sure returning to London to restart school after the lunch break was not going to be possible; not if he delayed things enough.

"It's not a bad place, they say," Alan volunteered.

"What sport do they do?" Owen asked him.

"Not sure. I failed the eleven-plus so I don't go there. But I suppose it's Football, cricket in summer, swimming, cross country."

He nodded. That sounded good. Something else occurred to him to ask.

"What was that football going on in the field near the road, first time I came down?" he asked. "Looked like tents there, too."

"Oh that," Alan scoffed. "That's the Boys' Brigade. They come down every year. When they're there I get a load of our Scouts, in uniform, and we go and walk past them messing about, then go up through one of the footpaths onto the Downs. Makes their officers furious, but they can't say anything."

"Don't you play them at football?"

"No. Why should we?"

Owen used one of his father's expressions: "Any excuse!"

Alan sniffed. "Scouts don't have anything to do with them," he said positively. "Come from London, anyway... oh. Sorry."

Owen laughed.

Back in London, the coin was constantly on Owen's mind. After school on Monday he walked down to the jeweller.

"Please could you tell me what this is worth?" he asked, putting the sovereign on the counter.

The woman behind the counter examined it, looked up at Owen and curtly told him to wait there. He was alarmed that she took the coin with her and was about to call after her, but it seemed too late.

Eventually she returned with a serious faced man and, Owen was glad to see, the sovereign.

"Where did you get this from?" asked the man abruptly.

"Er... we found it and wanted to know what it's worth," said Owen.

"Where did you find it?"

Owen was stung at the tone. Why should a complete stranger question him? He decided to tell part of the truth.

"Under a bed in a house we'll be living in," he said.

"And have you tried to contact the previous owner?"

"The house has been empty for twenty years. Look, I just want..."

"If we have someone like you asking us to buy a sovereign – you do know what that is, I suppose? – we have to be cautious in case it was stolen."

"I'm not asking you to buy it. I'm asking you what it's worth. And it hasn't been stolen."

"So you say. But we have to be sure."

Owen waited.

"Have you nothing else to say?"

"Yes," said Owen, "I'd like my sovereign back."

It was the man's turn to look uncertain.

"Well, I will give it to you, but I will be telling the Police about this and giving them your description."

Owen was now shaken, as well as angry. He knew he had done nothing wrong.

"Okay," he told the man, "You're very welcome to. My name is Owen Wilson, my father is manager of the mill up the road. All I want to do is to find the owner of this if I can, and tell him what it's worth. And return the coins and tell him the full value of them."

Another silence.

"You mean there are more?"

"Are you going to call the Police?"

"How many more are there?"

"May I have the sovereign back, please? I think I need to go somewhere else."

"Just a minute, just a minute… I will give you £5 per sovereign if you have them."

"May I have that one back please?"

The man reluctantly handed it over. Owen put it safely in his pocket and turned away.

"All right, £6 each, then."

He turned back. "What is actually the value of it? That is what I need to know."

The man sighed. "I could give you £8."

"So that's its value?"

"Something like that."

"So if someone else offers me more – say a coin collector – I can bring the Police back and tell them you tried to swindle me?" Owen wondered where he had found the courage to talk to the man like that, if not from his anger.

Waiting for no more from either of them he walked out of the shop, leaving them to close the door. He went home, still fuming.

"Muuum…"

That usually spells trouble, Barbara thought.

"What's up now?"

"Do you know anything about sovereigns?"

"What, kings and queens, or coins?"

"Coins."

"Well, they're not common. I think you can still get them but they were superseded by the pound note."

"What about old ones?"

"How old?"

"Oh, sort of 1914-ish."

She looked surprised, then thoughtful. "Well, we'd still have been on the gold standard then…"

"What's that?"

"When the coin itself was tied to the price of gold. I don't mean that a sovereign weighed sixteen ounces, but it was actually worth one pound."

"Oh," said Owen, deflated, "so if I had a sovereign dated 1914 that's what it'd be worth."

"Oh no. It'd be worth far more than that to a collector."

"How much?"

"I really don't know. You father might, but I doubt it. You really want to ask a collector."

"Do you know any?"

"No. But what's happened? Have you found one at Tide Mills or something?"

He was so tempted to tell her the full story but just said that he had, and wanted to know what it was worth.

"Dad'll be able to find out."

Max did find the value. "Just over £20," he said.

Owen was astonished, but pleased. Max was cautious.

"Look, old chap, if you're really found one it needs to go back to the previous owner. You can't just keep it."

"We're trying to return it. But we need to find out who the owner was."

"Just ask Jack Pentelow."

"I did – sort of. We think it's this Isaac Galley."

"But how did you know it was that – what was his name? – who owned it?"

"Dad – I just do, that's all. Ruth and I are going to try and track him down."

Max sighed. "Okay, but you're not to sell it or give it to anyone without talking to us first, okay? We just want to make sure it's all legal."

"The jewellers down the road wasn't legal," Owen exclaimed. "He tried to offer me £5 for it. Then when I told him I didn't want to sell it he increased it to £8."

"Hmm. Thank you for the warning. We'll give him a wide berth, then."

Owen wrote to Ruth, telling her the news and urging her to keep the coins safe. She wrapped them in some newspaper and put them at the back of the top shelf of one of her built-in cupboards, then wrote back to tell him.

The date of the school visit was set as the following Friday. The rest of Owen's class were envious when he told them and indulged in all sorts of raucous comments, which he ignored with a smile. He planned to persuade his parents to let him spend some time in London's main post office which, he'd been told, was at Trafalgar Square.

They arrived at the school at about 10.30, as requested. A boy who must have been only just eleven, and who introduced himself by the nickname of Scamp, directed them to Reception.

The headmaster seemed pleasant and welcoming. He had arranged for a pupil to show them round, a stony-faced boy called Malcolm Botting to whom Owen took an immediate dislike.

"He comes from Seaford too," said the headmaster. "He comes in by train, like most of the others from there and Newhaven. Your parents tell me you know a girl from your village – what was it? Tide Mills?"

"Yes, sir," said Owen. "It's actually Bishopstone Tide Mills."

"Ah, Bishopstone I know. Lovely little village."

Was it Owen's imagination but did their prospective guide toss his head?

After a little further talk the tour started. As they walked around they had many curious glances from just about everybody, to Owen's embarrassment. He found it difficult to concentrate on what the boy was trying to tell them. They were about to head upstairs when what seemed like a complete class thundered down them. They stood aside. One of the figures skidded to a halt, nearly causing a major accident.

"Hallo!" the figure almost screamed, before resolving itself into Scamp whose excitement at temporary freedom as well as seeing them again subsided when he realised that the senior Wilsons were there too.

"Hallo Scamp," said Barbara. "I hope you haven't damaged the rest of your class too much."

He looked round at the two who had been sent sprawling. "Mum says we bounce."

The casualties looked up, grinned and resurrected themselves, then noticed Malcolm Botting. Their grins faded and they walked off down the corridor.

"Having the tour?" asked Scamp.

"We are," Owen confirmed. "With Malcolm."

"Who?"

"Malcolm. Malcolm Botting."

"Oh I see. His smile had gone. "We just use surnames. Anyway, I've got to go – the tuck shop shuts in five minutes. See you!"

And with that he was away.

"Do we get Eric cannoning into us as well?" Max asked.

"No. He's still at Primary school in Seaford," Owen told him.

He nodded and Malcolm Botting continued the tour. The information they received from him was stilted and not very informative, but by careful questioning they gained a reasonable impression. The information was not what a teacher would have given them, but it was a little more perceptive and more accurate a description of the real feel of the school. At last, just as the various groups were returning – rather quieter now – to their classrooms, Malcolm Botting returned them to the headmaster's office.

To Owen's surprise and some alarm the headmaster asked him to go with his secretary and take a short test "So we can make sure you're not in for some surprises when you get here," the man said with a smile. Owen did, found it was pretty easy, and returned with a smile on his face.

"Was that too easy for you?" the headmaster asked, seeing the smile.

"Not too easy sir, but not difficult either."

"Good. I'll look at the result later and we'll see where we can put you. I take it you'll be travelling to Lewes by train, presumably with Ruth Decks?

Owen looked surprised. "Yes, sir, I think so. You know her, then?"

"We keep an eye on each other's pupils sometimes, and Ruth has come to our attention. It will be good if you are on the train with her each day."

The conversation continued until the secretary returned with a piece of paper which she laid wordlessly in front of the Headmaster. He read it and nodded.

"Now then, unless any of you has other questions that completes the formalities. We have room in January, Owen is a suitable candidate so far as a meeting and this quick test can prove. The results are very good, I must say. We will write fairly soon and give details about joining and everything else."

None of them had any questions. They made their way back to the station. Back on the old train that was to take them to Victoria, Owen dropped the bombshell that he wanted to go and look in Trafalgar Square Post Office for Isaac Galley's name in as many telephone directories as he could find.

"Oh really, Owen; why couldn't you do that at the weekend when we've got more time?" It was almost word for word the response he was expecting.

"Because you haven't told me if we're going to the Mills at the weekend. And I don't know if the Post Office is open on Saturdays."

They both looked exasperated. "But couldn't it wait until a more suitable time?" Max asked.

Owen nodded. "I really want to get the coins back to this Isaac Galley, or whoever owns it, if he exists and if I can find him."

"It's not just a ploy to avoid school this afternoon?"

"*Mum!* Anyway, it's one o'clock now. By the time we get back and have lunch – I'm starving, by the way – it'll be nearly time to come home anyway."

She looked at her watch. Owen was aware his father was smiling.

"Oh, come on. Let him have his way for a change. He's right, after all."

She paused, resignedly.

"You men!"

Increasingly, Owen seemed to be included in that sort of comment, one that promoted his age. It subtly pleased him every time. He instinctively viewed it as recognition that he was no longer a child whose opinion didn't matter; it was as if he was being accidentally promoted a step or two closer to adulthood.

They found their way to Trafalgar Square and walked to the vast Post Office. Owen spent a slightly frustrated forty-five minutes looking for "Galley, I" in all the directories local to Seaford that he could find, but without success. More out of desperation than in hope he started looking in the London directories.

There was a yelp from the directories booth.

"Found it?" asked his father, attracted by the noise.

"It's a Galley, I," said Owen, "That's who I'm looking for and that's the only one anywhere. Can I try him?"

"From home, yes. It's too expensive from here."

"Okay… shall we go, then?"

"Have you looked everywhere?"

"All the books covering Sussex, Surrey, Kent, Hampshire and parts of London."

"*All* parts of London? We don't want to come back here again."

"I *could* come on my own, you know. But as we're here…"

The remaining London directories were scanned, resulting in two more

Galleys but no "Galley, I"

With Owen clutching his note of the number and address, they made their way home. Max stood nearby as he dialled the number and was so surprised to hear a strong voice answer almost immediately that he became tongue-tied for a second.

"I… er… hallo, I'm looking for a Mr Isaac Galley, please."

"Well, you have found him."

"Oh…er… thanks. Are you the Isaac Galley who was at Tide Mills in Sussex in 1914?"

It appeared that Mr Galley was now the tongue-tied one. Cautiously, and in a more cautious voice: "Who is speaking, please?"

Owen gave his name. "My family are about to move there, and…"

Max had lifted up his hand to stop him.

"…and we think you might have lived there. Please could you tell me?"

A long pause. Then: "Are you anything to do with a man called Holden?"

"No." Owen said, "All I've been told is that he was a bully."

A shorter pause.

"I was shipwrecked there, in 1914."

Owen thought. "What was the name of the boat, please?"

"Look, what… oh well. The *Annie*."

Owen gave a gulp.

"Er… may we come and see you, please sir?"

"What could you possibly want to see an old man for, when the only thing you know about him is that he spent some time in a village you're going to move into?"

"But may we, anyway, please sir?"

Another pause. "I suppose so. But who would be coming?"

"My Dad and me, and a friend from Tide Mills."

"And what's his name?"

"She. She's a girl. Ruth Decks."

"Decks… there was a boy called Decks, I seem to remember…How old are you?"

"Er… fourteen, sir."

"I was sixteen… very well. Come this Saturday. Tomorrow. Two o'clock. I will give you the address."

Before Owen could explain that he'd found the address along with the phone number, he was given it again.

For once, Ruth was on the south platform of Tide Mills station. She was nervous, and excited. Mr Pentelow had visited with the message from Owen in London on Friday after school and despite protests from her mother Jack had lent her enough money to buy a return ticket to Victoria.

She was nervous about having to change trains at Lewes. It was something she had never done before. From there north the lushness of the countryside even in autumn pleased her. It seemed to surround the train on both sides once it had trundled its way out of the County town. But after an hour the surroundings grew greyer and more built up, then she crossed a river that made her familiar Newhaven Ouse look tiny. She realised it was the Thames. Entering the vast, dim cavern of a station she saw the name Victoria and grabbed her small suitcase, joining the stream of people heading towards the barrier. By then she realised people were showing their tickets to a man in uniform and she fished hers out.

At last through it she was relieved and ridiculously happy to see Owen. He had, for a change, been allowed to travel to meet her on his own, and took pride in taking her case and leading her away before apparently nonchalantly navigating the Tube – an eye-opener to the country girl – and the bus to the Wilsons' house.

Barbara and Max's welcome nearly swept her off her feet. Despite the vast size of the house compared with her own she was made to feel completely at home. All three had been kind and casual with her, just as if she'd met them by chance at the mill house.

After lunch they discussed the coin. Owen looked at Ruth, raising his eyebrows. She nodded. They told both parents the full story.

"You mean there are more of them?" Max exclaimed.

"Thirty in all, Dad," Owen admitted having once again checked silently with Ruth. "And we want to find out more about this Isaac Galley to see if they're his."

Max thought. "You realise that if he got them illegally, they'd have to go back to whoever the real owner was? And if the real owner isn't known after all these years then they might be treasure trove?"

"What's treasure trove, please?" Ruth asked.

"If you find something valuable and the owner can't be traced you have to declare it. But I don't know how, or to whom."

"But if we found it, then it's ours."

"No. That's the whole point. It isn't. The real owner isn't you, and if no one can prove it's theirs then it goes to the Crown, I think."

"What, the Queen? But she's rich already, and we could do with the money."

"But you said you were going to give it back to this Isaac Galley."

"Yes," said Owen. "But if it's not his, or he doesn't want it, then we can do with it."

"We're not that badly off, old chap."

"No, but *we* are. Ruth and me."

He found the three pairs of eyes focussed on him quite embarrassing.

"But anyway, Isaac Galley will want it, I'm sure."

Isaac Galley lived in a part of east London that which was being rebuilt after the war. They drove, not knowing how long it might take by tube and bus, and searched for the address on a road that was lined with young trees. The houses were pleasant, detached and seemed quite prosperous. They found the house. It was well kept, had a tidy garden with a well-kept patch of grass, and the brass number and other door furniture gleamed.

The door was opened by a tall man, slightly stooped, with white hair and a ruddy complexion. A pair of very bright eyes swept round them all before fixing on Ruth.

"You're a Decks," he said in a quietly powerful voice. "Is Micky Decks your Dad?"

Ruth looked confused. She met the piercing eyes, recognised them as having the same steady gaze as she had seen on some of the old Newhaven fishermen, and liked what she saw.

"No. My Dad's Arthur. But I have a grandad Mike."

"Grandad, is it? Ahh... I'm getting old. And you must be Owen, who called me and gave me a shock. And these are your parents?"

Owen nodded, and held out his hand to be shaken, as did the other three.

"And none of you is a Holden? Or even knows anyone called Holden?"

They all said that they hadn't met anyone with the name. That seemed to be the correct password and they were invited in.

The house was scrupulously clean and tidy. The room they entered was decorated with photographs of ships and a deep frame with examples of increasingly complex knots in it. Their host caught them looking round curiously.

"Yes, despite having nearly drowned before being washed ashore at Tide Mills I went back to the sea. Joined the Navy just before the War. The first one. And never really left it until they sort of retired me last year. Sit you down, sit you down."

They complied, and were handed teacups.

"And now you must tell me why you want to see me, apart from going to live in Tide Mills."

6 – Isaac Galley

"Well, you see sir, we're going to live in the old Mill House. And I said, as soon as I saw it, that I wanted the top floor, west facing room." Owen was determined he was going to lead this conversation and was deliberately not looking at his father in case of any censoring attempts.

Isaac Galley laughed. "And I spent a good long time in that same room until they let me downstairs a bit at a time. Proper poorly, I was. They said I was as near dead as I could have been when they rescued me from the beach."

"What actually happened, Mr Galley?" Ruth's voice, noticed Owen, could be really gentle and soothing when she wanted it to be.

"I'll tell you. But I want to know first how you found me. After all, when I left I went as far away as possible, and I've been watching out for any Holdens ever since and giving them all as wide a berth as I could, too."

"May I just check something, Mr Galley?" Max had broken in to the conversation. "How is it that you were on the *Archie* when she foundered?"

"'Twasn't the *Archie*. She was the *Annie*. I told your son that."

"You're sure, er…sir?"

The man looked daggers at him scornfully, the light of battle in his eyes. "You don't get chucked off a coaster without remembering her name, mister. If they was to saw me in half, *Annie* would be printed in black all the way through me. I've been in close calls since, but none came close to what nearly happened to me that night."

Max nodded. "What rank did you end up with when you retired?"

It was their host's turn to look surprised. "Captain, RN."

Max stood and held the man's gaze. "Captain Maxwell Wilson, RN, retired. Pleasure to meet you, sir."

The expression turned to one of astonishment and then to amusement. He stood too. The two saluted and shook hands.

"And you gave a ship a wrong name," Isaac Galley accused him.

Max smiled back. "Call that a test. I didn't really know who you were. I do now. And the *Annie* was a coaster, you say? From Newhaven?"

"No – Rye. If she'd had a Newhaven crew she'd never have been allowed to get so close to that lee shore before they started her engine. Newhaven men know the seas there too well. This lot only started the old donkey when they could see the shore and where they were. And that, onshore wind or no onshore wind, is what made the Revenue take notice later."

"So it was a smuggling operation."

"Must have been. All I knew was that Holden was part of it. One of the Rye boys had gone sick, he needed a deck hand and I was fool enough to be hanging around."

"So she got as far as Tide Mills and then foundered?"

"She was well away from the harbour, slipped away quiet, and was heading way out when there was a big old squall from sou'west and her main halyard gave. The boom missed one of the men by a foot and the gaff spun round and smashed the taffrails. It took us an age to clear things away so we could control the ship again, then she was so near the shore, just past the east Pier, that we could nigh on count the pebbles.

"I thought I should look in the hold to see if she'd taken on water. So I was doing that when I found I was being hauled out of it. By Holden. He asked me what I was doing, so I told him. I hadn't seen what she was carrying, anyway.

"Someone told him they were going to start the old donkey so as to get us out of danger. I remember the look in his eyes – sort of hunted, and furious. He said something about the Revenue men in Seaford hearing us, then asked me if I could swim. Like a fool I said I could."

He paused for breath.

"He gave a sort of false smile, like a crocodile's. 'I've got a present for you,' he said, 'but I'll want it back, so no running away or your parents won't see you again. Be sure I'll be back to collect it one day.'

"He rushed down the companion way and I started to get on with my job, thinking that was the last I'd hear of it. But he hooked me back again, and he was carrying two bags. 'Empty your pockets,' he said. Well, I had little enough to my name, but a good few pockets to carry it in. And he started giving me little cloth bags to put in any pocket I could find.

"When he'd finished he pushed me over to the port side, near where the gaff had all but taken out the rail, and told me to take my shoes off. I realised then that he meant me to swim to shore with whatever it was, and run the risk of being arrested. So I refused.

"I'll never forget his face, or his voice, when he spoke next. 'Well, it won't matter if you're alive or dead, anyway. I'll still find a way of getting it back.' And with that he barged against me so I fell through the gap in the rail and into the sea."

He stopped again, this time for quite a while. All that could be heard was the ticking of the clock on the mantelpiece.

It was Ruth whose quiet, gentle voice – whose effect was again not lost on Owen – asked him to continue.

"I sank for ages," he said grimly remembering. "But even in that moment I knew I had to get my shoes off. It took ages, the first one, and I had to fight up to the surface for breath. I thought one foot to swim with should be enough and did my best. But apart from knowing where the surface was, and having glimpsed the beach, I was struggling. Whatever was in those packets was so heavy, see, it was hard going.

"I don't really know what happened next. I think I was under water more than on top of it, and I couldn't tell you if I swam at all. I remember some voices, and that was it until I came to, feeling as sick as a dog, in that room you want, young man."

He looked back at the original questioner who was gazing at him in amazement.

"You were lucky to be alive," said Ruth's gentle voice again.

"That's what I thought at first," he replied, "until I realised that I was dressed in someone else's nightshirt and had no idea where my own clothes were. I started worrying about Holden then, and about the Revenue men too. And I thought that the Revenue would be a lot kinder than Holden. Afterwards, when I'd started recovering, they told me that the worry made it worse for me, and that I'd have to stay in that bed for a week or more."

Owen nodded, ready to start with the next part of the story, but he was interrupted again.

"I've never told any other soul this story, and I doubt there's any left in Tide Mills that remember it. I hope not, 'cos if Holden or his son get any idea – well, it'd be the worse for them, that's all. But I want to know, now I've let myself ramble on, how you know about the *Annie* and got my name, though I'm starting to guess, if these two young 'uns have been in my room."

He gave a sudden grin and focussed on Ruth and Owen. "Tell me. Is there a bed in there? An old bed?"

Owen, starting to smile, nodded.

Isaac Galley nodded. "So you found my note."

Owen nodded, and handed it over. The old Captain's hand shook as he took it and smoothed it out. He read it.

"Yes," he said. "Edna told me later that some men from the west camp [Note: military barracks] were down watching. They pulled me out and got the water out of me, it seems. She said they thought I was heavy, but anything is if it's waterlogged."

Owen grinned again. "Who's Edna?" he asked.

"Ahh… She was a wonder." Galley's eyes were gentler now. "She looked after me from the start. She'd just married the son of the miller there and took me on – don't know what her new husband thought but she didn't seem to get on with him very well." The eyes wandered again. "She spent so much time with me…"

They let him recollect.

"But no one came to look for you, or the money?" Owen was back in the conversation.

"Oh, the Revenue came, saying they were looking for some money lost from a ship. Well, I was too ill to be questioned. At least, that's what they thought. What Edna told them. And I wasn't going to respond, was I? Still unconscious, I was." He grinned. "But I heard Holden was prowling around like a caged lion, asking if any bodies had been washed up, or any near drowned sailors. But he found his match in old Fox. Mr Fox senior was like a squire, then, and everyone in Tide Mills treated him as if he was. Fox told him to get on his way. There was never any question of him coming to talk to me. He couldn't demand to come and see me in my sick bed like the Revenue men could.

"Both he and the Revenue kept coming back, many times, before they gave up. It was only the Revenue people who actually saw me, though. But in the meantime Edna had given me my clothes back and the bags were still in them. I kept telling her I would tell her one day what they were, but I never did. And then one day I hit on a plan, found a screwdriver, and – well, the rest I suppose you know."

"Mostly," admitted Owen. "But how did you get away?"

"Well eventually the Revenue people had had enough and surprised me doing some gardening for the family. They took me, searched me and questioned me for ages but found nothing. I was scared of Holden, so never said anything about the stuff he put in my pockets. And eventually I suppose the Foxes must have found the money and paid for my release. I was so scared that I got on the first train to Portsmouth and signed up to the Navy for as long as I could. Best thing I could have done, as it turned out."

"But it wasn't the money you hid that paid for your release."

"How do you know?"

Owen put his hand in his pocket and pulled out the sovereign, handing it to the thoroughly intrigued Captain. He gave a start. His expression was so surprised as to be almost comical.

"So you noticed there was something about the bed, did you?"

"It was your note that made us look. And after a search we saw the bed slats weren't touching the frame."

"Did you get them all?"

"Yes. All thirty."

He nodded. "Good for you. But who was it, then, who paid the fine and gave me my freedom? Holden? So he could grab me and get his money? No - he wouldn't have dared to go near the Customs office. Unless, I suppose, he was in with one of the Revenue men. Or all of them."

"I suppose we could do some digging," said Max. "There must be records."

Galley nodded again. "I'm not going to do that. I finished with all that part of my life years ago. It's not something I want to remember, apart from Edna. You've brought the memory of her back to me and – well – if only she'd not have been married…"

"You'd have stayed in Tide Mills?"

"I'd have taken her with me. But then she *was* already married. And if I'd had the courage and got her to run away with me – well I had no idea what I was going to do. When I decided that the only way I could make a life was to go to sea, I knew she would have had to be on her own so much while I was away, it wouldn't have been right. Then it was the start of the War… No, she was better off married to young Fox."

It was Ruth's and Owen's turn to sit up with a start. They each had a sudden idea, one that fascinated and horrified them.

Owen voiced it. "If she's Mrs Fox, well, there is a Mrs Fox at Tide Mills still. She's… well…" He tailed off.

"She's a rather bitter old lady," Max put in. "A widow, and not well off. But the new owners of the Mills are going to improve her living standards, I'm glad to say."

"Edna Fox? Is that her name?"

"I don't know her Christian name," Max replied, "but I can find out."

"Can you? Could you use the phone? Now?"

Max was surprised. "Well, yes. Someone will be in the office."

Galley rose and escorted Max to the phone. A short conversation later and

Max looked up at the Captain.

"It's Edna," he said simply. The man said nothing but wheeled round and limped back into the room, carefully sitting down. He stared for a long time at a photograph of an old warship on the wall opposite.

"All these years," he said slowly. "I've never thought she'd still be there. And a widow? And almost fifty years later I suppose Holden's dead – or about ninety if he's alive. Mind you, there's his son…"

As if coming out of a reverie he looked at Max. "When are you going down next?" he asked almost fiercely. "I need to see if it's the same person. I need to face the demons I've avoided all these years. And if Holden is alive, or his son, they'll be my age and I can deal with them."

"And you can have the rest of the money," said Ruth without thinking. Max looked round at her with a start.

"Money? I don't want that money! Got through crime that was, if I know Holden. You'll not find where that came from, even if there's any Holden left alive."

Ruth blinked. "But it's yours. You said that Holden gave it to you as a present."

"But he wanted it back," came the reply. "If there's anyone left to give it to, you can give it to them. And if it's Holden I'll tell the Police everything so he gets his comeuppance. If not, it's yours. I don't want it."

"Do you know how much it's worth?" asked Max quietly.

"No, and I don't care."

"It's worth about £600."

"Is it now? Well then, it belongs to your son and his friend. Or maybe to Edna Fox if she needs it and you agree, after all she did for me all those years ago. But that would be up to you two. The money isn't mine."

"But Captain," said Max, "if it isn't yours, then it must be treasure trove. And that means going to the authorities, so it might be lost."

The man thought. "All right. It's mine. I'll give it to Edna. Or to you two. But when can I go down and see her?"

"Any time you like," Max told him. "Tide Mills isn't private."

"But I can't go there on my own. People wouldn't believe it was me after all these years."

"I'm going home tomorrow," said Ruth. "You could come down with me."

"You're a Decks. I wouldn't know Micky's son, but if he's still around he might remember me."

"We see him quite a bit," Ruth told him. "He lives in Newhaven now."

"He would be surprised to see me. But so will Edna." Once again his eyes had taken on that far-away look.

They offered to take him out for a meal. He was surprised and pleased, but after a pause declined.

"I need to think about the past this evening," he told them simply. "But some day, soon, I'd like to take you out. Maybe with Edna too…"

Secretly, both Ruth and Owen were horrified.

Arrangements were made for Max, Ruth and Owen to meet Captain Galley at Victoria Station the following morning, even if it did mean diverting from their usual route. Approaching the departure boards, at first there seemed to be no sign of him. Uniforms were everywhere, even if it was Sunday. At last one of the uniforms detached itself from a crowd of railway employees, turned into a smart Naval version and limped towards them. Simultaneously they noticed the gold braid around the cuffs and on the cap.

Max noticeably straightened, faced him and saluted as the man, smiling, drew nearer. The salute was returned.

"I thought I'd surprise her," he said. "Give her a reason for my absence of nearly half a century."

It seemed to Ruth and Owen that the very alert yet casual man they had met the day before had grown in stature and importance overnight. It was hard to identify, but with the uniform had come charisma, an aura of capability and strength that had been only hinted at before.

The journey to Brighton was spent with the two retired captains yarning about their Navy exploits. The two younger ones were listening to some of these with incredulity. But the attraction of watching the scenery flashing by also kept them busy – the journey time was meant to be exactly sixty minutes, after all.

In the slow train from Brighton (which they had reached in exactly 1 hour, as advertised) to Tide Mills the carriage was quieter, though the wind from the south was stronger than it had been in sheltered London. Captain Galley was looking at a Brighton he scarcely remembered.

"There's so much *more* of it now," he exclaimed.

At least from the new outskirts of the town, through Lewes and down to the coast by the wind-whipped River Ouse, was mostly as he remembered it. Reaching Newhaven he wondered, once again, at the 'new' houses clinging to the hillsides as they approached the town. From there he was describing a continuous stream of familiar buildings and landmarks until they had passed the ferry terminal. After that speech ceased. He was silent as they left the town end entered the wilder area around the creek that carried the tide to the Mills. Max was concerned.

"How do you want to play it, Isaac?" he asked. "Should we go down together so I can introduce you, and then retreat?"

"I… I just don't know," came the reply. "I should just be able to go and talk to her. That seems the right thing."

"Don't forget she's a very – well, bitter – lady now. She has been through some hard times, it would seem."

"What hard times?"

"I don't know. She's not the sort of person who would take kindly to being asked things like that."

He nodded, and remained silent, looking seawards from the window toward the grey, rough sea. As the hamlet became clearer he sighed and looked at Ruth and Owen.

"I hope this is all going to be all right." And he turned back to the view.

There seemed to be nothing they could say.

Nobody was waiting on the platform. Taking their lead from him they walked slowly down towards the cottages, stopping to take a long look at Mill House before returning towards Mrs Fox's home.

Max pointed to the row of cottages. "The first one is the Bakers' and Mrs Fox's is on the other end. Ruth lives up, and opposite. The first one. If you really want us to leave you here, perhaps you could come and see them afterwards – Ruth, would that be all right, do you think?"

She nodded. "I'll tell Mum and Dad when we get there. I'm sure they'll welcome you."

Now so close, the uniformed Captain seemed to be reluctant to go any further. Nudged by Max the rest of them moved away so he was alone, and only then did he very slowly walk to the front door of the tiny cottage and knock.

Edna Fox was kneading dough to make a small loaf that might last her a day or two and wondering as usual whether the flour she had scavenged from the mill floor was so old it would fail to rise. At the back of her darkened mind she wondered how long the Mill would continue in business, even with this new man doing whatever it was he was doing. What would she do if it stopped? There was this Welfare State thing, but she knew that was charity, really, and that she would not accept. With the strong movements of her hands and their rhythm, she failed to hear a quiet knock at the door.

The light from her window was dimmed. She straightened, angry. Someone messing around outside – one of those pesky kids, probably. The shadow passed and she paused, undecided whether to go and accuse whoever it was of nosy-parkering or wait for the shadow to return.

There was another knock at her door and this time she heard it. Astonished, as no one ever called on her, she still wondered if it was one of the village children. Angrily she dusted off her hands and stomped off to answer the knock.

At the sight of the neat figure in the smart Navy uniform she stepped back, then scowled in her usual way at something new.

"Yes?"

The eyes stared right back at her as if boring through her. 'Those blue eyes, she thought, despite her ingrained antagonism. 'I've rarely seen any that blue. Not since Him.'

The man spoke. "Are you... I think you are... Edna Fox."

It was a quite cultured voice, yet with a tinge of something local to it. And there was something in it besides that.

"And what if I am?"

"If you are, you are the person I should have had the courage to come looking for years ago."

She looked at him closer. Those eyes. That voice.

"You look like someone I used to know," she said. It was almost an accusation.

The face smiled, a look that triggered another memory. "Someone you looked after? Someone who you nursed back to health?"

She was silent, but her brain was racing. Could this really be the boy she looked after all those years – decades – ago? Could this be the boy she had spent so much time with to try to raise his spirits? Could this really be the boy who once – and once only, she swore – she had comforted all through the night? Could this really be the boy who, she tearfully swore to her husband despite herself and against her better judgement after it had all come out, that she loved most of all in the world?

And here he was. Standing at her door. Healthy. Maybe wealthy. In a naval uniform that looked important. And he had no idea about... about anything. Anything she had done, anything she had had to do. Everything that had happened to her and the family as a result.

In her head, something snapped. She pulled back her arm and slapped his face. Hard.

He stepped back, the smile gone. His hand came up to cover the red mark that was already starting to appear. The eyes in front of him faded from fury to horror. Her hand came up to cover her mouth.

"I'm sorry," he said. "I thought after... after everything we went through you might perhaps – well – at least feel that we might talk. Even if I was no longer welcome. I'm sorry."

He turned and stumbled away, confused with the situation but angry with himself for being attacked out of the blue by an emotion he had not felt for years. He seemed unable to see properly. Him! He who had been through so much in two wars!

At the end of the cottages he wondered what to do. He felt like going home; straight back to the station and onto the next train. But that would be rude to the people who had brought him here, though now he wished they hadn't. Instead his feet took him south, against the wind, past the buildings, over the culverts and bridge, and on to the beach. With the familiar element of the sea, his second home, in front of him, he felt just a little more at ease.

What had he done to cause such hate?

Was it that he had been gone so long? So many years? But he had been too scared to return. How could he tell her that now? It was easy, at this late stage, to say that he'd been angry with himself for so long after he'd run away. That he'd given in to that instinctive horror of risking going back because the area bore the promise of retribution from Holden; a promise of retaliation made against him when he himself had been young and impressionable. And why should that horror have been stronger than the attraction he had felt for Edna?

Because she had been married, that's why. Because they had spent *that* night together. Because he was aware that all his actions then had been tantamount to having come between man and wife.

He buried his face in his hands. It was a mess. A complete mess. He should never have risked coming back.

A voice by the side of him, a gentle voice, older than he remembered but still with the tones in it that had comforted him when he had been in so much trouble, and sixteen.

"Why didn't you come back before now, Isaac?"

He wheeled round, shocked, having been so embroiled in his emotions. Her footsteps, even on something as noisy as shingle, had gone unheard.

He held her gaze, not knowing whether to feel guilty or still angry at having endured a hard slap to his face. The thoughts of the previous few minutes gave him a simple answer.

"Because I was scared, and because you were married."

"Scared of me?"

He shook his head impatiently. "Of course not. Holden."

"Huh! Him! That bully of a man. He tried to force us to tell him where you'd gone. He said you owed him money. We couldn't tell him, of course. We didn't know. I wouldn't have told Fox or anyone if I *had* known, but I had no idea. No one did – not even your father. This went on for over a year – he kept coming back when he knew neither Fox nor his father would be there, asking if I'd heard.

"Then one night he got roaring drunk in the Ark and must have fallen into the river. No one missed him 'til next morning when his son realised he hadn't been home. They found a body by Dungeness a year after that. His size, his clothes. End of Holden. And nobody was sad, except his son and daughter. People were more sorry for them than they were for Holden himself."

They looked out over the waves. In Isaac Galley's mind was a sixteen year old being washed ashore more dead than alive, helped by... who knows? Soldiers from the military encampment, yes; but he could put no face to the helpers. The person he could put a face to, days later and now half a century on, was standing by his side.

"And you?" he asked in a gentler voice. "What happened to you?"

Another silence. He knows nothing, thought Edna. Nothing at all. I hate him for not knowing, for not coming back, for not even trying . But... I loved him then like nothing else. Was it really all his fault?

"You don't know *anything*. Not one tiny fragment," she said, still uncharacteristically quietly. "If you had known. If *only* you had known." She let the sentence hang. There was no speech for a many moments.

"If *you* had known how much I wanted you with me, how lonely I was... No, not lonely, love-sick. There. For the first time in years I've had the courage to say the words. I never even said them to myself. For a fortnight or more I was physically unwell; couldn't eat, didn't – couldn't – do anything except what was expected of me as I was training to be a seaman. I wondered if I was still ill, whether I'd run away too soon. But as the Navy got into me, that illness faded, but I never, ever, *ever,* forgot you.

"And in the first War, at night, on watch in the freezing, gale-ridden Atlantic, you were by my side. Every time. Night after night."

His throat constricted. She kept her peace.

"And..." he forced himself on "...in the second War you were with me on the Bridge when I was commanding my ship in the Atlantic while we were hunting U-boats; well. You were there, with me. All the time. And on the rare occasions during it all that I got ashore I never found anyone else to match up to you."

Another silence. A thought clicked in her mind and her eyes switched back to his suddenly, showing astonishment.

"You never married?"

He shook his head.

It was her turn to look out to sea with emotions whirling around in her head. When he'd been rescued from both the sea and from Holden, she hadn't been on the beach to see when he had been dragged ashore. But she knew the story. He had told her. He didn't know hers, though.

"He was going to make me give the baby away."

His search through the memory of his early years in the Navy came to an abrupt stop.

"What baby? You had no baby."

A grim smile. "I could hardly have had one when I was looking after you or you'd have known and I'd have had no time to help you. No. The boy who was born about nine months after you left."

7 – Isaac and Edna

Slowly his face crumpled from complete astonishment into a look of deep emotion. Though he made no sound the tears ran down his face.

"Is he still alive?" he whispered.

She nodded. "Married. Living in Eastbourne. She won't let him visit much. Won't have me over there. Grandchildren too. Never seen them."

He gasped, and turned. Suddenly the old, crabby, dishevelled Mrs Fox was enveloped in an embrace that she had never expected to feel again.

"What happened?" he whispered after another long silence.

When she had recovered she was able to tell the story of how she had taken money from her husband – whom she was already regretting marrying – and paid for Isaac's release to ensure he was never chased or, if found, shouldn't be deemed to be guilty. Her husband discovered, naturally, and became violent. By that time she knew she was pregnant and had to scream the fact at him to stop his blows.

He was coldly angry. She was left alone, ignored by him for ages. That was when he started making arrangements for the baby to be adopted. She had discovered what he was about to do.

"I told him that I would not allow that and he laughed and told me I had no choice," she said. "I told him that the choice was that I would tell Holden that it was Fox who had taken the money from the boy I loved. Fox was a coward and I hoped that it was enough of a hold over him to stop him going ahead with it.

"He called me all sorts of names, words I never knew existed. And then he said nothing else, but nothing else was ever said about adoption. Fortunately, soon after that he was called up for the war. It gave me four years of peace to bring up young Isaac." She swallowed. "Apart from the disturbed nights, he was the best ever thing that happened since you…went."

"I've got to meet him."

She nodded.

"When Fox came home he was shell-shocked, like so many of them. He took most of the pain out on Isaac, and the rest on me. We had separate bedrooms, fortunately, and Isaac slept with me. He couldn't understand why the man who he thought was his father could be so unloving, so cruel, when his mother was just the opposite. The number of times I had to bandage that boy's back when Fox had thought he'd been disobedient…Can you imagine how I felt?"

Isaac was shaking his head, this time in both sadness and fury.

"Then when Isaac was seven, Fox sent him away to a boarding school in the north. Without asking me, or him. I only saw him at holiday times. And even then, had he been able to, Fox would have made him visit relatives. My relatives. But at last I put my foot down, and the holidays were spent with me. Fox would take himself off for days then, and at other times. It was the start of the Mill going downhill.

"As soon as he could, after he'd finished school, Isaac found a job in Eastbourne, then a girlfriend, and that was the beginning of the end. Fox and I weren't even invited to the wedding – Isaac was twenty-one by then and could please himself." She laughed, bitterly. "Just as well, 'cos Fox would never have let him get married otherwise. Out of spite."

Isaac had no words, but his hand slowly reached out and found hers. She looked surprised, then worried, then accepted it.

"He never even asked me to come to the wedding on my own," she whispered.

Another long silence as they looked out over the sea.

"And the grandchildren?" Isaac asked.

"A girl and a boy. She must be about fifteen. The boy about thirteen. He just mentioned them the first time he saw me after each had been born, as if I knew about them already. I could tell neither Isaac nor *her* wanted me to have anything to do with them."

"Why?"

She just shrugged.

"They told me Fox had died," Isaac said.

She looked sharply at him. "He caught pneumonia during one of his weeks away. Came back here but never recovered even when they took him to hospital. I wasn't sorry, but that made me feel dreadful. I should have been sorry. He was hated here, not just because he was a bully but because he didn't – wouldn't – run the mill properly. They could see it was all going to pot.

"The funeral – it puzzled me that arrangements seemed to be made without my having to lift a finger, nor even to visit an undertaker. It was meant to be a quiet affair, small, and I didn't want to go, but had to. Isaac never answered my letter telling him, and I can't really blame him.

"When I got there it was crowded. Turns out he was the star turn to a family in London somewhere – kids and all. They couldn't understand why the service was in Bishopstone church, didn't know who I was, and didn't like it when they discovered I was the wife. They didn't believe me when I told them what he'd done. They didn't *want* to believe me. Turned out telling me to leave the service, even if it was held in Bishopstone church where I'd been christened. The verger felt sorry for me and told me to stay at the back, and I stayed, and faced them again when they found I was still there."

The face closed in again to the expression that was so well known around Tide Mills.

"As if that wasn't enough, he left me with nothing except a few pounds. The mill was left to someone in his London family, and they sold it."

By this time her companion was seething with anger at the injustices she had suffered. But the greatest injustice, he felt, was the estrangement of the son. Their son. The son he never knew he had. And he vowed to do whatever he could to cure that.

"I should have come back." Now he was as bitter about the treatment she had received as he had ever been about anything in his life. "I should have had courage and come back. But I thought you were married and that if I came it would be like putting man and wife asunder. It would…"

She interrupted. "He had made absolutely sure we were asunder. All by himself. It was worse than going through a divorce would have been, even in those days. But I couldn't divorce him. It would have meant that Isaac would be called a bastard. No one around here would have understood. Not *really* understood. And he would have had his education cut short."

A band of rain swept at them.

"No wonder you slapped my face."

"I'm sorry. I really regret that. I was just so angry at seeing you suddenly looking so well and such a – a normal person; and me… well… what I am."

"It's hardly surprising that you're unhappy. Maybe even bitter. You've suffered. Suffered so much. I feel awful, now. Guilty at never having even tried to see how you were doing. If I'd had any idea of what was happening I'd have come in and taught that man a lesson… good grief, is that me talking like that? And I would have certainly taken you and the baby…"

He paused again.

"My son. *Our* son." He was about to say how much it meant to him, to have fathered a son, but felt it wasn't the time.

Steps approached from behind. He spun round; an ingrained instinct from half a century previously warned him this was trouble. Could be trouble.

But it was Max and Owen.

"I thought there was a problem," explained Max. "You've been gone so long, both of you."

Adding those three words was inspired. It stalled a shrewish retort from Edna Fox that all he was worried about was his friend, the Captain. But to know he seemed concerned about her on an even footing… well.

Isaac was about to speak, but held his tongue. She glanced back at him, then at Max.

"We are fine, thank you."

"As we see. I've been asked to offer you a cup of tea at the Decks's house when you're ready. It's quite cold out here."

"The Seaford Bay wind never stops," said the Captain.

"There's a chill in it that has been there for fifty years," said Edna Fox slowly, unexpectedly. "But maybe it's started to ease off now. I think."

Her companion looked at her, astonished.

"I said 'started'," she said. "I have never forgotten you, you see. To know that you are standing by me on Tide Mills beach where it all started is something I never dreamed would happen. This last half hour, when I have had to tell the story of my life, has made me calmer than I've felt since Isaac left home and Fox left me penniless."

Max and Owen could see they were not yet ready, even if the wind was now blowing a misty rain into their faces.

"Please," said Max, "don't get too wet and cold." They turned away.

Another pause.

"What are you going to do?" she asked suddenly.

He looked at her properly for the first time, wanting to tell her that he would make sure she had somewhere better to live, a more comfortable life, the comfort of a relationship with her – their – son and any grandchildren there might be.

"I have to do something. Not just for you, but for me too," he told her wisely. "Somehow I need to start to make amends for not being there when you needed me. For not having the courage to come back and face... Holden. And Fox if you'd told me what a husband he was being."

"He was no husband. Not in the proper sense of the word. Huh! Husband!"

"Yes... some husband. But first we should get to know each other. As adults, not as teenagers as they're called now."

"Why? Have you changed much?"

"Have you?"

It took her a split second to realise what he meant.

"I've only recently retired," he told her. "I rose to be a Royal Naval Captain. That's a different sort of person from the lad you were kind to; the lad whose main chance of employment seemed to be as a fisherman or as a Port worker. Though I suppose I'd have been drafted into the Forces anyway." He shuddered. "I'm glad I was in the Navy before it all started, not the army. All I lost was my leg."

"Your *leg?*"

"Lower leg, left. Thank a stray bit of shrapnel for that."

"But... but you're walking."

"Limping. I have an aluminium leg now."

"Oh God," she whispered. This time it was her hand seeking his.

He smiled to feel the contact. "So yes, I've changed. I'm more used to making things happen than I was at sixteen."

"And I'm laughed at, and usually avoided," she whispered. "They think I don't realise, that I'm half mad. But I have no money except the pension. And that's only just started a few years ago. Before that all I could do was work at the Mill – after that man left me, that is."

His hand sought hers again.

"The first thing I'm going to do – we are going to do, please – is to go to the Decks's house, have that cup of tea and get warm. And I want to tell them the story. That way it will get round how badly you have been treated."

"You mustn't do that!" She was horrified at the prospect of having her close-kept guilty secrets available for everyone to know.

"But you want – we want – to know our son. And his family. Don't you? We can't do that unless the truth is out."

"But everyone one will know that he's a bastard then!"

"Everyone will know he's a human being. Everyone will realise that we are to blame, not him. And I don't believe we are to blame. Not really. Not when your marriage was such a... a..."

"Farce?"

"I can think of a better word: disaster. An appalling, disgraceful, bullying disaster. Oh, no disgrace to you; you could only react, by the sound of it. And when people know what that man did to you and *our* son..." he paused to let the word sink in "... they will judge very differently. Anyone who doesn't will be no friend of mine."

She thought. The rain became less like mist and more like proper rain. She shivered, half in dread at what now seemed inevitable and half at the cold which was penetrating her thin coat.

They turned and walked back past the mill to the home of the Decks. Edna's mind was in a whirl, wondering what had happened – what was happening – to her. In less than an hour it seemed that the damp, dark, miserable cell of her life had been invaded by a chink of light. Light that shone from a trusted time, long past, when a beautiful possibility had become part of her existence for a desperately short, intense period.

For his part, Isaac felt angry, guilty, and desperately sad that a girl he had loved and who had meant the world to him should have suffered so much.

Another hour later and Barbara, Mary and Ruth still had tears in their eyes.

"If only we had known," Mary kept saying. "If only..."

The story had been retold. Firstly by Isaac, then by Edna. Their audience was rapt, only exclamations of horror and indignation interrupted the tellers.

Finally Ruth asked the question Edna had asked Isaac earlier: "What are you both going to do now?"

Edna's eyes were downcast, but Isaac had no doubts.

"The first thing is that, if you will... will you return to London with me, where we can talk? I need to make sure you have a chance of living a normal life. That's what you did for me all those years ago in the Mill House. I can't stand by while you continue living here in coldness and poverty; I just couldn't live with myself. If you decide to return, then that is different. But even then the least I can do is to make life easier for... for the mother of our child."

Edna looked up. "I told you that everyone will just look on him as a bastard now. They won't want anything to do with him. Or me."

"Rubbish!" A chorus of voices rang out at that.

"Ruth and I would never do that. Nor would our parents," Owen said vehemently.

"He's right, Mrs Fox," said Max. "No one, *no* one says things like that nowadays. If they have any sense or decency they don't even think it. And if any of our staff here have anything to say on the subject I shall have words with them." Max was certain there would be no dissenters. By his tone, there had better not be.

She held his eyes for a moment, then looked back at Isaac.

"I don't know what to say."

"For the moment, please say 'yes'."

"People in London will laugh at me. And at you. And I've never accepted charity."

"Charity? No one said anything about charity. Just as you felt your duty was to nurse me back to health all those years ago, mine now is to nurse your hurts away and give a you a chance of the sort of life you *should* have had.

And people won't laugh at you, I promise that. You had my respect when we were young, as well as my increasing love. Why should that have gone? It hasn't."

Her eyes returned to the floor. She knew this was a chance for her. So many chances for her. Maybe even chances for them both. If the love they had at that time was to be rekindled... well, she still had thoughts for him in her dreams even if she blamed him for making no effort to come back. Before now.

"Please, Edna," he whispered.

Almost imperceptibly, she nodded.

They arrived at Victoria Station. Edna had been almost silent on the journey, Owen noticed, keeping her eyes mainly on the passing scenery. Isaac had also remained quiet. It seemed that both were talked out, and Max hoped that it wouldn't be permanent. There was little of a practical nature that either of the Wilsons could say to offer support. Their departure from the Decks had been restrained, even between Ruth and Owen.

By the barrier, where the story of the day had begun, Isaac halted suddenly.

"I'm sorry," he started, and Edna looked at him sharply. "I've been lost in my own thoughts and memories for the entire journey, as has Edna – or so I imagine. I do apologise. I've just remembered that although you have my address – and its telephone number – I don't have yours. I – we – need to contact you soon, at the very least to tell you what is happening. After all, you, Owen, are the detective who found out and really persisted in finding me. You and Ruth Decks, of course. So it's only right..."

"You?" Edna looked at Owen doubtfully. "You found him? But how?" Curious, Owen thought, she doesn't sound as shrewish as he remembered from the Seaford train or the meeting at Tide Mills.

"I... I'm going to have the room in the Mill House where Captain Galley stayed," he told her. "We found a note there, on the bed slats."

She frowned. "The bed slats?"

Isaac interrupted. "There's more to this story than has come out, even during today, Edna. He and Ruth told me how they found me and I'll tell you. But not here. Not now. We have a lot to talk about, you and I. That will be the starting point, I imagine. But now, please may I take you back to my home? We will contact you one evening, Max, Owen. You aren't due to move to Tide Mills soon, are you?"

"Not until the house is ready and my wife is happy it is," Max smiled. "Probably a few weeks yet, but before Christmas."

Conversation was awkward between them to start with, but her eyes grew round at the story of how he had hidden the sovereigns in the bed in 1914 and how Owen had discovered them in 1963.

"If I knew they were there I would have done as you asked and used them, instead of using Fox's money."

"Just as well you didn't, in one way. Holden would have heard and you would have been in danger."

She acknowledged that.

"Just as well I didn't know when I had to retire seven years ago, or I would have broken in to the Mill House and taken them to live on."

"If no one knew whose they were, you could have done."

"But £30... or are they worth more, being real gold?"

"About £600, Max discovered."

Her hand flew to her mouth. "But I could have... but they weren't mine to use."

"No one knows whose they were. Holden got them illegally and gave them to me, as I said, but intended to recover them." He pulled a face. "Recover them from me or my dead body. As it is, I've laid claim to them so that they aren't regarded as treasure trove. If they were, we'd lose them."

"I'd heard of that. A typically unfair law."

"But then," he said, ignoring the hint of peevishness in her voice, "I don't need them. I have a Navy pension, an income which is good enough for my needs. And it was you who found the money to pay for my release, so morally it's yours."

"Mine?"

"Of course. Fox household money..."

"I stole it."

"No. It was household money; you were married. Morally you had as much right to spend it as he did."

"Not in those days. Not with that man."

"Maybe, but now..."

She was silent. He was burning to go and visit their son, but knew that the time wasn't right yet. They passed on to more recent, practical matters.

Later, he showed her to a light, airy bedroom with what he knew to be a comfortable guest bed. She thanked him and was left in peace.

Her room was too big. The bed was too soft. They had eaten, but she found the food that Isaac said was 'normal' was more in every way than she had been used to for many years. In consequence she had indigestion for much of the night.

She woke at 6.30, feeling tired and grumpy, and wondered if she was doing the right thing. Surely she was taking a chance in coming away with him so soon after meeting him. It felt like eloping. Shouldn't she have waited...?

...waited in that cold, crummy little cottage, with no food nor the money to buy any? In the face of a freezing winter, maybe as bad and as long as the previous one? All through the fallow, hated years of her marriage she had still been able to live in some comfort and had eaten well. Eaten the sort of food that she had enjoyed the previous night, in fact.

Oh well, he was trying.

She rose and enjoyed the untarnished delight of using an indoor toilet, complete with hot and cold running water to the basin. She eyed the bath, and longed for it to be the right day of the week for her to use it. It was big, and best of all, plumbed in; no doubt with plenty of hot water to use in it. Perhaps, if she asked…

But she returned to her room and sat, wondering what time he would get up. In the midst of her worrying she heard sounds from downstairs. He was up! She opened the door and went to the landing, looking downstairs.

"Isaac, is that you?" she asked, aware of being only in her aged pyjamas.

To her horror he came out of the living room and saw her. He was smiling. She dodged back out of sight.

"I hope you don't mind. I'm an early bird, you see. Blame the Navy."

"I'm usually up and about by now anyway… look, may I use the bath?"

"Edna, you don't have to ask. Any time you want. Twice a day if you want. More if you prefer. There are towels there for you. Just tell me when they're too wet."

He never saw, but for the first time in years the corners of her mouth lifted.

Barbara Wilson had been horrified to hear of Edna's harrowing story. She wanted to call the Captain and ask them both to lunch. With a husband back in Sussex and a son at school she felt she could so easily do that. But Max suggested that the older couple needed time on their own to talk and to become used to each other again. If they could do so after all that time.

The story had travelled round the Mill and its families. Jack Pentelow was feeling guilty.

"I should have known something was wrong," he told Max who was still sharing his office. "She was hardly ever seen once Fox came back from the war. And that son of theirs – he was either at school or recovering from something – we never were told what. Or he was at home and the father was missing and ignoring the Mill again. But though Edna was from a worker's family, like we were, once she was married to Fox it didn't seem right to interfere. And when young Isaac was sent away to school… Well, we did wonder because he was so young. But that sort of thing happened then; I think it still does now. But no child of mine would leave home that early in life."

Max agreed. "I know Owen would have hated it, and Barbara would have objected violently."

"The one good thing, by the sound of it, is that it got the youngster out of the father's way. Maybe saved him from quite a few more beatings. I remember him coming home for the last time, with his schooling behind him." Jack laughed. "That would have been – what – 1932. He was a big, strong lad of eighteen and taller than Fox. I think he would have been safe from the beatings by then! Pity the man's wife wasn't."

"1932…" mused Max. "So he'd have been called up."

"Yes. In fact I believe he went into the Navy."

"Well, at least they'll have something in common, him and his father."

Jack nodded. "I just hope beyond hope that the two of them are reconciled with the son and his wife. You said that she wouldn't come and visit Edna? What about grandchildren? Are there any?"

"I knew nothing about them," said Jack. "Didn't even know there was one of each."

"I suppose they do *know* they have a grandmother? And a grandfather now?"

"They won't know about Isaac yet, but I hope they know about Edna. You know, after all these years I can't get used to calling her Edna again. As kids we had to call her Mrs Fox as soon as she married the Squire's son. It stopped for a bit when he went to war and she begged us to treat her like a normal person. But when Fox returned and someone let it slip, he was furious. She's been Mrs Fox ever since."

"Neither fish nor fowl," murmured Max.

"I beg your pardon?"

"Sorry. Neither accepted by Fox's family as one of them, nor by the village as one of theirs."

Jack was silent at this.

"Do you think we were cruel to her?" he asked suddenly.

Max grimaced. "I don't think anyone can blame anyone else. She was in a corner, being poor through no fault of her own, but presumably too proud to tell anyone why. Everyone else saw a sad, bitter, shrewish old woman who wanted little to do with them, especially when she'd reached retirement age. Mostly, people like that have some sort of mental problem and it's hardly surprising everyone else steers clear of them."

"Perhaps we should have been more persistent."

"Easy to say. Maybe not easy to do."

It was Jack who grimaced this time. "And maybe we shouldn't have jumped to conclusions."

There was no easy answer.

"With some of your £600, would you like to come and buy some new clothes?" he asked cautiously. "I suppose there was precious little money available up to now."

"And what happens when that's gone?" she asked. It was a waspish tone, and he was taken aback.

"Well actually it was a joke," he said, still with caution. "The coins haven't been sold yet. Ruth Decks still has them, I believe."

"A child has them? But, really..."

He put his hand up. "Edna, Edna: they are good people. Good people don't take advantage of others."

"They didn't help me when I needed it. They ignored me, avoided me."

"But did they know your situation? Did they know what Fox had put you through? How did they really see you? Did you make it easy for them?"

"You're on their side."

"No. I am absolutely on your side. But at Tide Mills I'm assured that the people are good, solid honest types. Max says so, and he has far more knowledge of them than I. I don't believe there are sides. Maybe they would have treated you differently if they had known. But you were, quite rightly, very bitter about everything." He hoped that he was right to use the past tense about her anger at life.

"Can you blame me?"

"No. I can't. And had I gone back and been half killed again by Holden I should have been bitter too, though my bitterness wouldn't have been so deep or lasted half a lifetime."

He let the thought sink in.

"Yes please," she said, out of the blue.

"What?"

"I'd like some new clothes. I will pay you back as soon as those coins are sold."

Well, he thought, at least she's accepted those.

"We'll see about money when the time comes. Maybe we'll decide between us that if I'd come back sooner, and Fox had been thrashed by me for his cruelty to you and... and our son, it might be *our* earnings buying clothes for both of us."

"I'm not accepting charity."

"And I'm not wishing it on you. There are few ways I can even start to make up for not being there, but this is at least one of them. I should help provide things you needed these last few years in order to have a normal life as the person you *really* are. It's what I would have done had Fox divorced you, or you him, and I had been there to... to..."

She just looked at him, and her eyes closed. Tears ran down her cheeks. He threw caution to the winds and went to sit beside her, wondering if he dare put an arm round her shoulders.

Her sobs diminished, eventually. She wriggled free and was about to wipe her eyes on her sleeve, the only way available to her, when a large, very male handkerchief was offered.

To his delight she smiled – a real smile – and accepted it.

"Please keep it," he said when she offered it back. "We'll buy some when we go shopping, shall we?"

He could scarcely fathom the look he received, but thought he was being judged. He did his best to look grave, though encouraging simultaneously. But it was a manufactured expression, he knew it, and before long he was smiling at her. She sniffed again and dabbed at her nose.

"That's better," she said. "I always preferred you smiling. It meant you were getting better."

"And don't forget there is all that nursing time I have to recompense you for," he said. "Nurses don't come cheap."

She snorted, apologised, and used the handkerchief again. "You know there was nothing else I could do. How could I leave you to die?"

"I am very glad that you didn't. That you didn't prevail on Fox to get some nurse in from the town. But nurse me you most definitely did. And I loved you for it."

"How could I not nurse you back to health," she said again. "You were so young, so helpless... and I had noticed you around Tide Mills when you were younger and..." Her eyes angled towards the floor.

"And?" he prompted.

"I noticed you," she said defiantly. "There were a lot I didn't notice. A lot I don't remember."

"And *I* noticed *you*. I was horrified when you agreed to marry Fox."

Another long silence.

"I thought I could love him. He wasn't bad looking when he was young. And so persuasive. And what they call 'a good catch'." She sniffed. "A right royal fool I was."

"He swept you off your feet. I knew I wasn't good enough for you, compared with him."

She looked horrified at him.

"There was two years between you and me. I never knew you felt like that about me. And when Fox and I married you were fifteen. It was only when you'd worked away for that summer and then were rescued that I could see what a man you were. A *real* man. Not like *him*. And as you got better I learnt that you were someone I could talk to, not be talked at like Fox did. Small wonder that I loved you."

It was Isaac's turn to stay silent for a long time, trying to control his emotions.

"Do you think I didn't love you?"

"I know you did," she said simply. "We have a son to prove that."

After a while he said: "I've been a bloody fool, haven't I? As well as cruel."

Her head shook slowly. "Not cruel. That was Fox's province. You said last night that you were scared, and that I was married. You had no way of knowing what the situation really was."

"And I thought that no matter what I felt, I mustn't come between man and wife." He sighed. "Why is it, then, that it makes me feel no better? I should have come to check, to see you. But then – I suppose even had I realised, what would I have done? Thrashed Fox? Got myself arrested for assaulting a squire? That would have helped a lot, I don't think! Taken you and the boy away? With me away at sea and not well paid anyway? You wouldn't have accepted that."

"Wouldn't I?"

He thought. "No, you wouldn't. To start with I was living in crummy, dirty lodgings because I had nothing and could afford nothing. Then the war came and for ages I seemed hardly ever to go ashore. But when I did I started educating myself and got a foot on the promotion ladder. Dead men's shoes, sometimes…"

The eyes closed again and he shuddered.

"Did you lose your leg then?" she asked in a gentler voice than he had heard so far, a voice that took him straight back to that bedroom on the second floor of the Mill Cottage.

He shook his head. "I was lucky. I came out of that annihilation, that bloodbath, completely unscathed. It was the second lot that lost me the leg."

As it had last night, her hand reached for his. There was yet another silence.

"Come on," he said almost roughly, standing up with the usual effort and dislodging her hand as he did so. "We need to go shopping."

She looked up at him, surprised.

"I thought it was me who was meant to be abrupt and shrewish?"

He gazed down at her and saw again the lift of the corners of her mouth.

"You should hear me when I really get going. When I'm dressing down some sprog who's gone too far." He grinned. "Some of them were so young that by the time I'd finished with them they were in tears. And... and that always got to me because I'd always be reminded of myself when I spent my first night in Portsmouth, sleeping on a park bench."

Another grim smile. "They usually got off with just a hazing. I didn't have the heart to punish them properly, like I would a full-blown matelot."

He had thought that his pension might run to Harrods prices, but blanched when he saw their dizzying heights. She kept gasping at them too and the looks she gave him were saucer-eyed.

"I can't spend that sort of money on clothes," she gasped. "I'd be frightened to wear them. Scared of ruining them. Let's go somewhere else."

He was relieved, and she found Marks and Spencer.

It took her some time to grasp the idea that she didn't have to ask for his permission to buy something, even if she did ask him almost fifty times – or so he thought. Eventually, with prompting on the different circumstances she was buying clothes for, choices were made and paid for. As they regained the street he looked at her. It took her a moment to discover his inquisitive stare.

"Happier?" he asked.

And what he had longed for since first knocking on her door the previous day appeared.

Another full smile.

Unbidden, the arm unencumbered by carrier bags went round her shoulders again. She wriggled free.

"Now, now, young Isaac," she said. And this time there was not just a smile but a look of mischief that struck so many chords that he nearly broke down.

"I need a tea. How about you?"

He was being abrupt again.

Clothes shopping for him had been for years a matter of necessity only. Clothes shopping for her since Fox's funeral had been almost unheard of. She was starting to look longingly into shop windows. He was feeling the strain on what remained of his left leg. She had noticed his deepening limp and was becoming concerned.

They found a Lyons' Corner House and took a lift up to one of the restaurants. Thankfully Isaac lowered himself into a chair.

"I've tired you out," she said.

"I'm all right walking, but it's starting, stopping and turning that do it," he admitted. "But it has been worth it."

"Why? How can what we've done today be worth a lot of pain to you?"

"Because I witnessed a smile and an expression that came straight from my sixteenth year, Mill House, and of course, you."

"Behave."

"I'm telling the truth. You can't blame me for that."

"We only met yesterday."

"No, we met long enough ago to want to remember, and to make up for past mistakes. I do, anyway. I hope you might."

"Isaac... please... I really do need to get used to... to... all this." She waved her arm round to encompass the surroundings and nearly managed to slap a Nippy as she did. Isaac stared at her, wondering what the result would be if he laughed. But she once again gave a smile, a guilty smile, so he gave vent.

"Isaac... we could have been in trouble!"

"No, the customer is always right. I would have apologised, said she was closer than we thought, and that would have been that."

Her head shook, wonderingly.

At least, later, in the shoe shop, he could remain seated as she accepted his suggestion of trying new footwear. Hers were very old, and secondhand. Again, money changed hands and he led the way, even further laden, to a taxi rank.

"I can't face a bus," he said. "This will be quicker."

He must be really wealthy, she thought, and wondered if she was being unfair. Unfair on his pocket; he had made it very clear what he wanted her to do.

On the way back he asked the cabbie whether there were any really good ladies' hairdressers near his home. The man didn't know, but suggested phoning the local cab office in the morning and asking them. "One of their men will know," he was told. Edna's face was a picture.

8 – Young Isaac

After lunch just over a week later the telephone in the mill office rang. Jack Pentelow answered it.

"It's Edna Fox," said a voice.

"Er... er..."

"You know – Mrs Fox. From the village."

"Oh... yes, sorry. You threw me a moment. How are you?"

"Still trying to get used to living a normal life again."

"Oh... er... yes... Are you really all right, though?"

"Yes, thank you Mr Pentelow. Or really I should call you Jack as we were at the same school. Even if I was older than you."

He laughed, though it was a little forced. He thought back. There was nothing in his memory about her until she married the old squire's son. Then, at two years her junior, he saw that she was a good looking girl, even if really a year or two too young to be married. His parents had discussed that for months beforehand, in a 'no-good-will-come-of-it' way, as had many others in Newhaven.

"Indeed. Yes. I remember your marriage." He was furious with himself for mentioning it as a first memory. Tactless, he thought, now knowing the story.

But she laughed. With a start he realised that he had heard no such thing from her since her husband had died. Like others, he had put it down to the sorrow of losing a spouse. "I do too, just. It was the last time until Fox joined the Army that I was treated by everyone else in the village as one of them, as an equal partner in life. And even then – well, it was like being at arm's length. And you know how that marriage went. Now you do, at least."

"And all through that hell of a marriage..." he winced "...I wasn't really part of Tide Mills. And the more Fox mismanaged the business the less I was liked, it seemed. Hardly surprising that I had no one to turn to when he died and left me penniless."

"Facts that nobody here – nobody else here – knew anything about, of course," he said defensively.

"Maybe. But please – I need to come down and see you and – well – everybody. I want it clear in everyone's mind exactly what happened. And I'll come with Captain Galley. And maybe Max, Barbara and Owen. Is there somewhere we could meet?"

"I'm sure there is. If we can organise a get-together for the Wilsons we can for you."

"And do you think The Buckle – or an hotel – can provide a buffet? It'll be paid for by me, of course."

"Er... yes. Yes, I can lay that on. It was a joint village effort for the Wilsons, of course but... well, I'll call the Buckle now. When did you want it to take place?"

It was arranged for a Saturday evening the week following. Jack told Max when he came to use the telephone and he smiled.

"She and Isaac asked to come and see us last Sunday night," he said. "I suggested they came to talk everyone at the Mills and even to answer questions so that everyone has the right facts. And at the get-together I'll have a chance to give a progress report."

"Surely they've not finished the Mill House yet?"

"No, but it's getting on. All I want now is a blinking telephone line – as well as a kitchen to keep my wife happy. But they have other men becoming free from other jobs so they should be able to start on one of the cottages."

"No problems with the standard of the work, then?"

"None. I think it's a case of Martin keeping such a tight grip on what's going on that the problems – if any - get corrected before we see them."

"Talking about Martin, there's another Toads match next week. Are you up for it?"

Max laughed and felt his head. "I think it's just recovered from last time. Yes, I'd like to. That was good fun. What my wife and son will say when they're living here, I don't know."

"Another few years and Owen will be there too!"

Max winced. "Don't remind me. He's half way to fifteen now."

"Is he now? And how's it going between Ruth and him?"

"Haven't a clue. They just seem like good friends. There's been no shenanigans going on, anyway."

Jack grinned. "So far as you know."

"So far as... you don't know anything, do you?"

"No," said Jack with a laugh. "I shouldn't think they're really old enough for that yet, would you?"

"Perhaps not, perhaps not... We'll have to keep a look out."

"You're being too cautious, Max, if you don't mind me saying so."

"I keep thinking back to Isaac Galley. He was only sixteen."

"Owen's not in a bed being looked after by Ruth. Stop *worrying*!"

If anything prompted Max into the mindset that his son was really no longer a child in the fullest sense of the word, this conversation did. It caused no epiphany moment, but the subconscious attitude changed.

The Saturday of the party – as it had come to be known – arrived at last. As neither food nor beer had arrived by mid-afternoon as agreed, Jack walked along to the Buckle to see what was happening. The first thing he saw as he approached the pub was an important, black, Police Wolseley.

Entering the pub cautiously he found the landlord, who was harassed. "The pub was broken into last night," he was told. "We've had Police here all morning. I'm getting everything together for you but it'll be another hour, I'm afraid."

"Oh no... that's bad. Do they know who it was yet?"

"Just been dusting for fingerprints, so there's been a lot we couldn't touch until a short while ago. That's been the cause of the delay."

"Do you need a hand?"

"No – we're nearly ready, as I said. But one thing you could do is get a team to come and fetch it all. It's a bit of a bumpy old ride with the trolley along Marine Parade with its old rails, along to the bridge. I wouldn't want the barrel to fall on the food as we go! And the Police might want us here."

Jack walked back and started mustering a team. Most were in, and he was particularly pleased to be able to collar Jack Barden, the young man who lived alone in the southernmost cottage in the settlement. At the earlier get-together it had been noted that he was very interested in helping to eat and drink, but had been less helpful in preparing and providing beforehand and clearing up after it. He wasn't very keen to help now, but Jack had a few words with him which prompted a grudging agreement.

The group of about fifteen of them, including Owen, Alan and Eric but excluding Ruth, made short work of the portage. Owen was pleased to see Ruth happily helping to set up everything in the area they'd used before.

"I wouldn't have been much use carrying stuff," she said. "I'm better here."

"You're good wherever you are," he responded without thinking, then blushed. He received a sharp look which turned into a smile.

"Thank you," was all she said as she turned back to her arranging. The door opened and, as any alert person would do, she looked up. A stranger stood framed against the greyness of late afternoon, but details of the face were hidden. Somehow the figure was familiar.

The table Ruth was working on was nearest to the door. She was one of the few who, in the activity caused by the late arrival of the supplies, had seen. She looked closer. There was a tall figure behind, with an important-looking cap on, and white hair escaping from it around the face. She realised, and crossed to the door, stopping a few feet away in amazement.

"Yes, Ruth. A little different from when we last met. And more comfortable than for many years. And I'm in a spin because of the improvements, just as it looks you are."

"Mrs Fox..."

She was interrupted. "Can it just be Edna? Please? I know you shouldn't at your age, but I really feel as if I need to be a real part of the Mills again, just as I used to be when I was at school. I don't want to be the old woman who's known for complaining a lot and being sharp with everyone, whether they deserved it or not."

And, wonder of wonders so far as Ruth was concerned, she smiled. Ruth backed away to let her and the smiling Isaac into the light and this time everyone noticed the movement. They stopped, staring at a transformation.

She was hatless ("I can't get used to wearing a modern one. Not yet," she had said) and it was therefore obvious that a hairdresser of some expertise had been allowed free rein. The result was tasteful without any hint of flamboyance. The remainder of her choice was modern, stylish without excess. The result transformed her.

There were mutters from around the room which might have included the word "Wow!". She ignored them, removed her coat and hung it up.

"What still needs doing?" she asked in businesslike tones.

"We're just taking things out of paper bags and tidying up," said Jack Pentelow, coming over to shake her and Isaac's hands. "Hallo, Edna. Hallo, sir. You must be Isaac Galley."

"I am. I don't think we met when I was here last."

"A week ago? No, I wasn't told what had happened until after you'd all gone."

Edna returned to the table to help sort out the food.

"I meant fifty years ago, when I was washed ashore more dead than alive."

"Ah; well actually we did. We were at school at the same time, though you were about fifteen and I was ten, I suppose. I really got to hear about you, like everyone else did, when you disappeared. After that I didn't know of you until young Owen mentioned your name, and then of course the evening Ruth Decks came rushing round to talk to my wife, so full of information that I thought we'd been invaded."

Isaac laughed. "No – I think there might have been a build up to that happening."

"Like in the USA last year, you mean?"

The Captain's face went grim. "Like nearly in the entire world, last year."

Jack nodded. "I never want to be closer to a nuclear war than that. We read the survival manual and even that was - well, almost as good as saying that that was going to be curtains for every human being in the western world."

Isaac shuddered. "I've had to see a damn sight more than that. Part of our more recent training was to get to grips with the reality of nuclear war in detail. And I cannot stress enough how harrowing that is, and how the knowledge that pressing a button on a modern warship could wipe out ordinary people in towns over a wide area far away. It could have conceivably been the case that I would have to press one of those buttons. Certainly we would have been drafted in to look after our own people – many of whom were going to die anyway. I can't think of any part of a discussion on a nuclear war in a light way."

Jack looked at him in surprise. He was genuinely upset. He raised his eyebrows and received a small, embarrassed smile in return.

"Sorry. It was that training that told me, more than a tin leg and advancing years ever did, that it was time for me to go ashore. In the Navy I grew up with, the idea of mass extermination was anathema. So when the opportunity came to retire, I did."

"But you're still proud of the Navy. You're in uniform."

"I am. But that's because it's still my instinctive way of looking smart and showing that I was a part of something worthwhile. Old habits are hard to shed."

"It still is worthwhile, surely?"

"I hope so. I really hope so." He shook his head. "Yes. It *is* worthwhile. I think I was just getting jaded. The Navy has done a lot for me. And learning something about leadership has finally enabled me to face the demons of childhood and rescue Edna. That is something I should have done when I was a young man starting off in the Navy. If only I'd known the story earlier."

Jack looked uncomfortable. "If only we – I – had known what was going on, and latterly what had gone on. All I could see, firstly, was a woman who kept herself to herself, then when her husband died she became almost reclusive. Trust me that any attempt at help with food or physical help or particularly money were turned away and the would-be helper given a flea in their ear!"

"I know, I know. It was a surprise and a relief when she agreed to come to London with me. I think she was just getting tired."

Jack nodded. "Hardly surprising. How has she been?"

"It's probably best if she tells you. And I think she would want to tell everyone just the once."

Jack nodded. "I'm just pleased to see her looking comfortable and – well – less..." He foundered for words.

"Abrasive? I think I understand. I also think there were only two people who could have helped there. Our son, and me. And the son, Isaac – it's sad, but I don't think she really knows him now. If he started trying to help when she started needing it, after seeing her so infrequently for so long, he may well have come out of it with a flea in his ear. Just like the rest of us."

"This is me you're talking about, isn't it? I can still dole out fleas for ears, you know."

They swung round. A smart, determined looking woman stared back at them accusingly. But now there was a trace of humour in the expression.

"Sorry, Edna..." They spoke simultaneously, and to Jack's amazement she laughed.

"It's like overhearing Alan and Eric Baker saying something rude. Then they're embarrassed and stammer their apologies," she said. "You both have the same expression. I'm beginning to enjoy myself. Perhaps this won't be the ordeal I thought."

Isaac smiled. "As someone who had to stand in front of a parade of recruits, some up for it, some not, and tell them about how the ship is going to be run, I know something about ordeals," he said with a smile. You're lucky. These are friends, people you know."

"Are they friends? *Do* I know them? More importantly, do they *know* me? Only as an old widow with a sharp tongue."

"Part of what we want to do is to show them the real Edna Fox..."

"Can we just forget that surname, please?" she snapped. "It brings back memories I want to forget."

"The real Edna, then." Isaac was unphased by the snap.

"Edna Reed..." muttered Jack.

Her face softened. "You remembered!"

"Just came back to me."

"Well, do we leave you as just plain Edna for the time being?" said Isaac, then coloured as he realised what he'd said. "When I say plain..."

She interrupted with another smile. "Isaac, you've just spent a fortnight on helping smarten me up, even giving me the freedom to choose what I want so long as it wasn't going to make me look like an old maid. So if *you* of all people tell me I'm plain, what hope have I got?"

Thank goodness she's smiling, thought each of the men.

"You know I've never regarded you as plain. Not then. Not now. We've been through that and you should know it by now."

"And no getting fresh with me, either. People will get the wrong idea."

His head turned, and he was suddenly serious.

"I think it might be the right idea. Even after all this time."

For once she was speechless.

The room was starting to fill, and many of those who knew Edna well had to take second and third glances at this well dressed woman whose face they thought they had known. Somehow that face seemed younger, more at peace, and they wondered at the change.

Prompted by Isaac when they had met in London, Max stood on a chair again, wobbled and caught his balance thanks to Owen's shoulder which was conveniently near. In his best parade ground voice he called for quiet.

"We're all friends here. Eat first. Chat. Leave no one out. There's plenty. If you leave anything we have some tame gannets here who can help as they did last time."

They needed no second bidding. Soon the room was full of voices and Edna and Isaac found themselves the centre of attention. Alan and Eric hung back, being nervous of this smart person that was, yet wasn't, the person they usually tried to avoid. Edna noticed, and smiled to herself, and engineered her presence behind them as they descended for the third time to the food table.

They were about to refill their plates when each felt a hand on a shoulder. Knowing this was the usual parental sign that they were doing something wrong they nearly dropped their plates. Turning round they saw, to their horror, Old Ma Fox looking at them.

But this wasn't Old Ma Fox. This was a pretty woman – old, maybe – who had a twinkle in her eyes.

"I probably owe you lots of apologies," she said. "I've been unfair to you, shouted at you, probably snarled a lot too. You'll find out later how misfortune colours someone. But I just wanted to say that I'm sorry, and that I hope if I ever snarl at you again you have my permission to say to me 'But you said...'. And it will pull me up sharp and I'll apologise again. And another thing – you know my marriage was unhappy. I hate even hearing the name 'Fox'. So when later I ask everyone just to use my Christian name that includes you two.

"Now, for goodness sake, fill up those plates and eat! I don't want to see you fading away."

She was treated to two beaming smiles before they turned back to the table.

"She's not a bad old stick," said Alan.

"I've always liked her," replied his brother.

The Harveys barrel was being attacked by all the men, including Isaac who declared that he'd never found a better pint "even in Pompey, where we have Gales – the brewery, that is, not the wind. Although there are plenty of them too."

An hour later Max thought it was time he started talking and once again climbed on to the rickety chair, this time using Jack Pentelow as a prop.

"I know you've had a chance to chat to Edna, and to Isaac Galley. But this is their chance to tell you their story, and to answer any questions."

All eyes were on the figures in front of them, who exchanged glances. Isaac nodded.

"This is really Edna's day," he started. "But as the start of the story is mine I've been asked to set it all going."

He succinctly told the story they'd all now heard, of how he'd been saved from the sea. At the point where he was to all intents healed, he paused and looked with troubled eyes to Edna. She nodded, and before he had a chance to continue she took over.

"Yes," she said, "I fell in love with him then. Despite being married. But I'd already realised by then there was little love in that marriage and what there was seemed to be diminishing by the week. Fox was my life's biggest mistake. Had I known Isaac Galley – really known him – before he appeared in our spare room for me to look after and nurse, Fox would have remained a small, vicious little animal that delights in the misery of chickens."

A chuckle. It encouraged her.

"And yes, months after Isaac had run off out of Holden's way – and Fox's – to join the Navy, I soon realised I was with child. His child."

She glared round, as if daring anyone to criticise.

"And when Fox found out, well…" She continued the story up to the start of the war later that year when Fox had been recruited.

Isaac took up his part of the history, including the hiding of the coins. He hinted at the loss he felt at having to leave Edna behind and left his listeners to ponder his dilemma; whether to brave Holden and Fox and risk the sin of putting man and wife asunder, or doing what he did do.

There was silence when he finished. A dilemma indeed.

Edna quietly took up the tale again and, now without rancour, detailed her and their son's life up to the time that young Isaac married and left them both. Nothing was left out: not the beatings she and the son endured, nor the father's absences in school holiday times.

There were angry mutterings and several choice words were spoken by the men – and apologised for.

She spoke of the son's parting from the home and subsequent marriage, then paused again to let that loss sink in to her audience's imagination.

The bombshell, of course, was the discovery of the second family on the outskirts of London. The buzz at that was stilled only by the matter of fact way in which she reported how her legacy from the will amounted to an insult.

Isaac's let the uproar subside, then spoke.

"It's hardly surprising, I think you'll agree, that Edna should have felt so demoralised by this final blow that she behaved to everyone the way she did. It's also not surprising, given her life from 1914 until now, that she still had the pride to decline what she saw as charity, despite it being just her community trying to help. I nearly fell foul of this too, of course, when trying to encourage her back into normal life. Strong minded lady that she is!"

"You managed it though," she muttered.

"Yes. Just. And it's absolutely no more than you deserve. Surely we all believe that?"

There were murmurs of agreement and a lot of nodding of heads.

"Well, those are our stories. I should say really 'that's our story'. As to the future, I think we both need to adjust. Edna to real life and me to retirement. So no more questions on that score, please! But if anyone wants to ask us about anything else, now's the time."

He was almost certain that there would be few questions, if any. But Mary Decks put her hand up.

"If it's not too personal a question, have you made contact with your son yet?"

Isaac smiled. "That is a job for tomorrow. Literally. Young Isaac last saw his mother a month ago; he knows nothing of me at all. So we shall see. Please don't speak of that to anyone else until we've seen them. We have to discover why his wife has refused to meet her mother-in-law and we don't want her forewarned, please.

"Anyone else?"

Someone asked if they would be returning to Tide Mills.

"That's for the future, as I said to start with. It's a decision for Edna to make. I'm not going to impose my will on her. And by the way, if anyone decides that she and I are living together as man and wife, I advise you to disavow yourself. It would, of course, not be your business but I can assure everyone here that we have rooms at the opposite end of the house."

He looked around fiercely and was pleased to notice only two people's eyes drop away from his.

Max felt it was time for him to resume the talk, so stood by Edna and Isaac and lifted his eyebrows. They both nodded, so he gave the meeting an update on what was happening next and the progress so far. There had been a cautious finish date from Martin Killick for the Mill House – 10 December "Though what use it will be to me as an office when there's no phone, I'm not sure," he said. "If anyone knows a Post Office telephone engineer, you might ask, just in case there's something that can be done.

"I have conferred with the powers that be – Barbara and Owen – and they agree that we should be able to move in on about the 15th, and certainly in time for Christmas. There's a suspicion that there might be some sort of get together once we're in, but to save Barbara even more work I imagine that the Buckle might be asked to help again, if that meets with everyone's approval.

"And by the way, Edna asked if we could arrange this evening as her treat, and Jack's been making the arrangements. However, if she'll allow it, I note that no social event was organised when she retired. It's something that our employers always offer, so I see no reason why her retirement shouldn't be honoured by them now. So, Edna, with your permission it will be the Mill footing the bill for tonight, unless you would rather not."

He watched her carefully, as did Isaac. Her mouth opened, then closed.

"I'm sure this is really a plot. But I've decided it's a very nice plot, and when the youngest person here says 'I've always liked her' in response to a comment from his brother, I really feel that I've come a long way. So I'll be gracious, and accept, and give my thanks to the Mill owners."

Eric's face was as red as a beetroot. There was a round of applause, and he hid his embarrassment by turning back to the food table which was just behind Edna. Alan joined him.

"Idiot," he said. "You need to keep your voice down if you're making comments."

"I didn't know she was listening, did I? She was walking away."

"She's got very good hearing, young Eric, as you now know." This time both of them reddened, and Edna smiled and picked up a piece of cake. "I may be old, but my hearing's as good as it ever was!"

"Sorry, Miss…. Edna," they chorused as she turned away. This time they were silent and concentrated on eating.

"Are you really moving in in just two weeks?" Ruth asked Owen in another part of the room.

"Looks like it," he said happily. "Good, because it'll mean I'll miss the last week of school."

"Lucky thing! Can I come and help at weekends? And when I've broken up?"

"Yes please," he said positively. "I'd like that. What do you want for Christmas?"

That floored her. "I… I don't know. How about you?"

"There's one thing I want, but I can't tell you."

"Why not?"

"I can't tell you that, either. Maybe one day."

"You're annoying."

He nodded theatrically and grinned. "Always."

She put her tongue out, but it was a half-hearted attempt because she was smiling broadly too.

Edna had said categorically that she wouldn't allow Isaac to sleep in her cottage. "I can't take you there. It's… it's shameful. And there's only one bedroom."

With some relief he had booked two rooms in the Eversley Hotel on Seaford's seafront. They helped clear up as the guests were drifting way, then went to the station to catch a train in the dark.

"Sometimes they see you, sometimes they don't," Arthur Decks had told him, but he was talking about train drivers in the dark, not something more sinister. Arthur had been amazed to meet another Captain RN – even a retired one – so soon after meeting Max, and had spent quite a time swapping stories. This time the driver didn't see them, so Arthur, Ruth and Owen walked with them to the bus stop.

The terrace of houses had only just been built, that was obvious from the still-unsettled gardens and the newness of the brickwork.

They found the right number. They looked with approval at the bright yellow paint and polished brass on the door.

"Is this it?" Isaac whispered.

"It's the right address," Edna almost snapped. "Don't forget I've never been allowed to visit before."

He looked at her wonderingly. "There's more to this than meets the eye, you know. I can't imagine any son not wanting a visit from the mother who looked after him so well when she could."

"When I was allowed to."

"Exactly. Look, we should get on with this, surely. Shall I press the bell?"

She answered him by doing just that. Footsteps approached after a moment, by which point Isaac was almost shaking in anticipation. Edna felt an attack of shrewishness coming on. Why had her son so rarely visited? Why had she never been invited to visit him in Eastbourne? And why oh why had it taken Isaac's casual comment about visiting to persuade her to do so? She could – should – really have done so at any point since her son had moved out.

The door opened. An attractive young girl of about fifteen, with corn coloured hair and a pleasant face, smiled at the visitors.

"Hallo," she said, and then puzzlement crossed her face as she realised she didn't know them. And then a deeper puzzlement seemed to take grip as she really saw Edna's features.

"Did you want to see Dad? Or has Gerry been misbehaving again?"

Isaac smiled, despite his anxiety. He could see hints of the young Edna's face in front of him.

"I think we'd better see your father, please," he said.

The girl's expression changed to one of alarm. "Gerry's not hurt, is he?"

"No," said Edna, "It's not to do with him."

"Oh... oh, thank goodness. I'll go and find Dad."

She turned back. Each of the visitors realised she had omitted to ask their identity.

More footsteps. A middle aged man, very upright, with a similar halo of whitening hair to Isaac's, came to the door. He looked at them both, looked surprised to see Isaac's uniform, then managed a double take at Edna.

"Mum?"

"Yes, Isaac, Mum. Come to call on you at last, as I should have done years and years ago. And this is... well, may we come in?"

The Captain's eyes hardly left the face before him, noting the similarities and the differences between what was in front of him and what he saw in the mirror every morning; wondering what sort of brain and spirit lurked within that head.

Dazedly he nodded and led them into a room which turned out to be as neat and tidy as the front door. They sat. The girl smiled.

"Are you really my granny?"

Edna returned a smile which a month ago would have been unrecognisable as hers.

"Yes. I am. And I've taken far too long to come and see you. That's one of the reasons we're here."

"Good. I'm glad you have. Gerry will be happy too. Shall I go and make some tea?"

"Yes please..." her father started.

"No – please, not yet. What we have to say affects you too. And maybe afterwards we shall all need a cup of tea." It was the first time Isaac had spoken. The father and daughter looked round, astonished not just by his instruction but by the note of command in the voice of someone who, so far as they knew, was a stranger. Although a shadow of annoyance crossed the younger Isaac's face he sat. The girl followed suit.

"Isaac," Edna started, "I think it is time in both our lives for some explanations. Yes, I have changed, and the reason for that will become clear as we tell you the... our... story."

"*Our* story?"

"Our story. Mine, yours and his." She indicated Isaac senior, who spoke.

"Forgive another interruption, but your son – Gerry, did you say his name was? – is he due back soon? And your wife? This will affect them too."

His son shrugged. "It's Sunday. Gerry will have gone back to... to where we used to live, to play with his friends there. We shan't see him until lunch, I should think."

Isaac nodded, remembering times in his own childhood where he had started spending more time out of the house than in. His home in those days had none of the modern conveniences that this compact, modern house contained.

He nodded. "We will need to go over it again later, then, when he and his mother are here."

"I doubt if Gerry would be very interested, Mr. Er... Captain... er..."

"Galley," said Isaac. "Isaac Galley." He noted the surprised lift of the eyebrows. "The name means something to you?"

"Ye-es...." His son looked uncomfortable. "It was a name my wife used to mention sometimes. And we share a Christian name, of course."

"Indeed. But I think it best if Edna takes over now, then our part of the story will become clear. It sounds as if there's another story from your side, though."

He was about to be answered when there was a clatter in the hall and the door slammed. A mutter of young voices ensued, at the end of which was "I'll see if Dad's in."

Isaac rose and went to the door. "He is. Oh... what have you done?"

"Fell, and a piece of glass cut my leg. It hurts a bit."

"Gerry, why does it always have to be you? Come on. Into the kitchen with you and we'll patch it up."

He looked into the living room again. "Sorry. A bit of first aid to do. Won't be long."

"Do you want a hand, Dad?" asked the girl.

"No, it's all right, Bee. Billy's here."

A muttering from the hall.

"Oh, okay Billy. Thanks for bringing him home anyway. See you another day. Bee – yes please, can you come? Billy has to go home."

"May we come too?" asked Edna as Bee rose from the chair.

"Well... all right, then. The more the merrier, I suppose. Through here."

They followed Bee into a kitchen that was as clean and tidy as the rest of the house seemed to be. Isaac suspected the reason – Navy training, just as his own had been. In fact, here it was even more fastidiously tidy; to an experienced mariner that meant submarine training, where every inch of storage space has to be used and kept tidy.

A boy was sitting on one of the kitchen chairs He had the same corn coloured hair as his sister and a face that looked as if butter wouldn't melt in its mouth. He tried to get up when Edna appeared but his father stopped him.

"Move, and it'll get worse," he said.

The boy subsided, then caught sight of Isaac senior's uniform.

"A Captain!" he said with a smile.

"Retired," Isaac said briefly, "but a Captain nevertheless."

The boy grinned. "I knew looking at those old books would be useful."

"Old books?"

"Dad's Manual of Seamanship. His are very old – 1937."

"Mine are 1910," his grandfather told him."

"Is that when you joined...sir?"

"No. I joined in 1914. But they had a lot left over, I suppose. Just as they did in your father's time."

He nodded, then winced as his father dabbed the long, nasty cut with TCP.

"All the glass out of it?" asked Isaac senior.

"It was a thick piece," said Gerry. "No more broke off."

"Good," said both father and grandfather simultaneously, then grinned at each other.

"We'll see how it does in a day," said the first-aider. "If it doesn't look happy we'll go and get the doctor to put a stitch in it."

"I don't want a stitch!" exclaimed the patient. "It was bad enough cutting it. I'm sure it'll be all right."

"Depends whether you want it to mend or not," said Isaac senior. "Mine didn't. Now I have a metal leg."

"A... a *metal* leg?" the youngster faltered.

"Yes. Although the lump of metal that cut my leg was a bit bigger than a bit of glass. But it took so long for them to get help to me that the doctors said mine couldn't be saved."

The boy's expression was horrified. He turned to his father.

"I think I'd prefer a stitch."

Both men smiled at each other again as Gerry's attention returned to his cut. Skilfully his father and daughter bandaged it.

"Good work," Isaac couldn't help remarking.

"I had to learn. They made me a medic when I was in the boats."

"I thought you must have been a Deep. The house is so clean and tidy."

He had a grin in return. "When you have no space at all and you have to stow all your kit in it, it teaches you to be tidy. Even eighteen years afterwards."

"You were in for the war?"

"Yes. I thought I'd better join and decide for myself before I was drafted and chucked in anywhere. Living by the sea, the Navy was first choice. You're still in? I should be calling you 'sir' shouldn't I?"

Isaac smiled. "Not after eighteen years out of it. And I've just retired anyway."

"But still in uniform."

Isaac looked uncomfortable. "I had to look smart last night, and this is still my way of doing so. I thought I should do the same today. Look, if Gerry is all right now, may we all go and sit somewhere so that we can talk? Then the reason for the uniform might be a little plainer."

He received a puzzled look. Throughout the exchange Edna had said nothing, but her eyes darted from son to father as if she was watching a tennis match. Gerry limped theatrically into the living room and the others followed.

"Now then..." said Isaac junior. Edna looked at him, then at Isaac, who took a deep breath.

"Way back in 1914..." Isaac started the story. Both his grandchildren listened wide eyed as he described his adventure and how near he had come to death. Neither he nor they noticed the start that came over Isaac junior's face as he described what Holden had done and how he had tried to obtain information leading to the sovereigns.

"So it was Edna here who nursed me back to health. We became close. I knew that she liked me, and I her, and then one night... well. We became very close." He paused. Gerry still looked excited, not immediately understanding; but Bee's eyes opened wide again. Her father's jaw dropped.

"I knew what we had done was wrong. I had come between man and wife. I had to leave, not only to avoid anything further in that direction but also to get out of Holden's way before he found out I was better. I hid the sovereigns for Edna so she could bail me out or do whatever she needed to do, in case I was ever arrested or taken for questioning. One day I was doing some gardening, trying to repay the family, when the Revenue men came and arrested me. I was in prison for two nights, then they released me and I thought it was probably Holden who wanted to get hold of me, or Edna had found the money.

"But no one came to meet me from the cells. I walked over to Peacehaven to get out of Holden's way, wondered what to do until night fell, then carried on walking west. At Brighton I caught a train to Portsmouth and joined the Navy as a Ship's Boy."

"And I had no clue where he had gone," said Edna quietly, the pain in her voice plain. "But life settled down, as well as it could with my new husband, until it began to be plain that I was expecting."

She waited for a reaction. Slowly her son's eyes levelled with her.

"And I was born in 1915... Are you saying..."

His voice petered out but his eyes held Edna's. She nodded.

Softly she said: "You are my son. But you are also Isaac's. Fox, my husband in nothing but name, had no part in it."

Slowly her son's eyes swivelled to the Captain's and back again, then to the two youngsters, then back to Edna.

"But that means that you're our grandma and grandpa." Gerry had just realised.

Isaac smiled at him, and included his sister. "Yes, it does. So I'm glad to have helped bandage you up."

Isaac junior's mind was still on his life at Tide Mills.

"But look – does this mean that the way he treated me, the way he never spoke a kind word; all the thrashings, all the sneering, all the absences... were they all just because he knew I wasn't his?"

"Partially, yes," Edna told him. "But he was the sort of man who would have beaten his children anyway, just as he did me, his wife. It was just how he behaved, maybe how he was brought up. He was also shell-shocked by what he endured in the War, I suppose. No, that I do know. He would shout out in the night, sometimes so loudly that I had to go in and support him – even I, who had reason by then to hate him because of how he treated you and me. And every time I went into him it was wrong, and I had to escape back to my own room and lock your door and mine, Isaac."

The Captain muttered "Disgusting!"

She explained how the man had insisted that Isaac should go to boarding school as soon as he could be accepted there, and how the father had started leaving mother and son alone during much of the school holidays.

Isaac nodded, at last. "I could never understand why he was so cold towards me, and you were so warm. And why, when he was there, he always found fault and took the strap to my back."

His children were horrified. "How old were you then, Dad?" asked Gerry.

"Any age from about ten upwards until I left for good," he said grimly. "Even when I was seventeen I thought that I had to endure it because that was how all fathers behaved. It never crossed my mind that none of the other boys in the school ever came back after holidays with red weals on their backs."

Edna's hand crossed to his. He held it, and looked into her eyes.

"Why didn't you stop him, Mum?"

"I... I couldn't. I was beaten down by him. Mentally and physically. Oh yes, I suffered at his hands too. Like you I put it down to being normal behaviour for a husband; that and the effects of the War. But I knew deep inside that he was no man, that I hated being married to him, that he was cruel. And every time you came home and he went off I was relieved, but nevertheless I found that you were growing away from me."

"Because I didn't understand why you never stopped it. Or spoke to me about it. I wish you had. But I sort of understand now."

The youngsters were looking down at the floor. There was silence in the room. Outside a gull cried its lonely, mournful call and broke the spell. The older man's hand reached out to Edna.

"Sometimes we are beaten down so much that ordinary behaviour seems extraordinary, and what we experience in our own reality is what we must put up with."

"I wish you had come back then," she whispered.

"So do I."

The words came simultaneously from both father and son. They looked at each other, the younger suddenly aware.

9 – Grandchildren

"You really are my father, aren't you?"

The elder Isaac nodded. "And I hope you'll realise that had I been there and seen what was going on, Fox would have been thrashed by me, local squire or not, and even if it had cost me my freedom. And I would somehow have taken you both away with me – somehow, somewhere – and been a proper father to you and a proper husband to Edna. If she'd have let me back into her life by then."

"I wish you had."

The two continued their eye contact. Bee and Gerry looked up at them and realised that what was happening, what was being said, would change their lives in some way, without knowing how.

"But… there must have been a reason why you didn't."

It was a simple enough comment from his son, but Isaac knew the answers. He had given them so many times.

"I was in the Navy. I scarcely spent any time ashore. Even if I had, Edna was a married woman. Although I missed her with all my heart it would have been coming between man and wife if I'd gone back. I couldn't. And don't forget I knew nothing about what was going on. Not even that you existed.

"And there was also the unfinished business with Holden. He was known as a dangerous bully, and feared by everyone. At least until I was properly a man I would have been at his mercy if I'd encountered him anywhere. And it was only when I came to visit Edna at last that I learnt he had been drowned."

"Holden…" his son gave a start again. He sighed. "What you don't know is that Josephine's name was Holden and she hated Fox for some reason she would never tell me."

"Josephine?"

"My wife. My ex-wife, I suppose, though we're still officially married."

Edna gasped.

"I may as well tell you this now, though I've not admitted it to Mum. She left us five years ago. She found a wealthier man and moved in with him."

Edna looked horrified. "I wish you had come and told me! Why didn't you?"

"Because Josephine had always hated the idea of my coming over to see you so I'd… well, never got into the habit of visiting. And I had deliberately not visited when Dad – that is, Fox – was alive because by then I'd realised that he actively hated me. Because of him Tide Mills held too many painful memories for me.

"You know Josephine stopped me from inviting either of you to our wedding? I didn't care about Fox but I really wanted you. But she told me that if you were there the wedding would be off. And the only reason she'd give me was that you and he had made my childhood life so hellish that she wouldn't forgive you. It was easy to walk over me in those days." He gave a dismissive 'Huh!' "I'd had all the stuffing beaten out of me by you-know-who over many years.

"Besides, I knew that you had enough troubles of your own by then, and I didn't see that I should make them worse by sharing mine with you. And when my job vanished with the company I was working for I found I had to work every hour I could to pay the mortgage on this house and to feed us all.

"The final reason was that I didn't love Josephine any more. She had changed so much, become bitter, and hated being poor."

Edna took this in, but Isaac saw that the two youngsters once again had their eyes downcast.

"How about you two?" asked Isaac quietly. "How did you feel about that?"

The gentle voice brought Bee's eyes up to meet his. She pulled a face.

"At the time it felt like the end of the world," she said. "But the way she left, and how things had been for some time before, well... And afterwards, Dad was... different..."

She paused, and thought.

"Happier," prompted Gerry.

"Happier," she continued. "Everything was lighter, somehow. We started to think that – well, we missed her, of course – but... well... that it was better with just Dad. And she's never come back to see us, or anything."

For the first time since the conversation had begun, Isaac junior smiled.

"Thank goodness," he said. "I wondered all this time whether you had just said what I wanted to hear. I'm glad – we have had some fun since, haven't we?"

The two nodded. Bee crossed to him and gave him a hug.

"And now it's your turn," she said. "At last you've got a *proper* father."

Emotions can act like a spring. A story told slowly, with sad or happy incidents recounted, winds the spring. There comes a point where the spring has to release because the poignancy is at its height. So it was then. Tears were shed for the reasons any observer would by then have known. Alone, Gerry was the least affected, though he felt a pricking of his eyes as he watched the others and thought. His time would come later, when alone and able to think and re-examine how the others, his family, were being affected.

He wondered how he could escape the emotionally charged atmosphere. As do almost all boys, he found it embarrassing. Without fuss he limped into the kitchen and filled the kettle. Whilst it boiled he supported his arms on the kitchen table and stared at the painted wall opposite, seeing nothing.

"You never came to Fox's funeral," Edna remarked, expecting the reason to be that he had hated the man he thought to be his father so much that he had decided against it.

"I never knew it was happening until you told me afterwards," he said. "She had hidden both the letter telling me he'd died and the letter telling me where the funeral was. I only found it when I was looking through her stuff for something else. That was about two years ago. I visited you, but by then that was the least of your problems, as I said before."

"Why did your wife hate Fox?"

"She would never really give details. But maybe she blamed him – and therefore you – for the death of her grandfather, or for the loss of the money that maybe she regarded as the family's. Maybe both. Her father must have been the son of your Holden. She'd told me that he had drowned, but not when it happened, or why. But he hated Fox – the blame must have been passed down the generations. And she mentioned the name of Galley too but I didn't take much notice of that at the time as I had never heard it before."

Edna took a deep breath and told the story of the dreadful funeral and the discovery of the second family. When her son heard what she had been left in Fox's will it reduced him once again to silence.

"Can we do anything about it?"

"It was thirteen years ago, Isaac. I shouldn't think so for one minute."

"But surely…"

"It's something that occurred to me too," said Isaac senior. "I'm not sure if anything would come of it but I feel we should try, just to demonstrate that even after all this time we're not just allowing it to have gone on."

"But what… look, I appreciate what you're saying, but I don't have time or money to engage a lawyer."

"I'm not suggesting that. I have a lot of time to make up, and nearly half a century of ignorance of the girl I fell in love with to try to put right. Thanks to retirement I have quite a bit of time on my hands, so I might be able to do some tracing of my own. Leave that to me – if Edna agrees."

"Is the way that Mum's changed your work too? Or should I not ask?"

"It is entirely her own decision and choice. Don't forget that if I had been here with her, and acting as a proper husband, she would have wanted for nothing once I had risen up the ranks and started earning a decent salary. And do you really think that I could just leave her in that tiny cottage with nearly nothing to eat and almost no heating? Heaven knows how she managed over last winter when many people died because of a lack of heating in all that long cold stretch. No. I will continue to do what she will let me do, and what I should really have done years ago."

The talk continued for some time, with more snippets of information being remembered and shared.

There came a degree of comfort between them, an emotion nurtured by a shared history and hardships suffered in different ways. Two hours after they had arrived, Isaac noticed his grandson, who had returned from the kitchen with tea some time before, starting to fidget and looked at him shrewdly.

"Hungry?"

He nodded. "And nobody's even thought about the kitchen!"

His father looked at the clock with a shock. "He's right! I never noticed the time! Oh no… we have a joint, too."

"Can I suggest… no, grandfather's privilege: may I take my family out for a meal? If we can find somewhere?"

"I can't accept…"

"If you say 'charity', like your mother tried to say when I first asked if she would please endure some comfort for a change, it isn't. It's just practical.

Can you suggest where?"

"We never eat out."

"Then what are the good hotels in Eastbourne?"

"The Grand, but you won't want to afford that! There's..."

He listed some hotels, thinking that none of them would be affordable.

"I think we saw the Cavendish on the way to you," said Isaac. "Can we give them a call?"

"Well yes, but it'll be quite expensive."

"Let's see, shall we. May I use your phone?"

To everyone else's surprise, half an hour later they found themselves walking along the seafront. Gerry had been forced to change into smarter clothes. Bee did so without prompting, and a new, simple dress made her look even more attractive.

They introduced themselves at the Reception desk and were ushered into a large, smart restaurant. Both of the younger people were amazed at the bright decor – and the number of staff smiling at them in welcome. Edna had recently been taken to such a restaurant in London so knew what to expect, even if she was still unused to its opulence. Her son was almost as amazed as his children, but did his best to accept it as normal. Alone of them, his father was completely at home.

"That was the best roast chicken I've ever had," said Gerry as they were leaving.

"We've hardly ever had it," said his father. "It's been too expensive. Getting cheaper now, though."

"Can you cook it?" Gerry asked cheekily, and dodged the mock swipe at his head with a laugh.

They decided to walk along the promenade and stopped to watch the sea.

"What happens now?" asked Isaac junior. "What are you two going to do?"

Edna spoke first. "Too early to answer that. He only came to call on me three weeks ago, and the first thing I did was to slap his face."

"There were extenuating circumstances," murmured her host. The others looked shocked, so she had to explain.

"Nevertheless it's hardly a good start to any... any continuation of a half-century old love affair," she finished, and then wished she hadn't.

The expression on his face was unfathomable, but he kept his peace.

"I know one thing," said his son. "I want to be more fair to Mum. Now she knows what's happened to me, and I understand more of what she went through, especially recently, I hope we can see each other more often. And, I hope, we'll be able to get to know my father more too."

"Bravo!" said Gerry.

Bee smiled. "I'd like to see both of them."

"Should we change our surname to Galley?" asked Gerry, out of the blue.

His father's eyes widened as he took that in. "I... I don't think so. I don't know. I mean, we've been Fox for so long... to be honest it's not something I've thought about yet. I'm still getting used to – well, to so many new things."

The older man also looked astonished, but said nothing.

"Nice people, aren't they?" Edna commented as they returned on the bus to Seaford.

Isaac sighed. "*Nice* is wholly inadequate. I suppose that, like you I have a vested interest and that colours how I think. But when you see others and their antics it makes you glad to see pleasant, normal people. And that Bee... although she didn't say a lot, I'd like to get to know her better. She's obviously got a lot of intelligence. So yes, it was a baptism of fire and really gave us no time to get to know them properly, but... well, I'll be proud to call them Family."

"Will you come and visit them again?"

He looked surprised again. "Edna, I've just discovered my own son and my own grandchildren. Our son and our grandchildren. I should have been there when each one of them was born. Without the mother's evil influence..."

She made to protest. "No... not you. The children's mother, Josephine. Without her secret hate you would have been a part of their lives, all of them. And perhaps between you, you could have supported each other through the bad times. Damn! I never asked Isaac if they'd got any financial problems now."

"The last time he visited me he said that he'd done some training and was working for Post Office Telephones. Does that attract a good salary?"

"I have no idea. But to answer your question: yes. I hope to be seeing a lot more of them. Perhaps they could come up to London to visit. We could show them round..."

"You mean you can."

"Don't you want to?"

"I can't find my way around London! I don't have a clue where we are when you take me anywhere. I wouldn't know where to take them – apart from the Zoo, I suppose. At least I've heard of that. But I couldn't get them there."

"You sound as if you'd like to be shown round too."

"Of course! What do you think?"

"And I think those words answer your question."

"I beg your pardon?"

"Your question. Am I going to visit them again."

She thought, and smiled.

They took in the view over the Cuckmere valley in silence.

"What *am* I going to do?" she asked suddenly as the bus struggled up the hill westwards from Exceat Bridge.

"Visit London's sights with them and me, I hope."

"I don't mean that. I mean... well, where am I going to live?"

He sighed. "I wondered when we were going to start facing that question." He sighed. "Look, so far as I am concerned, all possibilities are open. There are two factors that I want to consider – no, three. The first is your welfare.

The second is the fact that I want to be in contact with our son and grandchildren now I've discovered them. The third is... is more difficult."

She looked at him quizzically. "Why difficult?"

"Because... because it involves us. Our being together. Or not."

It was her turn to pause.

He carried on. "You see, I can't presume anything. I don't know whether... what..."

She interrupted. "Do you want to carry on living in London?"

He was surprised, but relieved by the interruption. Perhaps this wasn't a conversation either of them was ready for. Not yet.

"Well, I'm not a London man by nature. I moved there because of the Navy and my posting. I have no roots anywhere really."

"Not even in Seaford? Or Newhaven? Or even Tide Mills?"

"My only roots are in the Navy, and that's not really being rooted to anywhere because the Navy sends its people all over the place. My father had come to Tide Mills just after I was born. He and I were never really close. I never knew my mother – I think she died in childbirth. Dad let that slip one day. What happened to him after I'd left I have no idea."

"He just upped and left one day," she told him. "He never really recovered, I think. Whether he was enlisted I don't know."

"I should try to find out" he muttered, more to himself than to her. She let the thought sink in and then tried again.

"So if you have no roots in London, had you thought about putting some down in Sussex? Near your new family?"

He looked at her from under his eyebrows. "How did you know that's what has been bothering me since lunch?"

"Bothering you?"

"Yes, because it's a big step. Bothering me because I've only just met them all. I don't know what their attitude is likely to be. Bothering me because... because you're not a city woman, because I can't assume you'd come with me if I moved, and because I refuse to leave you in that tiny cottage in Tide Mills."

"So we're back to the big question."

"Indeed we are. And I think it's still too soon to seek an answer. We barely know each other, even after these few weeks."

"We knew each other well enough in 1914."

A sharp glance pierced her, a glance that softened to a rueful smile.

"And the proof lives in Eastbourne, doesn't it."

She smiled back. "It does. We'd better get off just up here."

He had failed to notice that they were nearing Seaford station. They scrambled downstairs. The conductor rang the bell as soon as they were off the bus.

In the station's waiting room they found Owen, Ruth, Alan and Eric, so the conversation switched to the film they had all been to see. At Tide Mills – Ruth had made sure the driver would stop there this time – she, Alan and Eric alighted and Owen's parents boarded as previously planned, swapping

111

farewells as they did so. There was still no opportunity to continue *that* conversation, so instead they told the Wilsons of their meeting and how they had got on.

Tact ruled and none of the Wilsons asked about future plans.

When Edna and Isaac reached home the first thing Isaac did was to reach for the phone.

Eventually a treble "Hallo?" Came through the earpiece. Isaac thought a moment.

"Hallo Gerry. It's your grandad. I just wanted to say how much it meant to me to meet you all today. Can I speak to your Dad, please?"

"Oh.... Yes. Thanks. I enjoyed it too. And I loved the lunch."

Isaac smiled. "Good to hear it. I like roast chicken too. I'll be in touch, but now – is he there, please?"

"Hang on... DAAD!"

Isaac jerked the receiver away from his ear, grinning at Edna who had heard it squawk. There was a pause, then footsteps; and Isaac was hit by an emotion he'd only recently discovered when Gerry said "It's Grandad!"

He swallowed hard as he heard an amused voice say "Hallo?"

"Hallo Isaac. I just wanted to tell you we're home and that we each really enjoyed today. I suppose..." He felt it necessary to swallow hard again. "... I suppose you have no idea what it feels like to meet up with a son you never knew you had, and to discover that you have two really lovely grandchildren."

There was a pause at the other end.

"When we got back Bee asked the first question, and it was the obvious one. She wanted to know how I felt. At the time I was still shell-shocked, I suppose. But she and Gerry kept up the comments and the questions at intervals all the evening. Everything's more settled in my head now, I think, but I still want to sleep on the news."

His father nodded. "I think that's probably as well. But at least you sound as if you weren't completely horrified at the knowledge that you had this old sea captain as a father."

"The only thing that really horrified me was to discover why I'd been treated so badly as a boy by someone who I learned to fear and to hate. No; there's something else, too. I was horrified to hear how Mum was treated by him. I can't get over that. He must have been an evil pig of a man."

"That about sums up my views. To myself, I use rather stronger language and wish he was still alive so I could teach him a lesson. But maybe the more we think about him, the more his evil will become a part of us. I have every wish to ignore his memory, apart from recognising that some of the damage he caused to you and Edna will take a long time to heal."

"I take it you're not talking about physical damage?" his son asked with alarm.

"No. Damage to the spirit."

"I see what you mean. I suppose we should think about that, just as people had to get used to the occasional strange behaviour from those who'd gone

112

through the trauma of a World War."

"Indeed. I was lucky in the first lot, but I came across some men – well, boys, really who… well, let's just say they would never be the same person, a real person, ever again."

"I hope Mum's not that badly affected. I don't think I am."

"I don't think so, and I'm doing what I can to heal that. But now – she's making signs that she'd like to talk to you, so I'll wish you all a good night and look forward to seeing you again, and very soon. Here she is."

Edna put her hand over the mouthpiece.

"Can I invite them up in the Christmas holidays like you said?" she whispered.

"Yes, of course. Good idea. I don't know when the holidays are, though."

She uncovered the phone again and repeated Isaac's original message. "And we'll be down at Tide Mills in two weeks when the Wilsons move into Mill House. How would it be if you all came back to London with us – this is Isaac's suggestion – and do some sightseeing?"

"What – stay at his house, you mean?"

"Yes. There are four bedrooms, so if Bee and Gerry don't mind sharing a room, that would work."

"But… are you sure he doesn't mind?"

"As I said, it was his suggestion, and I think it's a lovely idea."

"I'm not sure if I can get any holiday, but I can ask. The children would love it, I'm sure."

"Well, you ask tomorrow, and see if you can. If not, we could have them to stay, and you could come up the following weekend."

"I'll ask them, and ask at work too. And – thank you both."

The three Wilsons found that week was mayhem. Max's employers, seeing how little time he had with his family in preparing for the move, persuaded four of their staff to come and help. It was still hard work. For Owen it was a time of mixed emotions since not only was he moving from the only home he had ever known, but the Friday would be his last day at his so-familiar London school. When he returned home, shaken by all the cards and wishes of goodwill, some from unexpected (and many female) sources, he found he had a nearly empty room to sleep in. The last of the furniture was loaded into the vans late that night. Only the essentials were left to be packed into the family car.

The small convoy started on its way just after dawn the following morning, so avoiding the possibility of the removals men having to work overtime on the Sunday. As arranged, the family stopped at the turning from the coast road on to Mill Drove to show the removal drivers where to turn. As they were waiting a westbound bus stopped and three people alighted. Owen noticed one was a boy about his own age with a tattered bandage round his leg and another a girl, attractive and a little older. They walked down the road toward the mill.

Finally the vans appeared. Max made sure he had been seen and drove down to stop near the Mill House. To his surprise Edna and Isaac were there, talking to the three people from the bus. The Wilsons uncoiled themselves from the car and stretched. The two older people came to join them as the vans lumbered down the narrow, uneven road. The younger three followed behind.

"Barbara, Max, Owen: may I introduce my son Isaac and my grandchildren Bee and Gerry?" There was no mistaking the pride in the older man's voice.

"*Our* grandchildren, Isaac."

"Sorry, Edna. *Our* grandchildren. I hope you don't mind, but when they'd heard your story and that you were moving in today, Isaac suggested that some help might be useful, and Gerry particularly jumped at the idea. I'm assured it wasn't just that he wanted to see where I'd hidden the sovereigns."

The two families looked at each other, grinned, and liked what they saw. They had little chance to talk. Two pantechnicons were approaching from the north and two young boys from the east, followed by an older girl, limping slightly. As if that was a signal, men seemed to appear from everywhere, grinning, and obviously wanting to help. Max wondered what to do for the best.

The two London based van drivers and their crews came to talk to him, apparently worried in case they were being held up. Max explained who everyone was and pacified them.

"We normally just put stuff where you tell us," said one.

"Well..." Max was still thinking hard. "Most of the stuff is labelled where it's got to go." He raised his voice so that everyone could hear and if the other retired Captain and retired Petty Officer recognised the tone, they smiled, remembered foul weather in the Atlantic, and the need to be heard over it.

"If everyone could take a lead from the three of us, and from what's on each item, we can identify things and where they need to go. Please also let the removals people take large or heavy things – we don't want any ruptures or squashed hands. Jack needs each of you in one piece!"

With so many people milling around, it was not as straightforward as it might have been. Fortunately the kitchen equipment was amongst the first to be unloaded, so Barbara enjoyed herself directing grinning men where things should go after being unwrapped. She intended to put the kettle on as soon as it appeared, but had only just filled it when there was a shout from outside and trays of what appeared to be cups and saucers from the entire village were placed unceremoniously on a table waiting to be taken in. Four large teapots followed and five minutes later all attempt at carrying had ceased and everyone was talking to everyone else.

Ruth and Owen, Alan and Eric, Bee and Gerry gravitated to each other and introductions were made a lot less formally than the adults had managed.

"Was it really you who found the sovereigns?" Gerry asked Owen.

"What sovereigns?" Alan asked, wide eyed. So Ruth and Owen had to retell the whole story, at the end of which both the other four were astonished.

"Treasure... real treasure," breathed Eric. "You never told us!"

"What have you done with it? Spent it?" asked his brother.

114

Owen looked at him with scorn. "It belonged to Isaac – Captain Galley. We couldn't keep them. It'd be wrong. And we couldn't tell you, not then, because we didn't know whose it was."

"Not even one?"

"What?"

"You haven't even spent one?"

"Not even one."

"We could've done with some last winter. Nearly ran out of coal, we did."

The winter of 1963 had been one of the harshest in living memory. Sussex had suffered less than other parts of the country, but the freezing temperatures and much snow lying on the local hills had lasted from Boxing Day until March.

"It was horrible," Ruth agreed. "At first it was fun, but after the first fortnight we were fed up with not being able to get anywhere."

Owen remembered the piles of dirty, frozen slush that had lain in London gutters for ages and nodded.

"What are you going to do?" he asked Bee. "You've got a grandad now."

"I know," she said. "It's so odd, just discovering there was a family just waiting to be involved with you."

"Are they?" asked Ruth.

"Yes. He phoned when they reached London that first time they met us, and he or Gran have called a couple of times since. We're going back with them tonight."

"You're visiting them?"

"Yes. They're going to take us round London." Gerry was naturally excited at the prospect.

"Well, Grandad is," Bee corrected. "Gran says she hasn't a clue where anything is."

"Hasn't she ever been there?" asked Owen.

"I don't know. Not for years, anyway. And it must have changed a lot during the war."

"I've never been," said Eric hopefully. His brother nudged him. "Well, I haven't," he repeated, rubbing his arm.

"We could probably take you both – and Ruth of course – one day. I know my way around."

The conversation veered off into chat about London landmarks, soon to be interrupted by Max bellowing as to his crew during a force eight gale that he was very grateful for the tea but he really should be getting furniture in before it started raining. As there was scarcely a cloud in the sky everyone knew he was joking, but they all started again. This time everything was unloaded and taken to more or less the correct rooms. The pantechnicons were turned and driven off, and everyone concentrated on the fine tuning of the household.

Owen found himself in his new bedroom with the other youngsters helping, and was hardly surprised when an irregular step was heard on the stairs.

"May I come in?" asked the Captain. A chorus invited him, despite it being Owen's room.

Isaac looked around the room, the colour on the window walls and the brighter, neutral colour on the other two to make the most of the light.

"Nice. Bit different from when I was last in here! Just distemper then, all white, I seem to remember."

Owen had placed his own bed exactly where the old one had been, and Isaac examined it and grinned ruefully.

"I'd like to have seen the original," he said, "but I can't blame you for getting rid of it."

"But I haven't. The others are sitting on it. I wouldn't just throw it away, and didn't want to put it anywhere else. It's part of my history now. As well as yours, sir."

Piercing blue eyes held his. "I seem to be blessed with really nice people," Isaac told him. "That was a really reasoned response and you obviously have respect for the past. May I see it?"

The others rose and made space for him. Owen lifted the mattress. Isaac stood, looking down, noticing the brighter slots on the screws holding the slats to the frame.

"I wonder where I got the idea from, to hide coins under those," he muttered.

"It's just as well I didn't know they were there," said a voice from the door. Edna had seen him come up and guessed where he was heading. The others made room for her. "I'd have broken in and stolen them as soon as Fox died. They'd have made the world of difference to me."

"They would, Edna, and they still can. That note of mine asked you to use them to free me from prison. You did that, but you didn't use them, so really they're yours."

She looked at the bed, then at him, then back to the bed.

She didn't see its basic woodwork, its slats, nor even the suspicious brightness of the screw slots. She saw a sick boy, nearly a man, whom she wanted to look after, in whose company she wanted increasingly to stay, a lover with whom she guiltily joined one night.

She remembered the rent in her life when he had been taken, the further horror of realising that he would never return to her. The love-sickness that had kept her silent, the mingled horror and delight on discovering that he had left her with a part of him; a boy to be born the following year into an abusive relationship with her husband – all these memories passed slowly through her mind.

The others were silent. Even Eric, the youngest of them was aware that this was a silence that was not a silence; a quietness that should remain unbroken. Isaac closed the small gap between Edna and himself and stood by her side, still looking down at that bed.

Something slid into place in her mind as she also remembered how he had treated her since the two had reconnected a few short weeks previously. Should she? Should they? This was the question that neither of them wanted to face, to discuss, let alone answer.

For Edna it had reduced to a simpler question: was this still *really* that young man she had nursed? Was the same smiling, mainly happy character still hiding under the Navy trappings and his success, just as it had bubbled out from him even under the weight of Holden's threats and his father's lack of care?

It seemed to her that it was.

She gave a sigh, and turned to look at him.

"Do you think we should?"

To Isaac's credit he knew exactly what she meant. He nodded slowly.

"I think we should. And I think now is as good at time as any to make the decision and tell people. Maybe not here, though."

"Downstairs? With Family?"

He nodded again. "Yes. Bee, Gerry, please will you come downstairs with us? I'm sorry to drag them away, but what we need to do has to be done with just the family. We'll tell the rest of you immediately after that."

Each one of them, even Eric, knew what was going to happen.

Downstairs there were fewer people left now, just the Wilsons and the younger Isaac. His father asked a harassed Max if he might use a room for a few moments, with Edna, his son and grandchildren in attendance.

"Use my study," Max said, pointing to it.

They did.

Five minutes later they emerged. The Captain called out: "Crew meeting, please!" in a voice that was used to being obeyed. In his turn Max recognised the tone, and half smiling, half annoyed at the extra delay, assembled with the others at the foot of the stairs.

The smaller the community the quicker news travels. Mrs Pentelow sacrificed a large cake that she had baked as a gift to welcome the Wilsons' the following day. Others made yet more pots of tea. All descended on the Mill House and embarrassed Isaac and Edna by their happiness.

"I've seen the change this gentleman has made to you," said Maud Pentelow, "and it's plain that you should have been together all these years, just like you wanted."

Edna shrugged. "All good things come to those who wait. We both know the wait has been too long, and it's been a wonderful surprise even to find him again. And I'm especially happy that our son and grandchildren have blessed our decision – and even happier that they're here!"

Poor Max finally managed to get furniture moving to the right places again. Fired by goodwill and then with the delight of the news everyone worked hard. If there were any knuckles bruised by being trapped between furniture and door jambs nobody mentioned them. In short order the front room, particularly, looked as if it belonged to a home again. One of the two rooms to have been wallpapered, the light, pastel yellows and reds pleased the eye and set off the darker furniture they had brought from London.

Finally the Captain, his fiancée, son and grandchildren were able to set off on the first part of their London-bound train journey. Seaford Station had been phoned so as to ensure that the train would stop at Tide Mills.

"I've just seen the clock," Barbara exclaimed shortly afterwards.

"Not surprising. I just put it there," said Max.

"I mean the time!" she said. "It's nearly seven o'clock. We need to do something about a meal. Should we go out somewhere?"

"Give Maud another half an hour and there will be supper at ours," Jack Pantelow panted as he planted his end of a table against the wall. "We didn't want to interrupt too soon after all the other interruptions had delayed you, so it'll be about half past seven."

"You're very kind, Jack," Barbara told him. "I was dreading the idea of cooking so soon after getting here – in fact I couldn't as there's no food in the house."

"Ah, but there could be, once the refrigerator has started," he told her. "We bought in some staples for you so you won't be without breakfast tomorrow, but you'll have supper with us tomorrow too, I hope. The Decks are expecting you for lunch."

Owen, fresh from putting the finishing touches to his own room, overheard that.

"You never told me!" he accused over his shoulder. Ruth followed him in.

"I don't tell you everything," she said.

10 – Christmas trees

It was a late night for all of them. The Decks had joined the Pentelows and the Wilsons for their evening meal and in the crowded living room afterwards the conversations had never stopped. Owen and Ruth sat together, saying little, each just pleased that the other was there.

Finally Max found a pause in all the conversations.

"Do you know, we have never, ever had an evening like this in London? Oh, we had friends to visit, but they almost always came because of an invitation made formally a week or so before the meal. Apart from providing snacks when Owen brought a friend round I can't recollect a spontaneous invitation like this. I think none of us has enjoyed a gathering so much. And so far as evenings with our London based friends are this is, to me, as it should be. Friendly, natural, spontaneous.

"It goes without saying that our home will be open to you all, especially if you have a need for a meal or a chat. I say that without referring to Barbara, which is wrong as she's the main cook. But, from your company tonight I just know we're going to enjoy it here. Thank you, all of you, for welcoming us like this. It's been wonderful."

"We look after our own in Sussex, Max," Jack Pentelow told him. "The Wilsons have quickly endeared themselves to us." He laughed. "Reminds me of the rhyme, that tells about Sussex folk and someone else who joined a community –

"... *But when he dwelt among us,*
Us gave un land an' love,
For Sussex will be Sussex
And Sussex wunt be druv."

Max laughed. "Edna said something like that, first time we met her on the train. And so did you at the first of the meetings. Where does it come from?"

"Written by a chap way back," Jack told him. "Don't know who, but it's exactly right. And anyway, apart from saving this Mill and deserving our thanks, you're nice people too. So think nothing of it."

Barbara thought that entering Mill House for the first time on their own, in the dark, would be cold and depressing after the sunny house in London. But as Max switched on the hall light and they really saw their own furniture established against the recently decorated walls and woodwork, she felt that this was now really a home. It looked right. It was warm. She knew that the new-fangled double glazing would help keep it so.

For completeness she opened the sitting room door, and gasped. In the grate a fire was blazing. On a table was a large bunch of flowers in a vase she recognised as their own. By it was a note: "Hope you don't mind. Thought it might be nice to come back to. Love, Mary, Arthur and Ruth. PS – your key is returned!"

"What lovely people," she exclaimed.

Owen saw Ruth's name mentioned and smiled too, then yawned

uncontrollably.

"Bed, you," said his father. "Bed for us, too, despite the fire. Don't know what to do about it, really. It's almost too good to waste."

"Cup of tea first?" asked Barbara.

"Yes please!" said Owen, though he could feel himself drooping.

"I wasn't talking to you... oh, well then, come on. But I'm not carrying you upstairs to bed. Nor is Dad."

Owen just looked at her. "I'll go and put the kettle on."

So it was he who first looked into the refrigerator and saw the bacon, sausages, eggs, and lard. Along with the tea, coffee, sugar, bread, butter and milk it was considerably more than the 'staples' they had been promised. Owen put the kettle on and returned to give the news.

"We will have to pay someone for it," said Max. "The thing is, whom?"

Owen had to be woken to be told to go to bed, the combined concept being something he regarded with scorn, tired though he was. Thanks to the new central heating and the double glazing his own room was pleasantly warm and although he wouldn't admit it to anyone else his bed looked very attractive.

Once lying in it his thoughts wandered. He imagined a young Isaac, just two years his senior, convalescing in a bed exactly where his was. He was being cared for by a girl only a little older than him... than Isaac... As his eyelids drooped he was surprised to see that the girl's face was Ruth's.

The next moment, it seemed to him, it was light. A knock at the door had woken him. "Tea!" said a voice outside it. This was new. Not only tea in bed on a Sunday morning but a parent bothering to knock at his bedroom door and not just sweep in. His first feeling was that of being pleased; perhaps he was being regarded as older now, suddenly, and all it had taken was a change of address. But another side of him was feeling that this was a removal of a tiny part of that unspoken fellowship between parents and child, a part of that unquestioning love. He could not decide whether the trade-off was welcome on not. But at least a simple "Come in!" solved the problem and he smiled happily when his mother accepted the invitation.

"This isn't going to happen every day, you know. *You* should be bringing tea to *us* in the morning... no, it's all right. We'll manage. But it's quite late, I saw Alan and Eric walking off earlier in uniform, so they'll be at some parade service, I imagine."

He nodded. He should ask about the Scouts and think about joining, even if they did have to get up early and go to church sometimes. Oddly, shorts and a quite adult-looking khaki shirt didn't seem out of place in the country like it did in London on the rare occasions he had seen Scouts there.

"Thank you for the tea," he said, still smiling as she put it on the table near him. Regarded as older or not, he was quietly pleased when she ruffled his hair and looked at him in her rather special way before leaving. He lay back, subtly more at ease.

There was a lot of work still to do, finding places for the less immediately needed furniture and the smaller items. Owen was kept busy carrying, unpacking, carrying, cleaning – yes, even cleaning! – and was pleased when the doorbell rang.

Ruth. With Alan and Eric, but still Ruth. Before she had a chance to say anything or even stop looking exasperated, Alan piped up.

"Hallo. Do you still want some help? We've got some time until lunch."

Owen thought quickly. He didn't really want the boys in, just Ruth, but couldn't think of a way of excluding them without seeming rude.

"I'll ask Dad," he said. "There's quite a bit of unpacking still to do so I should think so."

Barbara was just passing and smiled at them all as she wondered what to do with a magazine rack.

"Mum, we've got more help, if you and Dad want. Can they help unpack?"

"Well, yes, I should think so. But some of the boxes have glass in them and we don't want anything broken. Best if you all go very slowly and take care. And maybe do it on the floor so there's not so far for things to fall."

Ruth took the lead and sat on the floor of what was to be the dining room. Empty cupboards lined the walls and five packing cases needed their attention. It was as the first glass decanter was unwrapped from its paper that Eric found he didn't quite understand how easy it was to allow something to fall. The heavy glass container landed heavily on his lap, causing a squeak. He put it to one side and massaged himself.

"Eric! Really!" said Ruth, nevertheless watching him.

"Wasn't expecting it," muttered the victim, looking balefully at the glassware. "I'll know next time. Sorry."

They continued with few comments, and if the boys were awed by the glassware they were handling they said nothing.

Half an hour later there was a crash from the hallway and some very nautical language from Max. The four exchanged glances and giggled. Owen went to look, and found his father grimly stepping over some broken crockery on his way to find a dustpan and brush.

"Are you all right?" he asked.

Max bit back a retort. "No, not really. That was our best china."

Owen found nothing he could safely say, apart from "Do you want a hand sweeping up?"

His father shook his head impatiently. "My accident, my responsibility. Once it's clear I'll bring the rest in to you. That's where it was meant to be going, anyway."

Owen nodded and returned to the dining room.

"I never did like those plates anyway," he told the others.

They went over to the Decks' house for lunch, as arranged. Mary was less in awe of them by now, to the adult Wilsons' relief; Owen had never noticed any awe coming his way so knew no difference. It was inevitable afterwards that Ruth should very diffidently ask Owen if he'd like to come up to her room and play cards, which he accepted with an alacrity he didn't fully understand. The two men smiled.

"Arthur, I owe you for those stores you so kindly got for us," Max exclaimed as they were about to leave to continue unpacking.

"Oh, any time will do. It wasn't much."

"It was a lifesaver, so it meant a lot. So did the fire and the flowers – we haven't even thanked you for those. It was a very kind gesture and made all the difference. Going home to a lived in house was a pleasure."

"I hope you didn't think we were interfering too much," Mary said.

"Mary, it was a wonderful thing to do, as Max said, and we are very grateful." Barbara was sincere.

Barbara was about to call Owen but Max stopped her. "Let them play for a bit. Owen worked hard all day yesterday and he deserves a break. If the boys appear again we'll send one of them over to get him."

"You mustn't let them take over your home, you know And be careful, they're very clumsy, especially that Eric." Mary was being protective again.

Max laughed. "They've all got on very well indeed. And the only person to drop anything was me."

She looked horrified. "I hope it wasn't anything too valuable!"

"I don't know. It was a wedding present that neither of us liked, so it was only used for 'best'. I think we're probably glad it's gone. And we can always tell the donor that it was smashed in the move, and we shan't really be lying, shall we?"

Mary laughed.

The closing of the door made Ruth and Owen look at each other. She crossed to the window.

"They're going home."

"Don't they want us?"

"Don't know. Shall we go?"

"Do you want to?"

"I like the Mill House."

"Okay then. That was fun, though. Can you carry on teaching me some time? There's a lot to it."

"Yes. Crib's a good game. Dad plays it in the Buckle sometimes. I think there's a league, or something."

"If we're good enough, we could join."

"Dad would never let me go to a *pub*!"

"Not even for crib?"

"No. He says they're no place for children."

"Why?"

"I don't know. He goes, though."

Owen thanked her parents and they made their way back.

"He's a nice lad," said Mary.

"Good enough for our Ruth?" asked Arthur, smiling.

"Enough of that, Arthur! Let them grow up first."

"I know, I know. But by all accounts it was seeing Ruth by the station that made young Owen come back. And look where that led. All these changes!"

She nodded. "And we're going to have to move house soon, whilst they put heating and the electric and this double glazing stuff in here. We shan't know ourselves."

The tidying of the Mill House continued. Apart from one or two near misses there were no more breakages. Ruth and the boys left, the Wilsons went to the Pentelows for their evening meal and Owen was wondering what to do the following day. His London school was behind him and he would be free, but the others still had a week of learning ahead of them.

Monday's activity was decided for him as Barbara had to visit Seaford's shops.

"You'll come and carry things with me won't you, darling?" she asked, and both her menfolk looked at her with resignation. Owen decided rightly that the request was aimed at him, could think of no reason why not, and acquiesced.

They enjoyed exploring the town. Most people in shops seemed to want to talk to them, and were interested in their move to Tide Mills. Mother and son were amazed at the friendliness of almost everyone they encountered, and how helpful they were. It was particularly noticeable after London's bustle and matter-of-necessity trading. His fifteen minutes waiting for parents outside the station all those months ago sprang to Owen's mind and he told his mother about it.

One shopping trip proved inadequate, so the afternoon saw them return for more. Arriving home, they both collapsed into chairs with a cup of tea.

"I wish I could drive," Barbara said, "it would have been so much easier."

"You could learn," Owen told her, not without some misgivings.

"Your father would never trust me with the car!"

"Have you asked?"

She paused, teacup midway to her mouth. "Do you know, I haven't? We've never discussed it. And it would be easier to learn in Seaford than in London."

"Well, there's only one way to find out. Anyway, I want to learn to ride a motorbike when I can."

"You don't need one here," his mother told him.

He looked back at her pityingly. "But why not? It means I can visit Brighton sometimes…"

"What's wrong with the bus?"

"… and do it *quickly*. And Ruth can't ride a bike. She could sit on a pillion seat though."

"Well, you've got two years to go before you can ride one."

A pause. Barbara could almost hear the cogs turning.

"A year and a few months. And I can apply for my licence before that. And that means I could have a bike now."

"But there's no point if you can't drive it."

"I could drive it along the bank almost to the Buckle. And almost to the ferry the other way."

"That would be dangerous."

"No it wouldn't! If it's safe enough to walk, it's safe enough to ride. They don't go very fast. And anyway, lots of pedal cycles go along it."

She felt exasperated. "We'll need to talk to your father. We can get you a bike…"

"But Ruth can't ride one."

"But you can get anywhere on one. And are you sure she can't? Has she tried?"

That stumped him.

"I'll find out. But I really want one, just so I can get to places."

She thought of something else. "Are you sure you can take a pillion passenger on a bike if you haven't passed your test?"

"Er… I don't know. But if I get practice on the bike I'd be able to pass the test as soon as I'm sixteen, won't I?"

There was logic to that. She sighed.

"We'll talk to your father."

"Now?"

"No, he's at work. Although he works from home we can't just interrupt him for every little thing."

"You did with a cup of tea this morning."

"That's different."

One of the unoccupied cottages was being improved by Killicks and their foreman had to visit Max quite regularly. He had already been at the house three times that day whilst mother and son had been out. Barbara and Owen had discovered this at lunch, so when the door was opened by Owen later the man did a double take.

"I were expecting Mas Wilson," he said in as broad a Sussex dialect as Owen had heard so far. He was intrigued to hear the honorific 'Mas' being used in modern times, and referring to his father. "He'm out, seemingly."

"No, Dad's in his office. I can get him for you. Who shall I say it is?"

"Wilf Painting, that's me. I work for Mas Killick as his foreman."

"Oh, you've been here already, haven't you? Come in. I'm sure it's all right."

His father's door was shut. Owen hesitated, then knocked.

"Come in!"

Owen opened it, saw his father was writing and said "It's Mas Painting for you."

Max looked up and grinned. "You've picked that up quickly!"

Owen realised what he said and smiled back. "Shall I show him in?"

"Yes, and thanks."

Later, for something to do, he wandered down towards the expanse of wind-blown grey that was the sea. Even with the strong wind blowing he could see what he rightly assumed were fishing boats some way out, and wondered what it was like to be on one. Lumpy, he thought. Not comfortable. Perhaps in the summer with a calmer sea he would try and get taken out. There must be someone who knew someone…

He strolled slowly back across the bridge, noticing the water below flowing strongly through into the upper pond so as to be ready for an evening of

124

powering the mill. Passing the southernmost cottage he almost bumped into Jack Barden.

"Wotcher!" Jack greeted him in a mock London accent.

"Hallo," Owen replied, recognising both the accent and its falseness.

"Thought you were London, you and your family."

"We are."

"Just not normal London."

"I think we are. We were from south west London."

"Posh there, are they?"

Owen shrugged. "Don't think so. We were all sorts at school."

"Going to a posh school here, are you?"

"No. Same one as Ruth. Just like the one in London."

"What, the Grammar School in Lewes? Why not a posh school?"

"Why would I want to?"

That seemed to floor him. He shrugged.

"Goin' to be bored here, I reckon."

"I don't think so. There's plenty of hills to explore. And if I can go on a boat on the river or out to sea that'd be good too."

He was aware of a keen glance.

"Interested in boats are you? I've got a place on a fishing boat, so if you wanted you could come and crew on her sometimes."

"I'd like to try."

"Probably have to be weekends and school holidays to start with. We do some nights, too. Your parents let you out at night, would they?"

"I'll be fifteen by next summer, so they should."

"Right-oh, then. We'll let the weather improve a bit and you get to fifteen, then I'll see what I can do."

"Thanks... er... Jack, isn't it?"

"It is. And you're Owen, guv'nor's son."

"I am. Not that that has anything to do with it."

"Your own man, eh?"

"Something like that."

"Okay then. I'll let you know when the time comes."

"Thanks."

Finally Ruth and the boys broke up from school. Barbara gave them the job of finding a Christmas tree and installing it in the living room.

"Where do we get a tree from?" Owen asked the others.

"Newhaven," said Alan decisively. "We do jobs for the main greengrocer there and he'll give us one cheap."

"What about getting it back?"

"Probably use the ferry if we time it right."

"What? Are you getting it from Dieppe?"

"No..." Alan chuckled, "there's a little ferry goes over the river to take men who live on west quay to work for the railway depots on the east. It only runs when shifts start and end, so we'd need to time it right."

"How do you know the times?"

"Dad'll ask one of the locals in the Buckle tonight. He often goes down when there's darts on. Some of the workmen from the works come over to play."

"After work?"

"Sometimes when they're *at* work. Soon as they clock on, Dad says. If there's nothing to do at work they come over here or go to one of the Newhaven pubs."

"Blimey!" Owen couldn't imagine anyone from his father's London mill doing that, much less anyone from here. "So have you got this afternoon free?"

"Yes. We could go into town and ask Horscroft's to keep us one. We'll need one too. I'll ask Mum and we could bring them both back at the same time."

"Me too?" asked Eric.

"We'll need you."

With no ferry involved, getting to Newhaven was a matter of the bus ("Cheaper, and stops nearer the shops," said Alan). The old Clippie glared round at the four with distrust, followed them up to the top deck and to the front seats which, unusually, were empty.

"Make me walk, why don't you?" she moaned.

Owen smiled at her. "Were you on London Transport some time ago?"

"'Course not! What d'you take me for – a Cockney?"

"It's just that I knew a conductress who sounded just like you on my bus to school."

"It wasn't me, that's for sure."

"Ah well," said Owen dismissively. "We're going to... where are we going?"

"Bridge Street," Ruth prompted.

"Bridge Street, please," he finished.

The woman took his money, then held out her hand for the others' money.

"I'd like a ticket, please," said Owen. "So would they."

If looks could have killed, Owen would have fallen to the floor, bleeding. The others gave their money. Owen looked carefully at his ticket, then watched like a hawk as the others were issued theirs.

"What was all that about?" asked Alan when she had vanished up to the back of the bus again.

"Old London conductor's trick," said Owen. "Kids and old people don't usually check their tickets and most don't care if they get one or not. But if an inspector gets on, it's the passenger who gets done for not paying, or not asking for the right fare. I've been caught, so now I always check. She was trying it on."

"I never knew that!" Eric was quietly indignant.

"You're stupid, that's why," his brother told him.

There was a scuffle. Owen said something quietly as angry steps were heard at the back of the bus again. He looked anxiously at an elderly couple of about thirty who were sitting two rows back. The clippie looked at him, looked at the couple, scowled, and on the basis that she couldn't shout at *them*, returned down to her platform.

The others chuckled to themselves. The 'elderly' couple were completely unaware what had happened.

They found Horscroft's and asked about trees. The assistant was about to show them some when Alan stopped her.

"No use our choosing now. We need two, and we can't get them back to the Mills until we're sure of the ferry tomorrow."

"It's for the Mills, is it? Well, we had a Mr Wilson on the phone earlier, asking us to deliver one. We could drop these off at the same time if you like."

Owen spluttered. "That's my Dad! What's he doing?"

"Ordering trees, by the sound of it," the assistant smiled.

"Did he say where it's for?" asked Owen.

"He said it was for the Mill House. Cash on delivery."

They all felt deflated.

"Well..." Alan started, undecided. "I suppose we could get it delivered."

"Dad said we'd have one but he didn't have time to fetch it," put in Ruth. "If I ask Mum, would your father arrange one for us too, and get it delivered?" This was to Owen, who nodded. "We could call and tell you whether it's two or three we want," he said.

"By closing time tonight, please," said the assistant.

Owen nodded again. "Thank you. And do you know about the ferry? The one across the lower harbour?"

It was on the offchance, but the assistant knew the ferry he was referring to.

"There's not one until the morning shift books off," she said. "My old man's on that and he'll be home by two."

"So would they take us over?" asked Owen.

"They will if you get there by one o'clock. They take the afternoon shift over first, see, then collect the morning men. You'd best wear boots though. It's low tide."

Owen was puzzled. "You have to walk over the mud to the boat," said Alan in his ear. He nodded again.

They left the shop and turned left down Chapel Street, then made their way towards the fishermen's quays. A café opposite beckoned and they asked for teas. When they arrived they were taken aback to find they were served with pint size china mugs.

"How much sugar in one of these?" Alan wondered.

By the time they had managed to sink all that liquid – except for Eric who declared himself beaten – and had visited the café's toilet, it was nearly time to find the ferry. Alan and Eric led the way and they joined a group of men at the top of a ladder which led down to the mud that the ebb tide had revealed. Their arrival prompted some comments.

"You're going across?" "You ent 'arf goin t'get yer fortune tol' by your

127

Mum, see how."

"Why?" asked Ruth, to whom the comment was directed by a wizened old man.

"'Cos you ent dressed for it! Stands t'reason. That ole mud, she's proper clodgy."

There was a pause whilst Ruth decided how to retort. Owen broke in.

"Excuse me," his London accent in sharp contrast to the old Sussex, "but what's 'clodgy' mean?"

The old man laughed. "'Bout time you larned some Sussex, boy. An' you'll find what clodgy means dreckly minnit. The ol' ferry, she'm on 'er way.

Owen looked up. An elderly fishing boat was slowly coming towards them and ground to a halt when she reached the sloping mud. The only man on board came to the bow and hung a set of steps over the side to make it possible to board.

"Yew lot stayin' up there all day?" he shouted at the group good-naturedly.

There were some ribald remarks and the first of them started down the vertical ladder to the muddy river-bed.

Owen's feet reached the mud, leading him to discover exactly what 'clodgy' meant. He glooped his way to the boat with the others, a sound also manufactured by the rest of the group and resulting in a weird sound effect being reflected from the vertical wall they had climbed down. Ever the gentleman, he helped Ruth climb aboard. Alan and Eric lifted their eyes to the sky. Some of the men looked on approvingly.

The short journey across the river was delayed for a while to allow an old, unkempt, black fishing boat to pass on her way north. Her name was partly obscured by netting draped over the side and some of the letters that showed were eroded, but it seemed to be *Channel Pride*. Owen felt that the name and the boat's condition were hardly synonymous.

At the other side the water was deep so there was no more clodgy mud to be splashed up the legs of the four and the boots of the workmen. Instead they climbed another vertical ladder and gained the quayside, said their goodbyes to the crew going to work and set off between the remains of the big hotel and the customs buildings.

"Where are we going?" asked Owen as they left the – to him obvious – way down to the coast.

"We can't get past the ferry landing. They won't let us," Ruth explained. "We have to use the level crossing, then another one back to get to the path past the allotments. That takes us down to the beach."

They were held up at the first of the crossings whilst a small loco attached to a guard's van trundled past. Owen was interested to see that its name was *Fenchurch* as it reminded him of a central London street he knew quite well. Alan was quite excited since a steam engine shunting the quays in Newhaven was by then quite a rarity.

He let the boys lead and walked at Ruth's side, remembering that she wasn't good at walking long distances. At one point he asked her how her leg was.

"I'm fine, so long as it's on the flat. I'll be aching when I get home, but it's worth it."

There was a further level crossing as they neared the beach, though it was unattended. "Unused more or less, now," said Alan. "Not so many ships as there used to be."

Owen looked at him questioningly.

"Fewer ships, less cargo, fewer trains to take it away," he explained.

Their return to Tide Mills caused an exclamation from Barbara when she saw the state of their shoes and socks, and Owen's long trousers. She had also noticed Ruth limping and made her sit down whilst the others eased off their muddy footwear in the porch.

There was a rush to visit the toilet. Pint mugs of tea were taking their toll. The brothers used it together whilst Owen stood, cross-legged, on the landing.

Tea and cake were produced by Barbara whilst the four told their story. She went to check with Max about the tree and surprised him by telling them of the Newhaven visit.

He laughed. "Sounds like they had a good time anyway. Yes, let's get three while we're at it; one for the Decks, one for the Bakers and one for us. I asked for a five footer – is that all right for the others?"

Barbara went to check. The Baker brothers rushed home to ask and called in on Mrs Decks to check there too.

"We usually have a four foot one," said Mary Decks, "but if the Wilsons are having a five, so will we."

Max was told and ordered three trees of the same length for delivery the next day.

The trees were delivered, planted in pots, brought indoors to the three homes and decorated. Women in the hamlet of Tide Mills started making arrangements. The Wilsons held a discussion and invited Edna and Isaac, Isaac, Bee and Gerry for Christmas. They declined, embarrassed but pleased, saying that they were sharing Christmas in London. On the spur of the moment Max mentioned New Year's Eve; there was a discussion at the other end of the phone and they accepted.

Carefully Max discovered who would be in the hamlet over the holiday. Cautiously he gave out invitations and discovered that one of the old hands by the name of Archie Bullimore would be on his own, so suggested he join them for Christmas and Boxing Day, along with Maud and Jack Pentelow.

"You don't want us, Max," Maud was scandalised. You should have Christmas with the family."

"I am," said Max with a smile. "And they want you with them too, as do I. We'll have Ruth and those boys here until the last possible moment, I should think. And who knows, they'll probably be back with their parents later."

He cheerfully overruled all their other protests. They accepted and departed happy.

Barbara knew that many of the other families would accept their invitation to call in for a drink on either morning, or at any other time over the holiday. Max had already let it be known that a barrel of Harveys Old Ale was on order and had to be drunk before it went stale. Every time he mentioned it to a couple, both sets of eyebrows would raise; one in anticipation and the other in resignation.

It was all going to be a lot of work, but Barbara hoped she could rely on Ruth to help in the kitchen now and again.

In fact Ruth and the Baker brothers were hardly ever out of the Mill House, doing jobs from collecting coal to 'helping' to wrap presents.

At last it was Christmas Eve. Geese or turkeys were being prepared all over the hamlet so as to be ready for the oven the next morning. Ruth was helping Barbara prepare and for some reason Owen was showing an interest in kitchen matters too. Max visited Archie to bring him down to enjoy the start of the beer.

"You invited me for Christmas, Guv'nor. This ent Christmas yet!"

"Shush, Archie; I want an excuse to start the barrel. I can't unless you're there to share it with!"

The old man subjected him to a long stare and saw no guile.

"Wel, thass diff'rent, ennit? 'Long as I'm helpin', like."

When at last there was a lull in the preparations the crew in the kitchen found the two men swapping sea yarns in the living room, each with a pint of the dark ale in his paw. Any stiffness between them as employer and employee had evaporated and there was an argument – a friendly one – in progress, which stopped as the door opened.

Archie looked up, noticed Ruth and nodded.

"Goin' to give us a song, lass? Reckon you know some Christmas songs well enough by now, surelye?"

"Me…? Well no, not now. Not here…"

"Do you sing?" asked Owen.

"'Course she do. All the Deckses sing. She's sung solos in church afore now."

"I wish you would, Ruth," said Barbara. "It'd make it special, somehow."

"But…"

Owen knew that had he still been in London he would have joined in the mockery if someone his age was to sing voluntarily, and on their own.

"Please, Ruth?" he said, half to join in and half wanting to hear her.

"Can you get your box, then, Mr Bullimore? It'd give me something to follow."

"Ar. Right you are. I'll be back dreckly minnit."

When he reappeared he was carrying a wooden box shaped like a thruppeny bit, so it appeared to Owen, though it had fewer sides. It opened to reveal a concertina, but one that was larger than those Owen had seen in pictures.

Archie sat himself down again and played a couple of scales. The notes were surprisingly deep.

Archie saw surprise on his audience's faces. "She's a baritone. Gentler than one of they trebles. What'll you give us, girl?"

"Something unusual. How about the Coppers' Christmas Song?"

She started off, after Archie's introduction:

"The trees are all bare, not a leaf to be seen
And the meadows their beauty have lost
Now winter has come…"

"Thass a Copper song," said Archie when she had finished. "Rott'ndean they are, and as fine a bunch of singers as you'll hear. Record for the wireless, they do."

And that was the beginning of an hour's music. Ruth's voice was pure and accurate. She sang songs that none of them except Archie had heard, and some that were widely known. They all joined in, even Owen, whose singing was normally restricted to the bath.

At last, though, there was a knocking at the door and Arthur was anxiously asking after his daughter. She smiled at him uncertainly but was pleased to see him grin at her.

"So you've got her singing, have you? Reckon she should do more of it, but she says she hates being in church having to sit through the long sermons. But she's a lovely voice, for all that."

They all agreed with her. Archie patted her back as he put his concertina away. Owen was still entranced, and gave her such a beatific smile as she caught his eye that she almost blushed.

"Please, come tomorrow and sing again? And Boxing Day? And whenever you want to?"

She smiled widely and dropped her eyes, suddenly tired. The smile turned to a yawn and she looked up to apologise.

"It's late," he said simply. "And I'm tired too. We must be asleep for when Father Christmas comes."

Was he joking? she thought as she studied his face for signs of a joke. Her frown deepened as she noticed nothing, then a flicker at the side of his mouth gave him away.

"You nearly had me there," she said.

He laughed out loud. "I should have bought you something for your stocking."

"*I* should have bought you something for *yours*. But I'll sing instead, if you like."

"What, when I open it? You'll need to be up early!"

She put her tongue out. "During the day. And you can sing with me."

"Me?! Not likely!"

"You have an accurate voice, and I like listening to it."

"I've never done anything like that in my life."

"You have," said Barbara, who had overheard the last exchange, "I've heard you in the bath. It's a nice voice."

"Well then," said Ruth before he had a chance to object. "I'll come round tomorrow and we can try a duet. In your room. Then it's just us."

She wheeled away and followed Archie to the door. Owen shook his head and followed.

"Just going across with Ruth and Mr Decks. Won't be long."

It would never have happened in London, but neither parent even thought to object. Owen was half expecting a stop to be issued. At the Decks' front door she turned to face him whilst her father opened it. Owen found himself closer to her than he had expected and looked down, straight into her face.

Was this... could this be... was he – were they – too young... was he certain?

He threw caution to the winds, closed the gap and kissed her lips.

She had wanted to wish him good night and make some joke about Santa Claus to get her own back. But the look on his face, closer to her than she expected, reminded her of his expression when she had stopped singing. When his eyes held hers as his head approached she saw how his eyes closed she knew she could not just say good night.

From the door, Arthur saw the kiss and smiled to himself.

"Come on lass, we're letting the cold in. You've the rest of your lives ahead of you."

Owen realised her father had seen and he blushed furiously. Panic rose, Then he remembered those few closing words and felt still nervous, but better.

"Good night... sir," he said, and walked away without looking back. He didn't see the look of astonishment and the growing smile on the man's face as he ushered his daughter inside and shut the cold out.

11 – Christmas Day and after

It was the unaccustomed weight that Owen's right leg encountered as he turned over that woke him. Blearily he realised it must be early morning. Time to get up for school... no. No school... why? Was he ill...?

His brain clicked back into gear. The Mills. Christmas. Christmas *Day*. So what was stopping his leg from moving to the right must be... He looked down. Yes, a Christmas stocking. Nearly fifteen he may be, but his parents still continued the old tradition.

He gave an inaudible chuckle and the usual view of them both being just part of the furniture of his life gave place suddenly to a fierce love. It made him tingle for a moment, a feeling that delighted him as if he were on the outside of himself, looking in.

He sat up and reached down. The first item puzzled him. Chunky but round and with obvious lumps. Curious, he unwrapped it. Leather? Metal? A belt. He looked at it, at the odd dark metal clasp, the two loops at the side. A used, well worn Scout belt. There was a note with it –

> *I never told you when you said you were interested but I*
> *was in the Scouts. This was mine when I was 13. Hope it*
> *fits. Have fun! I did. Love, Dad.*

Dad, a Scout! Why had he never suggested that Owen should join in London? But here it would be better. More to do. And Alan wasn't bad. Eric was still in the... what? The Cubs? Or was he? He might be old enough for the Scouts now. Pleased, he delved on. An apple. He grinned and tossed his head. Different from an orange, anyway. Next, a package that was obviously a box. After a serious discussion with tape and paper he found the box contained a torch, but one that could hang on the belt and send its beam forward. Useful. Especially round here with no street lighting.

He delved on. Handkerchiefs...oh well. Then a little further down another lumpy package which opened to show a penknife. A good, chunky penknife with a tough blade, a screwdriver and a thing on the other side that he thought of as being for getting stones out of horses' hooves.

Wow. Better than the little pocket knife he'd had in London that he'd lost and found so many times. This one would hang on the Scout belt. Hallo – a note. He opened it out –

> *This was mine too. It probably has some of my blood on it*
> *but I did manage to keep all my fingers. Please try and do*
> *the same. Cutting fingers off is a silly way to lose weight.*

Owen grinned. Further down he found a smaller box; this time a compass and another note –

> *Tried to get a new map but no one has any at the moment.*
> *We have one downstairs. I'm qualified to teach navigation,*
> *I should think.*

He should do as a Captain RN, thought Owen. Ah well. He delved down further and found the usual sweets, chocolate and the inevitable orange.

"Do you think Ruth will be allowed to come over later?" he asked Barbara and Max after he'd thanked them for his stocking gifts. "I bought her something and – well". He swallowed, suddenly embarrassed. "I'd just like to be… to see her open it."

"It's not an engagement ring, is it?" asked Max with a smile. Owen's embarrassment deepened and his face reddened. "But anyway; don't forget she'll have some things under her own tree. I should think that would come first."

Owen made himself persist. "Can I ask her, though?"

"Of course, and I'm sure she'll come. But I think it would be best if she opened her gifts first, at home, and let you and us do the same here. Don't forget she might not have as much as you, and you wouldn't want her to feel like the poor relation… no, that's wrong. Disadvantaged."

That pulled Owen up short. He had missed that possibility and it made him feel awkward and overprivileged. Of course, his family was quite wealthy compared to Ruth's. The last thing he wanted was to make her feel bad. He hesitated.

"You can ask her soon anyway," said Barbara. "She's coming over to help prepare for the influx of people this evening whilst I do the vegetables and start steaming the pudding for lunch."

And she did. Alan and Eric had been told to get out of their mother's way and as soon as Ruth was seen heading for the Mill House they wasted no time in joining her. So potentially Barbara had three helpers in the kitchen – four with her son who, of course, had to be there if Ruth was. It was all a bit much, Barbara thought.

Soon afterward there was another knock at the front door and Archie stood there, complete with concertina. He grinned at Max who ushered him through to the living room as a long-lost friend and without a pause filled two pint mugs from the Harveys barrel. The two toasted each other.

"All we need now is a Toads table and we could be set for the day," Max joked.

"I heer'd you started down the Buckle," said Archie with amusement in his eyes. "And that Jack and this builder chap, they go too, seemingly."

"They do. But don't go thinking that Killicks got the job here because I play Toads with him. That was all done fair and square after all the contracts were in.

"Ah, but I did hear there was another crowd who should'a got it, but Killicks got it instead."

"Who's been talking? You can tell whoever it is they're talking rubbish. The lowest priced contractor would have done a substandard job. Their prices and their attitude on the phone established that beyond doubt. And I had to persuade the Directors that we should go to a company who were reputable. Fortunately Killicks are – and you know it, being a local man."

"So that was the way of it. 'Twas in a pub. I heard a man talking loudly to anyone who'd listen, see. Sounds like I better go back an' have another pint in there to put people right."

"You can broadcast that truth about wherever you can, please Archie. We..."

The door opened and the four youngsters came in. Two of them skidded to a halt when they saw the well-decorated tree with gifts piled at its base.

"Wow..." said Eric. Alan just looked.

Max took over. "Been thrown out, you lot? Better have a drink, then. Owen, can you?" Owen led over to a table the others recognised; they had helped to carry it in from a pantechnicon only a few days previously. He asked the right questions and provided the glasses. About to pour one for himself, he looked round to his father and Archie, still talking earnestly by the fire. He crossed to them, empty glass in hand, waited for a lull in the conversation and asked if he could try the beer.

Archie laughed. "I were drinkin' that a darn sight younger nor you. 'Bout twelve, I was, first time I sneaked a sup o' my ole Dad's."

"Did you like it?" asked Owen, conscious that his father was looking at him with what he thought was disapproval.

Archie gave another chuckle. "Didn' get a chance. Me Dad slapped me on the back so hard I near on broke a tooth on the glass. 'Iffen you want a beer, you go get it yoursel' like any god-fearing man,' he said to me in a voice that the whole pub heard. Well, I had a few pence in my pocket, see, and went up to the bar and got a half of my own. I turned, and the whole pub were watching, so I had to drink it, didden I?"

The others laughed.

"And did you enjoy *that*?" asked Owen.

"Not much," he admitted. "But it had to be done."

Owen turned to his father. "May I? Please?"

Max looked at him, remembered how his son had worked over the move and in all sorts of other ways, how their presence there could be traced back to his persistence following Ruth's presence on the platform.

"You've seen me draw a pint from the barrel," he said. "If you can draw a half pint like a barman; a full half, but not in danger of spilling, and without an inch of head, then you can drink it. But slowly."

Owen kept his look of surprise and exultation to himself, grabbed a glass, held it at an angle and allowed the beer to trickle down the side. He judged when it was half full, turned off the tap and turned to face his father.

Max noticed the glass. "I meant a half-pint glass! That's cheating!"

"That's not what you said, Dad; you said a half pint. It is. And there's no head, not really." There was a lacing of head at the top of the liquid, as Max noticed. The others, including Archie, were chuckling.

"Oi think you bin got there, Max – er – guv'nor. But he ent done half bad, choose how."

Max raised his eyes to the ceiling. "Go on, then," he directed. Owen drank. It was bitter, he was expecting that. Slightly fizzy, too. Probably not what he would have chosen, he thought; but it was a man's drink, the others were watching, and he was determined. He took another sup at it, grinned at his father and joined the others. The boys were impressed. Ruth just smiled at him.

"Dad doesn't allow me," said Alan, aggrieved.

"He's older'n you," his brother said. "When d'you open the presents?"

This was so obviously meant to change the subject that coincided with Owen's next sup at the beer and nearly choked him.

"After lunch, mostly," he said when he'd recovered.

"None now, then?"

"No. Family tradition."

The door opened. Barbara.

"Didn't you hear the knocking?" she asked. "It's Mr Baker saying that Alan and Eric need to head off to church now. Are you going too, Ruth?"

"Not this time," said Ruth. "I was singing at the late service yesterday. Are you on this morning?" This was to the boys, who nodded.

They left, with sorrowful farewells and a last look at the tree and Owen's half-full mug. Barbara followed their eyes and gasped.

"Owen, really. That's just too bad…"

"But Mum…"

"It's all right darling, he asked and I said yes to a half."

"Well…" she said.

"Can I give you a hand in the kitchen, Mrs Wilson?" asked Ruth tactfully.

"Yes – yes please. I suppose I must trust these men not to do silly things."

She looked at her husband.

"It's only a half, darling, and we've only got a pint."

"What about me?"

"Would you like a half, or something else?"

"I'm so hot I could do with a beer," she admitted.

"Owen? There are the half-pint glasses. Your chance to do it properly this time."

"How much did you spill when you poured that?" asked Barbara accusingly, wondering whether to fetch a cloth.

"Not a drop," said Owen. The men and Ruth laughed. To prove he knew what he was doing he poured a perfect glass full for his mother who just as carefully took a drink from it, smiled and returned to the kitchen with Ruth in tow.

"Betcha didden know they boys sang in the Choir. Good voices they have. Ruth too."

"I heard Ruth last night. She *is* good."

"How 'bout yew, then?"

He hesitated. Max, wisely, kept quiet. He too had heard his son singing in the bathroom and even stopped to listen on occasion. And even now the treble was all but gone, the result was still pleasant and musical.

"I don't sing…" Owen started.

"'Course you do, boy. 'Ere, listen to this."

He dug out the concertina and played a tune, then at the start of the chorus chimed in himself with

Sweet Bells, Sweet chiming Christmas Bells,

136

Sweet Bells, Sweet chiming Christmas Bells
They cheer us on our Heavenly way,
Sweet chiming bells.

"Try that," he almost ordered, and played the chorus again, and a third time. Cautiously Owen joined in. So did Max. As it was played again and the two voices grew stronger, Archie added another *"Sweet bells"* after the first. When the others tried the same he stopped and told them that was a different part and they should leave it, for the moment.

"Thass the chorus words," he said. "You'll know the verses, I reckon, as they're just "While Shepherds watched..."

He started the main tune again and it was so effective and simple that they caught it quickly and put the words to it.

In their small circle, concentrating on the music, they became aware of another voice, an accurate, pleasing soprano, joining in the verse. When it came to the chorus she took a higher line and as if he understood, Archie dropped down to a harmony. With only a little hesitation Max and Owen concentrated on the tune and keeping it accurate.

It occurred to Owen that being a part of this was a new feeling, a special feeling. It wasn't just him in a bathroom singing down to his toes. This was being a part of something, something that needed concentration, yes, more concentration than being in a football team in some ways, but less in another since you knew what was coming. It was a different, new experience, one that was fulfilling in a way he'd not encountered before.

When the last verse ended *"...and to the Earth be peace"* he looked round during the last chorus. Ruth's eyes were closed and her face was itself at peace. His father was smiling, more relaxed than he'd seen him these last few months. The old man was looking down at the concertina, concentrating still. Suddenly he looked up, grinned when he saw Owen was watching, and waved his head in a circle. Ruth took the hint and the others followed her into a second rendition of the chorus.

"That was a cross between a Scouts' campfire and being in church," said Max when they had ended.

"You got good voices, you two," said Archie, smiling. "'Twern't bad at all. Not at all. Now when we get they boys back we can really do summat, see how."

"Where does that come from, Archie?" asked Ruth. "I've always wanted to know."

"Yorkshire. 'Ten't all smoke and muck up there. There's good stuff they does too." He grinned again. "But we knows where God's Own County is, and it aisn't Yorkshire!"

The morning passed quickly in conversation and song, with Barbara coming and going. Finally Ruth looked at the clock and said she needed to go and help at home. Owen walked with her.

They bumped into the Baker boys, both looking unusually smart, who were returning from Seaford church with their father.

"We've been singing," said Ruth before Owen could stop her. "Owen and

Mr Wilson have really nice voices."

Owen wished she hadn't mentioned it and pulled a face.

But Alan answered. "It's really good when it goes well. It's only a small choir up there but they do what they can. We help a lot. They got Eric to start off "Once in Royal David's City from the back of the church. Everyone was watching and smiling at him."

His brother looked embarrassed. "I didn't see that. I was reading the words."

"You know what old Miss Armstrong told you after the service. She said you had the voice of an angel."

"It's about the only angelic thing about him," said his father. "But it was good to hear him do it so well."

Eric flashed him a sudden smile, pleased with the rare compliment.

Owen delivered Ruth safely to her door and wondered if he should kiss her again, but there was no opportunity. He could almost feel Alan and Eric watching his back. Returning home he saw the Pentelows leave their house and waited for them before opening his own front door. Max appeared from the kitchen, wet handed, and greeted them, asking Owen to take them to the front room and organise drinks. He happily complied. The easy chat continued between Guv'nor's son, Manager and Warehouseman, definitions having been blurred by the time of year and Max's even-handed treatment of all his staff.

The other two joined them and in the course of the greetings Maud Pentelow asked Barbara if she could help in the kitchen. Knowing Maud was still inclined to be shy, or perhaps stage-struck, Barbara welcomed her effusively "...but only if you'll call me Barbara, not Mrs Wilson," she laughed.

Ten minutes later Max, visiting the kitchen on the pretext of refilling a water jug, heard peals of laughter as he opened the door. Two faces beamed at him. He correctly assumed that the last remaining ice had been well and truly broken.

It was a traditional Christmas meal; soup to start with, a large, stuffed turkey with sausage and bacon rolls, with roast and fresh vegetables.

They did justice to it, and even Archie was rendered speechless.

"It's coming up to three o'clock," said Barbara as she and Maud cleared the plates away. "Should we watch the Queen's Speech first, then serve the pudding?"

It had been a day of thick cloud. By the time the Queen had been digested, so to speak, it appeared almost dusk. Barbara and Max returned from the kitchen, the first with bowls that were now nearly incandescent, and the second with a large Christmas pudding. Maud had risen to help but had been tasked with returning the guests to the table.

Max doused the hot pudding with brandy and poured more onto a heated tablespoon. In the gloom – the lights hadn't been switched on – Barbara struck a match and both stood back as the flames licked round the pudding and almost set light to Max's hair. He carried it at arms' length to the table where, unbidden, Archie sang and the Pentelows joined in, followed shortly by Owen's light tenor –

> *"Now bring us some figgy pudding,*
> *Now bring us some figgy pudding,*
> *Now bring us some figgy pudding,*
> *And a cup of good cheer.*
> *Good tidings we bring*
> *To you and your kin;*
> *We wish you a Merry Christmas*
> *And a Happy New Year"*

There was a cheer and a short round of applause. Barbara and Max smiled approvingly. As the flames died down Barbara dug into the pudding; for the first two bowls she managed to transfer a little flame but the remaining four were without.

"Best we've ever done," said Max in satisfaction. "Help yourselves. There's brandy butter, custard and cream."

At last they had done it justice and although it was by then quite dark Max and the Pentelows persuaded Barbara and Maud to leave the washing up and come for a walk with Owen and Archie. Each of them felt better for it; a short circuit to the Ouse, over Mill Creek, along the path and back down Mill Drove. As they passed over the railway Jack thought back to the previous year when the long cold spell had nearly killed off the remaining trade here, and that fateful journey some months after when the Wilsons had been on a train here and the son had seen this girl...

And that girl saw the lights of their torches weaving through the hamlet on their way, and with a call to her parents slid out of their cottage. The first Owen knew about it was a footstep at his side and a hand slipping into his.

He looked round, pleased.

"Can I come as well?"

"Silly question." His grip on her hand tightened. She laughed.

The others realised she had joined them but said nothing directly; she was becoming an accepted regular visitor. If Barbara thought back to their life in London, where people visiting had to be invited specially, she said nothing about it. And she liked the genuine friendly feeling with these people in Tide Mills who called at your door and accepted you as you were. It was all so much more *real*.

And she liked Ruth. Working in the kitchen with her that morning had enabled her to get to know the girl better. She found herself thinking that she would "do" for Owen, then was immediately ashamed of herself for thinking in such a snobbish way, like her mother used to.

Once they were all back in the living room Owen's eyes kept drifting to the tree with its wrapped gifts. He was agonising about the suspense of not knowing what he had been bought and not wanting to make Ruth – or Archie – feel they were somehow... there must be a word for it. Less? Underprivileged? Or was it that he was overprivileged?

At last Barbara nudged Max, who put down his glass. "I think it's time," he said in a voice that cut through the chatter around him. He found that everyone's attention had switched to him. Good, he thought. I haven't lost the knack yet.

"There's an untidy heap of boxes under that tree and I think it's about time we did something about it. I imagine Owen will have a breakdown if we don't attack it soon."

"Dad!" Owen protested, his feelings discovered.

"Over to you, old son. You decide what to do about it."

That was new. It had always been one or other parent who had distributed the gifts. Owen went searching, aware of a minor, added responsibility in his life. What to do first... Be impartial, that was it.

He looked round. Mum. She should come first...

Carefully, as she unwrapped her gift, he found a gift for Archie that he knew nothing about, and gave it to him registering their guest's surprise and pleasure. Then there was one for Ruth that similarly surprised him but delighted her. Slowly the pile decreased.

"Don't forget your own," said his mother with a smile in her voice.

He found a medium sized parcel with his name on it and with some trepidation started to open it, hoping it wasn't too embarrassingly valuable.

A transistor radio. A small one that would go anywhere with him. Oh wow. He grinned at his parents. "It's just what I wanted!"

They smiled, not just at his pleasure but at the oft-repeated phrase.

"And we don't want to hear it down here. Or at night!" he was told in mock-severe tones. He smiled.

Next was his gift to Ruth, whose eyes widened when she received it, the second unexpected present from this family. Yet this one was just from Owen and had "With love" before his signature.

She opened it and found a small box. Inside was tissue paper and a card. "Made in Sussex at Lewes," it read. With trembling hands she moved away the paper to find a pendant; a bright metal chain and clasp holding a detailed azure stone held in a silver-looking setting.

She looked long at it, letting the chain swing from her fingers, before lifting suspiciously bright eyes to Owen and hoping her voice wouldn't let her down.

"It's lovely, really lovely," she almost whispered. "How did you know I love blue?"

Finding himself close to her he whispered back. "I've been in your room, remember?"

She was looking straight into his eyes. More than ever he longed to hug her, to kiss her. But not with people looking on.

"Put it on for me?" she said in a quiet voice.

He did, knowing that he would be closer to her. He couldn't help resting his hands on her shoulders when he had secured the clasp. She turned, smiling. People looking on or not, he had his hug and his kiss. And returned them.

Though the hug was short, it was enough.

"I haven't got anything for you," she said quietly, for him alone.

He thought furiously, then said, equally quietly, the best thing he could have done. "You're here. That's all I want."

She gripped his hand. The look he saw in her eyes was all the confirmation he needed.

The pile of gifts diminished to just one small packet that was addressed to "Ruth and Owen", to his complete astonishment. There was no other identification on it. He crossed to her with it and they ripped it open.

Taped to a card there were two sets of keys. On the card was written "In the warehouse" and it was signed twice; the same words in two different sets of handwriting, "With love, Mum and Dad".

They exchanged glances. Max was holding up a key which they recognised as fitting the Mill office door. A glance exchanged, they hurried out of the room.

By now Owen knew where in the office the warehouse key was hung. He retrieved it and wisely gave it to Ruth before they walked down, now as excited as eight-year-olds, to the big doors. The key unlocked them and they were rolled back.

And there, leaning against a board to protect the sacks of flour from them, were two new bicycles, locked, one a man's, one a woman's. They gasped, though Ruth's pleasure was less than Owen's. She had ridden a bike before and knew that she would be too slow to keep up with him. But it was a better bike than her old one which was *very* old and far too small, so it would help.

They were so taken up with the cycles that they only noticed a packet on the ground when they were wheeling them outside. Ruth stopped and picked it up.

"It's to me from Mum and Dad," she said, puzzled. "It's got 'Don't get too excited!' on it."

It turned out to be a pair of plimsols. She examined them, even more puzzled, missing the note that had fallen from them. Owen bent to retrieve it and handed it to her.

'No,' it said, 'they're ordinary. Right pedal is higher than the left.'

She bent to look. It was. Some wizard with metals had added to the metal pedal top and put a lead counterbalance on the bottom so the pedal remained the right way up for use. The left pedal had also been weighted so the two were still in balance.

"Quickly," she almost shouted, "hold it for me!" Careless of her smart frock she sat on the floor and frantically struggled into the new plimsolls. They each found the lights, which fortunately had batteries installed. Ruth almost grabbed her bike and got on it.

"Come on, then!" Hardly waiting for Owen she set off up over the sluice bridge and up toward the railway, wobbling only slightly. Owen set of after her and had to set a fair pace, unaccustomed bike or not. He caught up with her at the crossing.

"It takes a bit of getting used to, but it's *so* much better than riding with those... that heavy shoe on," she said, her face shining. "I think I could almost beat you back to the Mill!"

He was thrilled to see her so light of mood and just said: "I'm not going to give you a head start! Ready?"

She nodded.

"Go!"

Owen forgot the railway line that came into the roadway as a tram track halfway down and nearly came to grief. His bike crossed it – just – after he'd made a last-minute swerve, but it meant Ruth reached the warehouse door first.

"You let me win!" she accused.

"I nearly fell off!" he said. "My front wheel all but caught in the tramway. Phew. Is it really all right?"

"It's wonderful. I really feel free on it. My parents… your parents… you know; I wondered why the present under the tree wasn't… well… you know." She gulped. "I tried not to show I was disappointed, but I know money's still tight after last winter and the awful summer when they reduced Dad's wages."

Her hand flew to her mouth. "Don't tell him I said that. He'd be furious."

Owen assured her that he wouldn't, but the knowledge was stored away for later.

"Can we cycle up home and show my parents?" she asked.

He said nothing, just remounted and looked ready, then set off when she did.

Mary and Arthur were almost as excited to see her expression as she was to be wearing it. In her mind she was seeing the prospect of freedom at times from the weighty built-up shoe, and being able to go where she wanted. Preferably with Owen.

They locked the warehouse and returned home with the cycles.

"Room in the shed in the garden," said Max. "It's rickety and damp, but it's the best we can do at the moment. I'll ask Killicks to use some spare wood and knock us up a new one we can lock. Not today, though."

Ruth changed her shoes and they returned to the house where one or two others from the cottages had arrived for a drink, having had the general invitation. Owen told his parents about Ruth's delight and was so pleased that he almost forgot about his own new bike.

"Just be careful on it," said his mother.

"Although they're light and have drop handlebars, the wheels and tyres are tough so you could probably take them on rough ground," said his father. "But keep a puncture kit with you in case."

With the barrel of Harveys, bottles brought to the house by the increasing throng, and the liquor the family already had, it was an alcoholic evening. Quietly Owen helped himself to a half-pint every now and again, keeping the glass out of sight.

It was an evening of song, board games and chat, interspersed by Barbara, Ruth and Maud calling out to people to come and help themselves from the food that had been laid out on the kitchen table. Owen found that he was feeling the effects of the beer he had drunk and was glad to get something solid inside him again.

At last the Decks family decided that they should be getting home, as did Archie who was noticeably slurring.

"I'll come over with you," said Owen, feeling more than a little unsteady. Max looked at him sharply. Owen went into the hall with them.

As soon as the door was opened and cold air hit him, he wondered what was happening. His slight wooziness seemed to develop sharply into unsteadiness and he had to lean against the wall to ensure he kept upright. Ruth was watching.

"I'll be over in a moment," she called to her parents who were just leaving, and went to him. Taking an arm firmly in hers she hissed in his ear: "come with me. Don't look round, just come with me."

He was so nonplussed by the sudden command in her voice that he meekly – slowly – climbed the stairs with her. For her part she was thankful that she was a slow climber; it meant that he could keep up with her without it looking too odd. She was relieved, for both their sakes, when they were out of sight of the door and at the first landing.

"All right now," she said as he once again leant against the wall. "You can make your own way. I'll tell your parents you were tired and have gone to bed."

He nodded, an unwise move, and blinked.

"Can you help me up the next steps too, please?"

"Oh, *Owen*! Oh, all right."

They arrived at his own bedroom and he unsteadily opened the door, then turned.

"Do I get a good night kiss?"

"No. Not when you're drunk. I'll see you in the morning." She turned her back on him and marched back to the stairs, looking back between the bannisters when her head was almost at floor level. He was watching her, a look on his face of almost comical surprise. She gave a slightly grim smile and put her tongue out and continued downstairs.

"Is he all right?" asked Max when he saw her in the hall.

"He's ok. I left him at his bedroom door. I said that I'd tell you he was tired and had gone to bed."

"I think he's learnt a bit too well how to pour pints from a barrel, don't you?"

She thought. What did he know?

"He's certainly been a good barman," she said with a smile.

"Yes," said Max, "mainly for his own benefit. Silly young idiot. That'll teach him. Thank you for taking him upstairs and for everything else you've done today. We'll see you tomorrow. Come early. You can wake him up and embarrass him. I should enjoy watching that."

She smiled at him and saw its echo on Max's face. Hers broadened. "Goodnight, Mr Wilson."

"Sleep well," he said, as if she were his own daughter. She was glad she wasn't, or a finding that she was attracted to Owen would be off limits. She shook her head to rid it of the thought. Was she? Apart from tonight, that was?

As she neared her front door she was smiling at the memory of Owen's little 'ways', his sense of the ridiculous, his concern about her when they were together. And his real delight, clearly visible on his face, when they had cycled together earlier and she had kept up with him.

As she lay in her bed, shivering with the coldness of the aired sheets against her, even with a nightie, she was still smiling. She would drag him out of bed in the morning and make him ride with her – somewhere. It didn't matter where.

Did he wear pyjamas?

And with that image in her head she found sleep.

The boat was rocking and Owen wished it wasn't. He was sure it was calm when he and Jack had left the harbour, but now it was rough and to make it worse his left shoulder was stuck in something and he had a headache. Also, someone seemed to be laughing.

Blearily, his eyes opened. The boat and Jack fled away on a wisp of sleep and were replaced by his mother with cup of tea. And Ruth.

His brain struggled to rejoin the previous night with the present. The partial lift of his head from the pillow gave way when he remembered what had happened. But Ruth was here...

"Hallo," he said with his eyes closed once again.

"Well, you were a lot of use last night," said Ruth. "I had to go home all that way on my own. Anything could have happened."

To give him credit, his eyes snapped open and he focussed on her, saw the smile and then closed again.

"Sorry."

"I should think so too. All those men waiting to take a poor little crippled girl home, or anywhere, and my knight in shining armour was absent without leave."

This time he did hoist himself up and looked at her. "You're not crippled. You just have one leg shorter than the other, that's all... Ow... my *head*..."

"Serves you right," said Barbara. "Next time you drink enough beer for an adult please make sure you are one. I have no sympathy. I think you should get up and go for a swim. That'll get rid of the headache."

"It's December," he said thickly.

"Better still. How *do* you feel?"

"Ow."

"Get up, drink some water, go for a run – or a cycle ride – and then come and have breakfast."

"Breakfast... I don't think..." His head sank back on the pillow.

Ruth grasped the bedclothes and looked up at Barbara with a question on her face. Barbara nodded. With one pull she had exposed most of him to the cold morning air.

He did wear pyjamas.

There was a shout and he scrabbled for the covers again but Barbara pulled them off the bed.

"Come on, you, or you'll be good for nothing all day. Ruth wants to go for a ride, don't you? You don't want her to go and meet up with all those men she was talking about, do you?"

He groaned.

Barbara laughed again and turned to the door. Ruth looked at him a moment longer.

"Come on, Owen. Please?"

The eyes opened again and he smiled and nodded, then shut his eyes with a wince.

"I'll be down in a minute.

To the surprise of both of them, he was. Pale of face and moving slowly, but he was there. He took one look at the boxes of cereal and turned away to find a glass and fill it at the sink. He drank, then turned round.

"Come on, then. Kill or cure. Let's cycle somewhere."

On their way out they bumped into Max who had been to fetch logs for the fires. He gave Owen a questioning look. Owen screwed up his eyes as if in pain and walked past.

"Twit."

That was all. It was enough.

12 – All change

With the new bikes at the ready and with Ruth's change of footwear they set off. To start with Ruth led down by the tram tracks to the seafront path. Owen was more cautious this time and made sure his wheels kept clear of the rail. At the junction onto the long siding from Newhaven they turned right.

"What's that?" asked Owen, feeling better for the breeze from the southwest across his face. He had seen a wide expanse of concrete extending seawards. A pair of tracks, far too wide to be a railway, added to the hazard of the siding rails.

"Dad says it was an airplane hangar," Ruth told him. "It was built for the first World War."

"And these tracks? Not a railway, surely? What were they for – a crane?"

"They were for the doors," she said, having asked her father the same question. "They must have been enormous."

They continued, Ruth leading over a narrow footbridge that crossed the mill creek and led to the railway.

"Best follow the tracks home," she said. "There's a footbridge over the railway there and it's very high."

"Okay," he said. "I'll follow."

The track followed the line of the railway. Soon the path diverged, crossed over a drainage ditch and led them to a junction.

"Left under the railway and home by road, or straight on to Mill Drove?" asked Ruth.

"How tired are you?" asked Owen, his headache now well on its way to being a memory.

"I'm not!" said Ruth happily. He looked round at her beaming face.

"How about under the railway, then?"

She led off. The path grew muddier and muddier and they were slipping all over the place.

"Are you okay with this?" he called at her bent back.

Incautiously she looked round.

"Yes! I don't get... oof!"

Her front wheel had struck an obstruction and her bike skidded sideways, depositing her onto the grassy bank on her left side. Owen skidded to a halt, almost dumped his own bike and ran to her.

"Are you all right?" he asked.

She pushed herself away from the grass. "Yes, of course." she said testily, rubbing her shoulder. "I'm not glass, you know!"

"Sorry... sorry... I was just being nice."

She looked round at him. "I know. Sorry. Probably best if we push them from here until it gets firmer. All right?"

"I'll follow you."

They pushed their way through the increasingly muddy, narrowing path. Soon Owen saw that the way was through a very low, brick-lined tunnel under the tracks.

"It's a cattle creep," explained Ruth's voice hollowly when she was half way through. Although Owen had never heard the term before he knew exactly what she meant.

The other side proved drier and they were able to remount. Owen looked back.

"We've gone under the platform!" he said.

"The beginning of it, yes. That's why it's quite a long tunnel."

"Now what?"

"Left, then right and we're on the main road."

She was aware that the wetness had penetrated the top of her new plimsolls and hoped her parents wouldn't be too annoyed. She refused herself permission to tell Owen, to say how uncomfortable she was, but just kept going.

The main road was very quiet. Being Boxing Day there were no buses and in the short distance to the Mill Drove turning only one car passed them, going the other way. Side by side they cycled down and over the railway crossing, coming to a halt outside her cottage.

"Aren't you coming back with me?" he asked plaintively.

"I can't come to your house looking like this!" she protested.

"You look all right to me," he told her.

"I've got muddy feet and there's mud all down the left side of my dress."

"Well? Pick up something clean if you want, but you can change in... in our house."

"I need a bath."

"Well? We've got one."

She thought a moment. "Actually, if it's all right, may I use yours? Mum and Dad will have had baths this morning and there'll be no hot water."

"It'll be fine," he said. "I'll wash your back for you."

He was given a look that made him grin widely, but hoped she didn't think he was being too rude. He was given the bike to hold; a few minutes later she was back carrying a bundle.

"I can't cycle and carry these," she said. "I'll drop something."

"Put them in the bag," he told her, pointing to the back of the saddle.

She looked. A bag was attached to it, nearly large enough to take school books.

"I forgot we had them," she said.

The reception they experienced at the Mill House was mixed.

"I thought people stopped getting muddy once they'd passed their thirteenth birthday," said Max, looking at them both. "Yes. Of course you can use the bath, Ruth. Leave it dirty for Owen; he can clean the mud off if he got you that dirty."

"I chose the route," Ruth admitted.

"You did... oh well, I take it all back, then. But you can still have a bath. And being the host he is, Owen will clean it, won't you? And how's the hangover?"

"*Dad!* It wasn't a hangover. It was a headache, that's all."

"I'm Navy, old son. I've seen too many hangovers not to recognise one. If it's better, good. But you're still a twit."

One of the bad things about his father, thought Owen, was that it was difficult to pull the wool over his eyes. One of the good things was that once he'd made his point, that was it. He'd move on. Even now Max had passed him and was going into the kitchen.

"Breakfast? Or will you wait for Ruth?" he threw over his shoulder. Max looked at her.

"I've had mine," she confessed.

"Tea or coffee?" he asked.

She smiled. "Tea please!"

"It'll be ready when you are."

And that was it. No nagging, no making you feel like an idiot; not like certain of his London teachers had been prone to do. He wondered what the teachers at the Lewes school would be like.

Ruth was half way up the stairs so he followed her.

"Use my room to change?" he asked.

She gave him a mock-serious glance. "Will you be in it?"

His turn to smile.

"I could be... but no. I'll be a gentleman."

She gave him a curtsey and turned to continue upstairs. Towel! Why hadn't he thought?

"I'll put a towel in the bathroom."

"Thanks!"

He ran down, asked for their whereabouts, followed his mother upstairs to see where they had been put, and put one on the towel rail in the bathroom. Leaving it again he heard his own bedroom door open and couldn't restrain himself from looking up.

Ruth. In his dressing gown. She smiled.

"Hope you don't mind. It's nice and warm."

"Please do."

Too late to say that, really, he thought. She was already wearing it. As he turned, somehow he couldn't get the idea of her wearing it out of his mind. His dressing gown.

He ate some breakfast, despite the earlier protestations.

"I'm told your father has called you a twit," said Barbara. "I'd have said more, but he assures me that you have no need of any lecturing after having to go to bed early last night and having the headache this morning."

"Yes, Mum," he said through a mouthful of cornflakes.

"*Men,*" she muttered. Owen registered surprise, though she wasn't looking at him. He smiled. It was almost worth the hangover... No. perhaps it wasn't.

He was starting on toast and marmalade when Ruth reappeared, looking clean and groomed. He couldn't help smiling.

"Would you like some toast?" asked Barbara before he had a chance to say anything. He rose, mouth still full and said "Eye oo 'i," which both Barbara and Ruth correctly translated to be an offer to slice the bread and put it under the grill.

"Ak oo," she imitated, and Barbara laughed.

"Make sure he washes his hands first," she said.

"*Mum!*" At least his mouth was by then empty.

They sat companionably over toast and coffee, Barbara and Max joining them.

"Well, when does the onslaught begin?" asked Barbara.

"I beg your pardon?" Max asked.

"When do we get the first candidates for lunch?"

"Oh. Well, it doesn't really matter, does it? There's the turkey to carve at and – well, I'm sure we've got more."

Ruth, knowing something about cooking and preparing for the occasional meal for others, was amazed.

"My darling husband: have you been blind to all the shopping and the mixing and the baking and the boiling and the cursing of husbands that has happened in this kitchen between when we took it over and Christmas day? Have you not looked in the replete larder and the groaning refrigerator and even thought 'that's more than we usually have'? Someone has been slaving away for days out here, even finding time now and again to bring in a cup of tea to the office occasionally."

He realised with a start both the corners of exasperation that she was trying to bury and the lift of her mouth to show that she was amused at him.

A sigh. "I'm sorry, darling. The simple answer is no, I have been blind to it; and no, I hadn't noticed. Sometimes I take it for granted, what you do to keep us fed and watered. Especially since the move and over Christmas. I have a lot to thank you for. And I do. We do. Don't we, Owen?"

He went to give Barbara a big hug, managing to beckon his son to come and join in. He grinned and did so.

Ruth looked on, amused, knowing that there were times when her own parents did just the same.

"Come on, Ruth. Join in. You did a lot yesterday and Christmas Eve."

Pleased, she limped over to them, aware that Owen was making a space for her next to him. She slipped into it, happy.

"Well, one thing you *can* do, since you offered," she said to their bemusement, "is to wash some potatoes so they're ready for the oven at about 11.30. I can part cook them and keep them hot for later to go with the rest of it."

They set to and were nearly finished when there was a knock at the door. The Baker boys, plus parents who were worried about coming so early.

"It's just that they kept on saying to us 'they said to come when you like' and 'we want to go and see Owen', and it all got a bit much. So we came, but we can go again if you'd prefer."

Barbara and Max laughed. "You're very welcome," said Barbara. "We're just getting the salad ready so we'll be through soon. Owen – can you go and be barman again, please?" She looked directly at him. No words passed but he knew what she had left unsaid.

"Let me help out here," said Jessie. "These men – they're hopeless in the kitchen."

To a mini-chorus of words like "Huh!" they went and attacked the barrel again, apart from Owen and the other younger ones who concentrated on squash and fizzy drinks. Archie was sitting in a corner with his concertina, just playing notes here and there with occasionally a dance tune thrown in. Max asked him what he was playing.

"I'm not, really. Just knurdling."

Max looked his question at him.

"Messin' about, see; just seeing what comes out."

"It's a nice background," said Max. "Thank you – but don't forget your pint!"

"Slim chance o' that, guv'nor, see how!" Archie laughed.

People gradually came, drank, chatted, ate, chatted, sang, listened, chatted and, finally, went. A stream of wives, some husbands and all four of the youngsters went into the kitchen and helped, washed and dried up, put away, got out, brewed tea and coffee... But when the last one had gone the kitchen was tidy and clean and just the Pentelows and the Decks's were ready to go.

"We'll give you Mill House back," joked Arthur Decks. "We've really enjoyed the freedom of this Christmas and the welcome – and when I say 'we' I mean the whole community. You have tremendous goodwill on your side."

"It was hard work for Barbara," said Max, "but today especially she's been so relieved to have help in the kitchen that – well, she had time to relax."

"I did," said Barbara. "It took most of them a while to realise that the Wilson family aren't ogres and that we genuinely like people. It's so different here from the formality of London; you can't believe the difference."

Smiles all round, and they were about to go. "Come on, Ruth. Give these people some peace." Her mother was aware that Ruth had hardly been away from the house all day.

"May she stay, Mrs Decks? Please? Just for a while."

The question could only have come from one person. Mary Decks looked at the Wilson parents, who just smiled and gave small nods.

"Well, if you want to... just for a while. And I'm sure someone will see you back home."

"I will, Mrs Decks; that's a promise."

"As if I can't find my own way!" said Ruth indignantly. "I told you I wasn't made of glass."

"He's showing that he's a gentleman, that's all. You wouldn't like him if he wasn't, would you?"

Ruth decided not to reply.

They settled down to watch the Boxing Day news and Maigret on television.

At 10 pm when it had finished he walked with Ruth to her house and again tentatively offered her a kiss. She accepted this time. He was sober.

He felt, going back home, that he was walking on air. Later, putting on his dressing gown, he thought back to its last use; Ruth. Back in his room he considered sleeping in it.

Even for the young, liquid consumption before bed produces certain results. Owen had to visit the toilet and noticed it was past two in the morning. A light shone through the window, a regular flash. He realised it was Newhaven's lighthouse. But there was another light below it, between him and it, nearing the beach at Tide Mills.

He shivered. It was cold in the house; he felt sorry for whoever was on a boat at that time of year.

Life returned to normal for a few days. Mill work for the men, including Max; housework for some of the women and jobs in Newhaven or Seaford for the others. Barbara felt guilty as she saw them trudge either down to the coast path or up to the station and felt she should be doing something. She asked Max, but all he could tell her was that at the moment the books were done by Arthur as he had for years, but that when the new machinery was active she would be involved.

Unknown to him or Owen she enrolled on a book-keeping course that she discovered in the weekly Brighton and Hove Herald. It was chosen mainly because its first set of textbooks and exercises would arrive just after Owen had returned to school.

In the meantime she set to baking again, knowing that the house would once again be full over the New Year. The Galleys and Foxes were coming to stay the following Monday until New Year's Day (Isaac junior had wangled some days off work in exchange for working the two weekends following). There was also the little matter of another evening 'session' planned for New Year's Eve. She reminded herself to ensure Max checked the level in the barrel.

When their visitors arrived they realised how lucky they were to live in a 3-story house now. Two spare bedrooms were on the first floor and two more – on the second – even if one of them was tiny and only had a camp bed. That one had been cautiously offered to Gerry on their first visit, and after looking at it he said he'd be very happy there.

They arrived late on the Sunday and almost immediately joined the family for dinner – another stretching of the culinary skills of Barbara, Ruth and even Owen. With the exception of slightly gritty carrots – Owen's contribution – it went well. Both Isaacs – and, cautiously, Owen – rated the Harveys highly.

Over coffee, Isaac dropped his bombshell.

"You know that Edna and I are officially an engaged couple because I asked her when we were here. Now I can tell you that we're going to get married," he said with no preamble. "We've talked long and hard about it and have come to the conclusion that we still are in love."

He paused to look at his fiancée.

"Tomorrow – I hope you haven't planned anything – we want to go into Seaford to look for a house down here. Ideally somewhere in Bishopstone – not the new houses they're just building but in the village itself. I suppose you don't know of anywhere that's for sale?"

Neither Barbara nor Owen had heard of anything in the village, nor had Ruth. She was there too as Barbara said that having done so much for the meal it was only right she helped eat it. And she had been party to the discovery of the coins too.

Congratulations were just starting to be given when Isaac junior stood up. Everyone else stopped with words on their lips, so to speak.

"Before you join with this part of the family in offering them congratulations, we have something to say, don't we? It was Gerry who brought up the idea first." He nodded to his son, who looked shocked and embarrassed, but after a delay stood up.

He was smartly dressed and for the first time wore long trousers, trousers that would doubtless become old before their time when worn to school, but which currently seemed to add two years to his age. He looked at his grandfather, who smiled back with a quizzical expression.

"We've talked about this a lot," he said, "and we've reached a decision about what we want to do."

He wondered how to say what he wanted to say.

"You see, Grandma and Grandad went through hell for most..."

"Steady on, Gerry..."

"Well, they did. They've both said it and so have you, Dad. They've been apart and Grandma was treated..." He paused again, wondering what word to use.

"Just 'badly' will do, Gerry," Edna said in a quiet voice.

"... so badly by... by the man Dad thought was his father. We think that... well, it's only right that we change our name to 'Galley'. If you'll let us, Grandad, Grandma."

Hurriedly he sat down with his eyes looking at the floor.

He missed the long look he received from the old man. He missed the tears that formed in his eyes and were impatiently dashed away. He missed the absolute astonishment on Edna's face which gave way to the crumpled expression that precedes tears.

He didn't miss the long silence that allowed all this to happen, and looked up, scared.

Isaac and Edna reached for each other's hands. Finally, Isaac looked up.

In tones that were the absolute opposite of the voice of a Captain, RN (retired), he said to his grandson: "Stand up, Gerry," and stiffly hoisted himself to his own feet. Gerry did the same, looking at the floor again and wondering what was coming. Surely it wasn't that much a cheek, was it? His Dad hadn't thought so.

He thought the handshake would never end, and hoped that no bones were broken. It did end: it turned into a hug.

"Join us please, Isaac, Bee, Edna."

When they were in a knot, he said, still in a choked voice: "That was the best Christmas present I have ever had. And I mean ever. Apart from finding first Edna, and then you three."

Lying in bed, unable to sleep, Owen was thinking back through the day's events. His parents and the guests had gone to their rooms an hour before and apart from the gentle sigh of the south-west wind there was no sound. Remembering the previous night he looked out through the west facing window, but saw nothing. He checked on the north window and noticed a dark shape at the other side of the level crossing, a shape that he'd not noticed before. He thought it looked like a small lorry of some sort. There was no sign of movement so he put it down to a night-fisherman's vehicle. A lot of people fished off their beach, even on a winter's night.

In the morning he looked again out of curiosity, but it had gone.

"What's your mother going to think?"

Whilst Edna and Isaac were readying themselves for breakfast, Bee, Owen and Gerry were outside looking over the new bikes.

"Don't know," said Bee. "She might be the only Mrs Fox left!"

"She left us," said Gerry, shortly. "She can't be Mrs Galley, anyway."

"Have you seen her since she went?"

Bee shook her head sadly.

"No," said her brother, but his tone was angry. "She just went. How could she do that?"

Bee had made up her mind. "We're better off without her now," she said. "You know how much better Dad's been since she went."

"And we've got a real Captain as a grandad!" Gerry crowed. "And I'm going to like being called Gerry Galley!"

Nine people travelled into Seaford by train that morning; the eldest two to look for estate agents, their son on an unspecified errand of his own, and the three youngest from Mill House augmented by three from elsewhere in the village just going in for fun.

"Never been to Seaford," Gerry admitted to Alan, to whom he'd taken a liking.

"We've been to Eastbourne a few times," Alan told him, "but it's full of old people. No model shops."

"No toyshops either," Eric put in.

"There are," said Gerry, "But not in the town centre. I could show you."

"Can we come over?"

"'Course. Any time. Weekends or holidays of course."

The others nodded.

"What's Seaford like?" asked Gerry.

"Oh... boring. It's all right. Better in the summer when you can go swimming off the beach. We do from Tide Mills of course, but there's no ice creams there. And too many motor boats out of the Harbour come to the beach. One nearly ran me over once. Someone in Hove got their arm caught in a prop. Had to have it taken off."

Bee heard the end of this and shuddered.

"Do you have to?" she said plaintively.

"*We* don't. *He* did."

They found that hilarious. Bee turned away to carry on talking to Ruth and Owen.

Released from the company of his children and parents Isaac made his way to the telephone exchange. With some apprehension he asked the person who came to the reception desk if there was anyone he could talk to about transferring there from Eastbourne.

The reaction was encouraging, as Seaford seemed short of technicians and even, at that time, lacked a Technical Officer.

"How about going for that?" asked the man who had come to talk to him.

"I only qualified as a Technician 2A a couple of years ago," admitted Isaac. "I wouldn't stand a chance."

"Probably some of the old timers here would get their feathers ruffled, but that's going to happen whoever gets the job. It's a question of attitude more than anything. You know the job – well, a lot of it – and the rest of us do too. Some more than others. And the good ones would help the Supervisor out if he was accepted as a reasonable bloke. It's them that throws their weight about that get ignored. That's what happened to the guy who's just gone. He thought the best way to get the job done was to bully people."

"I bet that went down well."

"It did after the chap before had been chucked out for doing free private jobs for his mates."

"You can't get away with that! Not with all the reporting there is."

"You're right. He didn't."

"Oh. Good. What was he like?"

"Okay, I suppose. Too busy going out on jobs to be a good supervisor. Sometimes you have to when it's complicated but not all the time."

Isaac nodded. "Sounds sensible."

"He wasn't!"

They laughed.

"Do you really think I'd have a chance of getting to Tech. Officer?"

"You're Union, right?"

"Yes."

"Come and see some of the others and see what they think of you. If they like you, you could be in with a chance."

"Why don't any of them go for it?"

"Some might. But it's difficult getting to be a supervisor in your own patch. If someone comes in from outside it's more difficult for the local guys to feel bad about it."

This made sense to Isaac, though he'd never heard anyone say it before. He was taken to the canteen where they joined others who were between 'jobs' or were waiting for instructions. He was introduced and was soon swapping experiences about his exchange in Eastbourne and what happened there.

Some time later he realised three hours had vanished, engineers had come and gone and he really should make his way back to his hosts for lunch.

"I only called in on spec, to find out if there was a chance of transferring here if I move," he said. "I've done nothing but rabbit for ages!"

The man who had first met him and had suggested he should apply for a supervisor's post smiled.

"Well, you see, it's like this. I'm the Assistant Exec Engineer here so it'd be me interviewing you if you applied. From what you've said and the way these guys talked to you, I think you should. But it's up to you. Talk to your own supervisor first and see what he thinks – that's only polite. He'll probably call me. I won't say you called in and you should keep it under your hat too. But send your letter in anyway if you want to progress."

If ever there was an offer of a job, and a supervisor's one, this was it. Isaac was thinking furiously.

"If you think I could do it, I'd like to give it a go."

"If I didn't think you were good material you wouldn't have got as far as the canteen."

Isaac looked surprised.

"Thank you," he said.

"Right, I'd better go. I look forward to getting a letter."

Edna and Isaac at last found Swain's estate agents and told the man there what they were looking for, and where. He tried to sell them one of the new bungalows overlooking the sea, but Edna insisted they would prefer the old village.

"We had someone in before Christmas who said they were thinking about selling a property in Bishopstone," he told them. "But as it was just before the holiday – about two weeks before – we suggested they would be unable to sell for at least a month. It's very quiet at this time of year and the main properties that go are rentals."

"Do you think they were serious?" asked Isaac. "What sort of place was it."

"Alas, we had no details of it. Nor do we have the address or telephone number."

"Hmm… Well, it's the only lead we've had so far. None of the other agents we've passed have anything at all in Bishopstone. Look – when the seller returns, please can you tell us, and send the details post haste?"

Their London address was noted and they left.

"What do you think about going to Bishopstone and looking round?" asked Edna. "If we could find someone – I know; ask the vicar. Vicars know everything in a village."

They had walked around the town and, although it wasn't as far as he'd walked in London on Edna's shopping trips, he was feeling the strain. They found a taxi.

Edna grew quieter as they neared Bishopstone village, a place as peaceful and as unspoilt as it had been for centuries – or so it seemed. The Vicarage was partly hidden behind the usual Sussex knapped-flint wall with a hedge appearing at its top, though the gate was open in welcome.

The knocked on the door and explained their search to the lady who opened it and introduced herself as the Vicar's wife. She invited them in, provided tea and showed them into her husband's study where they explained it again.

"It's an awkward situation," the vicar started. "I know the house you mean – the only one in Bishopstone that might be available in the foreseeable future. I take it that you're talking about the place down the road? About four bedrooms, I think. And two reception rooms. Is that the one?"

"The problem we have is that we know neither the property nor the vendor," Isaac told him. "All the agent said was that someone was wanting to sell, but as it was nearly Christmas it was the dead period."

"Hmm… I think he was reluctant to take it on his books, having bigger fish to fry. What he didn't know, or didn't tell you, was that the owner was suffering from a long-term illness. I'm sad to say he died just before Christmas."

They both made the appropriate noises.

"There's something of a mystery surrounding the place. It has something to do with the family that used to own the Tide Mills, apparently; the story goes back about three generations to when the family first developed the Mills site. Toby Vallance – the owner of the house who's just died – told me that his wife had been a part of the Fox family. Her maiden name was Fox. She married Vallance, but died in childbirth shortly after.

"He said that the house had been the Fox family's since about the early 18th century. When Tide Mills was built one branch of the family moved there but the other stayed as owners of the house you're interested in. It eventually came to Toby Vallance's wife, and when she died, to him.

"The difficulty comes with tracing the family so that the will can be read and implemented. You see, there was a cousin, apparently the man who inherited the Mill before the last owner. He was the last of the Foxes, it seems. He died – what – about ten years ago?

"This latest cousin had been a guest up at the house here a few times, often at Christmas, when others came too. But there were Fox family connections in London too, apparently. But this man always said that his wife was too busy looking after their sickly son, or was ill herself, so she never came."

Edna gave a gasp. She camouflaged it by turning it into a cough.

"When this cousin died, his will required the Tide Mill to be sold," the vicar continued, no doubt accustomed to coughs from members of his congregation in the course of a sermon. "The house in the village was Mr Vallance's, of course, having been left it by his wife. But no one has yet traced the London connections. I was appointed Executor, and I have had no time to investigate yet, I'm afraid. So we are at a standstill for the moment. At this stage at least I can't help you further."

There was a silence while this was digested. Isaac removed his hand from under Edna's where it was in danger of being crushed.

"Who were the undertakers?" he asked. "It seems logical that they are the first point of reference to discover who might be interested in selling the house."

"Indeed, and after the funeral takes place I shall be able to help you. It has yet to do so as the death occurred *literally* just before Christmas. It's to be hoped it will take place here as this is where Toby Vallance lived since the start of the war. The first one."

"I really hope so too," said Isaac, though not for the same reasons as the Vicar. "You see, my companion and I first met when I was sixteen and – well let's just say that circumstances kept us apart from then until a few months ago." His hand returned to hers again. "We intend to be married at long last and to live locally to the area which meant so much to us all those years ago.

"Currently we are living in my house in London – separately, so you need not worry – but we want to move as soon as we can. Neither of is as young as we were. So you see, we really need to try to find out what is likely to happen with this house as soon as we can."

"I wish I could help you. You know how it is over Christmas, though. Toby was taken into hospital and died almost the next day. I'm hoping to be able to contact the family and ask them to come and deal with the administration."

Isaac nodded, thoughtfully. Edna cleared her throat.

"Do you know of any family, or relations we could ask? You mentioned family in London."

"No – there were just family connections, that's all. He never mentioned family."

Edna gave a long sigh and looked at Isaac, who lifted his eyebrows and nodded. She continued.

"You see, vicar, Currently my name is Fox. Edna Fox. I was married to the cousin, the man who used to visit at Christmas; the man who told you lies about my son's and my state of health. When he was with Mr Vallance or in London I had no idea where he was. I knew that he did everything he could to be away when my son was home, but he would return to the Mill House when Isaac returned to school.

"So you see, I too, would like to know what is to happen under the will if the house is still in the Fox and Vallance names. But I have no idea where to start looking, just as you don't. That's why it would be very useful to know any clues you may have about the London aspect."

The vicar was frowning. "But surely you are not the woman who attended Mr Fox's funeral, claiming you were his wife, when the party who had made all the arrangements asked the verger to throw you out?"

"I am indeed."

"But... Oh, this is most irregular. I am at a loss. I am so sorry... But is it possible that you can provide some evidence that will verify that? Perhaps your marriage certificate?"

Isaac sat up with a start. "Edna, that certificate will give the names of the witnesses to the marriage. That might be a start to a search for the rest of the family."

"It would certainly be a good starting point," the vicar responded. "May I suggest you bring it here? The names might be familiar to me, or to members of our congregation. It might set you on the right road. I have a further problem in that all the funeral arrangements were made by the undertaker, so I have no addresses. The undertaker will, I hope. That is where I was going to start my investigations."

"I shall try to find the marriage certificate," said Edna without enthusiasm, "though it's a document I wish had never seen the light of day."

Only a pigeon broke the silence that held after that bitter comment. Somehow its call was soothing.

"One last thing, for the moment; please could you tell us where this house is?"

The vicar explained. The two gave their thanks and farewells and set off to look for it. What they saw entranced them.

13 – Brighton and Hove

The youngsters' return home had resulted in Ruth and Owen showing and demonstrating their new bikes. The other four were impressed, even if the first journey had resulted in a deposit of mud to what would otherwise be pristine paintwork. Alan and Eric were almost gobsmacked when the owners had a short race again, down from the railway crossing to a line made by a length of string across the end of the millrace bridge. It was all but a dead heat, despite the gender difference. And Owen swore that he had gone as fast as he could.

"No; I can say hand on heart that I didn't let her win," he told them. "It was all her own doing."

"Wish we had bikes so we could cycle to school," Eric commented.

His brother nodded and changed the subject. "What's happening on New Year's Eve?"

Owen explained that everyone was invited to the Mill House until the year had changed. "Dad says that they'll all have to go almost as soon as it has, 'cos they're all back at work the next day. Including him."

Later, with only the Wilson, Galley and Fox families left to sit down for dinner – even Ruth had gone home – Edna and Isaac detailed what they had discovered, to excitement all round. When the questions had subsided, Max remained thoughtful.

"Of course, this *might* mean that the house is yours, Edna. As Vallance's wife, nee Fox, died giving birth to the first child there would be no other children if he didn't remarry. If Vallance has no other relatives to will it away to it *could* be that you are the last survivor of that part of the Fox family."

She straightened, shocked, as was Isaac.

"Surely not? That can't be the case."

"It can if it had passed to this man Vallance through his wife. And Vallance would have known that Fox was dead at the time he was preparing his own will, so it couldn't have been left to him. Vallance knew nothing about Edna, but believed that Fox's wife and family in London were legitimate. He had no reason to think otherwise."

"I don't think we'd considered that, Edna, had we?"

"Certainly not. And I don't think it at all likely."

"If I may make a suggestion, could I recommend talking to a solicitor? You can put the problem to him and see if he can come up with any information. He'd need sight of your marriage certificate, Edna, and he would be better placed to investigate with the Bishopstone vicar and to be told what the will holds."

Edna and Isaac exchanged glances.

"It would take any unpleasantness out of your hands, Edna," Isaac said gently.

She nodded. "How much would it cost?"

He smiled. "I think we should present the facts to someone first and hear what they say about that. Compared with some of the cases the average solicitor takes, I imagine something like this might be quite an interesting investigation for them. Shall we look for the paperwork tomorrow, and see if there's time to find a solicitor later?"

She nodded, dreading having to go to her old cottage and expose its poverty to Isaac.

"Any recommendation on a solicitor, Max?"

"I imagine your best way would be to talk to Jack Pentelow. He's a Seaford man through and through."

It was over the coffee that Isaac Junior tentatively mentioned that he had visited the local exchange.

"Nice crowd. I spent ages talking to them. It turned out that the chap who saw me at the desk was local guv'nor and he all but offered me a job there. As a Technical Officer."

"Well done, Dad!" said Bee with enthusiasm.

Her brother agreed. "Will you get it?"

"I don't know," Isaac laughed. "But he seemed pretty enthusiastic that I should apply. Of course, if I got it, it'd mean moving to Seaford."

Gerry was wide eyed. "But we've only just moved into the new house!"

""Hardly 'only just', Gerry, it was three years ago. But what do you think about moving school? Because that's what it *would* mean. As well as moving house."

"But what about our friends in Eastbourne?"

"There are buses. And you'd have friends here too, don't forget."

"Who? Everyone I know lives in Eastbourne."

"Ruth, Owen, Alan, Eric… and all their friends."

"I'm having to move school, Gerry," said Owen. "So I'll be new too."

"It won't affect me," said Bee. "I could leave next July when they break up."

Isaac, father and son, looked shocked.

"Bee… I know we've not looked at it but you have the intelligence to stay on and go for the Advanced. In fact, I don't see why you couldn't go on to University, or at least a Polytechnic course. But we can discuss that. And if you're going on to an advanced course, wouldn't it be better to start a new school then?"

"So don't we move until next September?" Gerry persisted.

""*If* I apply for the job and *if* I get it, you mean. It's too early days yet to think of moving dates or even looking for a house here. If we were to move before September I think Bee should continue in Eastbourne, but you could move sooner or wait until then. We'd have to see."

That silenced them both.

"If you do get it, Isaac, could you hurry them up about providing what we want for Tide Mills? It's been months already." There was a grin on Max's face so it was obvious he wasn't expecting anything.

"I could certainly have a look, Max, but it depends on so much. And I can't give anyone preference unless they're a hospital or something."

"I know," said Max. "But an idea of when it's likely to happen would be wonderful."

The following morning they took their visitors, plus Ruth and the Baker boys, to Brighton by train. Max had a plan.

Their first stop was at the Clock Tower where they walked up Air Street towards an unprepossessing building at the top that looked like a warehouse. Puzzled looks were replaced by astonishment as they realised it was an ice rink.

That accounted for two hours of the morning and a small cut on Gerry's right calf which he cheerfully ignored. They found a restaurant and had a light lunch; Max was very insistent that they shouldn't eat a lot, much to the disappointment of the boys who, after all that unaccustomed exercise, pleaded that they were hungry.

A red and cream no. 11 bus took them along Western Road and through Hove, past the floral clock where a nondescript, slightly overweight boy of Bee's age joined the bus. She looked him over but ignored him. They passed the Victorian town Hall and the big library, then turned left down Hove Street, stopped at the Fire Station to let two fire engines out, their bells clanging their warning.

"Won't hear them much longer," Max remarked, "they're all sirens in London now, like the Police." This was news to the others, although Bee and Gerry had heard the sirens during their stay at Isaac's house.

They – and the boy – alighted at the sea front and walked towards a large brick building. Once through the entrance it suddenly became clear from the sounds and the smells that this was a swimming baths. All the younger people looked hopefully at the bags that Barbara, Max and Isaac had been carrying everywhere.

"Yes," said Max, "here are your things. We've got a bit of a trek – only the Minor pool is open in the winter and we go downstairs to the changing room. Follow the signs, somebody."

They did, and found the entrances to the changing rooms where they separated.

The three boys were lining up at the poolside when there was a splash beside them. They looked, but it was seconds before they saw the cause of it as a boy surfaced some way away and sped down the pool as if he was jet-propelled.

"Must have flippers," Alan sneered.

Later they saw him again. His trunks bore a badge with 'SSC' on it and he grinned at them before standing again with his toes over the edge.

"No flippers!" said Alan, wonderingly. The boy teetered on the edge and fell into the water with a bigger splash than when he had dived. He surfaced and hauled himself from the water.

"Don't need flippers," he said. "I'm a Shiverer."

"A what?" asked Max.

"Shiverer. I belong to the Shiverers' Swimming Club. They teach you to

161

swim fast."

"You were just now," said Eric with admiration.

He nodded, and before they had a chance to continue talking he had dived in again and was half way down the pool before Alan had a chance to say "Wow..."

Although well used, the smaller of the two pools in the King Alfred was not the most interesting place to swim, despite the games of mock water polo that the youngsters were drawn into. Half way through the afternoon they were ready to emerge and change – as were the three adults who had been languidly swimming lengths, talking, swimming...

"Come on, then. Last thing of the day," said Max, and led them from the subterranean changing rooms, along cream painted passages lined with large pipes and into a cavernous car park. They walked the length of it and ended up at double doors with *AMF Tenpin Bowling* painted over them. This was new to all of them – except Max who had seen an Evening Argus advertisement – and they crowed with delight.

"It's the first proper American tenpin bowling centre outside London," Max told them. "It's only been open a few years."

Being told to change their shoes for those the man behind the desk provided was an eye opener, as was the first ball from Ruth who was still getting used to taking the few steps without her built-up shoe.

"Oh well," she said as it went into the gulley with a wobble, "there's a first time for everything."

They watched entranced as the pins were lifted, the gate uselessly swept for downed ones, and all ten were carefully replaced. The next time Ruth was more accurate, and her slow ball succeeded in knocking nine of them down.

A combination of a new sport, its automated nature and the fellowship went down well and they were all sad to have to leave – even if it was to catch a no.31 bus to Brighton's Pool Valley to change onto their own no.12 toward Seaford. They were tired and hungry when they returned.

Edna and Isaac had visited her old cottage that morning and if Isaac was shocked at its bareness he didn't mention it. Edna searched everywhere she could think of and eventually found the marriage certificate. With it were Fox's and his parents' birth and death certificates, as well as the latter's marriage certificate.

"That should give anyone a good start," said Isaac cheerfully as they came away, secretly glad to be out of the place. Jack Pentelow had pointed them to a good legal practice he thought wouldn't charge the earth, so armed with knowledge and documents they caught the next train into Seaford.

Their visit at the office, unannounced, caused something of a stir, but the elderly solicitor grasped what they needed.

"I will see if I am able to interest one of our newly qualified young gentlemen in the case," he started. "I call them 'boys', but they are actually well educated and qualified, otherwise they would not be here. He can travel around and discover facts far more readily than I have the time to do. They

162

are quicker to take things in than we of the senior generation, and he might well relish the challenge."

He lifted the phone and called this 'boy' in. He was actually in his late twenties. The task was explained and the young man expressed his interest.

"May I have your address and telephone?" he asked, then expressed surprise when the London details were provided.

"I see, Sir, Madam. I take it that I may ask you for any other information if I need it?"

"Yes indeed," Edna and Isaac answered in chorus, then laughed.

"Then otherwise we will report back to you as soon as we start making headway. I imagine you'd prefer that any family or friends we find we left ignorant of the reason for the search?"

"Er... It hadn't occurred to me," said Edna. "But if you think it would be wise."

"It depends what we discover, really," He replied. "It would be best to tread carefully to start with and use our discretion."

Max's planning had omitted an evening meal; Barbara had noted that when he was arranging the day. When she was asking Mary Baker about their taking the boys with them they had naturally discussed the return time. Mary had volunteered to provide a big stew and, if Mrs Wilson didn't mind, could she use her kitchen to prepare it.

"We don't have the room here for so many people to eat," she admitted, "so it would really help."

Barbara had been delighted.

When they walked down from the bus stop Alan and Eric had to be persuaded to continue to the Mill House ("Mum and Dad will want to know we're back" Eric had said in an unusual flash of responsibility) but had been persuaded not to. The smell as they opened the front door sharpened appetites even more, and the appearance of the Baker parents caused smiles from all and hugs from two. Having served up, they were about to go home and had to be forced to stay and eat.

"You were good enough to cook it, you're very welcome and it's only right," said Max firmly.

There was no chivvying off to bed for any of the youngsters that night. At about ten o'clock Eric was found asleep in a chair, despite the music around him. Those who wanted to see the new year in – and finish off the Harveys – started arriving later and a few minutes to midnight they were all summoned outside by Jack Pentelow, much to their surprise.

As the radio finished playing Big Ben's preamble there was silence during the long gap as they waited for the first stroke. When it came, there was a chorus of 'Happy New Year' from everyone, and as the words died away they could hear sirens sounding from the shipping in Newhaven Harbour and from those out at sea, all of which added to the message of a new start, a new hope. Ruth found a pair of arms surround her and hoped – rightly – that they were Owen's. Edna experienced the same fierce protection from Isaac.

At last they trooped back inside to toast each other and the future of the Mill, aware all the time that bed was calling. Work started as normal the next day. Isaac, Bee and Gerry would have to leave in the morning so as to be home in time for Isaac's late shift.

"Though I don't know if I'll be able to keep awake," he joked.

The house seemed very empty once Bee, Gerry and Isaac had departed one way and Edna and Isaac the other. Ruth and Owen consoled themselves by cycling into Newhaven on the main road. Once again Owen encountered railway tracks, this time across the swing bridge, but was going slowly enough to be able to stop, lift his front wheel out and continue before anyone noticed apart from the car behind whose driver was most amused.

They spent the afternoon watching trains shunting on the sidings to the west of the river, the tiny little tank engine chuffing its way around importantly, Dark clad men waved it this way and that until it came up to a set of wagons with a clang. Owen made a mental note of its number – 32474 – so that he could tell his father.

He treated Ruth to a tea in the café they had used before but this time asked for smaller mugs. The proprietor smiled, remembering their faces, and brought them cups.

When they returned to Tide Mills the Baker boys were playing football. They were most indignant about having been left out of the plans.

"You weren't here when we went," Ruth accused them. "Bee and Gerry had to go, and you weren't there."

Alan looked uncomfortable.

"Overslept," he muttered.

"What are you doing this afternoon?" asked Owen, tactfully changing the subject.

"Could go and look at the roadworks," Eric started, "then go to the cinema?" This was more in hope than expectation after the Brighton trip, even though that had been paid for by Max.

"What's on?" Ruth asked. "Anyone got the Herald?"

"We have," said Alan. "Let's go and look."

They discovered that "Summer Holiday" was being shown.

"It's been out for ages!" Alan exclaimed.

"Not ages," Owen told him, doubtfully. "I think it was only last year."

"Well yes. It's January the 1st. It'll have to have been out last year!" Eric said.

"Okay okay, clever… Anyway, have you seen it?"

"Well… no. You?"

He shook his head.

"Shall we?"

Entrance fees were scrounged, lunches eaten and they met up again outside the Bakers' house as it was nearest the road. The brothers were going to be walking along the main road so they could watch the machinery that had been chewing its way through Hawth Hill, exposing the white chalk so that a new

164

road could be built straight into Seaford. Alan explained all this with enthusiasm before Ruth and Owen started their ride. To save Ruth's leg they had elected to cycle into town. Ruth wasn't interested in road works: Owen was loyal.

They enjoyed the film despite its love interest so far as the Baker brothers were concerned, and partly because of it for the older pair. And if Owen's hand slipped surreptitiously into Ruth's in one or two parts, neither was surprised and neither of the other two noticed.

"Must be lovely just to go off like that," said Alan as they reached the fresh air again. "Think of all that sun and warmth, and the swimming…"

"Like we do at the Mills in the summer, you mean?" asked Eric innocently. The look he received in return made him step back, straight onto Owen's foot.

They returned along Marine Parade, the cycles either wobbling slowly or being pushed along the pebbly parts where slow riding causes loss of balance. Ruth, still acclimatising to cycling after a long stretch of having too small a bike, was particularly glad to be able to walk, though she had to stop and put on her hated built-up shoe.

"Plimsolls and pebbles don't mix," she said. The alliteration amused Eric who repeated it like a chant until cuffed on the back of the head by his brother.

This time it was Mary Baker who provided tea and even cut into a cake she had been busy making.

That evening Max and Owen, rather against Barbara's wishes, finished off the Harveys. Barbara was busy in the kitchen – again. There was little of the beer left – probably for the best in view of Max's work and Owen's youth – and it was becoming stale. The evening changed into one of those rare events. Son is excited to be treated as an adult. Father is aware his son is growing into adulthood. A mid-point of age related attitude is approached from each end. The result is a freedom, a casualness, a mutual appreciation. It needs relaxation, mutual acceptance and liking between the two to work well.

Barbara returned to find them laughing with each other, and mellow. She said nothing but helped herself to a gin and french and sat.

"Are you okay?" asked Max eventually.

"Better now I've finished the drying up, thanks."

"Ah… sorry. I should have come out to help."

"It would have been nice. Nice to see you both in there sometimes."

Later, when Barbara had gone upstairs on an errand, Max looked at his son and just said "Oops."

"Mum?"

"Yes. We should have gone and helped."

Owen sighed. "Yes, but it's good to sit and chat with you. And there'll be other times."

Max nodded. "And there'll be other times to chat, too. Maybe we should invite Mum into the conversation too."

That wasn't what Owen wanted at all. He could talk to his mother at any time, but until tonight… he couldn't remember when he and Max had just chatted so freely. And it was good.

"Yes, we should," he started dutifully. "But... but... " He didn't want to spoil it by annoying his father.

"Go on then, old son. Spit it out."

"Well... when it's the three of us, it's just you and Mum talking, and you talk about – about things that... that..."

"Have no interest to you."

Owen nodded. "But just then, it was us, talking about things that interest us."

His father nodded in return and sighed.

"We'll just have to make some time. Sometime."

"I'd like that."

Once again, drinking shortly before bed had its effect and Owen had to visit the toilet. The house was silent. Nothing could be heard through the double glazed windows. He was in bed again, awaiting the return of sleep, when he noticed the curtains on his north facing window brighten momentarily, then go dark again as if someone had switched off a light outside.

Cautiously he stood on the bed and moved the curtain aside. A van was parking just above the railway crossing; he remembered almost seeing one there before. The darkness was almost complete, but the courtesy light had come on and he could see a figure climb out of each front door.

They were all but invisible, as well as silent, from then on. He thought he heard a small sound near the house and his heart thumped. But it must have been a loose stone; no further sound of people entering the house – which was locked anyway. London habits were still observed.

As there were no further sounds, nor anything to see, he returned to the warmth of his bedclothes and slept.

There was a knocking at the Mill House's front door, far too early to be welcome. Owen heard reluctant footsteps, the opening of the door, and voices. At length footsteps mounted the stairs to his room. A knock, and his father's face appeared.

"Morning, Owen... sorry, but please will you come down and tell this idiot policeman... I mean, this police officer... that we weren't gallivanting about at two o'clock this morning?"

Blearily, Owen looked up at the ceiling. Was he right? Did his father just call a policeman an idiot? And what...

"Come on, Owen. Please. I want to get rid of him and make a cup of tea."

"Ok, Dad. I thought it was some sort of joke."

"I don't make jokes at 6.30 in the morning."

Owen was struggling out of bed, aware that his dressing gown was hanging as usual on the back of the door which... that dressing gown. The dressing gown that Ruth had worn...

"I can't get my dressing gown – it's on the back of the door you've got open."

Max looked, understood, and closed the door partially.

The two of them came downstairs. There, in the hall, was a policeman in a flat cap instead of the usual helmet. He was looking impatient.

"Ah, here we are at last," he said as soon as the two appeared down the stairs. He was not the sort to wither under Max's RN (retired) glare.

"Now you can ask him for yourself, *officer*." The last word was stressed so as to avoid using the man's rank, which by his appearance was well above that of Constable.

"What were you doing last night?" The man rapped out.

Owen, on his home turf, was less intimidated than if this had been happening in the street. He raised his eyebrows.

"Talking to Dad, and having a drink..."

"Don't be impertinent. You know exactly what I mean."

"I don't. You asked me what I was doing. That's what I was doing."

"I mean what did you do when you went out later?"

"I didn't go out later."

"We know better."

Owen looked at his father for help. Max was looking straight at Owen's attacker and said nothing.

Owen felt himself get annoyed. "I didn't go out later. I got up during the night to go to the toilet..."

"What time?"

"I didn't see a clock."

"You must have a clock in your bedroom."

"I have. I couldn't see it. It was dark."

"Hmph. What did you do?"

"I went to the toilet."

"Then what?"

"I went back to bed."

"I mean when did you go outside?"

"Outside, outside, or out of my bedroom?"

"Ah, now we're getting to it. Outside. Into the open air."

"I didn't."

"Come on, what time was it?"

"I told you I couldn't see the clock."

"But you went outside."

"No, I didn't. I said that."

"And I said that we know different."

"Well you didn't see me, because I was in bed."

"You just said you went outside."

"I said I went to the toilet. I didn't go outside."

"And I said I know different. You'll have to do better than that."

Max cleared his throat. "Just one minute, *officer*. You are trying to browbeat my son. I will not have that. If he says categorically that he did not go outside the house, then he didn't. You have my word on that."

"And why should I accept your word over that of a suspect?"

Max glared at him. "What did you say your rank was?" It was a bark now, not a conversation.

"Inspector."

"And your name? And your number?"

"Sargent. I don't carry a number."

"Yet you are issued with one. What is it?"

The man glared at Max, who looked daggers back at him.

"If you must know, it is 32501."

"Well, Inspector 32501 Sargent, if you have evidence that my son was seen outside last night, present it to him now in my hearing or else leave this house."

"I am following a line of enquiry."

"You are not. You are assuming that as we have just moved here from London we are a soft touch for bullying. We are not. I have dealt with Metropolitan Policemen who are far tougher than you, but they are polite. As I said, identify to my son the person who has said he has seen him, and what Owen was meant to have been doing. And he and I will call that person a liar. Also, going out of doors at night is not a crime. It is inadvisable to interrupt your night's sleep but it is not a crime.

"So come on. Tell him who saw him and what he's meant to have done."

"And just who are you?"

"What on earth do you mean? You know perfectly well who I am. I am the father of this young gentleman whom you seem to think you can browbeat and trick. My name is Captain Maxwell Wilson RN (retired). I am the senior manager for the owners of this mill. Who is your superior officer?"

The last question was ignored. "The mill manager's name is Pentelow."

"It is indeed. I imagine you know that because you will doubtless have hauled him out of bed at this ungodly hour of the day too."

"But how can this place support two managers?"

"How does that affect your browbeating of my son? It does not, it is none of your business and I shall not answer it, just as you failed to answer my previous question."

The Inspector blinked. "And what was that?"

"I distinctly asked you who was your superior officer."

"And *I* don't have to tell *you* that."

"I think you do, and I shall therefore be checking with the Chief Constable. As an employer, and as an employer who will be developing this mill and employing more people, I imagine he will be giving me the time of day.

"In the meantime as you have produced no evidence or accusation that any of my family may have been involved in a crime, I require you to leave."

"But I haven't finished…"

"You have neither arrested anyone nor made a credible accusation. Kindly leave."

"But…"

"Leave!"

Even an admiral, a guest on the bridge of a destroyer under Max's command, would have quailed at that tone. Max pushed past the Inspector and opened the door.

"Out!"

"You will regret this, Mr..."

"Captain!"

"Captain, then."

"No, *you* will regret waking my family at this hour and trying to bully my son. All I have to do is telephone the Chief Constable. What you have to do is to worry until you have had him tell you your life story. You might find then that you... that you really are a Sergeant again."

The man had no option but to step outside. It was as well that Martin Killick's men had repaired the front door well. Had it been in its original state the slam would have done a lot of damage.

Max stood for a moment, breathing hard. Owen looked at him in alarm.

"You all right, Dad?"

"Cooling down, Owen, cooling down." A pause. "I suppose you didn't go out last night?"

"No! If I had I'd have told him. As you said, that's not a crime."

"No. What I'd like to know is, what crime *has* been committed. And by whom. I just hope it's not one of our people."

"Is everything all right?" came Barbara's voice. "You haven't arrested that policeman?"

Man and boy looked at each other and burst out into laughter.

"I'll make us some tea, shall I?" Max called upstairs.

"Lovely. Breakfast in bed too, I should think."

It was said as a joke, but Owen and Max shared an unvoiced thought.

"After last night?" said Owen.

"Good lad."

Barbara had told herself that five more minutes wouldn't matter, but had managed to drop back into a deep sleep. It seemed that only moments later someone was shaking her shoulder, someone she knew and loved, who was asking her to sit up. Oddly there seemed to be a smell of bacon in the bedroom. She shook herself mentally and hauled herself back to consciousness.

There were her two children, one adult and one now nearly adult – when did that happen? – looking oddly domestic in dressing gowns and aprons. She smiled and enjoyed the emotion... yes, all was well.

A tray appeared in front of her as she pulled herself up in bed. Her mouth opened in astonishment.

"I was only joking," she said.

14 – Unpleasantness

Max was about to go to the mill office to check for post and messages when four people knocked on the door. Ruth, Alan, Eric and a policeman, this time one with a helmet.

"Hallo Mr Wilson," said Ruth before anyone else could speak. "Is Owen awake and if not may I wake him?"

This prompted a giggle from the brothers.

"He's up, Ruth. Go on in, all of you. And how can I help… oh, hallo Jim. Didn't recognise you in uniform. Cup of tea?" The two had been partners in one of the Toad-in-the-Hole team a couple of times.

"Yes please, Max. I'd love one. It's a bit awkward, this, but I've been posted outside your house to keep an eye on your son's movements. But don't tell the Inspector that I've told you that."

"That Inspector… his attitude stinks. Bullying doesn't go down well in this house. It's all right between kids – up to a point – but from adult to child it's unforgiveable."

"I hope young Owen stood up for himself."

"He wasn't bad, not bad at all. I had to pull 'Captain RN' on him at last, though."

"I didn't know you were… sir."

"You as well?"

"Bosun, I'm afraid."

"Well, I never knew. And as we're members of the same Toads team and I'm retired anyway, Jim, this is Max speaking."

He grinned. "Thanks. I'm actually after two more favours. May I use your toilet, please? And I suppose you don't have a pair of gloves I can borrow? I was expecting to be inside today and didn't bring my own."

Max laughed. "Favours to be delivered preferably in that order." Jim smiled. "Go ahead, toilet's upstairs and the door's open; I'll find some gloves. Owen?" This in a louder voice. "Put the kettle on, would you? Cup of tea required."

The four visitors were sitting in the kitchen when Barbara came in and pulled up short to see so many people. Max introduced Jim to her.

"So what's this about, Jim? Why have you been posted outside our door?"

"What?" Barbara asked, shocked.

"There's been another break-in at the Buckle." He was interrupted by protestations ranging from 'Not again!' to 'That's the second time!'

"I know. Ridiculous, isn't it? But Sargent – the Inspector – has got it into his head that as you people are Londoners you're the most likely candidates. He seemed to think you son's in on the game. I told him about Owen but he's not interested."

Owen started to bristle.

"It's all right, son; *I* know you're nothing to do with it, and so do my mates. But this man – he's just joined us from Essex and I reckon they're glad to be rid of him. He has a bee in his bonnet. So I'm stuck out here, watching the house of my friends."

Owen grinned suddenly. "Well, we could be going out soon. How would it be if Ruth and I cycled over to Seaford? To do some shopping for Mum, of course."

Jim grinned. "I could follow on foot, I suppose. But chances are you'd beat me to it."

"No, this is ridiculous. Look, I'm about to go to the office. The first thing I'm going to do is to lay a complaint against that Inspector. I told him I'd do so and I try not to break promises. I won't bring you into it apart from saying that we have a Constable watching our house."

"Thanks, Max."

"One thing," said Owen slowly. "That man made me want him gone as soon as possible. He never asked me if I'd seen anything, and I have. I think I may have done, anyway."

He had his audience, and told them what he had seen – and, to his slight embarrassment, why.

"So you didn't tell this to the Inspector?" Jim asked, his notebook open and pencil in hand.

"He never asked me. He was too busy trying to tell me that I'd gone out in the middle of the night."

"You didn't, though."

"No! But he kept saying that he knew better."

"I think what has happened is that he heard that a slight figure was seen by the landlord with someone else, but they were then so far away that he could barely make them out. It was only later when someone came to deliver coal for them that he realised there had been another break-in."

"So you mean he put two and two together, and made five, accusing Owen as a result." Max put in.

"I'm afraid it looks like it."

Max suddenly laughed. "I suppose I could stroll along to the Buckle with Owen, carrying our empty beer barrel to return it! That would make him sit up!"

Jim laughed too, but became serious. "I don't think that would be a good idea, Max. It might spike his guns eventually, but in the meantime it might make life very difficult for you all, and particularly for Owen."

"I suppose so, even if you witnessed it lying top down over a drain as we let the lees pour out…"

It was Jim's turn to laugh. "Yes, although I'm not sure beer was stolen last night. Too heavy to lift. But it might just confuse the issue too much. No, leave that in the kitchen, please."

"Okay. I imagine that accepting an empty is the last thing on their minds down at the Buckle."

"And I must report in what you've just told me, Owen. Can you say anything about the people getting out of the van?"

Owen though furiously. All he could remember was…

"Yes," he said suddenly. "The driver was out of the van some time before the passenger. The passenger looked... bigger. Quite a large man, anyway."

"So it may be that the driver was the man that the landlord described as 'slight' but the other was – well, what you said. Bigger."

"Yes. Quite a bit bigger."

"That's good," said Jim, back in policeman mode. "How about as they were walking down the Drove – they did come that way?"

"I think so. It's so dark at night that I only noticed a slight movement near the house as they passed. I couldn't see any details."

"Where did they walk?"

"Pardon?"

"Were they your side of the road or the other? Or in the middle?"

"Er... the movement I noticed was right by our house, so our side."

"So it could be that they gave the cottages a wide berth but walked close to the Mill House knowing it had double glazing and no one would hear them."

"I heard a stone."

"What?"

"A pebble, or something. One of them must have kicked it."

He didn't add that he had knelt there, scared, imagining that the next sound to be heard would be their front door opening quietly.

Jim noted this as well. "Anything else?" he asked.

"No. I couldn't have seen anything else because my window looks north. I thought it was just... well, people walking; though I did wonder why they parked a van up there and walked from it."

"So you went back to sleep then?"

"Yes."

"Thanks again, Owen. Very, very useful. May I use your phone, Max?"

"Yes, you'll need to come to the office. The Post Office hasn't been good enough to provide any more lines here yet."

"Oh, haven't they? When did you order them?"

"About four months ago."

He nodded. "I happen to know one of the engineers at Seaford. I'll have a word."

Max's eyebrows shot up. "That would be *most* useful. Thank you."

They left for the mill office. Barbara went to wash up but was stopped by Owen.

"My turn," he said.

Barbara laughed. "Breakfast in bed this morning, and now my son offers to wash up? I must complain more often."

Owen looked at her guiltily. "Sorry, Mum."

She smiled. "We all get caught up in conversations at times. Thank goodness you – all of you, I hope – have a father who you can chat to. Many children can't, and the further back in time you go, the less real communication there was between parents and their children."

There seemed to be no answer to that, but Owen stored the comment away.

The four of them walked – it seemed fairer on the brothers – along the coast path later, and saw Jim at the Buckle. He waved to them.

"I've been relieved!" he called. "You're not under surveillance any more."

They were too far away for conversation so just waved their understanding and called out their thanks.

They wandered round the town, looking into shops. There were one or two junk shops rubbing shoulders with the more important ones, and the windows caught their attention. One was in a back street and they had gathered in front of a model engine when an unpleasantly piercing young male voice interrupted them.

"Oh look. It's that ghastly crippled girl with her little friends."

Owen gave a start. The others appeared nervous and weren't looking round.

"It's Malcolm Botting," Ruth hissed. "Steer clear of him. He's dangerous. He goes to the Grammar school and tries to lord it over us."

"He showed us round the Grammar School," whispered Owen.

For several terms Ruth had encountered Malcolm on the train and had suffered at his hands. He was older than her. Sixteen, she thought. But one moment... how old was Owen? And hadn't he got taller and broader since they had first met?

"They're treating us to the big ignore," Malcolm scoffed. "Typical working class peasants."

Owen turned round slowly. A flash of recognition crossed the older boy's face but his sneer diminished not at all.

"Are you talking to us?" Owen asked in a pleasant voice. "Or was it someone else?"

"Wasn't talking to you. Her."

He pointed rudely at Ruth.

"Ruth is my friend. So are the other two. So if you make unpleasant, untrue, bullying comments to them you're insulting me as well."

"Who are you? And what are you going to do about it?"

"You know who I am. But you actually know nothing else about me. And what am I going to do? I'll tell you. I'll tell you to leave her – us – alone and not talk in a way that makes you sound like a pig."

"I'll say what I like."

"I don't think you will after you've been asked not to. Or, if necessary, taught not to."

"What's it going to be?"

"Asked."

"No. I'll say what I want."

Owen smiled, far more casually than he felt. "Then I need to teach you."

"Yeah?"

"Yeah. Ready?"

"What?"

"I'll take that as a yes. One more chance... Ready?"

Owen moved towards him. A look of uncertainty crossed Malcolm Botting's face.

"Not here."

"Not anywhere. Just go away and don't bully any of us again."

"You goin' to put up with that, Malc?" one of his companions was getting out of the way as the boy took another step back.

"Only for the moment. The man in that shop threatened me with the Police if I came near his window again. That's the one that broke. But you..." This was to Owen "... had better watch out. I have lots of mates at school."

"Good for you. I hope they have the courage to fight, unlike you."

The boy gasped. Owen turned back to the window. The others stared at him; he wasn't looking at them but at the glass. The shop door opened just as Botting rushed forward. Owen saw the shop owner dash out, but in the window's reflection he also saw Botting's attack start and instinctively moved to protect Ruth.

The shop owner was quick, and caught the attacker's arm before he crashed into the window where Owen had been. There was a cry of pain.

"I didn't replace that window last time just to have you smash it again, you little hooligan. And don't think you can bully me like you've been trying with these youngsters. You don't mess with ex SAS men."

The boy's arm was being held, in a twisted position, behind his back so that to move either way would be to cause damage.

"You lot – scram."

It was the same tone as Max used occasionally. It was never argued with. Botting's friends shuffled off, looking back now and again.

"I saw all that. You – at the back of the shop you'll find the telephone. Call the Police, would you?" this was to Alan, who hesitated.

"Go on, boy. This little urchin won't hurt you any more. If he tries to move again he'll wrench his own arm out of its socket and be in hospital before the day's out. Oh, by the way, you; this is a citizen's arrest. When the Police get here it'll be a real arrest for disturbing the peace and attempted bodily harm."

"No...please...don't call the Police... My parents will kill me... Ow... you're hurting me."

"Go on, boy. Phone. And you – all I shall do is dislocate your shoulder. Hurts like hell and leaves it weak. But I won't kill you."

"No, sir, please?" said Owen decisively. "Alan, wait. Just let him go. I think he's learnt his lesson and..." Owen put his head near the shopkeeper's ear. The man smiled but kept his hold on Botting's arm.

"Well now, your victim has pleaded for me to let you go... hmm. What should I do?

Then, in a bark: "Name?"

"Ow.... Malcolm Botting."

"I think you meant 'Malcolm Botting *sir*', didn't you?"

"Yes... sir."

"Address?"

"12 Pelham Road... sir."

"School?"

"You're not going to...*OW*...County Grammar Lewes."

"I thought they taught manners in grammar schools. But then if they have to educate pigs I suppose it's difficult. Right: if I see or hear of any more of your bullying or bad behaviour from these people *or anyone else...*"

He paused to let that sink in. "I shall visit your parents and contact your school. And don't forget that if it hadn't been for this chap's request, you'd be under arrest by the Police by now. Hoppit."

He released the arm. Botting ran, rubbing his left shoulder. They watched him out of sight.

"Thank you, sir," said Ruth. Owen echoed her.

"Are you really an SAS soldier?" Eric asked cautiously.

He got a grim smile. "I was. Demobbed after the war. It's not something I want to talk about. And you, young man," this was to Owen. "Do you really have a black belt?"

"Yes, sir. But I'm glad you caught his arm. I'd been watching him in the reflection and it looked as if he'd have broken the window when I moved."

"He'd have probably injured himself badly, maybe terminally. Glass isn't something you argue with. You were probably wise to get me to let him off. Saves him getting back at you. Should do, anyway. If not, tell me. I meant what I said."

"Well..."

"I know. It's telling stories, isn't it? But you, young lady; you're in no position to defend yourself against someone like that until you get that leg sorted. And you two – if you don't go to the same school it's not telling tales. And you're smaller than him at the moment. So remember there's someone else on your side. Two of us – this lass's knight in shining armour, and me."

They repeated their thanks and walked off, hoping not to see Malcolm Botting again.

"'Knight in shining armour'" said Alan suddenly, and the other two joined in the laughter, Ruth rather less so. Owen just smiled wryly.

"What did he mean by a black belt?" asked Alan when they had recovered.

"Oh... just Judo," said Owen.

"*Judo?*" the three were nearly in unison.

"You never told me," Ruth said accusingly.

He was about to apologise, then thought back to when they'd just moved into Mill House.

"I don't tell you everything."

"We didn't know either," the brothers complained.

"It's not something I boast about," he said, unconsciously echoing their saviour of a few minutes earlier.

It was by then becoming decidedly cold. The usual Seaford south-westerly wind seemed intent on finding every aperture in their clothing. Ruth, in a skirt and Eric, in shorts, were becoming cold, so they found a little café and ordered the inevitable tea. Owen paid for a piece of fruit cake each.

"We'll spoil our lunches!" Eric said, paraphrasing their mother, when he saw his plate coming towards him.

By the time they reached the station and made sure the train driver would stop at Tide Mills they were once again cold, despite tea and cake. When they arrived the brothers ran down to their cottage leaving Owen to escort Ruth more sedately to Mill House.

Barbara took pity on Ruth and put them both in front of the living room fire to warm, providing lunch on trays to be eaten there.

"I went and asked your Mum if I could feed you," she said apologetically. "You did so much to help us over Christmas I thought it was the least I could do."

They both looked their thanks at her.

Conversation stopped to allow plates of food to be demolished. A cold day and driving wind causes healthy appetites along with the temporary discomfort.

Owen thought back to the day's unpleasant incident.

"I'm really glad that chap came out of the shop," he said suddenly.

"I've not thanked you properly." The comment was hardly consequential but it was important to Ruth.

Owen shrugged. "If I'd not been there and he'd tried it on, the man would still have come out."

She shook her head. "That's not the point. You stood up for me. Nobody's done that before. Not among my friends."

"Why not?"

She shrugged.

"*Are* they friends, then?"

She shrugged again. "They're people I like. But they're girls and they don't know what to do with a bully like Botting."

"You said you were bullied at your own school. Don't they help then?"

"When they're around, yes. But they can't be everywhere."

"And you can't run fast."

"Or far."

"What do you think... I mean, do you remember what that chap said?"

"What? Botting?"

"No, the shopkeeper. The SAS man."

"What about?"

"Your leg. It sounded as if he'd seen you before."

She shrugged again. "He may have done."

"But what..." he was talking slower now. "... what did he mean about getting your leg 'sorted'?"

She sighed, and hesitated. "He... well, yes; he's seen... we've met before. We've chatted when I was looking for a present for Mum and Dad. He said he had a brother who had the same thing. He was a sportsman himself, played anything he could, and seemed to be good at most. When he could he joined the army." She paused again. "He said it was to get away from his parents who... who weren't very nice." She gulped.

"When he'd left, his younger brother just moped around – he came back on leave and found him worse each time. He – the brother – said that he hated being there, hated his parents, hated everything. He couldn't join the army

176

and follow his brother. He couldn't do anything apart from office work, and that bored him. The last time they met, the brother was in such a bad mood that they had a row and he ended up walking out."

Owen almost knew what was coming. He hoped above hope that he was wrong.

"Our man had to go back to his regiment the next day. A few days after he arrived he had a telegram saying that his brother had managed to get to Beachy Head and had jumped off."

Owen was appalled. He could see that Ruth was on the verge of tears.

She continued in a very wobbly voice: "He couldn't forgive himself for having a row on the last ever time he'd seen his brother. He couldn't forgive himself for not standing up to his parents and getting them to treat them both properly. He vowed he would never forgive them. He had to be at his brother's funeral, but afterwards there was another row and it was his turn to storm out.

"He was so angry and bitter, he said, that he volunteered for the SAS, knowing that it was dangerous, but he didn't care. He said he just wanted to do everything, to risk everything, because now he had nothing to come back to."

Another long pause. Owen wanted to know what happened next but instinct told him that Ruth needed time to recover.

"He came out of the war, unscathed, only to find that his parents – they lived in London – had been bombed out on almost the last night of the Blitz. He said he couldn't mourn them, but instead set himself to thinking about his brother and what he could do."

Owen nodded, and gave her more time.

"He couldn't do much. He didn't have much money or any contacts, so he came down here and spent what money he did have on opening the shop." She sighed again. "It wasn't until the National Health started that he realised that he could try and persuade people like... people who had different length legs to have the National Health take them on and... and..."

Owen knew it was time to put his arm round her shoulders. She leant into him, still on the verge of tears.

He said nothing still. Then: "I should get it done. But I'm scared," she said.

The hug tightened a little. At last he felt it might be time.

"What are you scared of?"

"Being even shorter. What would happen if it went wrong? How would I cope? I might be in a wheelchair for ever."

He took a deep breath.

"What does the doctor say?"

"I haven't seen one."

"What?" He said it carefully, making sure there was no note of criticism in his voice. "You're worried about... about it but you don't actually know what needs doing?"

"They'd cut a bit of bone out of the other leg."

"Yes, but what have other people gone through who've had it done?

What's the recovery time? What will you be able to do once you're back up to full strength?"

She just shook her head.

"Can we... should you... find out?"

The fire lit her face, highlighting the wide mouth, the almost other-worldly elfin look, the sad eyes. This time there was a long gap.

"Can you come too?"

He felt his heart jump. Did she really think that much of him? Of what he thought?

"Yes. If I'm allowed."

"I want you to."

He sighed. "Parents?"

"They talked about it, years ago, but I... I wouldn't have anything done. Wouldn't even go to the doctor." She sighed. "And now: well, today happened, and you happened. And I *so* want to be able to do what you do."

"We can cycle."

"Yes. But not over the Downs."

"We could try."

"But I want to *walk*. I want to *run*. I want to play football with Alan and Eric. I want to play sports at school. You have no *idea!*"

She now sounded so frustrated that he felt his own emotions starting to get the better of him. He swallowed.

"Then yes, I'll come with you and your parents. And whatever you decide, I will be there."

He was looking at the fire, realising he had made a promise he couldn't break, even without using the word 'promise'. He felt a touch at his cheek. Ruth's lips.

It was some five minutes later that Barbara bustled into the room.

"Now look, you two. I'm really not going to act like a waitress... oh."

They separated, both faces burning red, though whether from the fire or from the sudden presence of Barbara wasn't certain. Owen took a deep breath.

"Mum, Ruth is going to the doctor to see about treatment for her leg. I've promised to be with her. We may need your help."

Barbara's next line was to have been 'What on earth do you two think you're doing?' Her son's nearly level voice and the request for help made her realise that she knew exactly what they were doing: standing in front of the fire, embracing, kissing; even enjoying the feel of each other's body so close, moving slowly...

Yes, they both had red faces. And hadn't hers been red when Max's parents had discovered him and her in a similar pose? All those years ago... Well, at least they were here, and not being furtive behind some shed or other.

"Sorry, Mrs Wilson," Ruth almost whispered. "Do you want me to go?"

Barbara shook her head. "What do you need help with?" she asked, for something constructive to say.

"I need to be with Ruth for moral support," said Owen. "It might mean... oh, I don't know. You talking to her parents. Me taking time off to visit her in hospital – that sort of thing."

Barbara tried to take stock. This friendship seemed to be moving faster than she expected – if indeed she had expected anything to come of it. And it was really moving too fast. They were only children, after all. Even if Owen was almost her height and his voice had deepened suddenly the previous autumn; and even if Ruth was now noticeably more shapely than all those months ago, they were only children. What would happen if... No surely not. Neither of them was old enough for *that*.

She drew a deep breath. Owen thought she was going to start a lecture. But she let it out again.

"Just go slowly, you two. Please. Ruth, if you're going to see a doctor about your leg I will do what I can with parents and anything else. And Owen will see you whenever he can. But you both start school in a few days and – at least for Owen – nothing must get in the way of that."

"What about Ruth?" Owen asked indignantly. "She's not going to be able to go to school if she's in hospital."

"She would have work brought into her. She'll need something to do that's worthwhile, or she'll be bored stiff. And she won't be in hospital all the time she's recuperating. She'll be home. Just remember, you two, that there are more things in life than each other."

It had occurred to neither of them that the only thing that mattered to them was being together. It was an eye-opener that someone might think it *was* the only thing. If anything, Barbara's comment served to bring the fledgling relationship more to the surface. It made them more aware of each other, of what each meant to the other, than before. As a warning it backfired, though neither of them could have put those words to it.

Building work on the cottages continued, with one of the empty ones being made habitable first. The family moving into it temporarily whilst their own was dealt with soon reported how much better it was, how much warmer. A new wave of optimism spread around the other staff. Killicks seemed to be able to move quickly, and started next on Edna's old cottage once she had appeared and removed or disposed of much of her belongings.

"There's still no news on the ownership of that house," she told them as a removals company loaded on to a van the better antique furniture, much of which had come from the Mill House in the first place. "The young trainee solicitor is getting to sound quite frustrated."

After a lot of heart searching, the Decks went to see their Doctor, but without Owen. Arthur persuaded Ruth and him that the first appointment would just result in a referral to a hospital specialist, but he would be welcome to come to that.

As it turned out, he was right. She was being referred to a specialist in the Royal Alexandra Hospital in Brighton. But the appointment would be at least a month away, so, with some misgivings, the four youngsters made themselves ready for a return to school; Alan and Eric to the Secondary and Primary Schools respectively, in Seaford, and Ruth and Owen to the two

Grammar Schools in Lewes.

On Owen's return late that afternoon the inevitable question was asked by Barbara: "How did it go?"

Owen thought back to his near-overwhelming confusion; the number of people; one diminutive prefect who Owen thought was younger than him but who turned out to be seventeen; the other prefects, aloof, tall, broad and seemingly all-powerful; the teachers who were approachable, interested and interesting; the teachers who were just doing the job the way they always had; the awareness that he was at first an oddity, then accepted, then laughed with; the cautious acceptance that it might actually be all right...

"Oh, it's ok," he said.

He had the same question from Max over their evening meal and this time was able to give an idea of his experience.

"I saw Botting in the distance once," he said without thinking, "but he left me alone."

"Who's Botting?" asked Max.

Owen could have kicked himself. "Chap who showed us round the school. You know. We met him in town yesterday. Not a nice chap."

Max nodded. "You get all sorts, everywhere. Hope you're not put in a position where you have to stand up for yourself."

"So do I. At least I can use Judo if he decides to do anything." Then once again he regretted saying it.

"That bad, is it?" said Max with some surprise. "Don't get into trouble."

"I won't," Owen replied automatically, hoping he was right.

There was another 'first' for both Owen and Eric the following Friday. Eric had turned eleven and was due to 'go up' from Cubs to Scouts. Scout Alan Baker (aka elder brother), plus parents, plus a bemused Owen, walked to Chichester Road HQ to watch the ceremony where a self-conscious Eric found himself stripped of his green Wolf Cub jumper to reveal a khaki Scout shirt. At his new Patrol a world-weary thirteen year old Assistant Patrol Leader (aka elder brother) could hardly keep himself still with pride, though he would have strenuously denied it if asked.

Prompted beforehand a man in uniform came up to Owen.

"I hear you might be interested in joining us... are you really only fourteen?"

"Yes," Owen admitted. "Fifteen in May."

"At your height you'd be better off in the Senior Scouts, I'd have thought. But Alan says you're a friend. Would you want to spend some time in his Patrol and then transfer when we start again after Summer Camp?"

This was going a little fast for Owen.

"I... I really don't know. Can I talk it over with Alan?"

A week after the start of term it snowed. They looked hopefully at it, thinking how typical of Britain's awkward weather that it should be snowing on a Sunday with school happening the next day. As much use was made of it as possible during the mornings and to a lesser extent the evenings when it was still dark so early.

Owen talked to Alan about Scouts, and to Ruth. She smiled.

"I don't want you round me *all* the time," she said laughing, and laughed still more when he looked like a kicked puppy.

The next Friday he went with Alan and spent the evening playing group games and tackling skills he'd never met before, like pitching tents and starting a fire.

He and Alan never stopped talking on the way home. Barbara and Max were amused by the spontaneous laughter that peppered his description of some of the things they had got up to. Scouting seemed to suit him, they thought, if just one week's experience was anything to go by.

Ruth's appointment was fixed during the next half term in late February. Owen asked her if she still wanted him to go with her and her parents.

"Yes please," she said. "I need you there."

Even if they were standing with her mother in the kitchen of the cottage he grabbed her hand and held it, looking into her face with a gentle smile. She smiled back.

"We've got to go slowly, remember?"

So slowly he lifted her hand to his lips and kissed it, then slowly let it down again. But he kept hold of it.

"Slow enough?" he asked.

Mary laughed along with Ruth. Barbara and she had discussed the exchange of a few weeks previously and what had been said, and Mary had agreed. They were both young. It should be discouraged. Did she want her to forbid the two to meet?

"Oh no," Barbara had said. "It wouldn't be possible and if any of us tried it would just drive them to... to be together out of sight. No. It's puppy love, and it's sweet, but I doubt it'll last. Puppy love never does."

Nearly a month had passed and the puppies were still seeking each other's company whenever possible. The Baker brothers had acclimatised themselves to it and, after a decreasing number of provocative comments, it had become accepted.

15 – The Alex, Brighton

There are few hills of any note around Tide Mills until you encounter the Downs' steep slopes. Ruth had been avoiding them because they made her limp worse. They had arrived at Brighton Station early one morning at the end of February and Ruth's heart sank as she saw Upper Gloucester Road rising away from them.

"It's not far," said Arthur, released from the Mill for the day.

"Not for you it isn't, Dad."

He looked down at her, realising with a shock that she was nearly his height, and took her hand. Owen manoeuvred himself to take the other.

There were fairly flat parts as well, so with breaks and a subdued cheer when the end of the climb hove into sight at Dyke Road, they made it. The Alex, as they now knew it was nicknamed, was just up on the left

For Owen the appointment was an anti-climax. After the inevitable wait they were seen by the specialist who expressed surprise that another child – as he put it – should have been brought along. His astonishment when Ruth told him calmly that Owen was her boyfriend was complete.

"You are far too young to have a boyfriend," he told her.

Owen bristled, but said nothing.

"Well, he is," said Ruth. "I asked him to be here."

"Are your parents not enough support?"

She didn't know what to say to that. Owen thought of what his father might say.

"Sir, it's a different type of support. And anyway, I'm here and want to be. Please."

The man looked at him, then at Ruth's parents and at Ruth. Seeing no evidence of giving way by any of them he started the examination, though much of it was done behind a curtain as it involved getting down to the skin.

"It all looks good," he said. "We'll need x-rays done of the femur on both sides. I'll arrange that and there should be a space for it to be done today. Then once we have the pictures back I can decide what to do. I take it you want her to have this done?"

The question was to Mary and Arthur.

"We would do what Ruth decides," Arthur said. "She and we, and she and Owen, have talked about it. She's also talked to other people. We've all talked about the good and not so good parts of it all, but we really need to know what happens next."

"And I want to know if I'll really be able to walk and run properly when it's done," Ruth put in.

"Well…"

It would all depend on what the x-rays showed, but after a quite long period of healing and some discomfort, and after sensible exercise there should be no weakness. If so, she would indeed be able to run and do what she wanted. If the x-rays came back as he thought they would, the bones would grow at the same rate for the next three or so years, stopping somewhere about the age of eighteen.

It was a great comfort to her – and to her parents and Owen. Brains tend to filter out statements that start with 'if' or contain 'should'. Ruth particularly seized the hedged promise of being able at last to run and walk without pain.

They presented their request for the x-rays, were given a time in the middle of the afternoon, and decided walk down to Western Road's shops for something to do.

Even at their advanced years, Gamleys in the Arcade was a draw for both Ruth and Owen, the former being glad just to stand for a few minutes after walking down the quite steep hill from the hospital. New games were marvelled at, old ones were reminisced over. Owen wanted to buy Ruth something but firstly didn't know what, and secondly didn't want to embarrass her parents by splashing money around. He made a mental note – again – to mention to his father that everyone's wages had been reduced by the previous owner.

They bought a drink and a roll in a little café. "I hate spending money on bread when we live in a Mill," Ruth grumbled. "Especially so much."

Arthur had to agree with her, but they needed lunch. "Has anyone thought about making pies from our flour to sell locally?" he asked no one in particular.

Owen thought. "Dad's not said anything about what's going to be happening," he said. "Not even to us. But I can mention it to him."

Arthur nodded. "So will I."

They caught a 38 bus back up to the hospital, even if it was only two stops, to save Ruth walking.

They found that Ruth had to change into a hospital gown for the x-rays and she was thankful that this time she could remove clothing without a doctor watching. The x-rays happened without a hitch, though this time nobody was allowed into the room for safety reasons.

As they walked back down to the station when the hospital had finished with them, Mary suddenly noticed something.

"Did you see where that 38 was going? The one that just passed us going the other way? Pool Valley! We could have caught the 12 from the Mills to Pool Valley, changed and it would have taken us all the way to the hospital."

They chuckled, Ruth wryly.

"Next time…" she said.

Life became a blur for the Decks after that. No sooner had Ruth returned to school than Killicks were asking them to move into Edna's old cottage, by then completed. It was to be a temporary move to give the builders a clear run at their own home. If Max noticed the single rent being paid for the two joined cottages he said nothing, and was pretty sure his Board wouldn't notice details like that. Jack Pentelow knew about it too and never mentioned it.

There was a rush of moving and trying to live in what was for them cramped conditions. The first thing they noticed was the warmth, the quietness and the un-fussy but good decorative order; it made them look forward to moving back to their home once that had received the same treatment. The arrival of a letter from the hospital a few days later concerned them. They knew it would contain another hospital appointment to see the results of the x-rays.

With everything else that was going on they had to arrange for Ruth to have a day off school. Owen told his parents that he was going too, and was furious when he was told he couldn't.

"It's only a half-hour appointment," he was told, "and you really can't miss a whole day of school for that. Ruth can talk to you in the evening when you get back."

"I said – I promised – that I would be there with her. I meant it. I need to be there."

"Owen, I'm sorry, but no. Arthur says that he can't go either – there's too much to do here. Jack Pentelow told him he could take the day off but he said it was only a short appointment, no decisions would be made and they'd discuss it tonight. Just like you."

Owen was mutinous. He knew his father's tone, though, and there was no argument to be won.

"Sir?" he said to his form teacher at the end of the lunch break on the day of the appointment. "Sir, I've been sick and I feel awful. I can't face lessons this afternoon. I'll need to be excused every five minutes. Please may I go home?"

Questions ensued. Owen had suffered from food poisoning before so knew the symptoms to talk about. In the end the man was more concerned about whether he would reach home without becoming too ill.

He walked to the station and caught a train to Brighton.

Ruth and Mary were astonished to see him waiting outside the hospital entrance for them.

"Did your Dad change his mind?" Ruth asked.

"No. I just knew I had to be here. I said I was ill."

"Oh, *Owen!* You are... silly. But... well, thank you."

"Your father's going to go spare when he hears what's happened," Mary told him. "Because he will. The school will tell them. They might even have called to check that you arrived safely."

Owen hadn't thought of that. He weighed up which was better: to hope his absence would go unnoticed, or to admit it now and stop worse trouble coming his way if his parents worried unnecessarily.

"Do you really think the school would call him?"

"Certain sure," said Mary.

He sighed. "I'd better find a phone."

There was a call box in the entrance hall. He had some money. Jack Pentelow answered.

"Hallo Mr Pentelow, it's Owen Wilson. Look..."

There was conversation coming his way. He interrupted it when he could.

184

"Mr Pentelow, please could you just give Dad a message from me? Just tell him I'm sorry, but I'm in Brighton with Mary and Ruth. I'll come back with them. I have to go now because I've run out of money. 'Bye."

He put the phone down, lighter of heart at having told the truth but apprehensive about the inevitable interview on his return.

"Is he all right about it?" Mary asked.

"Probably not. I didn't speak to him, I just gave Jack Pentelow a message for him. There'll be an inquisition when I get back. Probably a Spanish one."

It was an attempt at a joke, but he didn't feel all that happy about it.

The appointment time came and went, and they were still waiting. At last a nurse came to usher them to a room. The look that the specialist gave Owen was accusatory; it was clear that he still disapproved of his presence.

The x-rays were explained and the consultant said that apart from the difference in length the bones were normal and he could proceed with arrangements for the operation. But the operation he described was one that would actually lengthen the short leg.

"It will need some little time in hospital," he started. "They have to operate to make a small gap in the bone and attach a frame outside the leg. Once that's healed you can go home, but you will need to turn a little screw four times a day. That will lengthen the leg at the rate of one millimetre each day."

Silence. Ruth and Owen knew what a millimetre was; they'd learnt in Science. They described it to Mary, who went white.

"It'll take about ten weeks of doing that. And during that time you're going to be very limited in what you can do. You might need visits from a District Nurse to make sure there is no infection but that depends on how good you and your family are at keeping things clean. And every two weeks we would need to see you here to make sure everything is proceeding according to plan. It's only if there's something wrong that you'd have to go back up to London."

This was a bombshell that made everyone sit up.

"Er... London?" asked Ruth.

"Yes – oh, I didn't mention it as I thought you knew. The specialist team for us in Sussex for this sort of operation is in Great Ormond Street Hospital."

They had to digest this, each of them waiting for someone else to speak. Ruth felt she needed to know the worst.

"How long would I need to be up there?" she asked.

"It depends how it heals after the first operation. It could be two weeks, it might be three. Once it's healed satisfactorily and everyone one understands about cleaning it and dealing with it you come home. All the other appointments are here – unless, as I said, something goes wrong."

"And ten weeks..." Ruth was wondering if she could last that long.

"What *would* I be able to do?" she asked.

"I think you could walk using crutches, but very little weight can go on the affected leg at all. Just a few hundred yards at a time, perhaps. They'd tell you more in London. A lot of the time the leg will need to be supported, but again research moves on and they will tell you more after the operation. There will

185

be the weight of your lower leg to consider, you see."

She nodded, thinking ahead to a lost summer.

"Then once the legs are as close in length as we can get them you stop turning the screw and wait for another six weeks for the bone to heal fully."

Another six weeks!

"Then, of course, we have to do another operation to remove the rods and other metalwork. That means a few days in hospital and another six weeks in plaster this time to recover from that. Then a further six weeks while mobility returns and the muscles strengthen themselves. That can be uncomfortable, but you'll know the aches will be a sign that you're regaining strength. And for some months you have to be very careful. No rough games and no jarring the leg, otherwise it might break. It needs time to get as thick as the other one, you see."

Another silence.

"How long is it going to take altogether?" asked Mary faintly.

The doctor did some calculations. This time he looked directly at Ruth who was looking horrified and pale.

"About twenty seven weeks. That's about seven months, though the last few weeks the mobility will be steadily returning. It will take many more months to gain full strength, though."

The two supporters and the patient were trying to take it all in. Despite her problem Ruth was a very active person and the thought of such a long period of almost complete inactivity was appalling her. Mary secretly thought that she'd never cope. Owen was horrified at not being able to go out with her – *really* go out – for so long.

The question, of course, was whether it would be worth all that time of inactivity.

"Sir," Owen started, "is it guaranteed to work?"

He hesitated. "There are risks with all surgeries. This procedure has been used many times on bones which are healthy and bones which themselves have problems. Ruth's are normal. Unless there are infections or if there is a problem with turning the screw absolutely regularly, there will be every chance that she will be able to walk properly, and eventually to run and to do all the things she wants."

"Tell me again about the operation, please?" This was Mary.

The procedure was described again, the risks explained, the cure held out as a hope.

At the end of it Ruth found that she was being watched by her mother and her boyfriend. The consultant was just looking at Mary.

"I... I think so," said Ruth.

"You need to know so," the consultant replied.

Owen reached for her hand. He carefully kept his face impassive. She looked at him, then at her mother, then back to him, clearly undecided.

"May we have a few minutes together, please?" asked Owen suddenly. "The three of us."

"I have other patients to see, you know."

"Mrs Decks…?"

She nodded. "Please – just a few minutes."

"Very well." He was obviously put out. "I'll finish making up my notes. You go into the anteroom. I'll call you when I'm ready."

In the event they told him that they would tell him the next day when they had all slept on it. He was not amused, but eventually agreed.

"Well? What do you have to say for yourself?"

"Dad, I *had* to go with her. I promised that I would support her."

"And I told you that you could not."

"Dad, I *promised*. What have you told me about promises?"

"Don't throw that in my face."

"But what option have I got? A promise is a promise. It's not something you break, even when it'd be more convenient. That's what you've taught me."

"If you felt that strongly, why didn't you say so before?"

"I did, but you put on your Captain in command voice and that means there's no point in arguing."

Max thought back to the conversation.

"Owen, whatever the whys and wherefores, what you did is deceitful, it's not like you and it must never happen again. You will write to your form teacher to apologise and take whatever punishment he sets. I want an apology and so does your mother. I think we deserve it."

Owen thought. Did he just leave this here or…

"Dad, I apologise to you and mum for having to tell lies to my form teacher. I will write to him too. But I'm sorry, I *don't* apologise for not breaking a promise or for supporting Ruth. And Mary. I think it helped them that I was there. Mary isn't used to talking to doctors."

"That's not your problem. You should have minded your own business."

"It *is* my business, Dad. She's my friend. I made a promise to support her."

"You must be guided by us in this."

"I am guided, Dad. You brought me up not to break promises. And to help people when I could."

"There are limits. And you shouldn't have made that promise, a promise you couldn't keep."

Owen was silent, thoughts in turmoil. Then a light shone.

"What did you promise Mum when you first got together."

"That's got nothing to do with you."

"Dad, It's got everything to do with honouring promises. I'm almost sure you'll have promised her many things."

It was Max's turn to think. He felt he was losing ground. He should be able to control his son – at least in something like this. That time between them over Christmas came back to him and he remembered the lucid discussions they had had, each giving and receiving almost as good as they got.

His son was getting older.

"My concerns are these," he said, trying to recapture some of that spirit, that bonhomie. "Firstly, you have the O-Levels next year and you need all the schooling you can get, just like everyone does. Secondly, neither you nor I know how long this friendship is going to last. Friendships at your age hardly ever do, you know." Owen stirred and would have spoken but Max put up his hand.

"And thirdly it has disappointed both of us that you lied to be able to do what you wanted."

Owen detected the shift. "Dad, I know about the exams. I had a choice to make and I decided that half a day of school – three hours – was a small price to pay to honour a genuine promise."

It was his turn to hold up his hand to stop an interruption and was pleased his father allowed it.

"Thirdly, Ruth and I love each other. I think that's what it is. We want to be with each other. Like you and Mum we will support each other. I don't know what's going to happen in the future. I hope we stay together. If we don't, I don't want to be able to say that it was my fault for not supporting her when I'd promised to.

"I'll write to Mr Edwards to explain and apologise. I'll tell Mum I'm sorry. But please…"

He shut his eyes hard, hoping he wasn't going too far. "Please realise that I *have* to support Ruth. And that means going to London to visit…" He noticed the sudden surprise, but carried on. "… when she's in hospital, and helping her with crutches and making sure she's all right. It's a promise I made.

"And you didn't tell me just now that you never promised Mum anything, so I'm sure you did. And I'm also sure you never went back on that promise – those promises."

Max was becoming exasperated. This wasn't a child arguing. Not any more. This was an adult reasoning, making his point. Was this Grammar School? Or was it Barbara's and his upbringing?

He just looked at his son again. "No more school to be missed, no more lies," he said.

"I hope that there won't be another occasion in term time when I need to do what I promised," Owen told him as honestly as he knew how. "I don't know what the rules are about visiting when Ruth's in Great Ormond Street. If something happens and I have to go up, it may be that I have to tell you and go, despite what you said. If that happens, I will tell you beforehand. And I'm sorry if that is disobedient, but I will not break my promise to Ruth. Or to anyone." He was about to leave it at that, but another sentence came to his mind. "If I broke a promise, I would be letting you and Mum down."

There was a long silence. Max was looking at his son, wondering. Owen was wanting the interview not to continue and was looking out of the window. He had nothing else to add that he hadn't said already. Max's next words caused him relief.

"What has Ruth decided?"

"I don't know yet. I didn't go home with her, I came straight here."

Did you now, though Max. Well, that was something. You're not afraid of facing the music. Or maybe, facing your responsibilities.

He nodded. "You'd better go and find out."

Now Owen *did* look at his father, a clear, wide eyed weighing-up look.

"You understand, don't you?"

He received a similar stare to meet his own.

"I hope so. Find out, tell me, talk to your mother – I'll prepare the way – and write that letter."

Owen nodded, said no more and left the room and the house.

"Was it very bad?" asked Ruth when she answered the door.

Owen grinned wryly. "It started off that way. He started off by saying what I thought he'd say but I told him that I'd promised you I'd come. And I kept saying it. And I asked him if he'd ever gone back on a promise he made to Mum. I think that may have done it."

"Is that all?"

He grinned. "No. I had to tell him how I felt about you. He seemed to think we're too young for... for that. But he came round, I think. Perhaps all that he's really worried about now is that I apologise to Mum for having to tell a lie at school. And I've got to write to the form teacher."

"And what *do* you think of me?"

His eyebrows lifted. "Don't you know, yet?" She made no comment, but smiled tentatively.

He grabbed her and proceeded to demonstrate, until voices from inside the Decks' front room interrupted them.

That evening the Decks family, with Owen chipping in where necessary and holding Ruth's hand, talked the pros and cons round and round until Ruth's brain was spinning. Owen left at around eight thirty, aware that he had homework to do and a letter to write.

They walked up to the station as usual the next morning. Nothing was said until they were on the train and had managed to get a couple of seats to themselves. They would have a chance to talk until Newhaven when the train filled up with other Grammar School pupils.

Owen looked her in the eyes. "Well?"

She looked resigned. "I'm going to get it done."

He let it sink in.

"Your decision?"

"My decision."

"Sure?"

"Yes! Don't try and put me off, please. It took me all last night to make up my mind."

"I'm not going to give you an opinion either way. I can't."

"Good."

"You know I'll support you, don't you?"

"You don't need to. Not if it gets you into trouble."

"I told Dad that I had promised. In our family, a promise is something you keep come hell or high water, as he would say. If you need me or if I think you do, I will tell Mum and Dad and tell the school, and that will be that."

"It's not that easy."

"Then it needs to be. And anyway, it'll just be while you're in hospital. Once you're home I can see you in the mornings and when I get back, and that's only until you can start walking. And once you're really up and running you'll be up and *running*! Eventually."

She smiled wistfully. "That is exactly what I'm looking forward to. And walking on the hills with... with the Baker brothers."

His mouth opened in surprise. Before he could speak she added: "And you."

He would have said something rude back, but they had arrived at Newhaven Harbour to meet the influx of students onto the train.

It snowed again in March. They all examined the sky in hope but it was obvious this was not going to be snow that lay thick enough to have fun with. Once again it was a Sunday; by the time they walked up to the station all that was left was a thin layer of slush which Alan said was of no use to anyone. There was some left on the upper slopes of the Downs, though, and they all wondered if it would stay until the following weekend.

It didn't. To Max's amazement and relief, Post Office Telephones wrote to say that a new line was to be installed into the Mill House a fortnight later. The Mill office received a separate letter to say that the new business lines would be installed as soon as new cables had been laid for the new developments that were to be built eventually by the Bishopstone road north east of them.

Shortly afterwards the Decks, now happily returned to their own house, received a letter from a surgeon at Great Ormond Street giving the Tuesday after Easter as the date they wanted Ruth into hospital. The operation would take place the following morning.

Ruth didn't know what to think after she'd been told. Although she was looking forward to a time when it was all done, the presence of a date made it suddenly real. And scary. She had collywobbles when she joined up with Owen as they walked to the station.

She told him the news and added: "I'm scared."

Instinctively he took her hand and started off: "But..."

It was a conversation they continued for much of the journey to Lewes, off and on, as well as on the walk to their respective schools. As they were about to separate at the western end of Mountfield Road it seemed to Owen that a kiss would give her some comfort. He kissed her. Immediately there were catcalls and shouts, both male and female, and the two separated in embarrassment.

There were comments for each of them for the first few minutes. Ruth's companions divided themselves into the friends and the others, but she had a cocoon of people, friends, around her. She told them why that parting kiss had been given and immediately they were on her side.

Owen said nothing, and hoped that his face was no longer red. There was one small chorus of voices that every now and again when they had an audience, would break into a chant: "Owen Wilson pudding and pie, kissed the girls and made them cry…" He seethed inside but controlled himself as they walked past the houses towards the school. By the time he turned off the road and onto the strip of grass in front of the building he had calmed down – into mental stillness, and knew what he was about to do.

He knew that his only way of defence was Judo, and that Judo has to be started in a state of respect between the two combatants. He couldn't muster that and Botting – he was sure he'd be the ringleader – wouldn't understand.

On the muddy grass by the road he stopped and turned, now determined and still of mind and body.

"Who is the choirmaster?" he asked in a loud voice that was as cold as ice. The last rendition of the chant went into diminuendo. He saw a few 'singers' and made a mental note. One of them was indeed Malcolm Botting. Owen's attention switched to him.

"Not scared of that old man in Seaford now you're in Lewes, Botting? We all saw how you scurried off after he'd nearly twisted your arm off."

The boy laughed. "We? All? Anyone see me talk down an old man?"

Laughs rang out, though some of those who knew and liked Owen made sure there was space between themselves and the bully; they knew what he and his band of friends were like.

"Oh, my friends saw it all right," said Owen, "and so would yours if they hadn't all run and left you alone with him and us. But I saw them watching you from round the corner of Broad Street. Good sort of friends to have, that."

Someone shouted "Oy!" and would have come forward. Others could see the lack of fear in Owen's eyes and the stare he was giving Malcolm Botting. They kept by him.

"You don't know what you're talking about," Botting laughed.

"I do, in fact; because I was there and had no reason to be scared. You and your little friends are the ones who don't know what they're talking about." Owen was glad to be able to return that compliment. "So I'll tell you. All. That girl is my girlfriend. You wouldn't understand what that feels like, of course. Perhaps you never will."

"You little…"

"And…" Owen shouted to drown him out. "And she has one leg shorter than the other. And she's just discovered today that she's going to have a major operation on it to sort it out, and will be out of action for six months or more."

There was uncertainty about how to greet that news. Owen had an idea.

"And when she's back up to strength, I'll ask her if she'd like to fight you, Botting. Fighting a girl is about all you're capable of."

He turned and walked slowly towards the school, ensuring he didn't reach the edge of the grass, but aware that if they didn't move nearer they would be too far from any adult witnesses to be useful if what he thought would happen next did.

Before him his friends spread out and one shouted a warning. He heard running footsteps in the wet earth behind him and calmly turned and held up a hand like a policeman on point duty.

Botting ignored it and continued his charge.

He found suddenly that he was charging fresh air but that mysteriously his left foot had tangled with his right and he was falling, on his own, onto the grass and its underlying mud.

Owen, overtaken by Botting's flight, rubbed the toe of one shoe on the back of his trousers, ignored the muddy, winded figure in front of him and walked on.

Prefect or not, Malcolm Botting received a detention for being late to Assembly and for having a wet, muddy and untidy uniform. Protestations that he had fallen on the wet grass seemed also to have fallen: on deaf ears.

At break Owen was told how lucky he had been. A group had gathered round him. Some closer to him thought they knew better and smiled to themselves. At last he grew tired of their comments.

"It wasn't luck," he told them. "You know when you were in a crocodile and walking along to a field or something like good little boys, you can tip the heel of the boy in front and make him trip? Well, if you time it, you can do it from the side, too."

When they had stopped laughing he answered a few more questions and then took himself off to the shop.

Max heard about Ruth's decision that evening and made a call to Isaac in London. The readiness with which he received a positive answer to his request pleased him greatly. Arrangements were made.

Ruth's fifteenth birthday in March was celebrated with some style, though she was still apprehensive about the practical side of the decision she had made.

"It's not a nice birthday present," she said to Owen, "knowing that your present is going to be a summer spent doing almost nothing."

What was welcome news, however, was that news had percolated through the schools that an illegal radio station had started broadcasting. Hurriedly, on the night of that revelation, radios were tuned in, almost furtively, and many young ears heard the tones of Radio Caroline for the first time. Ruth was particularly glad; reception was better than Radio Luxemburg and it was more lively. She made a note to take her radio into hospital with her.

16 – Great Ormond Street, London

It was on Maundy Thursday that Owen found himself with just two friends on one of the school's pitches. They were due to break up for the Easter holidays a few hours' later. Owen knew that Ruth would be apprehensive. It would be many months before she returned to her own school. He couldn't be with her to support her at school; he was anxious, and just wanted to be with people he knew and liked, those who shared his outlook on life.

And it was on Maundy Thursday that Malcolm Botting had decided to make his move. He knew that any retaliation by his victim, or punitive action by the school, would either have to be instigated in a hurry before they broke up, or two weeks afterwards when they returned. With his usual gang of friends he had followed Owen until he thought they were far enough away from the school buildings not to be noticed.

"You need taking down a peg or two," he snarled at Owen, having waylaid the threesome. "I owe you for that detention. I owe you for trying to make me look a fool in front of everyone."

After the first shock, Owen looked at him and his entourage of six. He took it in and made himself look calmly back at the prefect in the same way as he had before.

"After last time I advise against it," he said equally calmly, and started walking away from the group, making sure he was walking back towards the Dripping Pan and obliquely across the windows of the school. He hoped that someone would be looking out and that they would be able to see that he didn't strike the first of any blows that might ensue. His two friends, to give them their due, walked with him, though a lot less calmly.

"Stop! Stop and fight like a man!" shouted Botting, incautiously.

Owen turned again. "So it takes a man to try and bully girls as well as boys younger than him, does it? I think you're wrong. It just takes a coward."

He turned back to his original direction, keeping his ears open for movements.

"If I say 'run', run down to the school windows," he said as quietly as he could. "Hammer on them, do anything, but get people to see what's happening. They won't attack you – not when they see they're being watched."

"Can't leave you to get slaughtered," said one of them.

"I'll be fine. Judo."

He was aware of a surprised glance just as hurrying steps behind him told of a problem.

"I said stop, Wilson. I'm a prefect."

Owen turned again. "Not for much longer, probably. By the time you get out of hospital the Head will know what really happened. If he doesn't already."

"You filthy sneak."

"Oh, I'll not say a word. But people judge, and anyone who bullies a girl is likely not to be too popular."

"Fight, you little…"

Owen was about to be surrounded by the six of them. His friends had somehow been excluded.

"Run," he said in a pleasant tone.

Botting and one or two of the others were startled and looked round. By the time they looked back Owen's friends had started running towards the school buildings. Fast.

Owen didn't see who tried to grab him. He felt it though, and twisted, held and pushed, and with a thump a boy fell to the ground with a shout of pain. Botting was next, though. Owen was glad that it hadn't been a simultaneous attack.

Being two years older than him his assailant was strong, and it took two attempts to dip himself out of the double handed grasp and to butt the boy's stomach. He could hear the air coming from above in a gasp and knew Botting would be winded for a few moments.

He stepped out of the way of any ground level, grasping hands. Another of the group stepped backwards to escape an attack.

"It's been an interesting show for the people in school," Owen remarked. "Look at them, gathering at the window. I imagine there are some teachers on their way now to pick you both up and dust you down."

He turned again and once again walked towards the Dripping Pan.

About ten seconds later a teacher *did* appear around the corner of the building. But once again there were footsteps behind him. Owen turned, surprised that his assailant hadn't learnt from his previous experience. He judged his moment and once again pushed against one ankle. Botting flew through the air again and this time hit the earth with a thud.

The boys behind him saw the teacher and ran, only to be caught by others who were appearing around the further end of the building.

An ambulance had to be called to remove Malcolm Botting to the Victoria Hospital for some stitches in his face where it had coincided with a sharp flint. They gave him a painful anti-tetanus injection for good measure.

Owen and his two friends had to give a full account to the Headmaster. Owen included in his report the incident in Seaford and the name calling on the way to school previously.

"How did you manage to dispose of two of them almost simultaneously?" asked his inquisitor. "And what have you to say to your so-called friends who ran away?"

Owen smiled. "I have a black belt in Judo, sir. I hardly used it there but there is a discipline in Judo that helps you think before retaliating. That I did use. And my friends – I'd like to thank them for doing as I asked and running to hammer on the windows and attract attention."

He was looked at sharply. "I wasn't expecting that," said the Headmaster. "And knowing that you have such a Judo qualification makes it unnecessary for me to ascertain that you were attacked first, that someone else struck the first blow. I'm aware that Judo will be an Olympic sport in next winter's

Games so have seen the need to teach myself some of its ethos and rules."

This was news to Owen, who looked pleased. "I didn't know that, sir. Good."

The Head nodded. "Very well. That's all. And all of you - if there's any more trouble from that boy please come to me first. That applies to his friends, too."

"Yes sir," they chorused, knowing full well that to do so would be against the ethos of any school pupil anywhere. They were about to go when Owen turned back.

"Sir?"

The Headmaster looked up again from his notes. "Yes, Wilson?"

"I... I wrote to Mr Edwards last month – about that time when I had to tell a lie to get some time off school to go to the hospital with... with a friend." He paused.

"Yes. Young Ruth Decks. I understand you are walking out with her."

Owen was startled. He'd not heard the term 'walking out' in that context before, but realised what was meant.

"Er... yes, sir."

"I do get to know far more than people think, you know. Anyway, that is water under the bridge, I gather."

"Yes, sir, I hope so. Mr Edwards accepted what I said about having to honour a promise. But... well, as I'm here, I just wanted to apologise to you as well. I am not normally a liar. But that time... well, you know the story."

The man nodded. Again Owen was held by a gaze not unlike his father's, a gaze that seems to penetrate to the soul.

"Thank you, Wilson. I don't want it to happen again. And your education must come first; you know that."

Owen took a deep breath. "Yes, sir. But just as I have higher standards than to tell lies normally, I also have other standards. I'm not prepared to break a promise I've made. I promised that I would support Ruth. And if she needs my support away from school in school time, I'm afraid I will have to tell Mr Edwards – and you – that I *must* go, and accept the punishment."

That deep stare continued, and Owen returned it calmly, glad to have levelled with this man, with his father and with himself. He felt at peace. Honesty had been regained.

"You're not a usual sort of person, are you Wilson? We'll just have to hope it's not necessary. But if it does, I shall know that you're not swinging the lead. Do you know what that means?"

"Yes, sir, my Dad's a Navy Captain."

For the first time there was a smile. "Then tell him from someone who was in the Wavy Navy that he's a lucky man. That'll be all."

"Thank you, sir."

"How did you get on?" the question was asked in chorus as Owen and Ruth met on the way to the station.

Ruth spoke first. "You don't know girls. My friends were fine, intrigued, almost envious." She stopped and gave a forced laugh. "Some of them had noticed you before and... well..." Another pause. "...had mentioned you."

She didn't tell him some of the comments about him and his looks and build that even her close friends had made. They were too descriptive for his ears and she didn't want to make him think that other, more attractive, girls might be open to advances.

"Am I that famous?" he asked with a grin, the comment threatening to chip at the block she thought she'd just built.

"No," she said defensively, "just 'noticed'."

He smiled. "Just as well you're here, then. It'll save them time trying to notice more."

She weighed that up, uncertain what was meant. Owen knew what he meant but wasn't happy that he'd quite said the right thing. Ruth decided she understood.

"How about you, then?"

He went into the day's events. She gasped when he airily told her what had happened to Botting and friend.

"What are they going to do to him?" she asked.

He shrugged his shoulders. "Don't know. It's not the sort of thing you ask a Headmaster. We'll find out next term."

There was no sign of Malcolm Botting's cohort on the road to the station, or on the platform, or on the train. Botting himself was still at the hospital.

That evening Max visited Mary and Arthur Decks to tell them that either or both of them was expected to stay at Isaac and Edna's house in London. "For at least Tuesday and Wednesday nights, when she's had the operation. And if you want or need to stay longer, they would love you to. Arthur, you have compassionate leave for as long as you need it. Jack knows."

The two were speechless. Travel to and from London had been a worry to them, financially and practically. They stammered their thanks. Ruth and Owen listened and smiled.

"Well, we did get them their sovereigns," said Ruth, smiling, and was accused of being ungrateful.

Alan and Eric were fed up. Neither of their friends were around for most of Good Friday. Ruth and Owen had elected to take their cycles and see if the path from Bishopstone and Norton was good enough to cycle on. It was, with some dodging through mud. They enjoyed it so much that they went again the next day, feeling a little guilty as the brothers had no bikes.

"We have so little time alone," said Owen.

Ruth and the brothers had to be in the choir on Easter Sunday and their parents would be going too. They were occasional rather than regular churchgoers. Owen decided to persuade his parents to go with him and was pleased when said that they had already planned to. He had felt that he should go, just to support Ruth.

Or maybe there was more to his sudden desire to attend a church service.

"I've invited the Bakers and the Decks to lunch," Barbara said to Owen as they all walked up to get a train.

He looked astonished. "You never said!"

"No, I just told Mary and Jessie that I'd made a mistake and bought far too big a joint and please would they help us eat it."

Owen remembered something, but it needed just him and his father. As they left Seaford station the choir members hurried off ahead so as to get ready and he engineered it that Max and he were at the back of the small group.

"Dad, it's work."

"What have you done now?"

"No, not my work, yours. Did you know that the previous owner of the Mill had decreased everyone's hourly rate before you took over?"

"Where did you hear that?" asked Max, surprised.

"There were two of the wives chatting, and they didn't know I was there. I overheard."

It wasn't true, and once again Owen was the victim of a promise he'd made. He had told Ruth that he wouldn't repeat her unguarded remark about wages.

"Did they say any more?" his father asked.

"Only that it happened before last winter. She said it was the summer before."

"Who did?"

"I… didn't recognise her. Her voice."

A pause. He wondered if his father suspected the real source of the information.

"Okay. Thanks, Owen. I'll look at the old records and find out what went on."

The church was already quite crowded as they entered, the closing of the door almost deadening the sound of the bells ringing. The Wilsons, Decks and Bakers sat separately, where there were spaces. As the choir processed, Owen had a tingle in his spine when he heard the brothers singing their hearts out with the processional hymn. It seemed so angelic, so completely different from the ordinary, mischievous kids he knew them to be. Ruth passed too, and her melodious voice sent another shiver down his back.

By the end of the service he was more used to what was coming and was hardly surprised to see a cheeky grin on Eric's face as he passed. Ruth stole a brief glance at him and smiled too; that made his day.

They all gravitated to the Mill House where Max opened the door and ushered them through

"Sorry, Arthur, Ernie. No barrel this time."

They grinned back at Max and held up a shopping bag each. "Our turn, boss. You've done a lot for us!"

And if Owen is right I might be able to help a bit more, Max thought, even if the London crowd doesn't like it. It's amazing they've stuck it this far.

That afternoon and the following day – Bank Holiday Monday – all four of the younger contingent spent together, walking, mucking about, laughing, playing board games; just as if it was a normal, slightly grey, holiday day.

Barbara, sensitive to Ruth's feelings, had suggested to Owen that it should be so, as ordinary but as filled as possible, so taking Ruth's mind off the events to come. It seemed to work as the boys were pleased to be included in it, and reacted with the humour that was their trademark. A great deal of laughing was done.

It continued the next morning. But as lunchtime drew closer Ruth became quieter and quieter as she put the few things she needed into a case. Her parents were packing too, so she was left to her own devices. Owen was at home, also packing.

Max had volunteered to take the family – and Owen who insisted on it – to London. He dropped them at the Hospital and said he'd park the car and see them in the hospital foyer when they were ready. The Decks and Owen went in.

"I feel as if I'm going in to hospital to die," she whispered to Owen as they slipped behind her parents.

Frantically he grabbed her hand. "You're going in to be made better. Never forget that. And it's only an operation. You'll soon be out."

"But then months of sitting about…" He gripped her hand harder and she winced.

"I'll be in whenever I can. I promise."

On the ward they were met by an elderly, forbidding looking Sister. She looked disapprovingly at Owen.

"He's the brother, is he?"

Owen could see Mary was about to say something. "Yes," he said firmly.

"If you visit, you'll have to come with an adult. We don't allow children to visit on their own."

Owen bristled. "What age do you need to be?"

From the look he received it appeared she felt he was hardly worth talking to.

"Sixteen, of course."

"Then I just qualify, don't I Mum?"

To give Mary her due, despite hating the idea of leaving her only daughter behind in the hospital, she nodded. "Yes. Sixth December."

Her husband coughed suddenly.

"And if you have germs I'd be glad if you would keep out, please." It was his turn for an attack."

"I'm fine," he protested. "Just not used to the heat in here."

Owen examined the floor, then looked up at Ruth with as carefully composed expression as possible.

"Very well," she rattled on, "the nurse will tell you visiting times and they are to be strictly observed. You will not be allowed in at any other time, and all other children must be accompanied by an adult."

It was Ruth's turn to look at the floor.

It was a large ward, well lit by good-sized windows. Beds were occupied by boys and girls of all from just under school age upwards. Some had curtains around their bed. One was crying.

Ruth felt her courage melt away. She wondered if it was too late to change her mind, but knew that it would create inconvenience to her parents and to the hospital staff. And she would have to continue with the hated built-up shoe for the rest of her life. She had decided – not agreed, decided – and must now go through with it.

She looked at Owen. "I'll be all right," she said defiantly. "Please, just come when you can?"

He grabbed her hand again, his way of showing comfort, sharing comfort. "Of course I will."

The Sister took them down to a bed. "This will be yours," she said. "We've been inundated recently; children seem to be having more accidents than usual. So that's why you're on a mixed ward and with the young children. The doctor comes round at six o'clock and will want to talk to you then. You need to be on the bed, but needn't get undressed until later as you don't have the operation until tomorrow. I'll get a nurse to come and talk to you."

She sailed majestically away back up the ward like a cruise liner embarking from port..

"Gosh," said Owen. "She's a bit of an old tartar, isn't she?"

"Is there anything you need?" Mary was clutching at straws, thinking of what to say to ease Ruth's transition into patient-hood.

She shook her head. "I've got everything, I think. At least I'll have plenty of books and the radio so there'll be something to do."

Owen was holding her hand again, unwilling to give her up to the hospital. He felt that if he let go, that would be like saying goodbye for ever.

A young nurse came to them, as pleasant and breezy a person as they could wish for. She introduced herself as Susan and explained the visiting hours as 2 – 4 in the afternoons and 6 – 8 in the evenings. "We're more flexible here nowadays than they are in the adult hospitals," she explained.

Susan looked at Owen, who looked at Ruth. She saw the hands that were still together. She looked at the parent Decks. She smiled.

"Sister told you, I'm sure," she said to him. "that it's really only relatives who are allowed to visit, and then only when they're over sixteen, and it's only at visiting times anyway, didn't she?"

Owen nodded. "I'm her brother and I'm sixteen," he lied again.

"Well, *brother*..." He was aware that she was looking at him from under mischievously raised eyebrows. "Sister retires on Thursday. I meet her replacement tomorrow and I'll check with her but I'm sure she will say the same. So long as you're her *brother*. It's good to find an older *brother* who's so attentive to his sister." Again he saw that look, tried a smile in return and was rewarded with an acknowledgement.

"It looks as if you're happy with his coming in like that?" she asked Arthur and Mary.

"We'd be pleased if he could. He's a really nice lad," said Arthur without thinking.

Owen was alarmed. Susan smiled again. "*Brothers* of pleasant girls usually are," she said.

They stayed, passing the time of day with an odd awkwardness, until the Sister sailed her way down to them in her disapproving way.

"I have to remind you that you are here just to drop her off, to place her into our care. Visiting time has passed and I really must ask you to leave. You may telephone tomorrow evening to ask how the operation progressed but it will be pointless to visit as the girl will still be under the influence of the anaesthetic. But please do not telephone too often. We are very busy."

Owen was sure that his father would have had something to say to the Sister. He felt tongue-tied in her presence. Neither Arthur nor Mary were the arguing type and Ruth was in no position to say anything.

They said their farewells.

"I'll be in tomorrow, whether you're awake or not," he whispered to Ruth. "I'll be holding your hand."

With kisses from all three, they left. Owen waved and blew another kiss from the door. He felt his throat constricting and his eyes unaccountably wet.

Ruth felt that the sun had gone behind a cloud.

It took the boy in the bed next to hers two attempts to attract her attention. She looked over. He was, she thought, a little younger than her – about thirteen – and propped up on pillows. The arm and leg nearest to her were both in plaster, the arm in a sling, the leg suspended on a frame. She immediately felt sorry for him.

"Hallo," he said again. "It's all right really. They're not all like the Sister. Susan's nice."

She nodded dismally.

"I was brought in," he told her. "At least you walked in."

That was a different take on it.

"What happened?" she asked.

"Mucking about with friends on a bomb site whilst Dad was in the pub," he said. "I didn't know there was some concrete and stuff waiting to fall on me. It did."

"Oh! Hurt much?"

"I only woke up in the ambulance, then wished I hadn't bothered. Then they had to clean me up before they operated and that was worse. The best bit was the anaesthetic taking hold and the pain just fading away." He sighed. "Woke up in here yesterday night and they told me to go back to sleep. Then they woke me up about 6.00 this morning and wondered why I felt awful."

"How's the pain now?"

"Just uncomfortable, really. It's okay. What're you in for?"

She explained. "Blimey!" was his reaction.

They exchanged names and life histories. His was Freddie Strange

"That wasn't your brother just now, was it?" he said when talk had paused.

"What makes you say that?" She was trying not to tell a lie.

"Brothers and sisters don't hold hands. And he looked really unhappy until Susan showed him she was on his side."

200

She nodded.

"Well? Boyfriend?"

"If they think he's not my brother he won't be allowed in."

"I won't tell."

She nodded again. A pause.

"Looks strong."

Ruth smiled. He sounded hopeful.

"I think he is, but he doesn't fling his weight around. He does Judo, though."

She got a round-eyed stare back.

"Wish he'd teach me!"

"Why?"

"School. I get picked on."

"We got picked on recently by a bully who lives in Seaford and goes to the same school as Owen."

"That's his name?"

"Yes. The bully ran at Owen but he made him trip himself up."

"How'd he do that?"

"You need to ask him."

"Good skill to have. Nice chap?"

"Who?"

"Your... er... brother."

"Well, I think so."

They chatted for some time before the conversation faltered.

"I'm... sorry. I have to call a nurse," said Freddie.

The next few minutes saw a scene of well oiled teamwork as curtains were drawn, a lightly disguised bedpan taken in. Nurses departed, there was a wait. A quiet voice summoned them back, an item was removed and some moments later the curtains were drawn back again.

"Sorry," he said in a small voice.

"Why?"

"There's a lot you can't do with an arm and a leg that mustn't move. It's embarrassing."

Ruth smiled and shrugged. "It has to happen."

He smiled back.

It was a car of silent passengers that made its way to Edna and Isaac's house. The welcome from the two was warm and helped dispel their anxieties and the feeling that they couldn't escape, the feeling that that there was something missing. Mary and Arthur started to express their gratitude at their offer of help but were interrupted by both their hosts in chorus. Edna and Isaac exchanged glances. Isaac gave way.

"Your daughter and Owen found a fortune that Isaac left for me. Instead of pocketing it themselves they put themselves out to find Isaac. He found me. Really, Ruth and Owen brought us together again and so has done each of us an immeasurable service. We've each rediscovered happiness.

"In return, if we can thank them in any practical way, we will. We've already decided that if she's up here and you have to return to Sussex, we'll visit her every day. So let's hear no more thanks and so on – it makes me feel awkward and I know it does the same to Isaac.

"Now: a meal before Max has to go home."

They had smelt something good cooking as they entered the house. It turned out to be a steak and kidney pudding. "Never could afford to make these since Fox died," admitted Edna, "but my Mum used to make them."

Forty five minutes later Mary, herself a good cook, asked for the recipe.

They all helped clear up. There's something about working alongside someone in their kitchen that breaks down any supposed barriers. When the last dishes were in their cupboards and the place cleaned to Isaac's Navy standards the atmosphere was relaxed.

"How about a pint?" Isaac said. "The pub round the corner is friendly."

"I won't, if you don't mind," Edna said. "I'm still not used to eating a heavy meal and then drinking on top of it."

"May I keep you company?" said Mary quickly and was pleased to see the smile that was returned. It was a long way from the straight-faced, shrewish Mrs Fox of Tide Mills.

"We can chat or watch television," said Edna.

"One day we'll get a TV, though I don't know when." Mary wondered if she should have said that with her husband still there. It seemed disloyal.

He smiled grimly. "One day, indeed. Once the mill is really earning, eh Max?"

Max nodded, reminded of his son's comments on Easter Sunday.

"I was looking at some of the old books," he said suddenly, "and it looked as though the hourly rate was cut at one point. Can you remember that happening?"

Arthur looked uncomfortable. "Summer before last," he said shortly. "We reckoned at the time the Mill wouldn't be lasting much longer. A few of the families left then and got jobs on the docks or somewhere."

"And nobody said anything?"

"Wouldn't have done any good. The decision was made and that was that."

"I meant that nobody has said anything to me. Or to Jack."

"Don't know about Jack, but the rest of us thought that we should wait until the Mill was earning again before we mentioned it. Seemed only right."

Faced with that comment, Max wished he didn't feel so exasperated.

"I wish someone had told me before now," he said. "I think everyone's too loyal for their own good. But I'm so glad they are!"

"Well..." Arthur left his rejoinder hanging.

"So are you happy that we go to the pub, Edna? It means you two can gossip if you want to."

"Huh!" said Edna with spirit.

Owen was very quiet through all this, though thankful his father had approached the question of an hourly rate so tactfully. The pub was a different matter. It sounded as though Isaac was including him. On the other hand he knew that his father was against his going into pubs until he was legally old

202

enough. He kept quiet and sited himself next to Arthur so as to be included. But Max, being Max, noticed.

"What are we going to do with you?" he asked no one in particular but looking straight at his son.

"Ah…" Isaac said with a smile. "They've got a little room with some pub games in it – a gentleman's bar – that's usually quiet. And the landlord doesn't mind too much. It's noisy young kids he won't have in the pub at all, and they have to stay outside with a bottle of pop or something. Owen will be all right."

Owen, knowing his father, wondered if he *would* actually be all right.

"It doesn't have a toads table in it, does it?" he asked.

Isaac laughed. "Where did you hear about that?"

Max had to describe his experiences with Jack Pentelow and Martin Killick.

"No," Isaac smiled, "but it's got bar billiards."

The three men (as Mary described them) went off. The pub was accommodating and the landlord had no problems about "my seventeen year old son" as Owen heard himself called, though it did shake him. Was he really that tall? He was swiftly shown how bar billiards worked and after a few tries became adequate at it, though might have done better had his mind not been partly on a young girl waiting in a hospital.

Time passed, and it was only when the clock struck that Max realised it was nine o'clock. He said a rude word and apologised.

"I should have been on my way hours ago," he said. "It'll take over two hours to get back, and after those two pints I'll doubtless have to stop at a tree somewhere."

"Good pints though, weren't they?" asked Isaac.

"Not as good as Harveys," said Arthur with a smile. "But not half bad."

It was an evening of firsts for Owen. Not only was he in a pub, he had been playing bar billiards, and now his father was leaving the pub without him. It felt most peculiar. But once again his thoughts turned to Great Ormond Street and a vulnerable girl whom he thought was probably waiting for sleep to take her.

It took a long time for sleep to take him as well.

"What time does the operation start?" he asked in the morning.

"We don't know. We've just asked each other the same question," Mary told him.

"Can we phone? Can we go in and… and see her before she goes in?"

"I don't think we should," she said. "They didn't want us to telephone a lot."

"But she would like some support as she goes in, I'm sure." Owen was on tenterhooks. It seemed certain to him that they – that he – should be there to hold Ruth's hand as she went under the anaesthetic.

"I'll call," Isaac volunteered. "I can say I'm an uncle or a grandparent or something. If we can get there in time it would be nice."

They agreed. He made the call. She would be going into the theatre at ten-thirty, he was told. He asked if they could come in and just be with her until then.

"Well, it's not usual," said the Sister; fortunately a different one from the previous night. "But if you're quick, yes"

Owen's eyes lit up when he was told. He jumped up and started looking hopeful.

"Steady!" Arthur cautioned. "Mary and I want to see her just as much as you do, you know. But we can't get there much before half past nine. They've got to have breakfast, then there are the doctors' rounds. No, we're best leaving at about nine, then we'll get there and only go in when they're ready for us."

That meant moping around the house for another half an hour, thought Owen. He slowly cleaned his teeth, washed his hands and wasted time. Finally they were off. He felt like a coiled spring during the tube ride into the centre of the city, and only a little better on the short walk from Russell Square station to the hospital.

They negotiated their way past various white coated people by using the name of the Sister who had agreed to their coming in. There was a fifteen minute wait whilst the doctors left the ward; the same sister escorted them down towards Ruth's bed.

"She's going to be a little woozy," she told them. "The doctor gave her an injection to calm her down before the surgery. Not that she needed it, she seemed calm enough but it's just what's done."

Ruth looked almost asleep. The boy in the bed next to hers smiled at them.

"She's had an injection," he told them.

"We were told," said Owen, for some reason on his guard.

"You're the brother," said the boy in a loud-ish voice. Then, so only the visitors could hear: "officially."

This time Owen took more notice. "She told you?" he asked, equally quietly.

He nodded. "Said you did Judo. Will you teach me?"

Owen was saved a response by a sleepy, happy "Hallo" from Ruth. He swung round and smiled. She looked vulnerable. He felt something warm happening inside his head, and a tingle ran down his spine. Mary and Arthur just saw a tired daughter.

"Hallo," they said in chorus, smiling back.

"I wasn't expecting you back," she said. "You needn't have bothered, really. I don't want to be a nuisance."

That floored her parents. Owen stood by her and touched her shoulder. "You aren't a nuisance. Never have been, never will be. We just wanted to be here before... before..." He tailed off, uncertain.

She smiled up at him and he felt that sensation again.

"You're good to me," she said. "They've given me something and I'm very tired. I don't know if I can keep my eyes open much longer."

Owen threw caution to the winds and kissed her. She smiled again. He was so nice. What had she done to...to deserve...

204

And she was asleep again.

"Now what?" asked Arthur, after a moment or two.

"I'd like to stay, please," said Owen before Mary could speak.

"Oh, we'll all be staying. Until she goes in. And we'll be back tonight." Mary was being very firm, for her. She was aware that her daughter was no longer her more mature self but once again a child who needed her Mum's presence, even if there was now a boyfriend in the equation. She looked at Owen again, as if seeing him for the first time. He *was* serious, wasn't he? And she had wondered about puppy love. Well, it might still be, but at the moment he was most certainly in this with them.

It took her a moment to get to grips with the idea.

There were movements nearby.

"You need to let her come with us," said the Sister. "It's time we got her ready. You can come back this evening if you want, although she will still be under the anaesthetic, of course. She'll be in the recovery ward – you'll see it on the way out." She nodded toward the door, partly to show where it was and partly to hint that they should go.

First mother, then father, then boyfriend kissed her again and were rewarded by a faint smile. They turned away as two porters came in with a trolley. Owen didn't trust himself to look at her neighbour, though Arthur remembered his kindness earlier and smiled at him.

He nodded and smiled back. "She'll be okay," he said. "They're good here."

Mary overheard, turned to look at him and said with every ounce of sincerity she had: "Thank you."

Freddie looked after them, sadly, as they left. He hoped he was right and that Ruth would be okay. He couldn't bear to think he might get the blame from that lady if he wasn't.

At the door, Owen looked back to where staff were fussing over Ruth. He found he couldn't see properly. He never saw Freddie wave to him. He stayed effectively blind all the way to the stairs. Mary wouldn't trust the lift.

The three of them went for a walk with Edna soon after regaining the house. Isaac carefully suggested it once he saw the anxiety that kept all three of them sitting on the edge of their seats and unable to listen to the wireless or even watch television. He said he would start on a light meal for when they returned.

By this time Edna had learnt her way round the area, so took them to a local shopping area where she managed to get them to smile at the antics of a small group of late-teen boys. It seemed they had been experimenting with some of the fashions that were becoming all the rage in the city centre. Their version of it seemed to have been to visit the women's shops in the quiet local shopping area, there buying the most colourful blouses and scarves they could find. One of the shopkeepers was outside her shop, looking vaguely scandalised.

"Apparently they normally shop round a place called Carnaby Street," said Edna. "It's near Soho, and I do know what that stands for. Always has. Even known for it in Sussex."

Owen didn't know what she meant, and didn't give his ignorance away by asking. He made a mental note to visit both it and Carnaby Street when coming to London to visit Ruth.

Between people watching, window shopping and wandering, the time vanished. Their mood had lightened, though Owen was still aware of a lingering, background anxiety.

With lunch over, Isaac wondered what to do with them for the afternoon. There had been no contact from the hospital, something Mary and Arthur were secretly dreading. He volunteered to take them down to the Thames and show them where he used to be stationed, then maybe to Tower Bridge in the hope that it might open.

"Flood tide, just reaching the top," he explained. Only he and Arthur understood the significance of this so he explained. "Incoming ships will use the tide to come up river. Saves on fuel and saves plugging against a current when you don't have to. If any need to come above Tower Bridge they'll open it."

Mary hesitated, worried about hospital phone calls.

"It's all right, Mary. You call me every so often from a phone box and I'll tell you if they've rung. I'm sure it's all going well, so don't worry."

Despite all the worrying, and because of almost hourly 4d's worth of phone calls to Edna, they enjoyed their walk. They wandered from Isaac's old Command on the Thames to a place where they did indeed manage to see a reasonable sized vessel sail under the raised Tower Bridge. Even for ex-Londoner Owen that was a treat, and the Decks's were enthralled. Most of what they knew of the bridge's opening had been gathered from photographs, especially from a newspaper back in 1952, when a double-deck bus had been on the bridge as it opened and had to jump the gap. Owen had been three at the time and couldn't really say whether or not he remembered his parents talking about it.

Back at the house a phone call was made to the hospital. They all gathered round Mary Decks, whose hand on the receiver was white knuckled. She waited impatiently to be connected with the Ward Sister. It was the older woman they had first spoken to whose peremptory tones answered.

"She has only just come out of surgery," was the brusque answer.

Mary waited. Nothing else was forthcoming.

"Was... was the operation a success? Is she all right?" she asked, almost fearfully.

"Of course the operation was a success, and of course she's all right. We would have telephoned to you had it been otherwise."

The earpiece was away from Mary's ear by now and everyone heard. Isaac put out his hand for the receiver, lifting his eyebrows to seek permission. He held the receiver to his ear.

"Madam, my name is Isaac Galley. I am... the grandfather." He shot a look at Mary and Arthur. "Let me ask you this: if your daughter had gone through an operation like that, would you be happy to be palmed off with that little

206

information? It really isn't helpful, and we *are* her family, you know."

There was a silence at the other end this time.

"And while the patients are minors their parents have them as *their* priority. And that's every single moment of their lives, not just while they are in hospital. So perhaps with that in mind you'll understand the level of anxiety that a mother or a father feels. Even when it's to an English hospital they have entrusted their daughter or son; somewhere they are confident of the best care in the world."

There was an audible sigh at the other end of the line. Then: "What exactly do you want to know?"

His brows beetled. "We're glad that the operation was successful and she's all right. When will she be awake? And may we come in this evening even if she's not, just to hold her hand?"

There was a change of tone. The Sister now sounded tired. "Yes. Yes, you may. She won't be awake yet and she probably won't be until tomorrow morning. But yes, come in."

They entered the ward in pairs. Mary and Arthur first. Owen, unable to wait, sneaked in whilst no one was looking; then the new 'Grandparents' came to join him whilst the parents tactfully waited outside. The bedclothes over her right leg were being held away from the skin and made the site of the operation appear gross. Owen had to swallow as he approached the bed. No, she wasn't awake, but they were all able to see her and touch her hand and in Owen's case wish he had the nerve to kiss her after her parents returned to say goodbye, and of course they *did* kiss her.

It wasn't until later, when once again the menfolk had vanished to the same pub, that Arthur mentioned their visit.

"You never kissed her," he said to Owen quietly when Isaac wasn't listening. "Don't go off her now, whatever you do. She's going to need you when she gets home, more than ever."

Owen was unused to being pleaded with, because that's how it sounded to him. He weighed up what had been said, then replied in as sincere a voice as he had ever used.

"I will be there for her. I promise that. And the only reason I didn't kiss her was that I... I couldn't. Not in front of everyone there. I wanted to, so much."

The look he received as a response was unfathomable until Arthur nodded. He put a hand on Owen's shoulder.

"Thank you." Not much to say, perhaps, but enough. Owen enjoyed a warm glow.

17 – Bikes and Freddie

The phone rang at seven the next morning. By the time Owen had reached it Mary was already there, fearing the worst.

But it was their friendly Sister this time. "I don't know what you said to my colleague yesterday but she was most insistent I call you as soon as it was a decent time. I hope this is? Anyway, Ruth is awake. All is well. She's in some discomfort at the moment, but that's only to be expected. If you want to come in, please do. About ten o'clock would be best, once the doctor has finished his rounds."

Mary thanked her, almost weak with relief, and relayed the news.

They had been warned that she would be still woozy after the anaesthetic, and she was. Quite naturally she was pleased to see them and was receptive of the kiss that Owen gave her. This time he was aware that he had her father's encouragement.

The obvious questions were asked: how she felt, was she in pain, was she happy it had been done, and so on. She gave vague replies and the thing that she said most was that her leg felt funny.

After a while she dropped off to sleep again.

Their Sister was hovering nearby. "I was going to say that little and often is best for her. She's still under sedation because the skin around the rods that are holding her bone is healing. It's a painful process so we keep her like that to dull it. In a few days she'll be better and we can let her come round a bit more. Then she'll be a lot brighter."

That made sense. They decided, reluctantly, that returning at the regular visiting time that evening would be best, but restricting it to a short visit depending how she was.

"I'm going to be expected back at school before she's really well enough," Owen complained.

They were about to leave when a plaintive voice from the next bed caught their attention.

"Hallo. I've been looking after her, you know. She'd just come out of recovery and started tossing and turning, so I called the nurse." Freddie sounded aggrieved.

Mary crossed to his bed. "Thank you... sorry, we don't know your name."

"Freddie," said Freddie.

"Then thank you, Freddie. We'll be in again tonight at visiting time. Is there anything you need? Or will your parents bring you something?"

"It's just my Dad. He won't be coming, I doubt."

"Not coming?"

He shrugged his shoulders.

"He'll be in the pub."

Mary didn't know what to say.

"One of us will sit with you for a bit, Freddie. We can't all crowd round Ruth's bed, there's too many of us. I know – do you like the sea and stories about it? Real life stories?"

Freddie's eyes lit up and he nodded enthusiastically.

"The people we're staying with – he's a retired Navy Captain. He can tell a tale or two. And he, Owen and Edna can tell you the story of how a treasure was discovered. Would that be all right?"

His eyes gleamed even brighter. "Blimey! Would it! Thank you!"

The story they told Isaac about him made him smile. But the smile soon faded. "I can't imagine how a man with a son chooses to go to the pub rather than come and visit his injured son. What sort of a man is that? I ignored mine for long enough, God knows, but that's because I didn't ever imagine he existed. But this little lad... well. Of course I'll sit with him and yarn."

Early that evening, two parents, a young lad, a smart woman and a distinguished looking man in full Navy uniform descended on Great Ormond Street Hospital. The Sister they first saw, and whom Isaac had charmed on the phone the previous day, was on duty. She took one look at this apparition and was captivated. Even with her years of experience, to have a full-blown, uniformed Captain visit her ward and know that she had spoken to him and been persuaded by him, impressed her.

He smiled at her and in a voice that was designed to carry around the ward, told her that he was grateful to her for agreeing with him during their phone call. The party then sailed off down the ward to Ruth's bed and to Freddie.

The latter's eyes had again widened when he heard the voice from the door, and now were almost popping out of his head to see Isaac coming straight down... to see him. A grin spread across his face. When Isaac sat by his bed and carefully – firmly – shook his hand, he knew that the eyes of every patient in the ward were on them both.

Mary, Arthur and Owen were doing their best to communicate with Ruth, who was still sedated, as they had been warned. In a gap between stories, as Isaac took a drink of water, Freddie told him that he was still looking after Ruth as best he could. "I've got nothing else to do," he said. "I'm bored out of my head. Especially when they tell us we've got to have an afternoon nap."

Isaac nodded. "How about a book?"

Freddie looked down and muttered. "Haven't got one. Don't really like reading."

Isaac tilted his head and looked directly at him. "Nor did I when Edna looked after me when I was sixteen," he said. "Sixteen, and I could hardly read! We left school at fourteen in those days. But when I ran away to join the Navy I found I *had* to learn to read if I was going to be any more than an Ordinary Seaman all my life. It was hard work and took me ages, but I managed it. And now – well, I give any book a chance. Most of them are worth it."

He thought from the silence that he might have hit gold. But the next question was on a different tack.

"What were you running away from?"

So started the next story.

They left a still groggy Ruth and an excited Freddie when the other visitors were ushered out.

The next three days followed a similar pattern. On the Sunday evening Arthur had to return to Sussex for work, so it was just Mary and Owen, Edna and Isaac who went to visit. Although their dragon of a Sister had retired one of the others was inclined to be rule-bound and insisted that only two visitors per patient at any time were allowed. The four of them took it in turns, with two by Freddie's bedside and two by Ruth's.

The days fell into a pattern; sightseeing by day and visiting Ruth – and Freddie – in the evenings. She was gradually better able to talk sense, though she still tired quickly. But after the Sunday visit Arthur and Owen knew they had to return to Sussex; it was the end of the Easter holiday. and Owen had school. It was with a kiss that he left her, and a lingering hand hold. He hurried to the door, eyes blurry yet again.

Isaac had told Freddie of the plans and the boy had immediately become straight faced.

"What's the matter?" asked Isaac, noticing.

"That means you won't be in any more."

"Of course it doesn't! We'll come in with Ruth's Mum, so you and I can still talk. And who knows, your Dad might come in sometime in the weekend."

He looked toward the ceiling. "No chance of that."

"Mum, then?"

"She died."

For once Isaac had no idea what to say. He pulled a wry face.

"Sounds like you could do with a bit of company... I'm sorry about your Mum."

Freddie just nodded. This time his eyes were downcast.

"I promise I'll be back tomorrow," said Isaac softly. "Perhaps we can work out how we're going to get Owen to teach you Judo."

That brought the head up again. A weak smile fixed itself to Freddie's mouth.

"Please?" he said. Isaac touched his shoulder and walked towards the door after a final wave to Ruth.

"He's fun," Freddie told Ruth, who nodded.

Arthur and Owen reluctantly took their leave from the London house and journeyed in near silence back home. Barbara had taken pity on Arthur and told him he had to stay with them while Mary and Ruth were still in London.

"You can't do a full day's work and feed yourself afterwards. And you'll be nearer a phone here for when Mary wants to talk to you." Their line had finally been installed in March, to the Wilsons' relief.

He was astonished and embarrassed, but pleased; and eventually accepted with relief.

School was a shock to the system for Owen. So much had happened since the unpleasant encounter before half term that he had all but forgotten it. There was no sign of Botting anywhere and he only realised it when they were released for the day. There were sightings of one or two of his gang, but none of them came near Owen.

On the train he found another prefect sitting across the gangway from him and nodded a greeting. The lad gave a rueful grin.

"Sorted Botting out for us, didn't you?"

"Did I? Self defence, that's all."

"Bloody good self defence – Head said it was Judo. That right?

"A bit," Owen admitted.

"He's not a prefect any more, thank goodness. And he's not back till next week. In fact he nearly got a caning, by all accounts."

Owen looked uncomfortable. "I didn't want it to go that far..."

"He's had it coming for ages, the way he's been bullying people."

"Yes, but..."

"Oh, nothing to do with you. But he bullied a girl – your friend – and the Head won't stand for that. So he's been told that the next time, he's out."

"Expelled?"

"Yes. It's just a suspension this time, but his parents aren't happy."

"I just hope that when he comes back he doesn't try it on again."

"He'd be a fool if he does. The Head'd kick his arse from here to... well, Seaford."

Owen laughed, a little grimly. "I hope you're right."

Alan and Eric were pleased to see Owen briefly that evening. Life without either of their older friends had been noticeably more boring, and they told him so. Alan managed to get Owen on his own.

"Do you think... I wonder if... Could..."

Owen waited patiently.

"She'd never agree, though."

Owen just continued listening, expectantly.

"Would Ruth lend me her bike while she's in the hospital?" It came out in a rush.

Owen blinked. "You could ask Arthur... Mr Decks."

Alan looked uncomfortable. "I didn't like to. Could you ask him? If he says 'yes' I could take that pedal off and put an ordinary one on, then it would be easier to ride. And when Ruth can ride it again she won't need a special pedal anyway."

Owen hadn't thought of that. Of course Alan was right.

"But what about Eric? He hasn't got a bike."

Alan looked uncomfortable again. "I know."

He looked so downhearted that Owen wondered if he should ask his father, but that might be frowned on by the boys' parents. Something struck him.

"Would he mind a secondhand bike? We could probably find one that doesn't cost a lot."

"It's worth a try. I'll ask my parents."

Owen had another brainwave. "Why not find a bike somewhere and see what they want for it? Then we can come and ask."

"Okay... said Alan slowly. "It'd have to be dirt cheap, though."

Owen longed to tell him that if his father was able to, all the employees would be better off shortly, but thought better of it.

"I'm sure we can find a way," he said.

"But can you ask Mr Decks? And Ruth? Please?" It obviously meant a lot to him.

"Okay, I will. I'll be able to ask Ruth this weekend when I go up again. On Saturday before I go to London we could have a look round some secondhand shops for bikes, if you know any?"

Eric was back with them. "Bikes?" he said, his eyes round.

They explained what they'd been thinking.

Arthur was surprised to be asked about Ruth's bike, not because he thought it was a cheek – he didn't – but because it had never occurred to him that neither of the brothers had one.

"Of course he can, so long as he doesn't damage it. But what are we to do about Eric?"

Owen explained, adding "I'd want to ask Ruth as well. It's only fair."

Her father nodded. "Quite right. But I'd be disappointed if she says no."

They started their search – on foot for Eric's sake – at the shops along the Ritz Cinema building, one of which was a motorcycle and cycle engineers called Clarke's. Alan had remembered seeing a secondhand bike for sale there once. The brothers were cautiously looking around, trying to find anything appropriate. Owen was looking at some of the new, small motorbikes.

"He said he had one that would have done, but that was last week," Alan said ruefully when they had joined up again outside.

"Did you ask a price, or if he had any idea where any others might be on sale?" Owen asked him.

Alan shook his head.

"Come with me."

They returned to the shop and Owen asked the question of the, by now bemused, shopkeeper. He was told to try the local paper.

"No other shops?" he asked.

Two other possibilities were mentioned and Alan nodded to each one, indicating that he knew where they were.

"What now?" asked Alan when they were once again outside.

"Local paper," Owen said. "They might be cheaper in there."

They found the newsagent and bought that day's edition. Reading the small printed advertisements in Seaford's persistent wind was a challenge until Eric pointed out the station waiting room.

To their surprise a "sm bys bike good cnd £2" was available in nearby Clinton Lane. The three looked at each other and Owen raised his eyebrows.

"Worth a look," said Alan, doubtfully. "Not sure that Dad would stand that, though."

"Let's have a look? Please?" asked its intended owner in a hopeful voice.

Alan nodded with some resignation. "Don't get your hopes up."

They crossed the road and headed down the hill, turning right into the narrow lane. The house was noticeably decrepit, with paint peeling from the attentions of sun and wind. Alan knocked at the door which after a wait was opened by a haggard looking man.

"You... you've got a bike advertised," asked Alan. Eric was tongue tied.

"Yeah..." said the man, unhelpfully.

Eric blinked and frowned.

"Is it my size?" he asked.

"Dunno. Better look at it, ent'ya?"

He backed into the tiny house, navigating over cracked linoleum. They hesitated.

"Come on, then," he called over his shoulder. "It's out the back."

Eric's over-imaginative mind thought of being locked in the back yard of the house and being held to ransom, a ransom he knew his father couldn't pay. But his elder brother had no hesitations, even if he did wrinkle his nose at the smell of rancid cooking that seemed to hang in the air, thick as cobwebs. They all breathed easier once 'out the back' where a large and a small bike were propped against the fence.

The smaller one looked just right and Eric measured himself against it.

"Saddle will go down a bit," said Owen helpfully.

Eric mounted it. "Feels all right."

"I'll hold it," said Owen. "Put your feet on the pedals and make sure you're not too low. Or too high."

After some testing they decided they had hit gold at the first attempt. Eric looked at his brother and Owen hopefully.

"Well..." said his brother.

"Are you sure?" asked Owen.

Eric nodded.

"Two pound and its yours," said the man. "Good nick, innit?"

"Can we afford it?" asked Eric.

"Dunno," he was told. "Have to ask Dad."

"Will you keep it for us until we can find out, please?" Owen asked, aching to put his hand in his pocket to where he knew he had put his savings against this moment."

"Give me five bob deposit," said the seller, "then I won't sell it to anyone else for the rest of the day. Come back and tell me if you don't want it, or you'll lose the money. Come back and buy it and pay the other one pound fifteen and it's yours. Deal?"

It was the most he'd said since he'd first opened the door.

Again the three looked wordlessly at each other.

"Should we?" asked Alan.

"Buy it? Or do what he's saying?"

"Either."

Owen sighed and pulled the two pound notes from his pocket.

"Pay me back when we get home? Or when you can? Or I shan't be able to get to see Ruth."

He'd known Alan for four months, just as a casual mate, someone you rub along with happily but occasionally find a nuisance. The look he received from the thirteen year old pulled him up short; made him re-evaluate how he saw him. Gone was the 'anything goes' twelve year old he'd first met. This look said volumes about a developing character, someone with feelings.

"Thank you," said the mouth. The eyes said a lot more.

Eric's face was as excited as either had ever seen it.

The man pocketed the money and they wheeled the bike through the house's thick atmosphere to the outside world. Immediately Eric was astride it.

"Stop!" Alan commanded. "You've got to learn to ride it yet! And a public road isn't the place."

"Can't he ride?" asked Owen.

"I tried at school," admitted Eric. "Someone lent me one to try."

"What happened?"

"I fell off."

Over that week Max had been looking over the previous few years' mill accounts, wincing at the diminishing returns again and wondering why the owner had done nothing to improve its fortunes. He saw the sudden reduction in the staff's hourly rate and winced again.

Jack noticed. "Problems?" he asked.

"What we've done – what *you've* done – since our lot took over has improved things financially over what I see here. How can anyone not take even the simplest steps to increase trade? It's criminal. So was reducing wages like that. How did I miss that to start with? How did the Board?"

Jack shrugged. "Perhaps they just ignored it."

"Well they shouldn't have done. I need to put that right. Can I put Barbara to work on calculating what should have been paid to everyone since the take-over? It'd show that we'd value her input – I certainly want her to feel a part of the Mill as well as its community. Then we can surprise everyone in a few days."

His wife was glad of the small challenge. It meant proving herself – mainly *to* herself but just maybe to her husband and to Jack Pentelow. It was also, she found, a useful mental exercise. Her view of the accountancy correspondence course had been jaundiced to start with, where everything she was being taught was blindingly obvious to her. But she had surprised the remote administrators by returning their tests, accurately completed, with all speed. In return they had equally speedily sent more material. At last she found that the real nuts and bolts of formal bookkeeping were there to be tackled and she was relishing the challenge.

The exercise Max had cautiously proposed to her was not strictly bookkeeping but required the same organisational skills and accuracy, so she had set to and had fairly quickly arrived at the figures needed. She had given the results to Max the Thursday before the boys' trip to Seaford.

Quietly, late that Friday night, Max had delivered envelopes to each of the cottages of the Mill staff. The comments from his addressees when they read the contents would have made him blush.

Alan and Eric stood in front of their father, hands behind their backs. Ernie

Baker knew that this either meant that they were after a favour or had to admit to some misdemeanour. The brothers were rendered speechless when their admission of having borrowed money from Owen to buy a bike was met with just "Did you now?" and a smile.

Alan recovered first. "We'll pay it back to you out of our pocket money but please can you pay Owen back?"

Ernie smiled again. "Both of your pocket money?"

Alan gulped, knowing what this would mean to his sweet purchasing ability. "Yes," he said in a small voice. "It's only fair. We were all in it together."

"But you're not asking Owen to contribute, are you? You're saying he was there too, stands t'reason."

Alan looked uncomfortable. "But he's not family, Dad."

"No, he's not. And I don't like you borrowing off other people. But I don't see any reason why Eric shouldn't have a bike, so I'll pay Owen back and the bike's Eric's. How's that? And while we're at it, it's about time your pocket money went up, now we can afford it. I'll see what you're each worth and tell you, shall I?

"Now, let's have a look at this machine."

By that time Arthur and Owen had caught their train to London and the hospital, having arranged to meet Edna, Mary and Isaac there. They found Ruth in some pain, and under medication for it, but otherwise bright. So was Freddie in the next bed, especially when he saw Isaac.

"He's happy," Ruth told them so that Freddie could hear. "He's coming out of traction tomorrow and they're putting a cast on his leg. He'll be able to get around a bit."

Isaac, himself seemingly more animated than usual, congratulated Freddie and said how glad he was. "Soon have you playing football again," he said.

"A proper ground to play it on would be nice," he responded with a grin. "Only got the street outside."

"What about a football club?"

Now he looked down at the bedclothes. "Can't afford that," he muttered. He looked up into compassionate eyes.

Once they had returned to the house Isaac sat them down. Both he and Edna seemed to be bursting to tell them something. They exchanged glances. Isaac nodded to Edna.

"It seems that one of Fox's predecessors sold or left the original family house, the one they lived in in Bishopstone village, to a relative by the name of Vallance. This Vallance died before Christmas and no one knew at the time what the will said. Your Dad, Owen, wondered whether it had been left to Fox's London so-called family – the crowd that came to his funeral. If the will had mentioned a Mrs Fox, then there is no such person as he wasn't married to her. Or if he was, it was bigamy. I'm the only Mrs Fox left – apart from our son's ex-wife, and she doesn't come into it."

She paused for breath.

"The solicitor has worked hard. It appears that Vallance was misled by

Fox, my hated husband, about having a wife now living in London. Vallance wanted to will the house back to the only family he thought he was connected to and specified a Mrs Fox in London by her illegally gained surname as the beneficiary.

"That means that we have had to prove that he married me first, that the second marriage – and indeed there was one – was bigamy and therefore null and void, and that as a result the house has to come to me."

She stopped. The other seemed bemused, hardly able to take all this in.

"We heard a couple of weeks ago that the proof about the second marriage being bigamy had been accepted," Isaac started. "But it was only yesterday that a Court decided that Edna was the proper beneficiary of Vallance's will as she is the only Mrs Fox who was legally married.

"So, in essence, Edna owns a very attractive, five bedroomed house in Bishopstone village. And we have decided that as soon as the paperwork has been finalised we will be married in Bishopstone Church and move into it."

Owen let out a low whistle. There was silence for a while.

"Do Mum and Dad know about this?" Owen asked.

"You are the first we've told. Not even our son and grandchildren know yet. We had the phone call just before we came out to the hospital. But we're so full of it that we had to tell someone. And it's right that that 'someone' should include one of the two people who reintroduced me to my past by unscrewing a bed.

"By doing so…" He spoke slower. "You and Ruth reintroduced me to Edna, introduced me to my son and grandchildren, gained Edna a wonderful house, and opened up a future for all of us into the bargain. I'd never actually put that into words before, but it's true. We have you two to thank for that.

"And neither of us have any idea what we can do for either of you."

Owen thought hard and ended up shaking his head.

"We don't want anything. We just did what we did."

"But think," Isaac commanded. "If you had just taken those sovereigns to a dealer and sold them for – what was it? – £600, I would never have known about anything. My life would have gone on to its dead end. Edna would never have been reconciled with her son and would have died in poverty. Isaac would never have known his real father. Bee and Gerry would never have had grandparents."

"And my Dad would have thrashed me for being dishonest," said Owen with a smile. "And I think Ruth would probably have given me up as not worth knowing, if I'd been that dishonest."

He almost squirmed under the piercing eye contact from both Edna and Isaac but made himself hold up and return the gaze.

"I'm not a saint!" he protested.

"You have moral fibre," said Edna. "The sort of moral fibre I didn't have all the years I was married to that pig. I should have left him. But in those days I would have put my son at risk if I'd done so. Not at risk of physical harm; he was already receiving that at Fox's hands. But the risk of no education and a lack of food.

"What we mean is that if there's anything you need, tell us. I can't believe it would be something trite, like wanting a new bike, but something that is for the good of your and Ruth's families. Something like that."

"Well, there is something, since you mention a bike," Owen said slowly, reminded about something. "Whilst Ruth can't use it I'm going to ask her if Alan can borrow her bike. We can get the special pedal taken off because Ruth won't need it when she can walk properly. But that would give Alan something he needs. Today, hoping it was going to be allowed, we bought Eric a secondhand bike to make it fair. I paid for it and Alan's going to pay me back. If he can. When he can. But with all three of us with bikes we can go *anywhere*. And when Ruth can ride hers, perhaps I'll be able to get a bike for Alan. Secondhand, obviously."

A look passed between Edna and Isaac.

"How much did this bike cost?" asked Isaac gravely.

"Two pounds," said Owen.

"So after all you've – effectively – done for us, you're asking for two pounds to help someone else. Is that it?"

Owen didn't know how to answer, didn't know what was in his mind. He decided that what Isaac had said was the truth of the matter, shrugged and nodded.

"Stand up, will you?"

Cautiously Owen complied, watching as Isaac hauled himself to his feet and motioned Edna to do the same. The crossed the room to where Owen was watching them, bemused, apprehensive.

"Give me your hand."

Still worried, Owen held out his hand, only to find it held in a grip like a vice and pumped three times. Still those Captain-on-the-Bridge eyes were holding his... or were they moist at the edges? Owen was shocked. He was more shocked to be pulled into an embrace which lasted a brief two seconds.

Impatiently the old Captain brushed his sleeve over his face in a gesture that he felt had become almost too frequent these last few months. "And that, Owen, is how you shake the hand of someone you *genuinely* respect. For their own worth. Not because you have to. So don't use it on a schoolteacher."

Edna almost elbowed her partner out of the way and without ceremony just gave Owen a gentle hug.

"Your Dad's a lucky man. Ruth is a lucky girl, too."

Despite his feeling that he had only done what he felt was right, a bell rang in his head, reminding him of a similar comment he'd heard recently. Ah yes. His Headmaster. '...not a usual sort of person, are you Wilson? ... tell him from someone who was in the Wavy Navy that he's a lucky man.'.

Oh well. Perhaps he wasn't so bad after all. He smiled.

"Thank you," he almost whispered, embarrassed.

Isaac looked round at Arthur and Mary. "I don't think we need lend Ruth's bike to Alan, do we? I think that Alan should have his own bike. We'll say that Owen wants someone he can cycle with, and that he's got the people and just needs the bikes. And that Owen's done us a favour so we're returning it.

Would they accept that?"

Arthur smiled at him. "They might, Isaac, they might…" Christian names between them all had been insisted on by their host. "But if not, we can just provide them and say they're for use by anyone. Can't imagine anyone else taking advantage of that. And the boys will soon make them their own, come what may."

Owen felt a glow inside him.

In the dark of the very early morning the shrilling of the telephone bell woke them all. Edna knew that Isaac would have to strap on his metal leg before he could get downstairs to answer it, and was about to do so when a door opened and Mary ran downstairs. Edna's heart skipped a beat. Ruth. Of course. Something must be wrong. She wrapped a dressing gown round herself and hurried downstairs.

She had heard the scared tone of Mary's "Hallo?" and stood by her side.

"Oh… oh, thank God. But what's happened?"

She listened for some time. Arthur joined them, white faced.

"Oh no. Oh poor little lad. Oh, I'm so sorry…"

Little lad? Who was it? Edna was puzzled.

"Yes, he's here… well, upstairs. I'll fetch him. Please will you hold the line?"

Edna looked enquiringly at her has she put the phone on the table.

"It's Freddie," she said. "The Police have just been in. His father was drunk and fell in the Thames. By the time they pulled him out, he was dead. Freddie's in tears, though I don't know why with a father like that. He kept on saying 'Ask Captain Isaac', 'Get Captain Isaac', so they put two and two together and called us here."

All this was being said as they mounted the stairs again. Owen was standing at his bedroom door, wondering what he should do. The relief when he saw faces that had returned almost to normal was immeasurable.

"Is she all right, then?" he asked.

"She's fine. It's not her… ah, there you are."

Isaac had emerged from his room.

"It's little Freddie…"

She went over what she'd heard. His face grew grimmer.

"So now he's an orphan," he said shortly. Then, with a question in his voice: "He's asked for me?"

Edna nodded. "Should we go in?"

"Yes."

"They're still on the phone."

"I'll be down."

They regained the front hall again. Isaac picked up the phone, introduced himself with his name and rank, then listened.

At the end of it he said, matter-of-factly: "I'm coming in."

A squawk on the phone, and a babble.

"If the Police can tell him at this time of night, I can come and offer him comfort at this time of night. I'm coming in. Now."

The receiver was replaced on the cradle with a bang. He turned round to look at his partner, battle in his eyes. His mouth opened, then closed again.

"I'm going in to see him, Edna. It'd be good if you could come too. Please?"

She nodded. So did he, in satisfaction.

"Good girl." Her eyes beetled.

"Sorry…" Another hesitation.

"Edna, if I was still on my own and this had happened, I would just say 'I'll take him on. He can live with me.'" He didn't add 'To be the son I never had', but the words crossed the mind of all who knew his history.

He stopped again, wondering what else to say, how to say it.

"He's got to you, hasn't he?"

"He's a nice lad. He's actually quite intelligent, I think. He asks sensible questions, anyway. He's just so… so *unfortunate*… To have a father like that, who ignored him. To be living in poverty while his father piss… sorry – drinks away whatever money there is coming in, or so it seems. And now his father's dead and he has neither parent alive…" He stopped and swallowed. "Well, he's not the only one, I suppose."

Another pause. And then, almost fiercely:

"But he's the only one we know about. The one we've befriended. The one who we *can* help, if you agree…"

He looked at her, hopefully.

"What will Isaac, Bee and Gerry say?" she asked.

"I beg your pardon?"

"Well, you were thinking about adopting him, weren't you?"

He crossed to her and caught her in his arms, then held her away from him.

"I *love* you."

Their journey was by taxi. There were no buses running at two in the morning.

They found the ward, in semi darkness. The duty Sister was astonished to see them.

"I never thought you meant it," she said. "He's been put in a ward on his own so he didn't disturb the others. The girl in the bed next door was upset and was crying with him, wanting to get out of bed and comfort him. So to stop her damaging herself we had to move him."

"That's Ruth. Our friend. Is she asleep now?" Edna asked.

"I think so."

"May I go and check? If not, I can tell her something to calm her down."

"Are you sure?"

"Yes. I know the way."

She was off before the Sister could object.

"And I need to talk to Freddie," Isaac said, grabbing the opportunity before she could say anything else.

"But he'll be asleep," she said.

"Doesn't matter. I will tell him something that will make him sleep better too."

"This is most irregular."

"Being told your father has been killed is a bit irregular too, don't you think? I imagine he had to be woken up to hear that, too."

She read the signs of battle in his voice and face and led the way to a small ward on its own.

Freddie was lying on his back, as he had been since his accident. Thirteen years old he may have been, but his eyes were red, his face puffed, his hair tousled. As Isaac entered the room he looked down to see who it was and his eyes first widened, then closed, with the tears starting again.

Isaac sat carefully on the edge of the bed, took the hand nearest him and the boy looked up at him, astonished.

"Is Ruth all right?" he asked.

"Fine, so far as I know."

"I thought you were here because she… because…"

He looked slightly relieved.

"I've come to see you. I heard you needed me."

Despite himself, Freddie just shrugged.

"Was I wrong?"

Silence. He let it spin out.

"*Was* I wrong?"

There was a nearly imperceptible shake of the head.

"Just as well I'm here, then. I heard what happened. There's nothing I can say that will change that, or how you feel."

Silence again. And tears.

Then at last: "He wasn't a good father, but he was still my Dad."

Isaac nodded. He thought back to his own father, that very distant man who he hadn't minded leaving, not really. The lie to that had come to him six months later when he regretted never having said his farewells.

"Sometimes they're not very good, fathers. Sometimes they're very good, like Ruth's, like Owen's. Mine wasn't, so if you think yours wasn't, we have that in common. But it didn't stop me missing him, in a way." He couldn't describe what he felt, and wondered whether Freddie couldn't put his feelings into words either.

Silence again.

"What's going to happen to me?"

So this was it. Isaac thought.

"You said your mother isn't around."

He shook his head. "Died years ago."

Isaac gripped the hand he was still holding a little tighter, and sighed. "Well, there are three things that could happen. Firstly you could go into an orphanage and stay there. Second you could ask the council if they can find you a foster home or someone to adopt you."

The eyes were downcast. The door opened and Edna came in. She took in the scene in front of her.

"Or you could come and live with us. We're in London at the moment, but soon we'll be moving down to Sussex, where Ruth, and Owen and their

220

friends live, and you'd come with us."

As the first sentence had been uttered Freddie's eyes became wide as saucers, red-rimmed though they were. They stayed that way as he looked straight into Isaac's, seeking the possibility of deceit in them, and finding none.

"Do... do you mean it"

"Yes," said Edna from behind Isaac. "Yes, he does. We do. If you want to. We have a son, older than you, a grandson your age and a granddaughter a little older. They'll live nearby. And as Isaac says, there are the others who live nearby too."

Freddie beckoned her closer. Not without some discomfort and risk to the wires and frame that held his leg, he sat up. An arm went round Isaac's neck. Edna came closer and the other, plastered arm circled her as well as he could make it.

He sank back onto the pillow, exhausted from the unaccustomed effort, by emotion and by the release from most of it.

He sighed, and just said: "Yes, please."

The two adults consulted, wordlessly. If there were tears in their eyes now neither of them was ashamed.

Edna looked back at the patient, now lying at peace, his eyes closed.

"Do you think you can sleep now?"

A nod. The eyes opened slightly.

"Thank you."

"Good night, ol' son."

"Good night, Freddie."

"G'night."

They were nearly at the door when a voice from the bed asked: "Will you be in tomorrow?"

"Later today, you mean!" said Edna. "Yes, we will. Of course we will. Good night."

"Good night, Mum."

Edna froze. Slowly the tears came. Isaac held her and they stood just outside the closed door.

"This time we'll *both* be there during the growing up."

18 – Accommodation

Freddie was back in the place next to Ruth by the time they all descended on the hospital the next day. Ruth had heard of the exchange of the previous night – in fact she had heard little else – and was really pleased for him whilst still being sad at the loss of his father. Edna and Isaac waved to Ruth as they approached her end of the ward, but made directly towards Freddie. He was smiling so mightily that the ends of his mouth threatened to meet at the back.

"Look!" he almost shouted, "No frame! No wires! I can move!" Then his face softened and a tinge of anxiety came over it. "You meant what you said last night? Didn't you?"

It was Edna who made it to his bedside first, compassion on her face. "Of course we did. Absolutely. We were both brought up to be truthful, and you've got to trust a naval Captain, haven't you?"

He smiled at her. She wondered how he could be so cheerful and so naturally easy to get on with, given the probably dreadful upbringing he had endured to date and, now, the death of his father.

"I'm glad to see you as cheerful as you are," she said carefully. "Have you got over the shock of last night?"

The face clouded over. "Not really. I still can't hardly believe it."

Obviously he was thinking. The smile had gone. He seemed to be focussed on the other side of the ward.

"It's like… It's like he really died when Mum did," he said slowly. "He was great up to then. But after that happened he went out every night, and came back late, and I learnt to be in bed before he came in. He started work early too, before I went to school. So I had to get breakfast, have a school lunch and get some chips in the evening – when he could give me any money.

"We only saw each other on Sunday mornings before he went to the pub. Then he'd come back and sleep in the chair. I never saw him, really. It was horrible."

Now he was looking really downcast.

"How long was all this going on?" asked Isaac gently.

"Years. Since Mum died."

"Do you remember when that was?"

Silence.

"Christmas – what? About three years ago? She was ill in December, we didn't have a Christmas meal, then she went into hospital the next day. Two weeks after that Dad said she'd died. I never even got the chance to visit her. They wouldn't let me."

Now the tears were running again. Hardly surprising, Edna thought. Her arm went round his back. Eventually he was able to look at her, then at Isaac and gave a watery smile.

"Must have been ten, mustn't I? Poor old me."

"Poor old Freddie indeed," said Isaac in a voice Edna had rarely heard before. "But now – now we can at least start to put things right. It'll take some doing, and we'll have to talk a lot so we know how things are settling down. The first thing we've got to do, if you're *really* certain you want to live with us, is to make sure the hospital people know what we've decided, and that your school knows what's happened and that you won't be back. At least, not to attend; but there will be friends you want to keep up with, won't there?"

He shrugged. "Some. Not many. It's not that sort of school. And at home I had to get a meal. That meant being there when Dad got in from work and washing up when he'd gone out again. Then homework." He shrugged. "I knew Mum wanted me to do better than him, and I knew how working on the docks made him exhausted. I didn't want to do that as a job. So I knew I wanted to get exams and that.

"But a year after Mum died, he wouldn't let me take the eleven plus."

He stopped talking. Edna and Isaac could see he was angry.

"So I just go to a crummy school with boys who don't want to learn. So we don't."

Isaac nodded. "Then the sooner we can get you into Seaford's school the better. One of the boys at Tide Mills goes there. He's doing all right."

"Does Ruth? What about Owen?"

"They passed the eleven plus, so they go to the Grammars in Lewes."

"Oh."

He could see it was a sore point, and not for the first time found himself angry at the injustice of a once-only exam taken when the candidates were scarcely old enough to realise its importance.

Around Ruth's bed the talk was all about Freddie and what had suddenly happened.

"I hope they're doing the right thing," Arthur said so that Freddie and his visitors couldn't hear. "They just don't know what he's really like, and they won't until he gets home with them. He could be a little thug."

"I don't think so," Ruth put in equally quietly. "He's been really nice with me – looking after me. You know."

Owen blinked and his eyebrows raised. "You know I'd be here all the time if I could."

That surprised her. "You don't think... no. It's not like that. I know they wouldn't let you be here any more than you are, and if you were you'd be as bored as I am. As Freddie is. It's just that he looks out for me, like I do for him."

He nodded, although not completely convinced.

When their visitors had been chased out by the Sister Ruth asked Freddie how their talk had gone.

"They're super," he said enthusiastically. "It sounds as if they really want me to live with them. They promised they're going to talk to the hospital people to see what they have to do next. Though I don't know why it's anyone else's business but theirs and mine."

"I suppose there are rules," said Ruth.

"Well, there shouldn't be."

"What about if it was someone else who thought they could take you on?

Someone you didn't like?"

"I wouldn't go."

"But they'd make you."

"I'd run away."

"And do what?"

"I dunno. I can look after myself."

"With a leg and an arm in plaster?"

He looked uncomfortable. "Eventually I could."

"But wouldn't it be better if you tell someone else that you don't want to go with a family who you don't like? I suppose it's them that Edna and Isaac have to talk to."

He thought a moment.

"P'raps."

Presented with the news, their son in Eastbourne was at first silent, then amused, then worried.

"You've done *what*?" had been his first question when told about the rescue of Freddie.

His mother explained again.

"Well... I could imagine you taking him on for a while, so he could recover properly, but to foster him... well!"

She had been about to tell him that if it worked out they were thinking of adopting him, but the reaction didn't seem to be appropriate for that information. Perhaps once they'd all met him it might be better.

"Do you know what you're letting yourself in for?" he asked. "Don't forget he's a cockney boy, more or less, and you don't know what sort of character he's got."

"Isaac, you'll have to trust our judgement. He's a lot nicer than you make him sound, and intelligent, too. If he's a London version of young Alan Baker, then all to the good. We've got the job of countrifying him, but I'm sure he'll prove a nice lad, like he's been in the hospital. I'm sorry it's so sudden, but he's got nobody else in the world. We couldn't just sit there and talk to him, knowing he was going to be sent to an orphanage for the rest of his childhood. Yes, I know they're called Children's Homes nowadays, but orphanages is what they are.

"Do you want to talk about it to Bee and Gerry? I hope they're happy about it."

He agreed to do just that. It was an hour later when Isaac answered the phone again. This time it was Bee.

"We've talked about Freddie," she said, "and if he's really as nice as you told Grandma then we're happy with him. In fact we're looking forward to meeting him."

The following Monday Edna and Isaac indeed started trying to discover who 'the authorities' were concerning Freddie. Someone had to care that they would be taking him on. Freddie had told the couple that he had no relatives that he knew of and had never been to a doctor. He told them where his school was, though.

Visiting the school was a frustrating experience. The Headmistress seemed to have no idea what should be done. Whilst sad that he had lost his father she could help no further "Unless we are contacted by the Police," she ended.

At last Isaac called the hospital. The surgeon who was looking after Freddie eventually came to the phone and Isaac was able to put the position to him.

The response was that it would relieve the hospital of finding a Children's Home for the boy, so if they were serious about it, well, he was grateful.

"Doesn't what Freddie want matter?" Isaac asked with some asperity.

"Well, I'll talk it over with him, of course. But surely if it's what you want then it's going to be better for him than a Home of some sort. And eventually, if you want to, you can adopt him."

"If it's what he wants, too."

"Yes. But then what would the alternative be? He just stays with you until he's... what age? Twenty-one when he attains majority? That's up to you to decide."

"And him."

"Well, yes. But he's a minor."

"And you're sure the only person we need to convince that we're serious is you?"

"Well... yes. If you want to adopt, then the Children's Officer service for your area would have to be contacted, of course."

"What a system!" Isaac exploded to Edna once off the phone. "He doesn't seem to think that any child needs to have any input into what happens to him. So long as something's provided, that's it. We can foster. And only if we want to adopt would we have to contact the authorities."

"Very wrong," said Edna.

There was the matter of Freddie's belongings to consider. The boy had given Isaac a door key and provided an address. A visit had to be made to the house to find any documents the lad needed, and to pick up everything else that seemed appropriate. The house turned out to be as grim as Isaac had feared, almost worse than the squalor that Edna had been reduced to in Tide Mills. They had taken a taxi there, and its driver was dubious about the address, and waiting there, until Freddie's story was told.

In the musty atmosphere of the place they found the pathetic remains of food, unwashed plates, festering rubbish and general dirt. There was no electricity; the windows were filthy. In a drawer in the kitchen were some school reports and the all-important National Health documents. At the bottom they discovered birth and death certificates. Isaac took them all. Upstairs, in the one room that was remotely clean, they discovered Freddie's worn clothing, a few toys, and a nearly threadbare teddy-bear. Elsewhere there were photographs in frames. All were put into a case.

"Phew," said Isaac as they locked the place again, aware that he was shutting the door on the first thirteen years of Freddie's life. "Poor old lad. I should think he's well out of that."

They started walking back to the waiting taxi. It was then about four in the afternoon. They saw a shadow dodge behind one of the buildings down a blind alleyway as they walked up to the main road where the taxi was waiting. As they passed it Isaac saw a boy, ragged, who was watching them. He stopped on an impulse.

"Hallo - do you know Freddie Strange?"

"Might do."

"Well, if you do, you'll be sad to know his father was drowned some time ago."

"Knew that, didn't I?"

"I see. So did you know that Freddie is coming to live with us? And later, he'll be moving down to Sussex with us?"

The boy shook his head.

"Used to play football with him."

"He can't at the moment. He's got an arm and a leg in plaster."

"He's okay though, is he?"

It was Isaac's turn to nod. "He'll be right as rain in a few months."

"Tell him… tell him Jake… tell him hallo from Jake, mister?"

"I'll do that. Got your address, has he?"

The boy nodded.

"Then I'm sure he'll write to you. Maybe ask you down to visit."

That made the eyes fix onto Isaac's, and the mouth drop open.

"Would he… would you let me?"

"Why not? We'll be in touch. 'Bye."

"'Bye mister, missus…"

They were aware of the stare all the way to the taxi.

Edna sighed. "How many more of the unfortunates are there?"

"Millions, probably."

A phone call to Max that evening tasked him, Owen and Alan with buying two bicycles that were Alan-sized.

"What does he want bikes for?" Alan muttered to himself, keen on finding some that were his size so he knew what he could look for if ever there was the chance of the Bakers being able to buy one. He had seen Owen's, of course, and felt that something like that would be best. And, in Seaford's excellent cycle shop, they found it. Max bought two and asked them to be delivered to Tide Mills once they had been properly prepared.

The next weekend was the third of Ruth's time in hospital. They arrived to find her in a chair at the side of the bed, one leg propped up in front of her and the other on the floor. Next to her was Freddie, in a similar condition but with a plastered arm in a sling across his chest as well.

The Sister was pleased with her, she said, as was the surgeon.

"She can go home on Tuesday," she said. It wasn't something they were expecting. "We'll be telling you and her what to do. But she needs to visit the Royal Alexandra in Brighton every two weeks to be checked on and x-rayed."

It was news to Freddie too. His face dropped, even with his new family there. There was some more, excited chat between them all; even Edna and Isaac were listening in, trying not to ignore Freddie in the process.

Once Susan had finished with Ruth she turned to Freddie and the other two.

"I hear you're taking Freddie on," she said. "That's very nice of you."

Isaac spluttered. "It's not *nice* of us!" he exclaimed. "We've grown to like him. It was me he asked for the other weekend, and that showed me that he liked me – us – too. It's a question of mutual appreciation, not anyone just being 'nice'.

"He's agreed to come back with us to London, and then down to Sussex when we move."

"I see," she said, slightly taken aback. "Then when you move we'll need to make arrangements with the Royal Alex for him too."

"If that's the Brighton hospital that Ruth's going to, then yes, please. If that's all right with you, Freddie?" Isaac was remembering the surgeon's attitude.

"Yes please," he said.

"Do you want to go home at the same time as Ruth?" asked Susan, delivering her thunderbolt. Freddie's head jerked up. The look of hope on his face made Edna and Isaac smile.

"Yes... please?" he said, the question implicit in his tone.

"I'm glad it's so soon," said Edna, keeping the panic from her voice and expression as she thought of all the reorganisation to be done in the house.

Isaac grinned at him. "I wondered how long it'd be, now that you can get about a bit. Good. We'll need to do some rearranging because there's no way you can get up and down stairs one sided. And not even for you am I going to rig up a bosun's chair and hoist you up to the toilet."

"Oh..." The patient realised with a shock what that would mean. "But you don't want to... to..."

"You forget I've had a son," Edna said softly, "and he's had his illnesses. So yes, we can cope with that. Easily."

"I'll try not to... to..."

"You just live normally. As normally as a plastered leg and arm can allow," said Edna. "It's not for ever. And once you're walking properly you can bring us breakfast in bed once or twice."

She was aware of a sudden shifting of Isaac's eyes from Freddie to the side of her face, and realised what she'd hinted at. And why not, she asked herself fiercely, aware of a heat to her cheeks.

Much scratching of heads was done at both the London house and the Sussex cottage. The latter, despite being two knocked into one, had only an upstairs lavatory (the outside privy had been converted into a shed, like all the others, during the improvements) and it seemed unfair for Ruth to have to trail awkwardly and painfully up and down stairs. Mary and Arthur tried all sorts of solutions, but could come up with nothing that was practical whilst giving privacy and dignity to Ruth, especially as it would be for so long a period.

Finally, Arthur went down to see Max, who listened carefully and thought.

"I know the simplest solution, but I doubt whether you or Mary, or Ruth for that matter, will like it."

Arthur raised his eyebrows.

"We have a bathroom, a small one, downstairs here. Most of the time we don't use the dining room – except when we have Mill get-togethers – so it could be made into a bedroom. Then Ruth has a level walk to what could be her bathroom – just hers. You and she would have a key to the house, so you could see her when you wanted.

"I'd need to run it past Barbara, of course, and I know Owen would put up no objection. But that seems to tick all the boxes."

Arthur just wondered what to say. A feeling of relief washed over him. Never in his life had he been treated in this way by a guv'nor; but then Max was also a friend. In fact one day they might be tied by family. Maybe.

He heaved a heavy sigh, aware that would answer just about all the questions apart from their wanting to be with Ruth in case she needed help.

He shook Max's hand. "I'll have to talk to Mary, of course, and Ruth. But it would be the solution to a major problem."

"Let's go and talk to our respective guv'nors, shall we, and meet up once we have.

Unsurprisingly both guv'nors were happy with the idea. Mary came straight over to visit Barbara so as to talk about food and money and all the other arrangements.

Owen jumped nearly a foot in the air when asked, mock-tentatively, about her moving in. Almost fifteen he may have been, but the shock and excitement got to him.

"Do we take that as a 'yes', then?" his mother asked with a smile. He just gave her a hug, then rushed outside where he was almost run over by a small wobbling bike with a worried looking eleven year old on it. The near accident caused an even more major wobble than before. Human and machine parted company.

Eric sat up, rubbing his arm. "I can't get this," he said despondently. "No matter how careful I am, I fall off."

"If by careful you mean slow, then you need to go faster – at least while you're learning. Not too much faster, but a little. When you want to stop, use the back brake first – that's that one." He showed him. Eric was soon on the bike again.

"This time I'll run with you, holding the stalk under the seat, then you don't have to worry. Mind the railway tracks. Don't get stuck in them."

For the next thirty minutes he was running up and down Mill Drove. Gradually Eric became more confident. Eventually his human stabiliser told him he was exhausted.

"Carry on for a bit on your own," he said. "Don't forget that when you have to stop, don't slow down until you start wobbling. Stop decisively. But use that back brake first!"

"Why?"

"Because if you lock up the front wheel the rest of the bike will do a somersault over it and you'll hit your head on the road. That hurts."

"Have you done that?"

"Yes. That's how I know."

Edna and Isaac, themselves trying to shift furniture to make a living space for Freddie, were phoned by Mary from the Mill House. They were amused to hear the question they were asked to pose to Ruth that evening.

"I'm guessing, but I'm fairly certain there's a young man who's jumping up and down with excitement at the prospect," said Isaac.

Mary laughed. "Max said he almost took off when the idea was put to him – then rushed out and spent the next half an hour holding Eric's new bike, running up and down the Drove. I think he's calmed down now."

Ruth's enthusiastically positive answer was tempered with the words 'if Mum and Dad don't mind', and it was telephoned through to the Wilsons the next day. Max spread the information, although everyone had taken it as a *fait accompli*.

Two new bicycles were delivered to the Mill House the next day. Max and Owen took one over to the Bakers' cottage and knocked on the door. Jessie took one look at them and called Alan.

"It's not bad, is it? The other one's the same?"

"Exactly," Owen told him. "The thing is that we've run out of space to put this and wondered if you could look after it for us. In return, of course, you could use it."

It was worth the subterfuge just to see the look on Alan's face.

"*Use* it! Are you sure?"

"Yes. It seems only right... Oh, look here. The truth is that Edna and Isaac wanted to give Ruth and me something to say thanks for finding the money and getting them together and all that stuff. I've got a bike and I thought you could do with one so we can all go where we want to. So really it's yours. The other one is for Freddie when he can ride one."

Now Alan's eyes were flicking between the bike and Owen.

"But really, it's yours. Or Ruth's."

"But..."

Slowly he put his hands on the handlebars and was about to climb on. But...

"Mum!"

Max repeated what Owen had said, but in different words. Jessie Baker didn't know what to say. After a few protestations from her Max had to explain what Isaac had said to Owen and what the latter's reply had been. Owen felt embarrassed. He found that for once Alan had a completely serious look on his face and that his eyes were locked into his own. Slowly the boy's right hand was extended, seeking his own. He thought, desperately and had a brainwave.

"I thought Scouts used their left hands." He extended his. Immediately the smile returned to Alan's face and he swapped, shaking Owen's hand vigorously.

"Thank you. Thank you so much. Can we go for a ride somewhere?"

"I'll beat you to the Buckle."

He waited a moment for Alan to mount the bike, then set off. Fast. That was the last that was seen of them for an hour.

Max had arranged to take the Tuesday as a holiday but had forbidden his son to accompany him to London to collect the two patients from hospital.

"There's not enough room in the car, if you think," he said, carefully avoiding the issue of promises and school. "We'll have to move Freddie first, then Ruth. Both of them have to sit across the back seat, so that leaves one seat for the driver and one for a passenger. Mary's coming up, and she's the only passenger."

Owen thought furiously, but could work out no way of including himself.

"And we shan't be back until after you've returned," said Max, "so coming home early is pointless." This time the gimlet stare had a smile with it, something Owen read with a reluctant acknowledgement that his father was right.

Freddie, rescued first from the hospital, almost bounced into the house. His face was a picture. There were lots of exclamations of 'cor' and 'real class' as he hopped his way into the front room using the single crutch that he had been given since he had just one arm able to use it. He sat himself down hurriedly, suddenly feeling tired beyond his expectations.

"Lie back on the settee, Freddie. You're bound to be tired having been still for so long. I'll get you a cup of tea."

"Aww... you don't have to bother."

"I think I do, for the moment, don't you? It's all right. Don't forget it isn't for ever."

When she returned with the tea he was asleep.

Max's journey back home with Mary and Ruth was uneventful. He found he had to make himself think ahead more and brake earlier so as not to dislodge Ruth, who was, as planned, lying across the back seat.

They stopped at County Oak, just north of Crawley. Fighting his way through crowds of coach passengers, Max bought three cups of tea and found he had to argue to get the people serving to let him take the cups out to a patient in the car.

"We don't want to steal them," he said plaintively. She relented, thinking how good looking he was.

At the car Ruth was showing her mother the quarter turn she had to give three screws that ran between the sets of three rods at top and bottom of her thigh.

"Four times a day," she said. "So it'll be when I wake, then dinnertime, then supper time, then when I go to bed. Eleven o'clock."

Mary looked shocked. "You can't leave it that late! You'll never be up in the morning."

"I've got to," she was told. "It should really be every six hours, but that would be in the middle of the night. No, this is what they told me."

Mary looked as she used the tiny spanner.

"Does it hurt?"

"It feels odd, but doesn't hurt yet. It will, but they've given me something to take. I've got to keep the skin very clean, though. I've got the stuff they use in the hospital."

They drank their tea, Mary insisted on returning the cups, and they continued.

Bumping down the drive towards the Mill House Ruth could see a knot of people standing there, all waving. To her surprise the entire Mill staff and their families had turned out and for a moment the noise was overwhelming. A tall figure pushed himself in front of them and without hesitation crossed to the car. He and Max helped her out and onto the crutches they had provided, and the first thing the beaming Owen did was to kiss her, and in front of everybody. There was a cheer despite their more-than-friendship being by then public knowledge. It didn't stop either of them blushing, though.

With almost continuous expressions of thanks to all her friends and acquaintances she was allowed to swing herself on the crutches cautiously to the open front door and through it, there to be welcomed with relief and concern by her father and Barbara. Mary followed and wanted to fuss over her.

"It's all right, Mum, really. I dozed off on the journey. It's just so good to be home. Er..." She had seen the look on her parents' faces. "...Second home, anyway."

At last she was persuaded to lie on a sofa, legs supported but body upright, in the same pose, had she known it, as Freddie was some sixty miles away. She was awake, though. Gradually people drifted away; Arthur and Max went back to work for the last half hour of the day, Mary and Barbara to the kitchen. Only Owen and Ruth were left. He scooted himself to kneel on the floor beside her and was about to speak, but she held up her hand.

"If you or anyone else asks me how I am, or how I'm feeling, I shall scream."

As that was exactly what he was going to ask, he grinned.

"How am I meant to find out, then?"

"I'm all right if I don't say anything. If I complain, then I'm not."

"As simple as that?"

"As simple as that. The thing's a nuisance, it's uncomfortable, but eventually it'll be fine. I'll be able to race you on that bicycle of yours, walk over the hills with you, run, play football with Alan – and maybe with Freddie – and kick other people who try to bully me at school."

That surprised him. "Has it really been that bad?"

"Sometimes. And your friend Botting was always someone I could rely on to start things off."

"Friend! I don't think so."

"Well, you know what I mean. I hope he's improved."

"I don't think he'll try anything on when I'm around. Not with me. And if he tries it with you, I'm not sure it'll be Judo I use."

"No. Don't do anything they can blame you for. Defence is one thing but attack is another."

"I know. I just hope I have the words to fight him with so he attacks me first."

"Just make sure *you* don't end up in hospital."

When Arthur and Max reappeared, tea was ready for Ruth, Mary and Arthur, and dinner for Barbara, Max and Owen. It was the same meal, at the same table. Much teasing had taken place about what it was to be called and it was in good spirits that they sat down together. Ruth's leg was supported by a plank, itself supported at one end with the other under a cushion on her chair.

"This is just for tonight," Mary said. "We'll take over from tomorrow and you must join us for a change."

Barbara was about to suggest taking it in turns but thought that Mary might feel that a little independence, and time spent alone with Ruth, would be welcomed. So all she said was "She's always welcome. As are you two."

Freddie was woken by a wonderful aroma of food, something that smelt even better than the amazingly plentiful hospital food he had eaten for the previous month. It had been the first time since his mother died that he could remember being pleasantly full. But this... what was it?

It was meat. Real meat. Red in the middle, fading to brown outside. Beef. He remembered seeing advertisements. And this must be Yorkshire pudding. And roast potatoes. And carrots. And peas. And gravy. And so much of it... He looked up.

"Is this really for me?"

Isaac's lips twitched, but he looked suddenly sad.

"The first time I woke up in Mill Cottage and found Edna giving me food, that's exactly what I thought, and what I said. It was for me. Just as that's for you. Oh – damn. I forgot. You can't use your right arm. You'll need it cut up. May I?"

"Thank you."

He watched with alarm as the plateful was taken from him and put on the dining table whilst Isaac set to with knife and fork. Part of him wondered if it was all a joke, and that was Edna's and Isaac's meal. But the plate reappeared on the tray on his lap. He was about to pick up a piece of gravy-soaked Yorkshire pudding in his fingers, but saw that neither of the others were doing so. He followed their lead.

It had never mattered when eating alone for the previous three years when his father was seldom with him. And even in the hospital it had been more convenient. And at that point there came the embarrassing realisation that Ruth must have watched him eating with his fingers.

He wondered: what else would he do wrong?

It was two weeks later that Edna and Isaac received the final paperwork from their solicitor proving and certifying formally that the Bishopstone house was theirs. It was a letter that caused a relief which in turn caused great celebration, to Freddie's amusement. When he learnt from Isaac how it had come about that Edna had gained a large house that she had known nothing about, he was amazed.

"What luck," he said slowly. "What bleedin', amazing luck."

Edna had given him the background to her life. He couldn't help but contrast it to his own, and his recounting of thirteen years of life experiences caused Edna to wonder if she had been so badly off, after all. But then the remembrance of never having had a genuinely happy period of her life since Isaac left confirmed to her that she had been – spiritually – worse off than Freddie. At least he had been happy, if poor, when his mother had been alive.

He realised it too, but couldn't erase from his awareness that he was with two people who now had everything that he never had, that food would never again be scarce, that he would have attention and – it seemed – something like love. He remembered from his parents' attitude to him until his mother had died what family love was, and hoped that what he had seen in the previous few weeks that these two were genuine. They had given him no reason to think otherwise.

Isaac bought a car.

Freddie's eyes opened wide when he heard, and he was helped out to look at it.

"It's a Police car!" he exclaimed.

"It used to be," Isaac told him. "It's roomy and quite fast, so while we're going up and down between here and Sussex it's just the thing."

"Wow…"

Leaving the house unlocked Isaac took Edna and him for a short drive, enough to give them the feel of riding in it. They were both impressed by its smoothness. Freddie enjoyed being able to sit across the back seats as he had on the way back from the hospital.

"It's better than Mr Wilson's," he said when they were back. "More room and more comfortable."

That pleased Isaac, whose choice the Wolseley had been.

By arrangement, the following day they travelled down to Seaford.

If your thirteen years have been spent surrounded by buildings, with only a wide but dirty river and a few visits to anything remotely green to relieve the scenery, the vista that had greeted Freddie as they left the remnants of south London behind had made his jaw drop. Everything he saw that was growing, or in the case of buildings, old and comfortable, amazed him.

The Solicitor who had done all the work met them at the house with a locksmith, since there had been no trace of a key in Mr Vallance's clothing – which had been destroyed by then anyway. It took the locksmith a very short time to gain entry and to add a modern rim lock to the solid door.

"I'll have that old mortice lock off for you so you can get the holes filled and repaint the door – or are you going to replace it?"

"What do we think?" asked Isaac. "I vote to get keys made for the old lock and replace it. We can use it at night and the Yale during the day – if we need to lock it at all when we're at home."

Edna, remembering her time in Tide Mills, agreed. Freddie, remembering some of the escapades of his school acquaintances during their forays to the better off areas of east London, wondered. But he realised that the two adults knew this area better than he did.

They had explored the inside of the house and discussed redecoration.

"We could ask the company working at Tide Mills," Edna suggested.

Isaac looked pleased. "I hoped you'd recommend them. They seem to have done a good job there."

"Yes. I feel I could almost live in that cottage now, from what Mary tells me."

"Don't you dare. I need you with me."

She smiled, pleased.

Decisions were made about rooms, and Freddie was very happy to be helped upstairs by the other two so he could choose one.

"Whichever one you like," Isaac told him. He visited them all and almost immediately asked for the smallest one.

"Well, you can, of course," Edna told him, surprised. "But don't you want more space than that? It's very small – we were wondering about it as a storage cupboard."

"I thought you'd want the bigger ones for visitors. You know, important people."

They both looked astonished.

"But *you* are an important person. We want you to enjoy this place as much as possible, like we want to. Why shouldn't you?"

"But I'm only... only..."

"Only what, Freddie? If you were 'only' anything, we wouldn't... we'd probably not be where we are now, and more importantly, nor would you. You're bright, good company and a nice person, so you're becoming Family."

He stayed perfectly still, and silent, leaning his good side against the little room's door jamb. As Edna watched his eyes fill. He wiped his face with a sleeve.

"I haven't felt part of a family since Mum died." He said, his tone echoing the emotion on his face. Edna carefully put an arm round him.

"You'll meet Isaac soon, and Bee and Gerry," she told him. "We'll make sure you're on an even footing with them. Now, you choose the room you really want, then we can think how it's to be decorated."

"Decorated? What, for Christmas?"

She smiled. "No. Painted or papered. What colours."

He trapped his lower lip in his teeth and looked up.

"Blimey."

Edna sketched the layout of the place and wrote their proposals for using the rooms on it.

"I was thinking we could call in to the Mill House on the way back and see if we can contact the decorators," Isaac said. "Freddie could see how Ruth's getting on."

19 – Cycle rides

The day Isaac brought the car home had been Owen's fifteenth birthday, though neither party knew of the other's celebrations. Owen had once again asked about a motorcycle but had been discouraged; he had been expecting that, especially as Ruth would have been in danger had she ridden with him with her leg in such a tender state. And that would remain the case until he had become experienced at controlling a bike, and her leg was at last free from the supporting rods.

She had experienced no problems with her leg, just discomfort when the screws were turned and stretch was imparted to the skin around the rods. Each time she went to Brighton to be checked on it had been Max who took her. At last Owen realised that she was now in good hands and that, unless anything went wrong, she was happy to cope without him.

His experience at the Grammar school had settled down. At home he was increasingly involved with the Scouts who had accepted him readily, especially when his judo expertise had been discovered. Also he had found and joined a newly started judo club locally. Having been adopted as an Olympic sport it was gaining in popularity. He found himself not only learning, but helping to teach beginners.

The builders had finished the last of the cottages and were now tackling the more challenging work of preparing the Mill buildings for new machinery. Some of it had already arrived by rail, causing great excitement from all concerned. They were used to short trains of covered wagons trundling down the tramway running through Mill Drove. Such trains had been delivering grain and removing milled flour since the railways had first been built. But to see low loaders with tarpaulin-covered machinery on them cautiously navigating down the line between the cottages had been fascinating, and did more than anything else so far to prove that the Mill had an exciting future.

Killick's men were also building substantial viewing platforms for the public within the mill and the grain store. Part of the latter was to be used as a machine room. Much head-scratching by outside experts had produced ways of extending the machinery powered by the windmill, one of the Mill's obvious features. They had also worked out a way to power the machinery using electricity in the event of inadequate wind.

"Fat chance of no wind in Seaford," Jack Barden scoffed, and for once others agreed with him. But all were pleased that repairs and redecorations were happening along with the installations. The changes increased pride in the combination of the business and the hamlet.

Life was settling down.

The approach of what looked like a police car late one Monday afternoon caught Ruth and Owen by surprise. They were sitting outside the Mill House shelling peas, and looked up at the sound of an engine. Owen, remembering the offensive Inspector of some months previously, became apprehensive. His brow wrinkled as it approached. Although it *looked* like a police car the usual sign in front of the radiator announcing it as such was missing. It came to a gentle halt opposite them.

They both smiled as Edna and Isaac alighted and waved to them, then opened the nearside door. Owen realised.

"It's Freddie!" he exclaimed, leaping up and almost upsetting the bowl of peas onto the ground. Ruth smiled and saved it from falling.

Owen went to help, and soon a happy looking boy was hopping his way towards Ruth. Owen rushed to find a chair. Isaac fetched a plank from the boot of the car and Freddie was soon sitting with the other two, leg supported. Owen took Edna and Isaac in to see Barbara.

"You look well," Ruth remarked, seeing his improved colour and less scrawny appearance.

"Food's better than ever I had at home," he offered. "I'm probably getting fat."

"You don't look it," she said. "How's the leg and arm?"

"Ok, 'cept that I'm fed up with not being able to use them. And everything itches! Mum's had to give me a knitting needle so I can get down the plaster and scratch."

She noted the 'Mum', but didn't comment on it.

"How's your leg doing?" he asked Ruth.

"Oh, okay. I'm bored a lot of the time and I really, really want to cycle somewhere. Anywhere. Or do anything at all."

Owen, back now from the house, took her hand. Her frustration was well known, and existed even though she knew why it was all necessary.

There were whoops from the road as two bikes appeared around the parked car and skidded to a halt.

"It's not the police!" called a voice. "Oh... hallo. You must be the boy from London."

"His name's Freddie," Alan corrected his younger brother. "Hallo."

"Wotcher. You the two that Ruth was talking about? The Baker brothers?"

Eric nodded. "That's us! The Fabulous Baker Brothers."

"Blimey. What's the fabulous bit?"

"We just are, that's all. How did you do that?"

"What?"

"Break an arm and a leg."

"Playing on a bomb site and a lump of concrete fell on me. Took them ages to get it off."

"Hurt?"

"Like..." he remembered that he was now with people who thought in different ways compared with his London school acquaintances. "Like hell. I was glad when they gave me the anaesthetic."

"I bet you were." It was a different voice this time. Isaac had emerged from the house and was grinning down at them. Freddie looked back at him. What had he heard?

"When I got that lump of shrapnel in my leg I said a lot more than "hell". But I was in the Navy and there was no one else around." He pulled a face.

"That was the trouble. Anyway, if ever either Freddie or I pick up an injury like his or mine ever again, and I hope to God we don't, there will be a lot of east London and Navy words around. It's excusable. But anyone who uses that sort of language as a matter of course has lost his use of real English, so Freddie was quite right to refer to the pain as just 'hell'. It's enough."

He understands, Freddie thought. He knows what it was like. Once again a feeling of fierce love for the old man went through him.

"Just going to see Max and, with any luck, this bloke Killick. Then we can start getting the house sorted."

As he limped away Freddie was aware of the questioning looks on the others' faces. The next five minutes were spent in answering questions.

Martin Killick, telephoned, was discovered in his office, but volunteered to come straight over to talk to a potential new customer. He arrived fifteen minutes later, waved at the younger contingent as he drove past on his way to Reception, and went inside. A short time later his, Isaac's and Max's cars were full of people – including the Baker brothers with parental permission – and on their way to Bishopstone village. At the house they spent a useful hour looking round it again, and making so many suggestions that Edna and Isaac were completely confused.

At last Martin Killick called them all to order, told them it was Edna's and Isaac's house...

"And Freddie's!" said Isaac.

... and that they should allow those three to say what they wanted.

"We were only trying to help," said Max.

"And you have," Edna told him. "We have a lot of ideas now thanks to you six. Now we just need to sort them out and decide what we like best."

"Do you want to call me from London when you've made your decisions?" Martin asked. "I've got colour cards and sample wallpapers in the car, and they will help you on your way."

They thanked him and told everyone else that they would discuss it and call in to the Mill House again on the way back. If Martin was still there he'd be given details, or Isaac would phone from London otherwise. He and the others got the message. They went to their cars, waved their farewells and drove off.

Edna and Isaac had almost decided on what would happen to the ground floor when another car stopped outside. Three people emerged and stood, just looking at the property. Edna glanced through the window and exclaimed "It's Isaac and the kids!"

Freddie sat up in alarm. This was the meeting he had been dreading, even if he knew it was inevitable. From the window he saw a middle aged man who looked so like Isaac he had to look inside the room to make sure it wasn't the same person – even if he did appear younger. He saw a boy with a cheerful face – now with a slightly astonished expression – and a bandage round his calf. He saw a girl...

Maybe for the first time in his life he felt a shock, a shock that made him sit up straighter.

She was beautiful.

She was way, way beyond his confused dreams, but beautiful nevertheless. He shook himself. No. Don't even think about her. She's too old, anyway. He had seen girls at school in London coming out of the girls' entrance as he and his acquaintances came out of the boys'. But they were small, grey, mousy and – well – ordinary. People. Kids. Girls, maybe, but kids.

But this tall, elegant looking, blond haired creature just glorified the name 'girl' and rendered it onto a different level.

He knew she was not for him. She was too perfect. She could have the start of a career on the stage. She would ignore him, maybe look at him when he said 'hallo', but after that, ignore him.

He didn't know whether to whimper, look away, or cry.

But the three from the car were on their way to the front door, and the moment of truth was coming.

A pause. Someone was pressing the bell. Silly really, because nothing would happen. It didn't work yet. Edna and Isaac were on their way to the door when he heard it open a crack and a man's voice called out.

"Hallooo... Anyone at home?"

The older couple were by then approaching the door. He heard voices. Five separate voices, happy voices. He heard footsteps. The door of the room he was in opened again. The two younger ones bounded up to him and looked down at his injured body, smiles on their faces. He could feel a smile blossoming on his own face, although he knew it would be only for a short time, until Bee got bored.

"Hallo," said a gentle, friendly voice. A voice with a smile in it. "You must be our new brother."

Brother. Again a shock. Of course. That was it. No more. But good. That meant acceptance. Shakily he looked up at her, still with a small smile on his face.

"You all right?" asked the boy. "You look a bit shaky."

With some difficulty he shifted his gaze. Another friendly face. Phew. And *she* wasn't bored yet. He swallowed hard.

"No... I'm fine, thanks. You must be Bee and Gerry."

"Yep," continued the boy. "I'm Gerry. The tall, gormless one is Bee."

"Take no notice of him," the gentle voice said as her arm nudged the boy none too gently. "He's just jealous that I'm older than him."

"I'd rather be me," came the retort.

Freddie smiled again.

"When do you get the plaster off?" asked Gerry. "You can't do much with that lot on, I should think. Must be difficult even having a..."

"Gerry, that'll do." A firm voice behind him shut him up instantly. The man who looked so much like his hero came up. This time there was no smile, just a non-committal look. Freddie knew it was Isaac junior. He knew the story.

"Hallo, sir," he said. Did the expression soften a little? Difficult to tell.

"Hallo. You must be Freddie. Pleased to meet you." The voice was similar to Isaac's, the accent somehow posher. Why? Was that the boarding school? Must be. Toffs' school. Not the Navy. "And please don't call me 'sir'. I'm not on the boats any more, and even if I was I was never called that there either."

Freddie nodded. "Well, I'm still pleased to meet you... er... what do I call you?"

"Well... I..."

"How about 'Isaac', Isaac?"

Father and son held each other's eyes. The younger remembered the welcome and ready acceptance both his children had given Freddie. The word 'brother' had not gone unnoticed. He remembered that this little lad had been horribly injured and in agony, must have been helpless and alone even when Ruth had been given a bed beside him, had then been bereaved and had had no mother to comfort him.

He looked back to where Freddie was lying on a window seat; to where he was now looking gravely up at him.

His antagonism towards an apparent interloper started to evaporate, slowly but surely, as his common sense and sense of humanity took over. His suspicions that the youngster might just be a gold-digger started vanishing too.

The long silence saw a lowering of the eyes in front of him. Was something glistening at the bottom eyelid?

I have two children, he thought. I know their friends. I have bandaged up their friends – especially Gerry's – and during none of those times have I ever doubted the display of honesty of a young human being in front of me.

Why now?

No. This wasn't fair.

He held his lips tightly together for a moment, exorcising his final doubts, and took a deep breath.

Freddie wondered what was coming.

Isaac's eyes lifted.

"Good idea," he said with conviction. "Isaac. And yes, Freddie, I'm really pleased to meet you. I know Mum and Dad are working out what they want down here, but have you chosen your bedroom yet? And do you know what colour you want it? Or are you having wallpaper?"

Freddie looked up, now more hopeful. He saw a different expression on the face.

"I... I was going to have the little room," he told Isaac, still in a serious tone, "but they told me I deserved a bigger room than that. So I chose the one at the end, the one with two windows."

"May we see it?"

"Yes. It's the one right along the corridor..."

"I mean, can you show it to us?"

"Okay... yes. But I need help up and down the stairs. Please."

He hopped into the hall and stood at the staircase. Gerry was his height; he put his arm round Gerry's shoulders and clung onto the bannister with the other hand. Isaac was behind to make sure they didn't overbalance backwards. Bee had been invited gravely by Freddie to go up in front of them, even if he'd prefer it to be her shoulders that were supporting him.

They made it to the top. Freddie hopped along and showed them the little room.

"That's the one I chose first," he said. "I thought they'd want guests to have the big rooms, but they said I should have a good room. So I chose this one, along here."

He hopped to the end room and opened the door. The window opposite looked over land that fell gradually away to the sea, with Newhaven in the distance. To the right, on the end wall, the larger window looked towards the Downs.

"It's lovely," said Bee. "All that countryside to look out at. Are you going to be allowed to paint it? Or will it stay whitewashed like this?"

Freddie's head swivelled at the sound of her voice. "It can be painted, or wallpapered. Whatever I like. But I really don't have a clue what to do with it."

She nodded and looked round at the walls that the Wilsons, the Baker brothers and so many others had seen and made suggestions about.

"Well, how about a warm colour on the wall that faces the sea? Maybe a wallpaper? And a light paint colour for the rest of the room to make it bright?"

He couldn't remember if anyone else had suggested any of that, but Bee had, and that was enough. "That sounds perfect!" he exclaimed. "Can you help me choose the wallpaper? Please?"

They got him downstairs again, Bee this time with her arm round his waist. He went as slowly as he could, a tingle running down his spine, and regretfully sat at a table where the wallpaper sample books were. He thought she would leave him there, but to his delight she sat at his side. Gerry was at the other and Isaac, with amused eyes, sat opposite.

Edna and Isaac had more or less completed their choices on decorating the downstairs and what would become their own bedroom. They returned to the room where the others were and were happy to take in the scene of acceptance in front of them. Soon they became part of the group, and with the aid of Isaac's hastily sketched plan described what they were considering for the downstairs rooms. Bee's ideas for Freddie's room pleased them. The lad himself was obviously enthusiastic about it.

They called in at Tide Mills on the way back but Martin had gone.

As they opened the door of the London house later they discovered a letter on the mat. It was from the hospital asking if they knew how to contact Freddie as he had missed an appointment to have the casts removed from arm and leg. The patient bounced up and down, partly in anticipation at getting them removed and partly in annoyance at having missed it.

"We told everyone where you would be living from now on," Isaac said, also annoyed as he walked into the hall to make the phone call. Another appointment was made.

His next call was to Martin Killick, who requested sketches so he could be sure which rooms were which and what was to happen to them. Isaac busied himself with pen and paper.

A few days later a very happy Freddie had the plaster casts removed. He had been astonished at the thinness of both leg and arm as they had been revealed and it had been explained to him that the lack of use of the muscles caused that. As soon as he was free he carefully swung himself to sit on the edge of the bed and cautiously put his foot on the floor for the first time in seven weeks. He was horrified to feel himself overbalancing. It was nearly useless. Similarly his arm felt as if it hardly belonged to him. It too was weak, as he discovered when he tried to grip part of the bed he had been lying on.

The instructions were to go very gently with everything, and when the muscles ached – as it would, he was told – he should stop to avoid damaging them. To start with he would need to spend most of the time with both leg and arm supported, but would need to do daily exercises to build the muscles up.

He attempted to stand again and managed it, just, although swaying, an adult each side of him and in front. He managed it, the swaying lessened, and he grinned.

"Back to normal!" he said, and took a step. The leg all but crumpled and the nurse supported him with a grin.

"Not quite yet. But the bones are mended. Now it's the turn of the muscles."

He sat normally in the car on the journey back to start with, but after only ten minutes found that the leg was uncomfortable and he had to support it along the back seat.

Back at home, very cautiously he tried again, and managed to stand with the leg for about a minute before it became too uncomfortable.

Well, it was working, anyway, he thought, promising himself that he would get it up to strength sooner than the hospital had said. The arm seemed almost all right, except when he tried to grab something for support, when it felt it had all the strength of a baby's limb. He sat down again.

Half term started after school that day. Next morning Alan and Eric visited Owen to ask if he could cycle with them over the Downs. Ruth, hearing the conversation from her settee in the living room, told him he should go and not to make a fuss over her.

Though he wanted to be with her, he also wanted to get out and about. Her attitude was all he needed so, with cycles, drink, snacks and permission from parents they set off. A route from Bishopstone was chosen; they all wanted to see what was going on with the Galleys' house. With Eric, an inexperienced cyclist, holding them back, it took longer to climb Rookery Hill by the path, climb further towards the rookery itself, and freewheel down to the main Bishopstone road. Eric pleaded a break and dismounted, rubbing muscles in his thighs that he hardly knew he had.

Despite it being Saturday the house was in turmoil, with men washing, painting, fitting new cupboards in the kitchen, installing electrical sockets and all the time shouting to each other. One of them emerged from the house for a smoke and saw the boys. He recognised them and they chatted for a while.

"Where are you going?" he asked.

"Oh, just for a ride. New bikes." Alan was proud. Quietly, so was Owen.

"So I see. Well, make sure you don't pick up a puncture. Not too bad up Norton way, see, but if you go up Poverty Bottom it starts getting mighty stony. Especially after the waterworks."

Alan assured him they had puncture outfits and would take care. Owen noticed Alan's Sussex burr deepened when talking to the man, and rather liked it. He wondered if he would start talking Sussex eventually.

The path continued up the side of the valley. It became stonier, as promised, as well as more overgrown. To save their tyres they dismounted and pushed the seemingly increasingly heavy cycles upwards until, panting, they came to a junction.

"Downhill! Please, downhill!" Eric gasped.

"Want to go on?" his brother asked.

"So long as it's downhill and we have a rest here."

"If we go down, we'll have to come up again later."

"Yes, but downhill now!"

Cautiously, riding now despite the lumps of chalk and flint, they went down. What should have been a cooling experience turned anything but as the sunken path was rutted and had what looked like sheep droppings at intervals. Eric was muttering to himself; the others ignored him.

At the bottom of the hill the world levelled out. True, they were hemmed in by Cantercrow Hill – that they'd just come down – and Gardner's Hill ahead of them. But to the right was Poverty Bottom and to the left, currently unexplored except by Alan, was Stump Bottom. It was grassy, level and inviting. Eric stopped muttering.

"Everyone fit?" asked Alan who, despite being younger than Owen, naturally took charge. Not only did he know where they were, he was a Scout, a Patrol Leader by now and becoming accustomed to telling other Scouts what to do.

They agreed, and he set off along the valley – the Bottom – at a good rate and almost immediately fell off.

It was his turn to mutter something.

Remounting, he set off again, but slower, followed by Eric and Owen who managed to avoid the deep rut he had run into. The path became smoother. They followed its gentle bends until a band of woodland swept down the hills on either side. A path bent off to their right through the woods, but straight on was a gate. Alan opened it and made sure it was shut once they were all through.

Straight on, the path followed a fence on its right and went up, and up, and…

"Up there?" asked Eric faintly.

"No. Just up here a bit we turn left."

"How much further?" Eric complained. "I need a drink and a rest."

"And that's what we'll have," his brother told him.

On their left they found a valley separating from the main hill and running with a bank of stunted trees on their left. It started off to the left but shortly swung very gently right. The trees receded a little to leave a steep bank on their left which came to an end in a small spur. Alan dismounted and pulled his cycle up behind it. He turned to face the cliff.

Totally unexpected except by him, they found a plateau of about forty feet round, bounded at its end by small trees and bushes, between which could be seen raw chalk. On the right the trees and bushes climbed the side of the Down. To the left the bank dipped to the path that had brought them there, before rising again to form a typical, gently rounded Down. At their back the path continued to the base of a line of trees that seemed to be the valley's boundary.

There was not a sound, apart from birdsong.

Owen looked round, feeling strangely at peace.

"Where are we?"

"Home Bottom. Up there – " Alan pointed to the trees and the hill " – is Fore Hill and a few miles further south west is Denton. The way we could have gone, up the long hill by the fence, is Blackcap. There's a farm up there. But here… we stopped once for a brew up. It's just a great place."

Owen had to agree. There was something special about it. He'd never encountered feeling like that about a place, a tiny area in this extensive spread of countryside that everyone just referred to as 'The Downs'.

"How do you know so much about it?"

"Maps," Alan said grimly. "Ernest is keen on them and makes us learn them by heart, almost. You'll find out." Ernest was their Scoutmaster.

Even Eric, who had by then recovered his breath, could find nothing to complain about. Apart from…

"Water, water," he croaked theatrically.

"Okay… I thought we might brew a cup of tea. You two – go and get some wood – all thicknesses." He explained what he meant. At the hint of starting a fire Eric found his thirst was less.

The first time they returned they met with a single word. "More!"

Two armfuls later they saw what Alan had been doing. There was a patch of bare earth and stones around it with a kettle perched across two of them. Off to one side were four cut turves.

"That's why my bag has been so bulky," he explained. "I wondered about a flint and steel, but matches are lighter, so here goes."

He'd done it before, that was obvious to the others. They were impressed; he was smug.

They sat round the fire, watching nothing apart from the gentle swell of the grassy Down in front of them, listening to the skylarks' non-stop singing and the other birds in the bushes around them. It was a moment of magic for the town-bred Owen. Nothing was said for ages whilst they drank in the scene.

At last the kettle boiled, Alan removed it from the fire with a forked stick and piled tealeaves into it. Owen, frequent tea-maker at home, gasped.

"Five minutes and it'll be brewed," he said. "Eric, in your bag there are three mugs and some milk and sugar."

They spent a good hour from the time they arrived to when they reluctantly left. Owen watched as most of their remaining water – and tea – doused the glowing sticks which were then unceremoniously stamped into the ground. The unburnt fuel was returned to the old quarry behind them and the turves, carefully cut by Alan to make the fireplace, were replaced and watered and trodden on to flatten them.

"There. No one will know we've been here," he said.

"Apart from the kettle," said his brother nodding to where it had been left on a log. Alan just glared, trying not to appear shamefaced, and put it in his bag.

It was noticeably cooler on the ride back down Stump Bottom. There seemed to be a pall of grey ahead, a pall they encountered as if it were a physical boundary. They shivered.

"Fret coming in," Alan observed.

"Fret?" Owen hadn't heard the word.

"Mist off the sea. Happens now and again. We'd best get going. I was going to take us up Denton and down that way 'cos it's a long fast hill, but we'd best head straight back. Less traffic."

They retraced their route. As they came up to the path down Poverty Bottom Alan looked up.

"Looks lighter ahead. P'raps if we go up Cantercrow after all, we'll come out of it."

Pushing the bikes up the long, rutted hill was a struggle, especially for the inexperienced Eric, but near the top they broke through the mist into a hazy sunlight, and were immediately warmed – though the hill climb had seen to it that they were no longer cold. Cautiously they made their way over the ridge and regained the hard road.

Alan was right. The freewheeling down the hill was exhilarating, even if they did meet the mist again as they passed the Flying Fish. The ride down to the main road was more circumspect, and that along it even more so.

The return was welcomed with mixed relief and annoyance by Mrs Baker.

"Idiots," she said. "You should have come back as soon as the fret came in."

"We did, Mum. We were up Home Bottom and it never reached us there."

"You saw it coming, sure as eggs is eggs."

"No, Mum, honest. We never saw it at all until we were nearly at the end of Stump. Then we were in it, then out of it at the top of Cantercrow, and in it again at the Fish."

She tried to make sense of what he was saying. "You and your bottoms and such. I'll tan yours if you do that again. Worried sick, we were."

"But he's right, Mrs Baker." Owen thought it was time he put a word in. "We never saw a hint of mist until we'd already started off. And then it was too late. Alan took the right route home, the quicker one, and we were very careful."

That threw her. She had let off steam and had almost nothing else to say.

"Well, with you with them they've got one sensible head, anyway."

"But *he's* the Patrol Leader, Mrs Baker. He knows better than me what to do."

"But he's younger. And you're Grammar school."

Owen winced and hoped it didn't show. "He still knows the way round the Downs, and I don't. And he knows what to do far better than me. I'd still be up there if I was on my own. *And* if we'd got lost, he's the one who can start a fire to keep us all warm."

"Well..."

She was now completely out of words.

"Shall we put the bikes away, Mum?"

"Yes, 'course. Then you can keep out of my way. I'm baking."

"Okay, Mum."

"They can come over with Ruth and me if you like. It'll be my turn to make the tea."

"Phew," said Alan when they were all but out of sight from everything between the Bakers' cottage and Mill house. "Thanks for that."

"Just telling the truth. And glad to be of use."

Owen never saw his expression. He was still full of admiration for the way that Alan had taken the lead in everything they had done.

Barbara and Ruth were glad to see them and pleased when Owen put the kettle on.

"We were getting worried," said Barbara. "The mist came in so suddenly, and that was hours ago. Did you get lost?"

"There was no mist where we were," Owen told her. "And Alan knew exactly where we were."

Alan flashed him a grateful look. "It was odd," he said, "we only met the fret when we were at the end of the bottom we were in..."

"I beg your pardon?" Barbara had never heard the expression either.

"Stump Bottom. It's the valley that the Blackcap path comes down into. The fret started at the end of that. So rather than go slowly down Poverty we turned right up Cantercrow Hill. Near the top we found the sun again, and weren't back into the fret until we were down through Denton. So most of the ride was in the sun."

This was an exaggeration, but Barbara was obviously impressed by his knowledge of the area if completely befuddled by the names and expressions.

"I'm pleased you were there, Alan. Good that someone knows what he's doing."

"Mum!"

Her smile took the sting out of the comment.

That week saw other outings by bike, including one memorable, nearly tragic ride. Alan led them through Newhaven and up the west side of the river towards Piddinghoe. Sailing was taking place on the pond there – "It's a new club," said Alan – and they had been watching the antics of the youngsters learning to sail, Eric with particular enthusiasm. Setting off again along the river bank north of the pond they had just reached the end of a landing stage when Eric noticed what looked like a waterlogged sack drifting down towards its end.

He was casually watching it when something in the sack moved.

He gave a strangled shout. "There's something alive in that sack!"

They followed his pointing hand. The sack moved again.

"Come on!" It was Owen's turn to lead. "It might be kittens or something. People sometimes drown them."

He ran out to the end of the jetty and judged where the sack would float past. He hung over the edge, glad the tide was fairly high or he'd have had no chance of reaching it. Without being asked, Alan and Eric held on to his legs.

The sack proved heavy, so heavy he couldn't do more than lift it a little more up in the water.

There was an angry shout behind them. Someone thought they were fooling around and was objecting. When he could get a word in, Alan swallowed his anger and calmly explained what they were doing. The man watched, then lay down beside Owen on the jetty. Together they lifted the sack onto the woodwork. There was now no movement visible.

An evil looking knife appeared from the man's pocket. Eric gave a cry.

"It's to open the sack." His voice was gentler than it had been when he had complained about their being there.

He felt along the top of the sack to make sure there was nothing there to damage, then cut his way along the join. He peeled back the top of the sacking. A black nose appeared.

"It's a dog!" Alan stated the obvious.

"Not a young'un, either," said the man. "Heard of people drowning kittens – bastards. Sorry, but they are – but never a dog like this."

He had carefully cut along the long side of the sack and folded it back to reveal a slightly open muzzle with fur that was becoming white with age and eyes that were partly closed in exhaustion.

"It's an old Labrador," he said wonderingly. "Another few minutes and she'd be done for. Got to her just in time, we did."

He now had the whole dog revealed. It was indeed female, a Labrador bitch, black apart from the muzzle and a white tip to the tail.

"Keep talking gently to her, and I'll get a towel. We'll get her dry and see how she is."

He retreated toward the nearest building, a boathouse at the landward end of the jetty.

"What do you say to a dog?" asked Owen.

But Eric and Alan had no doubts. Between them they just continued a low, soothing muttering; one treble, one now noticeably alto. After a while the dog's tail moved and the two brothers smiled at each other. Footsteps behind them heralded the arrival of a towel and the dog was soon being massaged and dried. The tail thumped a couple of times.

"I think she'll be all right," said the towel bearer. "She's getting a bit stronger already by the looks. So long as no water's gone down the wrong

246

way she should recover."

"Who would have done something like that?" asked Owen.

The man shrugged his shoulders. "Who knows? Whoever it was, if they were the owner, they don't want her. Perhaps they never cared for her at all. Maybe... maybe she was just used for breeding from, and now she's too old. There are some who just use dogs like cattle, and once they're no use that's it; they're out. Most try to sell them or give them away, but whoever had this one's a real bastard. Sorry."

"Well, one thing's for sure," said Owen decisively, "they're not having her back. But what'll happen to her?"

He was aware that the head of each of the brothers snapped up, and he looked at them. It was obvious what was going on in their minds.

"You two?" he asked.

"Always wanted a dog," Eric said.

Alan nodded. "Mum and Dad would never have one. Said we couldn't afford to feed it."

Owen bit back what he was about to say about having more money now. He thought. "I suppose... how about we share her? Ruth could perhaps do with the company during the day, when we're all at school. And she could come and walk with us when we're back."

"Suits me," said the man. "I've got two dogs at home, so an old girl like this wouldn't fit in at all well. She'll need taking back by car, though. She's not going to be able to walk for a bit; she's absolutely exhausted."

"I'll cycle back and ask Dad to come up," Owen said. "I think I can persuade him. If not, perhaps one of the builders can help. It's not far."

"Where are you from, then?"

"Tide Mills."

"Oh – where they're doing all the work. Good place for a dog, I imagine."

"Hope so," said Owen, wondering what the reaction from both families' parents would be. "Is it quickest to go along the bank from here, or should I go by road?"

"Go by road," he was told. "That way you'll know where to direct the car to on the way back."

Owen set off, fast. So fast that when he arrived he could hardly speak, alarming Barbara beyond words.

"Is it one of the brothers?" she asked. "You need to tell..."

He was shaking his head.

"Is Dad in his study?" he asked as soon as he could.

"No – he's in the Mill, I think. But what's happened?"

As succinctly as he could he described the situation. By this time Ruth had hobbled on her crutches out of the living room and caught the end of the story.

"We've got to rescue her, haven't we?" she almost stated. "Please may she come here? Or to my home?"

Owen explained what they'd all but agreed. She was pleased to have been thought about.

Max was in deep conversation with Martin Killick but looked round when Owen appeared. He had to look around, so different were the surroundings. It was gradually changing from a building site to something approaching a factory. He saw Owen's flushed face and sensed trouble.

"What's happened?" he asked in a resigned voice. Owen explained.

"Well done for rescuing it, but I don't know if we really want a dog…"

Owen explained about Ruth, and sharing ownership with the boys.

"What do the Bakers say?"

"I've not asked them yet. We need to get her back here and safe first, Dad. Please – can't you just nip up and get her with me? It won't take long. She's only at Piddinghoe."

Martin interrupted. "One of my guys can go up in the old van while we sort out this problem, Max. It'll only be about half an hour."

"But…"

"*Thanks*, Martin. I'll go in the back with the dog."

"Chances are you'll need to bring those two scamps back with you too," said Martin. "Truck's big enough. I'll come and make arrangements. Excuse me a moment, Max."

"But…"

Martin was off. When he got outside he said to Owen "Some things need to be acted on quickly, eh? Sort out other problems later."

He found one of his men and quickly gave instructions. Ruth was fetched from the house as quickly as she could make it, They set off with her in the passenger seat and Owen sitting on the hard floor in the back, trying to stop himself getting bumped about too much up the uneven surface of Mill Drove.

A man and two boys achieved a double-take as a truck with 'Killick Builders' appeared by the boat house. Walking footsteps and an unsynchronised crunching announced Owen's and Ruth's approach.

"Is she all right?" was Owen's first question. To answer it a tail moved quite animatedly and black-clad legs fumbled about before the head dropped back to the ground with a sigh.

"She's still exhausted," Alan told him. "But she's gained some strength."

Owen nodded. Killicks' driver came up and introduced himself as Neil.

"I know you, Neil. I was at school with you." Their co-rescuer was now grinning widely. His face was examined.

"Bloody hell, Rod? I thought you'd moved away!"

"I had. We moved back."

The two shook hands and started exchanging stories. Owen eventually cleared his throat.

"Sorry," Neil laughed. "I'll come back after work, shall I? We could have a pint in the Royal Oak.

With difficulty, because she kept trying to move, they carried the heavy dog to the truck. Neil scratched his head, loaded the two cycles at one side and strapped them so they couldn't move. The three boys sat the other side with the dog between them, and now covered with a new, dry towel. Ruth and he regained the front and they set off for home.

248

20 – Wedding

Barbara had spoken to Jessie Baker who had first expressed horror, then a non-committal acceptance. When the two noticed the van's approach from their respective homes they emerged.

The human passengers from the back climbed out and stretched. The dog's head lifted gingerly. The first person she saw was Jessie Baker.

"Oh, you poor old thing," said that lady, all resistance melting away like snow in August. "What have they done to you?"

"You'd better bring her in," said Barbara. The truck had stopped outside the Mill House as that would be less far for Ruth to walk back. Carefully, using the towel, they transported the dog inside.

"Kitchen, I think, near the Aga. She can dry properly there."

"We did our best, Missus," said Neil.

"I know you will have done, and thank you on her behalf. But she's had a shock and I think warmth and food might do the trick."

At the word 'food' the dog's head raised again and the tail thumped the floor.

"She's famished!" Barbara exclaimed.

Jessie laughed. "Dogs are famished all the time. But you're right. Maybe she's not been fed for ages. But a little now, and then some more later is best."

Alan looked at his mother in amazement. "How do you know about dogs?"

"We had them all our lives until you were born. Then soon after, old Guy died and I didn't have enough time to look after you and a dog – or so I thought. Then along came Eric and I *knew* I wouldn't have time. So that was that.

"But now, you don't take so much looking after, just a lot of worrying after, so it's you two who can darn well look after the dog."

"And Ruth, Mum. She'll be hers as well."

"And Ruth too, then. And the sooner I see her walking with that dog and then running with her, the better we shall both like it, I'm sure. But for the moment you two need to walk her before school, then she can be with Ruth and not under my feet all day. Then you can take her for a walk when you get home and before you go to bed. And don't forget she's not a young dog, and you'll lose her a lot sooner than you'd want to. She won't last for ever."

Whilst she was delivering this speech her hands were gently massaging the dog's ears and head, actions not lost on any of her listeners. It gave the lie to her tone. Owen and Barbara learnt something about her and realised why, despite her sharp tongue, the boys defended her if anyone made a criticism. Put simply, she cared: they loved her for it.

She stood up again. The dog looked up and the tail thumped again. A smile split Jessie's face, lightening it as if the sun had emerged from behind clouds.

"You know, I've not been able to do that for years," she said. "Now, is there any food we can tempt her with?" She looked hopefully at Barbara, still

249

with the smile on her face.

At the word 'food' the dog looked up again and the tail thumped. There was a movement of legs and she almost managed to stand, but collapsed again.

Barbara went to the kitchen. It had taken a dog to get Jessie to thaw towards her – not that she had been antagonistic, just cautious and a little too formal. She hoped that was over.

Some scraps were taken in a bowl to the other room and were held out to the dog, who accepted them gratefully.

"What's her name?" Ruth asked suddenly. "We can't keep calling her 'The Dog'!"

"She's got no collar, so no tag. I checked," said Owen.

"Try some names. See if she reacts," Barbara suggested.

Between them they ran through all the girls' names they could think of, including 'Ruth' and 'Barbara' and even 'Jessie', though that was suggested by Alan whilst well out of reach of his mum's hand. There was no reaction.

"You could call her 'Ouse' after the river we fished her out of," Neil suggested.

"It's an idea," said Ruth, "but Ouse isn't a very pretty name, is it?"

"What about some of the others, then?" he persisted.

"You can't call a dog 'Cuckmere'!" Owen protested.

"There's 'Rother', 'Bourne'..."

"Bourne?" Owen interrupted. "Where's that?"

"It's another name for a stream," Neil told him. "Like East Bourne."

It had never occurred to any of them.

"Then there's the Arun, and the Adur..."

And at the word, the dog's head lifted again and looked round. This time the legs scrabbled around and found positions under her, and she slowly gained her feet. Now the tail drooped from exhaustion, but she stood for a while before cautiously sitting and looking round.

"Ada – food?" asked Jessie. The dog looked at her and the eyes somehow looked more alive.

"Well, more by accident than design I think we've found her name," Barbara said. "Thank you... er..." She realised she didn't know the name of the man who had brought the dog back.

"Neil," Owen prompted quietly.

"Neil. Sorry. And thank you for bringing them all back. That was kind."

He grinned. "Happen you'd best thank Mas' Killick for that. He asked me. And he did me a favour, 'cos the man who helped them get the dog out of the water was an old school mate of mine who I thought had gone to live in Devon. Seems he's come back – with a wife."

"Then I'll thank him too. Now, though, as Jessie's promised her some food I'll go and get her some more. And you two need to rescue your cycles from the van. And then I must get on and leave looking after the dog to the rest of you."

Ada was able to eat a small bowl of food unaided this time, then lay down again by the Aga and slept.

"And I must get going too," Jessie said, "or there won't be a meal on the table tonight. Come on you two, bikes, then you can go and get some dog food from a pet shop."

They dispersed. Cycles were rescued, Neil drove the van the short distance back to the mill and the others set off for Seaford.

By the following Sunday progress was to be seen on many fronts. At the mill a walkway had been installed to allow visitors to watch the mill wheels turning and the grain entering and, if they went down some steps, they could see it emerging as flour. Heavy doors allowed access to watch the new machinery which mixed their just-milled flour with other ingredients to produce cake mixes, bread mixes and other flour-based mixes which just required water to be added before mixing and baking.

The old crossing-keeper's cottage at the north of the hamlet had been bought – it had belonged to British Railways – and had been converted into a bakery and shop with a flat above, all currently awaiting a tenant who would be the baker.

At the Bakers' cottage and at Mill House a dog lived, a dog who was increasingly strong and certainly very happy to have so many humans who cared for and loved her. She was, despite her advancing years, alert and active, along with being able to display an impressive canine dignity, when appropriate. At other times she could be mad. The freedom that came with Tide Mills, where people were already getting to know her, seemed to amaze her. If she ventured too far from people she would look back anxiously as if to ensure she still had a home.

School resumed. At her hospital visit the following day Ruth was coaxed to bear some weight on her leg – weight that the framework would take. Cautiously she did, and found it odd, slightly uncomfortable, but acceptable. They returned, she with instructions to spend five minutes more each time with weight on the leg until it became awkward for her, and then afterwards to use her sense but "Don't overdo it. Don't start on long hikes. No swimming. And carry on making sure the skin is clean and isn't going angrily red."

Edna, Isaac and Freddie made regular journeys down to Bishopstone to check on progress and catch up with news at Tide Mills. Freddie had grown to like Alan and Eric who decided they enjoyed his instinctively cheeky ways and inclination for low-key mischief.

It was later in the month that Edna and Isaac delivered wedding invitations to the Tide Mills families.

"We're moving in to the house the week before," said Isaac with a laugh in his voice, "so for a few days we're going to be living in sin as if we were twenty again."

Edna didn't know whether to say something sharp to him or smile. It was a measure of the spiritual distance she'd travelled that she chose the latter. Freddie would have commented – had he still been living by the docks in east

London. But by now he instinctively knew better.

"And Max has kindly agreed that we can use the Mill for the reception," Isaac added. "This time we'll get everything in ourselves, so don't think that the Mill is paying for it all!"

Walking, even with crutches, was now a lot easier for Freddie. He had been told he could put all his weight on the leg but still should use a crutch to support it. His arm had been able to get more exercise, although it tired quickly and he had to return it to a sling if it started throbbing.

He had examined the four cycles with admiration and commiserated with Ruth about her not being able to use one.

"Yet," he said, just as Owen did. She smiled at them both.

Isaac's eyebrows lifted and he nudged Edna. They retired to the back of the group.

"He said his birthday was in February, didn't he?"

"Yes," Edna responded, "the thirteenth."

"When did he have the accident?"

She thought. "About a month later. Maybe a few weeks. Why?"

"He never had a birthday present."

"Huh! From his father? From what I hear that would have been some sort of miracle."

"How do you feel about our giving him a wedding present?"

That puzzled her for a moment. "What – on our wedding day, you mean?"

He nodded.

"Well, I suppose so. But what?"

"That's easy. the cycle, so he can have some freedom and come down to be with this lot."

"The cycle… I know we bought the other one for him, but will he be able to ride one yet? Has he ever ridden one?"

"He can wear himself into it gradually. And as to learning to ride, everyone has to start some time. The road through Bishopstone is quiet enough, and these youngsters can teach him. And there must be people around who can teach the rule of the road. We can buy him a Highway Code too."

She nodded. "Do you really think he will be strong enough by then?"

"We'll find out. It'll help him get stronger. And when he is, he can cycle to school."

They had already visited Alan's school in Seaford and made sure a place would be available for the start of the summer term. Alan had been told and was pleased, and promised he would look after him as the two would be in the same form since they were only two months apart in age. To Freddie's disgust but grudging acceptance his old London school had been providing him with work. Secretly he had been glad of something to do. Lewes Grammar had been doing the same for Ruth, who was more openly accepting of it.

On the Monday before the wedding Freddie was pronounced fit enough to walk without a crutch so long as he took care. After the appointment the three of them walked down to Brighton's Clock Tower, by which time he was noticeably limping. Edna noticed first and firmly guided her charges into the

252

nearest café. Freddie sat down with relief.

"Not quite there yet, are you?" Edna asked.

He shook his head. "That crutch made walking so much easier. But being without it is great – it's just that I'm not used to not having it yet. What can I get you for a wedding present?"

The relief on his face having finally been able to speak the question that had worried him for weeks was almost comical. Isaac was at the counter, ordering food, so she motioned him to wait until he'd returned and sat.

"Now, Freddie. Would you repeat what you just asked me, please?"

He looked round at them both, wondering if he'd made a mistake, and that he shouldn't have asked. Or offered.

"I… I just wanted to know if there was something I can give you when you get married. If it's wrong to ask, sorry, because I didn't know."

Edna looked at Isaac, who looked gravely at Freddie.

"There's something you can do, Freddie. I'm going to ask our son Isaac to be my best man. We're going to ask Bee to be the bridesmaid and Gerry to be something they do in America; they have Groomsmen. So he's one of two who will accompany us down the aisle and stand by our sides through the ceremony. Would you agree to be the other Groomsman? To be with the other three as our family?"

The transformation of expression from worry to delight, with the wide grin that accompanied it, melted their hearts.

"I'd *love* to," he said. "Really. But can't I get you something?"

Edna sighed. "If we were starting out in life, say if we were in our twenties, and if you were our age and earning, then yes; I suppose there would be something. But we're not in our twenties, we have most of what we need and…" she laughed suddenly. "I felt at first my financial contribution to us as a couple was about nil. Isaac provided everything. But I've just realised that, by chance, I've been able to provide a house where we can all live. That makes me feel a lot better – even if I've not had to work hard to earn it."

"You worked hard bringing up our son. Never forget that."

"Well, yes, but it's not the same as *earning*, is it?"

"It may have been paid only by cruelty, but by God you've earnt that house."

She smiled at him.

"So is there really nothing I can get you?" Freddie was persistent.

"The best present you can give us is to walk down that aisle with us, without crutches, and be there with us," Isaac told him in a serious tone. "And the great thing is…"

He left the lad waiting, looking at him expectantly.

"…unlike a present, you don't have to wrap yourself up."

Isaac, Bee and Gerry travelled to London on the Friday evening before their moving day so as to help. They, with Freddie doing what he could with frequent cries of "don't be silly – you'll damage those mending muscles" ringing in his ears, moved, directed, re-moved and unpacked just about all day. They were invited down to the Mill House afterwards and all were glad to sit and do nothing for a while. Freddie, although hungry, was more tired and more aching than he thought was possible.

He was astonished to see Ruth using both legs, even if she did have a stick.

"You're tall!" he exclaimed.

She smiled. "I have to be, so as to be able to see Owen without craning my neck."

"Oy!" responded Owen, "you make me sound like a skyscraper." He was indeed by then almost as tall as his father and could see the top of his mother's head.

Later the boys, Bee and Ada went for a walk along the beach. Ruth would have gone but from experience knew that walking on pebbles put too much strain on her leg. They were chatting idly. Freddie, still only just used to the immensity of the sea having been acclimatised only to the width of the Thames, had his eyes on the beach. It was pure chance that he saw a stone of a light blue hue hiding amongst the pebbles and stopped to pick it up. Looking at it, he gasped.

"It's a jewel!"

They crowded round him. It was a curious heart shape, dulled by the action of the sea and sand, but looked somehow exotic.

"It's glass, said Alan in a matter of fact tone. "We get quite a few on the beach here. Most aren't as big as that, though. Wonder what it was?"

But Freddie was looking at it still. "It'd do," he breathed. "If only..."

They waited.

"How much would it cost to have a hole drilled in it and a chain through that? Like a necklace?"

They looked at it with new eyes.

"I know someone who could," Eric volunteered. "My friend's dad is a jeweller. I could give it to him at school on Monday."

"How much would it cost?"

Eric shrugged. "Dunno. Who's it for?"

"Don't tell her, but it's a wedding present for Edna.

They looked closer at it.

"Something old, something new, something borrowed, something blue."

Attention turned to Bee, whose voice it was, and she blushed.

"Well, it's old and blue," said Owen, "But what about borrowed and new?"

"If Eric got it done, it'd have a new chain," said Alan.

"And if I don't pay for it until after the wedding, does that make it borrowed?" Freddie looked hopeful. They laughed.

"I suppose you could stretch a point," Owen told him. He looked pleased and handed the thing to Eric who promised to ask the question as soon as he could. In the event his friend's father was so confused by the story and the personnel it involved that he just took the glass on the Monday, thought about it, remembering the words 'wedding present' and worked on it the next day. It was returned to Eric on the Wednesday. He opened the box and with trembling fingers held up the result.

Silver wire had been attached to the sides, curving to the top to enhance the heart shape. At the top was a ring, and a silver coloured chain formed a necklace with a clasp.

Eric shouted out something to his mother and raced with it up to Bishopstone. He found the house in confusion still, but managed to persuade Edna to let him see Freddie without asking why. The two found somewhere out of sight. Freddie's eyes widened when he saw the results, and his jaw dropped comically, just as Eric's had done.

"It's beautiful," he exclaimed. "But it'll cost *pounds*. How much did he say?"

"I forgot to ask," Eric admitted. "I'll ask tomorrow."

He did. His friend, too, had forgotten to ask.

Very early on Saturday morning, woken by a quiet alarm clock muffled by his pillow, Freddie reluctantly hauled himself from sleep and bed. The packet had been carefully wrapped. He had hesitated over what to put on the little label but had screwed up his courage and written 'For Mum, with love, Freddie'. As quietly as he could he tiptoed downstairs and put it by the kettle, thinking rightly that it would be the first thing to be used in the morning. He stumbled back to bed, thinking he'd take ages to get to sleep again but was out for the count sixty seconds later with a warm feeling inside.

Isaac woke without the need of an alarm sharp on 6.30. In the usual way of waking up his initial thoughts were muddled, but like a bolt from the blue came the recollection that, over fifty years late, this was the day he would be married. He felt a thrill go through him, one that would not have disgraced a young man in the prime of his life.

As if to remind him that he was ageing he was delayed in getting up by having to fix on what he still described as his tin leg.

He found the little box in the kitchen and read the label, and another little tingle went through him. The little rascal! He'd done something, bought something, after all! But what with? He knew that there had been a couple of occasions in shops where too much change had been offered by shopkeepers, and there had been discussion about why Isaac had handed it back. He thought they had been lessons which needed to be taught. How, then, had this been afforded, whatever it was?

The tea made, he made his way upstairs with a tray and two cups. For the first time, he entered Edna's room, which was now his too, without knocking. It felt odd.

He gently woke her.

"Happy wedding day, Mrs soon-to-be-Galley," he said.

She smiled up at him. Amazing, he thought, how despite the addition of all those years, that smile was the same as the look that welcomed him each morning in 1914 when he was recuperating. The smile that made his body tingle as it was doing now.

"What's this?" she said, spotting the package.

"You'd better look at it. I know as much as you do."

She read the label and caught her bottom lip in her teeth.

"The little varmint… and after all we said."

The little varmint was listening outside, wondering what he'd just been called. He heard the paper being torn, the box opened, then a pause, then…

"Oh *look*! Oh, Isaac, look it's beautiful. How could he…"

There was a catch in the voice. Surely she wasn't going to cry over it? But then people did, he remembered. His mother now, when he had given her something Dad had found and paid for on her birthday many years ago. She had wept. He felt his own eyes going misty at the memory.

But there was more talk in the room.

"He's marvellous. And I'm going to wear it today."

"Not a bad lad, is he? I'm so glad we saw beyond those defences – and so glad he saw beyond ours when he was in trouble."

That was enough. He tiptoed back to his room and sat on the bed, smiling.

When he finally headed downstairs, dressed in his new suit which he had submitted to only after some soul searching, he received a hug from a suddenly damp-eyed Edna that nearly squeezed the breath out of him.

"I used to collect those off the beach when I was little," she said, showing that she was aware of the origin of the 'stone'. "But never one that colour, or that size and shape. And where did you get it mounted like that? It's wonderful!"

He was thankful that she hadn't mentioned price, but smiled.

"Something old, something new, something borrowed, something blue," he repeated. "All in one."

"Borrowed?" She was suddenly shocked. "I don't have to give it back, do I?"

His mouth dropped open. "No…no! It's just that… well… the chain… I haven't been able to pay for it yet. Nobody's told me what…"

"So that's why it's borrowed," she said, relieved. "I think that's very clever. So it's for me to wear today, is it?"

"Yes. Please. And whenever you want, of course."

He had another hug, gentler this time.

"I'm *glad* you're here."

And again his smile nearly met at the back of his head.

Preparations were made in the Mill. Martin Killick had offered to oversee it.

"I don't really do churches," he had said. "So many thanks for the invitation and I'll happily come to the reception. Best thing I can do is make sure the caterers do it properly."

When the catering company appeared, he was waiting for them, looking cross and official. They quaked a little to find it was just him they had to deal with, but soon he was allowing himself to be directed to carry chairs and tables, and to help generally.

Everyone else was dressing themselves up, then starting the mile long walk to the ancient Bishopstone Church. Edna and Isaac, Ruth and Freddie were taken by car in view of one 'tin' leg, one with a brace round it, and one set of muscles that still tired quickly.

It was a happy occasion, un-stuffy, and it left the congregation in no doubt that this was a couple who would do things their way. There were no formal clothes on show apart from the Naval uniforms worn by Isaac and various friends of his who had been invited. Perhaps, though, the co-ordinated shades of blue of Edna's and Bee's dresses, and the boys' new suits, could be termed formal and on show. Bee felt a little self-conscious but was aware of how good she looked. Secretly, each of the boys felt special in his suit, especially Freddie whose first ever suit this was and almost the first pair of long trousers. None of them would have admitted to feeling any different from usual. Fortunately the vicar was on the side of informality and managed to be light hearted whilst still dignified.

As arranged, Martin returned an hour later with the car to ferry the same party back so that the new Mr and Mrs Galley could ensure everything was correct. It was, and Martin and Isaac poured a pint each to celebrate the fact.

"I'm going to have to go carefully," said Isaac with a grin. "I have a speech to make later."

Martin just smiled, downed his pint and said with a smile: "I haven't."

The two laughed. Edna rolled her eyes. "You men…"

But Freddie's face was unsmiling, worried. When he could he spoke to Edna on her own.

"He doesn't get drunk, does he?"

She received a sharp, astonished look.

"No. Never. Not…"

She suddenly understood. This was a boy whose father had returned from the pub on an all too regular basis, roaring drunk and best avoided.

"No," she said. "And if when we celebrate he gets a little too happy, he is absolutely not the sort of man to be violent or unpleasant. If he was, he wouldn't have made Captain. And if he was, I most certainly wouldn't have married him. But let's go and see what he says."

Freddie was reassured by the first comment but horrified about having to repeat his disquiet. There was no resisting her, though. She led him to Isaac, whose broad grin subsided as he saw their looks.

"What's happened?" he asked.

"Nothing. But Freddie just saw Martin downing a pint as if it was from a thimble, and it reminded him of his father. He wanted to be reassured that you're not the sort of person who would do the same sort of thing. I told him that you weren't, obviously."

Isaac looked at his foster-son and nodded gravely. "And I promise you that I shall never be the sort of person who will be dangerous to you or anyone else after a beer or two. Or more. In fact, if I have too much to drink I just get quieter and quieter and take myself off to bed. And I rarely drink more than a pint or two anyway. Yes, I understand absolutely why you're worried, but you needn't be. Should you ever think I'm making a fool of myself you can come and tell me off."

"He'd be the second in the queue," said Edna, an element of shrewishness in her voice.

"Then I'd better be careful, hadn't I?" he said smiling and ignoring the slight sharpness of tone.

Yes, I had, he said to himself as he and Edna moved back to the tables, leaving Ruth and Freddie together.

"You're lucky," she told him. "They're good people."

"So were my parents, once," he said sadly. He heaved a sigh. "But that was a long time ago, and yes, I'm lucky it was those two who found me. I could be in a children's home with... with nothing."

"But you're not. You've got us. You've got Isaac and Gerry. And you've got Bee."

He looked sharply at her. "Bee?"

"Yes. Bee. I don't know if she realises it, or if anyone else has noticed. But I've seen the way you look at her. She's very pretty, isn't she?"

He was embarrassed. It was something he'd hardly had the courage to admit to himself. What did he think of her? Really?

"Yes," he said, throwing caution to the winds. "She's very... beautiful."

Ruth smiled. "She is. And she's a nice person."

He nodded. "I don't think you can be one without the other."

"Oh yes you can," Ruth's words held a vehemence that brought him up short. "One of the best looking boys I've ever seen turned out to be one of the most dreadful bullies of young girls with one leg shorter than the other that you will ever find. Yet Owen... well, he's good looking, but he's not film-star-drop-dead gorgeous. But he's..."

She drew in a breath.

"He's Owen. That's all."

Freddie visualised the tall fifteen year old who seemed so much more worldly-wise than him, and could see what she meant. He would never be that sort of person. He would never be good enough to start thinking of Bee as anything more than a beautiful looking girl. He sighed.

"You're not still worried, are you?" asked Ruth.

He shook his head. "It's just... well, I'm lucky, I know, but I'll never be... well, the sort of person Owen is. Or that Bee... would like."

She shook her head slowly. "Do you know what it's like not to be able to do much walking, almost no running, and never to be picked for a team because you can't keep up and get tired too soon? No, you don't, but it's horrible. I felt like you do, maybe. But over a year ago a boy saw me from a train and walked all the way back here from Seaford because he wanted to talk to me. That was Owen, and that was the start of it. The start of his family's coming to live here and sort the mill out. Suddenly my life seemed better.

"So don't get downhearted, that's what I'm saying. If you want, there's plenty to do here. Owen does judo and he's just joined the Scouts..."

"*Scouts?* You mean the Brussels?"

"What?"

"Brussels Sprouts – Boy Scouts. We laugh at them."

258

"But *we* don't. Let Owen tell you about when they could have been lost in a fret on the Downs. It was Alan who got them out of that. His Scout training."

"What's a fret?"

"Sea mist. And he'd made a fire and brewed a cup of tea too. So we think the Brussels are worthwhile. And Alan plays football…"

This time his eyes lit up. "There's a club?"

"Yes. I think Owen might be joining it too. He used to belong to one in London."

"Cor…"

As the guests returned from the Church, they were greeted by Edna and Isaac with their extended family. It would have been an impossible job but for the hint they had all been given: "Introduce yourselves first, and then the other people have got to tell you who they are. But don't expect to remember their names!"

There was some serious mingling happening. Seeing the crowds could manage without them for a while, Edna and Isaac herded their grandchildren and foster-son together.

"Thank you all for what you've done so far, and I really hope you'll carry on supporting the family just as you have been doing. Now, we're in the lucky position of being able to give other people gifts on our wedding day – some people anyway – rather than them buy us things. So here is an envelope for each of you which you should open now."

There was a muted chorus of thanks and a lot of tearing of paper. Copies of the Highway Code were pulled out. Each had a note pinned to the top:

"Look round the back of the Mill House."

They looked at each other, eyes wide, and made a dash for the door. Ruth and Owen, Alan and Eric all were in on the surprise and followed, allowing some of the adults a better chance at loading plates with food.

And there, at the back of the building as promised, were three new cycles, each with a label on. They were tenderly examined, touched and marvelled over.

"But we can't ride!" said Bee sadly.

"I can." Freddie was suddenly the centre of attention. "Mum had a bike and I used to ride it. Couldn't sit on it – it was too big. So I had to stand on the pedals. But at least it means I can teach you."

Owen laughed. "So can we. But I think we should take it in turns, that way no one crashes into anyone else."

Freddie's gaze was back at the bike, taking in its gears, its gleaming chrome and the shiny leather of the saddle. Suddenly he pushed it gently back against the wall and rushed off in a fashion that only a weak leg can allow you to rush.

"Where's he going?" asked Gerry.

"To say 'thank you', I should think," Bee told him. "As we should. Come on."

Regretfully Gerry looked at the bike again and leaned it back at the wall so he could follow his sister back to the celebrations in the mill. There they found Edna being embraced by a suddenly tearful Freddie, a Freddie who turned to face the wall as he realised the other two were there. He slipped away, only to find a blue uniform in his way. He saw the sleeves, recognised the rank, knew who it was and looked up at a smile and a pair of happy looking eyes.

"Approve?" said the smiling mouth.

His answer was in the hug.

The Best Man's and Groom's speeches were each an emotion-charged account of discovering each other, and the impact the discoveries had made on their families and friends. There were many pauses for laughter - and for the speaker to overcome the rushes of emotion caused by recounting their experiences.

At last they were all able to chat and enjoy themselves until Max stood and announced that there would be music for a while. He introduced old Archie Bullimore who summoned Ruth, Owen, Alan and Eric.

Without preamble Archie launched into song:

"Come write me down, ye powers above
The man that first created love
For I've a diamond in my eye
Wherein all my joys and comforts lie
Wherein all my joys and comforts lie

So now his trouble and sorrow is past
His joy and comfort has come at last
That girl to him always said nay
She will prove his comforts night and day
She will prove his comforts night and day."

After the first line he was joined by the Baker brothers, now treble and alto, and later by Ruth's soprano with Owen singing the tune as a tenor.

When they and the applause had finished Archie told them it was a song of the Copper family, also called 'The Wedding Song', and went into that family's history just as he had in the Mill house at Christmas.

He played a note, looked round at the others and started off another song, this time with four parts, including Owen who had been specially trained in secret to sing its tenor line.

There followed dance tunes on the concertina and more songs, and then there was a natural pause whilst Archie picked up his concertina again. To their surprise another low treble voice, shyly at first, started singing *"Love Divine all loves excelling...".* The audience parted slowly and revealed Freddie, now deep into his task and with his eyes closed, giving a clear and mature rendition of the old hymn. He sang only the first and last verses but it was enough to show that here was another voice, and one that equalled Ruth's and the brothers'.

When he had finished there was an audible 'Wow' from many and a pause

260

before the applause started. Edna, astonishment still on her face, wiped her eyes. Freddie was prevented from slipping away to the back of the mill and was pushed forward until everyone had stopped clapping. His face was red.

Isaac held out a hand to be shaken, saw the lad's embarrassment and led him away towards the food table, then spun him round and held his shoulders.

"You keep surprising me," he said. "Where on earth did you learn to sing like that?"

The lad gave his trademark shrug. "Had to get out of the way on Sunday mornings, didn't I? Nice and warm in the church, and they had music…" He paused, a faraway look in his eyes. "Didn't take me long to learn the tunes. The words came too. Then one day I hid and they locked me in between morning service and the evening. I just sang. Most of the time. It was so good, singing with that echo. You can play with it, make it work for you. And then, Christmas, I went up to the big shops and just did some carols. Earnt me some money, so I thought I might be all right. At least he and I ate well that Christmas. Well, I did. I had to chuck most of his away after he'd started snoring. It'd gone cold."

Silence.

More comes out every time we talk, thought Isaac. Poor old lad. He hadn't been living, only existing.

"Well," he said eventually, "I'll tell you this: you can sing. And if you love it and want to, then join the choir with Ruth and the others. And maybe look for shows. Could be you've got another two years to that voice before it goes down…"

"Started already."

"Has it? Well, what you do is up to you, but sing all you want to here, and people will love it. And I mean here in Sussex, and not just tonight! And when you can't get up to treble any more we'll see how it settles down. But you have music in you too, so don't waste that."

"I've never been taught."

"If you want lessons in sight reading, then we can do that. It'll open up a new world for you."

"What – read all those dots? I could never do that!"

"Not to start with. But gradually… you'll see."

"You'd really do that for me?"

"And why not? After what you've done for me?"

"What've I done for you?"

Isaac drew in his breath, thinking how to put it.

"Gave me someone else to fight for. Made me laugh. Helped me stop feeling sorry for myself. Got some stories out of me I thought were lost and buried for ever. Been good company. Made me think I was doing something useful. Agreed to be part of my family. Supported us today. And sung like that, just now."

He was aware of eyes that were looking into his, trying to read him. A right hand was offered, this time by the boy, and was shaken.

"Come on," said Isaac, his voice not quite its usual self. "Let's get something to eat."

It was about midnight that taxis arrived to take people home. Edna, Isaac and Freddie, along with Isaac and his family, were staying at the Mill House. Owen had enjoyed the Harveys again, though this time not to excess. It nevertheless prompted him to require a visit to the toilet in the early hours of the morning. He had slept and dozed fitfully for some time, hoping that he would not need to get out of bed but knowing that he would feel no better until he did so. A sound from outside, audible even over Freddie's quiet snoring, made him get up. He listened, but heard nothing else. Oh well, he was on his feet...

As he returned, he found Freddie and Gerry, who were sharing his room, standing, listening. They jumped as the door opened and then relaxed when they realised it was Owen.

"Shhh!" he said, unnecessarily.

"What's up?"

"The dog. Then a sort of creaking. And the dog growled again. Didn't you hear her?"

"No. How long ago?"

"Couple of minutes. Should we go and see?"

21 – Voices, publicity and the leg

They hauled on trousers and jumpers, then tiptoed downstairs in bare feet. Ada was standing, bristling at the door. Shoes on and done up, Owen was about to open the door when he paused and turned off the light.

"Okay?" he whispered. "Let your eyes get used to the dark, then tell me."

There was a pause.

"Okay, I think," said Gerry.

And "Okay," from Freddie.

He opened the door slowly. They could barely see the cottages and glasshouse opposite. Ada pushed past them and sniffed, then growled quietly again.

"What is it, girl? What can you see?"

There was a movement just visible, up towards the railway crossing.

"Keep in the shadows," Owen hissed. "If anyone comes this way, stay there and keep absolutely still, even if you think they've seen you."

It was easy when there were walls by their side to shield them from the very little light from Newhaven's port and street lights, but when there was nothing except low scrub they had to move very slowly. Half way between the last of the cottages and the old crossing-keeper's house there was a light ahead, and they froze. There were two muffled clicks and it went out. Owen was reminded of the van whose silhouette he saw in that very place some months previously.

An engine started, a shape moved. If it was a vehicle – it must be, thought Owen – then it had no lights. The engine sound diminished. Owen wished there had been a car on the main road whose lights would shine on it, but none came. But along the road, nearer Newhaven, was a lay-by whose surface was chalk. Dimly a movement could be detected which might have been a car.

They could hear it no more. Each of them relaxed.

"So what was it?" asked Owen, more to himself than anyone else.

"Morris Minor." Freddie and Gerry spoke simultaneously, then grinned at each other.

"Where did the men come from, then? Has the Buckle been robbed again?"

"Has it been?" asked Freddie, not having heard the story.

"Tell you tomorrow. Let's go down towards the beach, see if there's anything there. Ada?" he pointed the dog towards the sea. "Seek!"

Ada had no idea what the word meant. It would be surprising if she had if all she'd done for most of her life was lie in a shed, pregnant or feeding puppies. But she walked happily enough beside the three, down to the beach.

It was dark. Still the only light was the dim glow from Newhaven. They gained the beach itself, then Owen held up a hand which the other two sensed more than saw.

"If we go down, the pebbles'll give us away," he hissed. "See what we can see from here."

They stood, now shivering in the south-westerly wind that was coming straight at them. All eyes were drawn to the lights on the two breakwater arms guarding Newhaven Harbour.

"There!" whispered Freddie, pointing. "In line with the flashing light."

"They're both flashing. Which one?"

"The outer one. Look! There."

With the gentle swell at the right point, they could just make out a vessel, a small vessel, no more than a large dinghy. She was either sailing towards them or towards the harbour – they couldn't distinguish. It was just a shape, all dark.

"Black sails, maybe?" Gerry this time.

"I think she's heading away. But it does look like she came from here."

"I think that's all we're going to get tonight," said Owen. "Back to bed for all of us. Pity we didn't catch them, though."

Freddie had experienced more thumps and cuffs from adults he'd seen in suspicious circumstances than any of the others, so he wasn't so sure.

"Is it?" he muttered.

It all seemed so unlikely the next morning in the usual bustle of preparations for church. Any attempt at conversation about it was stalled by one or other of the adults asking them to hurry up and use the bathroom or have breakfast or put on a *clean* shirt. They were all going, and a car was needed for Ruth, Freddie and for Isaac senior. Given that, everyone squeezed into the two vehicles and it was only the Baker brothers who had to cycle into Seaford; an opportunity they seized with glee.

Isaac noticed with intense pleasure his ward's gusto in joining in with the hymns, sometimes without referring to the words. Owen, quietly equipped by his father with a music version of the hymn book, muttered along as best he could with the tenor line, until he had it more or less correct, and then was disconcerted to discover that the last verse seemed always to be sung in unison.

After the service they chatted for a while to people who had been sitting near them who had heard Freddie's contribution and who seemed genuinely affected by it, to his embarrassment and quiet pleasure. Conversations finished; Ruth and the brothers were walking from the vestry towards them but they had a young man with them, a young man dressed in a black cassock.

"This is Mr Treadgold, our choirmaster" said Alan, grinning. "He asked if we could introduce him to the boy singing treble somewhere around here."

Mr Treadgold had already fixed Freddie with a friendly, wont-take-no-for-an-answer stare.

"Your voice I could hear, was it?"

Freddie, once again embarrassed, nodded and muttered "Sorry."

"Sorry? Don't be sorry, be grateful. You have in your throat an instrument, a well crafted instrument that is a delight to listen to. Come with me for a moment, would you? If your family can spare the time, that is. Do you live locally?"

Freddie had no chance to refuse without appearing rude. At the chancel steps he looked back at the others and shrugged as if to say 'what can I do?'. Isaac gave him such a positive nod that, encouraged, he all but tripped on the step as he turned to follow again.

The others were listening to Eric and Alan telling them how he'd just taken over from an organist who had retired. Ruth, who had only just rejoined the choir now she had been encouraged to walk a little, nodded her agreement.

"He's really keen to get what he calls the pure choir sound again, and contrast it with the older voices," she explained. "He…"

She was interrupted by the organ starting to play Tallis' Canon: *Glory to Thee my God this Night*. They could see Freddie nod. He started again. Freddie joined in, quietly. The organ stopped. He was told something and turned towards the opposite wall. Another start, and this time they heard him, but only just. Another stop; another muttered instruction. Freddie turned to face them.

"Ruth," Mr Treadgold called, "Can you go to the back door and tell me if Freddie's too loud or too soft, please? Actually, tell him, not me. Hands behind the ears if you can't hear properly, finger on the mouth if he's too loud."

Another muttered instruction and Freddie came to the top of the chancel steps and clapped once. The sound reverberated around the empty church.

"Fill the space so you can hear that reverberation. Now: I'll count you in. Got the note? Good. Start after three and use that voice of yours to *fill* the space!"

The first three words he sang were tentative, but after that Freddie had, in his mind, returned to those afternoons in the East London church where he would do just what he was being asked to do now. The sound came back to him, and somehow it gave confidence and a fullness to his voice he couldn't detect, but which left the others open mouthed.

The organ accompaniment stopped and he faltered but un urgent 'carry on!' made him do just that. The first verse ended. The hymn book drooped in front of him, but he continued. *"Forgive me Lord…"*

The pure voice rang round the church. The vicar, on his way to close the main door, stood, silenced and entranced. Mr Treadgold stopped Freddie after the second verse.

"Was he too loud?" he called to Ruth at the back.

"No. Just right."

"Good. Well done, you. Now, let's try this again. Alan, you take the second part, Eric the third. And Ruth the fourth, please. And don't forget, we're trying to fill this place with sound and charm the old ladies. And anyone else who's listening too. Okay: here's the start note… One two three…"

Once again Freddie started. Alan came in with the same part at the end of his first line, Eric at the second and Ruth's more mature pure soprano at the third.

With Freddie's example in their minds the other three gave of their best. The four of them did indeed fill the church with sound. At last the echoes of

Ruth's voice faded and silence reigned.

"Now, *that's* what I was trying to do last week when you lot were mucking around," the young man called, as severely as he could despite his pleased smile. "That was excellent. And you, my new soloist; please will you join the choir? What's your name?"

Freddie told him.

"Whom do I ask to give you permission?"

Freddie was still recovering from the unexpected delight of being asked to sing loudly and wholeheartedly, and even being complimented on it by so many people. He was wearing a broad smile and a beatific expression, and was unusually voluble in making introductions and giving explanations.

Edna and Isaac were delighted that he was interested in singing, and agreed promptly. The others gave a shout, then remembered they were still in church.

Later, the three boys gave an account of their night time interruption and actions to Max, Ernie and Arthur.

"I'd heard there might be something going on," Ernie Baker said slowly. "'Course, they might just be landing fish or crabs or something, but why here?"

Deliveries of machinery to the mill by road and by rail had been progressing gradually. Engineers and Killicks' builders had done some head-scratching and emergency re-siting but had by that time achieved a Works that was ready to be commissioned. The Monday after the wedding a stock of ingredients was delivered, and along with representatives of the machinery manufacturers the processes were described to the mill staff. Flour and other items were loaded in the appropriate places, specially printed paper bags placed at the other end of the machines, and the first very few examples of each new product were created.

Max was pleased, but cautious. "Now we get our volunteer cooks to follow the instructions on the bag and make the bread or cake or gravy or whatever," he said. "Once we're all happy they're acceptable, we can get going."

"We've done all that for you," complained one of the manufacturers' representatives. "We've told you what the proportions should be."

"Yes, for the water you have in wherever the machine was tested," said Max. "Our water is different, harder perhaps, and I want to be absolutely certain that what we're selling is top notch. We might need guidance on how the adjustments we need to make to get it to top notch, and that's where you come in. All this was explained in the tender documents."

His comments silenced the man, who had been hoping for a short stay at the Mill, a night in a hotel and a free day afterwards.

Various of the mill staff took bags of the mixes to give to their volunteer cooks. The remainder dispersed back to the business of flour milling. Test time came very soon afterwards for the gravy mix, a very few hours after for the cake mixes and not until late afternoon for the bread mixes. There were adjustments to be made, as all the local people were sure there would be, and a further series of tests which delayed the muttering representatives still further.

At around six o'clock Max and Arthur declared themselves satisfied with most of the products except the bread mixes and explained that the next test batch would be available the following day when he would see that particular representative again.

The man wasn't happy.

By the following afternoon, after two more batches of bread had been baked and sampled, Max and Arthur declared themselves happy with the results and signed off the installations. Max called his Managing Director and gave him the good news, and was immediately told that he would be visiting and wanted to see everything, preferably working and producing.

"I shall now be able to give starting dates to the other four additional staff I've found," Max told him. "Two of them are wives of the staff, so they would be able to produce cakes and bread for the shop here almost immediately, but we do need the publicity campaign to swing into action now so that our salesman can assure local shops that they will be supported."

"Ah, yes; publicity. We should get on with that. I will ask our people to design something as soon as I've seen the site."

"But surely, there must have been a campaign worked up and ready for our commissioning here?" Max asked.

"We had no idea how much longer that would take."

"How strange. I have been providing detailed time scales as requested."

"You must leave that side of things to us. We have a department to cover it, as you obviously know."

"Then please – might you be able to get some signs done and brought down here, showing people what we have and telling them that they can visit a live mill? We – and I mean the Company – need them in order to get the name re-established."

"I'll see what I can do."

"Really," Max said when he had broken the call, "it's as if it's someone else's money they're spending, not the Company's. Think of all they've ploughed into this place, and they seem to be in no hurry to start selling! Ridiculous."

That week Freddie was dragged unwillingly to a Scout meeting, where he started off with an inbuilt feeling of scorn. But later he was seen to grin, then to join in with the likes of Eric, puzzling out how tents were pitched, and at the last was shouting encouragement in a game with the rest of them. Owen remembered that he had to go carefully because of his recovering injuries, and told the Patrol Leader running the game why. He also warned Freddie, who wanted to ignore the ban on using his right side limbs too much, but saw sense when it was explained that he might break one of them again.

The Mill's Managing Director paid his visit, along with the other Board members. They were shown the old and new machinery working (fortunately the tide was ebbing so that the mill could operate).

"The new stuff's not water powered, is it?" asked the Director who had been against the scheme from the start. He sounded peevish, as if he didn't want to be there.

Max explained that it could be operated by wind power, and only by electricity when the wind failed. He described with pride the speed with which their new sales lines were being produced, whereupon the same man asked him what sales were currently being achieved. Max gritted his teeth.

"Our new salesman is out and about in Seaford and Eastbourne at the moment giving free samples of product and its results. I'm told there is significant interest, but that one question is always being asked. It concerns our publicity campaign. There hasn't been one yet."

"Why not?" asked the man.

"That is a question I cannot answer, sir, as the publicity is done by the specialist department in London."

"Have they been instructed?"

"Again, I have kept the Board and them fully updated with progress and the anticipated commissioning date, but it is not I who have the authority to commission a campaign."

"Hmphh!"

He and the Manging Director were to be seen in earnest conversation soon afterwards. Max could only hope that there was a chance of pressure being brought to bear, especially as he had to field similar questions from the other Directors during the afternoon and gave them similar answers.

Finally the party was shown the bakery and shop. Max explained his strategy in using the old signalman's house for it.

"The smell from baking will entice people in as they are thinking of leaving," he told them with a smile. "Once in there we can also offer to sell them knick-knacks as well and wring a few more shillings out of them."

He was asked what knick-knacks meant to him.

"In this case," he said, thinking on his feet, "anything from bread boards to ivory handled cake knives. And a lot in between, no doubt."

The signalman's house was to double as accommodation for the baker's family when they were engaged. Max had decided, and told the Directors, that there was no point in giving his preferred candidate for the job a starting date until there was a reasonable demand for the bread and cakes. Until then, any special requests could be accommodated by the ever-resourceful Mary, Jessie and Barbara, along with other wives who were keen to earn some extra money.

The old buildings opposite had been tidied and decorated, and even landscaped after a manner, and the old yard would contain tables and chairs for visitors visiting the little cafe he was considering establishing there "As soon as we can advertise what we can do here," said Max to his Managing Director.

The man drew him to one side. "As to that, I understand you have been telling everyone on the Board that there is no advertising. I find that very disloyal, Wilson, and you should be careful what you say in future." This was said quietly. Some blessing, thought Max.

268

"Well, sir, Many of the Board have asked me how sales are doing and I have had to tell them where we stand. That we have some really good products, flour and mixes that will make proper bread, and we have examples for people to try. I've had to give them the reason for the lack of sales when they ask me. And that reason is that nobody knows we're in operation apart from an increasing number of shopkeepers as our man goes round. But even they are hesitant at stocking our goods without the public knowing what we're doing.

"You'll appreciate that I can't lie to the other Board members and they won't accept flannel from me – they are Board members, after all. And I won't lie to you, or evade the issue. It's not what you would expect; that I do know."

It was his Managing Director's turn to grit his teeth.

"Publicity is not in your sphere of influence, Wilson."

"No sir, it isn't. But the effect of the lack of publicity is to undersell what we have achieved here, all at great cost to the business and despite heart-warming goodwill from our staff. I realise that financial performance will improve with time, but I'm keen to see Tide Mills being a profitable part of the main business without delay and as soon as it can be achieved."

The man looked at him again. He nodded, told Max that that was all, and walked away.

The next Monday a stranger appeared in the office and introduced himself as the publicity manager and asked to be shown around "if the workers don't mind."

Jack Pentelow was affronted, and showed it. "All our staff here just want to get going with all this stuff," he told the man. "If you've come to do some publicity Max and I will show you round with pleasure and you'll be welcomed by everyone when they know what you're here to do. We're not Union here. We work for the firm because we know it's for our benefit."

"But haven't you been approached by the Union to get people to join up?"

"No. If anyone comes, any of our blokes can talk to them. But they all know that if they think something's unfair, they can talk to Max Wilson and he'll sort it or give them good reasons."

"But what about pay?"

"What about pay? The best thing is for us to get the publicity round and get the profits up, then there'll be some extra money coming in, some of which will come our way. Stands to reason."

"I doubt if the Union will see it that way, Mr Pentelow."

"Then they haven't got the sense they were born with and they don't know Max Wilson. And if they try to force our blokes to do anything, they'll be onto a loser. They don't know Sussex people. We wunt be druv."

"I beg your pardon?"

"Talk to the blokes as we go round. You'll find out what it means. I'll get Max down here."

"I can walk up to his office. That'd save time."

"His office is in his home. He, on the other hand, needs to be here to show you round." He reached for the phone and dialled.

By the time the visit to the mill, the new plant, the bakery, the shop and the potential café had been completed Mr Publicity's mind was reeling.

"I can't put most of what I've learnt in writing," he said. "If the attitude here got out to the Union they'd strike."

"Strike about what?"

"About... about the men... how they just get on with it. How they have no opportunity to talk to Union people. How the place isn't unionised at all."

"Their best Union representative is Mr Pentelow here, and failing that, me. We're both staff members, you know."

"But you're not Union."

"I fight my own battles with the Directors on behalf of the staff. Often I win them. I have authority to improve the conditions and wages of everyone here – in fact the first thing I did was to make expensive improvements to the staff cottages. How many cottages, improved or not, does the London mill have?"

There was no response.

"There aren't any, are there? No, we give – well, rent at a peppercorn rent – a cottage big enough for their family. The previous mill owner lowered the hourly rate. When it was pointed out to me – by my son who overheard a comment, may I add – I restored the pay to what it should have been, plus back pay, plus a bit extra. But don't ask me, ask the staff if they have any issues. Ask them if they want a Union here. But before you do anything, tell me what the problems are and if it's at all possible I'll put them right."

"What does your son do here?"

"I beg your pardon?"

"You mentioned your son. Where does he work?"

"At school."

"Oh... I thought..."

"The fact that he's a minor doesn't mean he's oblivious to what goes on here. Like me, like all the others, he has an interest in this place doing well."

"Why?"

"Why? Wouldn't you? Isn't it normal to want your father's responsibility to work well?

"I... I don't know."

"Perhaps we look at things differently here. You'd best stay over tonight in one of the hotels locally and chat to some of our people in the Buckle tonight. That'll give you an insight into their thinking." Max had no wish to offer the man hospitality at the Mill House.

"I have to get back to London tonight to work on a publicity. The MD wants to see an outline scheme tomorrow."

"I'm glad he's making it a priority. Any delay, of course, means more time when we can't add to the business's profits."

"You are making a profit, then?"

"No. I meant to the overall business. Not just the Tide Mills branch of it."

The man thought, trying to find any flaw in the arguments he'd heard and could find none.

"I'll see what I can do, Mr Wilson."

It was Wednesday and Owen, Alan and Eric had gone to Scouts, meeting up with Freddie on the way. Ruth was fed up and felt slightly out of sorts. She had spent almost three months unable to do very much. Her boredom had been seasoned only by Owen's presence and by Barbara and Max's kindness. Her main activities seemed to struggling back to her real home in the mornings with a crutch to ensure not too much weight was put on the leg, struggling back when Owen returned from school, the occasional visits by car and, of course, to choir and church to sing. She longed to be able to walk; to walk properly.

She noticed Ada. The dog seemed restless. "Do you need to go out?" she asked. The tail thumped. Grabbing the hated crutch as a support she swung herself to the front door and watched enviously as Ada made her sedate way, as befits an elderly dog, up the cinder track. It was good to be outside, she thought. Perhaps she should sit out here now it was warm. At least she would be able to see what was going on. And it would give Ada more freedom too.

There was the usual short whistle from a train as it approached the halt, warning anyone on the crossing to get off it. It was such a regular occurrence that she thought nothing of it until it dawned on her that there was no sign of the dog. The train whistled again, this time a prolonged blast. The noise of a train that was slowing down for the station was also usual, but not like this, not a scream of metal on metal.

Her heart in her mouth, she stood, forgetting the crutch, and started to run up towards the crossing. The train was now at a halt, by the side of the platform – she could see that as she hobbled up to it as quickly as she could.

A movement at the further end of the platform caught her attention; the driver, shouting something to a passenger – it looked like Jack-the-lad Barden. He raised his hand in acknowledgement and boarded.

So it hadn't been to try to avoid a dog that the train had stopped so suddenly.

And then there was a rustle at her right hand side and a black nose appeared from the bushes with a canine grin on its mouth. A sense of relief washed over her. She turned to the dog and told her she was silly before realising that her leg was aching and she had no crutch with her. How on earth had she managed to reach this far up the track without it?

Carefully, slowly, now aware that for the first time there was a real pain in her leg, not one that could be put down to unaccustomed use. She wondered if she could hop home.

By part hopping and part using the leg as a balance, she made it, and collapsed thankfully on a chair, hauling her leg up so as to support it. The pain eased. She wondered if she should tell anyone. Ada seemed aware of her discomfort and leant in to her unaffected side in support.

Barbara was in Seaford, shopping. Max had been called up to London to check on the publicity drafts. Her parents were at work, one in the mill and the other in the bakery. She decided it was probably all right, and even dozed off for a while.

She was floating – no, she couldn't be; she knew she was bent in the middle. Sitting. That was it. But still floating. Worse, she felt sick, but couldn't move. And there was a dog barking. Why?

Ada couldn't understand why her mistress was asleep in the middle of the day. She couldn't understand why the leg that looked so different from the other one and every other human's was now smelling peculiar. Dangerously peculiar – she knew that. She whimpered, and then barked again, loudly.

Get out. She must get out. She scratched at the door. No, a human always had to make that work. What else. She padded into the kitchen and focussed on the high scullery window. If she'd still been a young dog, the dog she'd been before she started to have so many puppies, she could have reached it easily. But now?

How about the shelves under it, the shelves that held so many lovely things to eat? She knew she shouldn't be in there, It had been made very clear. But there was danger...

She gathered herself, and made it up two of the shelves, dislodging some tins from beneath her. The remains of the Sunday joint lay at her side and she whimpered gently at it as if to tell it she'd be back.

A gathering of muscles again and she jumped across the corner of the scullery, gaining a shelf's height as she did so. Now she was just under the window but the last shelf was immediately above her. Another whimper. She looked around.

How...? then she realised it. She walked over a jelly to the other wall, sat and licked her paw, and jumped the crazy oblique angle from there to the deep-set window.

The stonework dug into her side and she wheezed, but got a paw-hold on the window ledge. Then it was a jump down, a jump that jarred her old joints far more than she expected it would. A quick shake, a listen. Sounds from the Mill. That was it.

Limping, but making all the speed she could, she found the door she had seen a lot of people use. She knew because of the smell. Standing outside head on one side, she barked for a few moments, then scratched at the door.

Jack Pentelow was struggling with columns of unaccustomed figures, those provided by the mill's new activities. After the third bout of barking and scratching he said a rude word and went to the door. The dog backed away, looking at him.

It took a second or two for the figures to banish themselves from his mind and he realised that Ada needed to be let in, presumably to the Mill House, where she should be. But how had she got out?

The dog led to the Mill House door. Jack knocked. No reply. He thought it would be all right just to open the door and let the dog in, but Ada stood in the opening, looking at him, then into the house, then back...

"Something wrong, gal?" he said quietly, and allowed himself to be led by her.

Thirty seconds later he was dialling the emergency services. Half an hour later an ambulance with the new-fangled two-tone horns bumped its way down to the Mill House where Mary and Arthur had run when they'd been told by a breathless Jack Pentelow, and were now holding Ruth's hands and looking with near-panic at the rising fever in their daughter's face. It was another hour before she was admitted to a bed in the Royal Alex. In her delirious state she was aware that, although still apparently floating, she was at least no longer in a sitting position. Her arm hurt. But she knew also her parents were there.

"But I've *got* to see her... I'm sorry, but I've just got to." It was a worried voice from some way away, a voice that meant so much to her, someone she badly wanted to see, and to have hold her third hand... no. No that was wrong. She shook her head and almost smiled.

"Owen?" she whispered.

"Yes," two voices answered her. Then Dad: "Do you want to see him?"

As best she could, she imparted a look that said 'what do you think?' but actually only nodded.

He was allowed over, much to the nurse's chagrin. To everyone's surprise, including his own, his hand found Mary's where it gently held Ruth's. He was rewarded by a faint smile from Ruth and a tearful nod from Mary.

"You're a good boy, Owen," she said.

"Came as soon as I got back. Mum told me on the platform, so I dumped my bag and took the same train back. Is she any better? What happened?"

"An infection got in," said the nurse briefly. "She's had the first injection of a course of antibiotics. As she's now starting to respond, I think we've got it right. Her specialist has been sent for from London, as he did the original operation and is the expert."

It was five o'clock that evening when Ruth's specialist from London saw her. He made arrangements, and tired though he was he prepared himself for an emergency operation.

"Just an exploratory," he said. "And we'll see how she's doing with the lengthening at the same time. You need to leave her with us, at least overnight and tomorrow morning, then you can come in when she's out of the anaesthetic."

Ruth's heart sank. The question she wanted to ask was the same as the question Arthur put to the surgeon.

"How much is this going to add to her recovery time?"

"That's what we're going to find out. We'll be able to tell you – all – tomorrow. Actually, the people down here will tell you, because I have to be back in London tonight or my wife will kill me."

Arthur jumped up. "And all this time... Doctor, thank you so much for coming down for her, for us. We really appreciate it."

He smiled. "I have an interest in her. You see, I've long felt that there was an improvement I could make to the placing of the rods in cases like this. Ruth is the third patient to receive that improvement, and all the others have been successful. If I find what I expect to find, we will be dealing with just an infection, and no mechanical problems with the bones – if she's been tightening the screws as she was told."

Another, gentle smile on Ruth's face.

They took her to the operating theatre soon afterwards. Her visitors, slightly encouraged but still worried, left.

There was a discussion at the Mill House that night. Owen, remembering his success at winning an argument previously about the same subject, was being deliberately level voiced and calm.

"Dad, I've got to leave school early tomorrow to meet up with the Decks' and visit Ruth. We break up tomorrow, so there's nothing important on in the afternoon."

Max's eyebrows lifted. "Well, so long as you square it with your teacher and the Head, fine. Give her our love."

It was Owen's turn to look surprised. "Er... thanks. I thought you'd object."

Max grinned. "And if you hadn't asked I'd be worried."

"What, that I might just go?"

"No, worried that you didn't feel about Ruth the way you have been feeling. Go on with you. Find out what time they're going and meet them there."

As it was, it was only the last half hour of school he had to miss, and this time his form teacher accepted the reasons almost readily. He ran from Brighton station up to the hospital, to find the Decks' already by the bedside and a nurse once again trying to block him.

"I'm really sorry," he said at last. "I was visiting her last night, with her Mum and Dad, I've just rushed from school which I left early with everyone's permission, please don't try to stop me from seeing her. You must understand." Once again he was using the calmness that he discovered worked so well, and it was partly this that persuaded the nurse that he might actually be an adult, or nearly one, and could perhaps be allowed in. And he was tall and good looking.

"Go on, then." She sighed, and watched him march down the ward. *Was* he an adult? He didn't look broad enough. Well, it was done now.

Ruth was awake, though still tired, but in good spirits. "At least this time I've been told some facts," she said with a smile. "It was an infection, but one that had been getting worse for some time. What happened yesterday just brought it out, sort of thing."

The looked relieved. "Are they treating it?" asked Mary.

"Yes. Injections of antibiotics every few hours. Including through the night, they tell me. That'll be fun."

Owen nodded. "They just want to make sure you don't get too comfortable here and not want to come home."

She put out her tongue at him, smiling.

"What did happen yesterday, Ruth?" The question was Arthur's, but they all wanted to know. She explained her part in it, and Ada's as far as she could.

"So Ada was with you in the house, the wrong side of a closed door?" Arthur exclaimed. "Yet the next minute she was barking outside the mill office, getting old Jack to come and find you."

This was news to Ruth, who looked suitably surprised. "She's a good dog," she said.

"She's a miracle worker if she can get out of a closed house," Mary told them.

"I think I might know how she did that," Owen offered. "Mum complained there was a mess of tins on the larder floor and a jelly had a paw-print in it. She was going to say something to the dog but that's when Jack appeared with the news. So Ada must have got out that way. And it takes some doing, especially for an old dog. I wondered why she was limping a bit."

Three pairs of eyes bored into his. "Are you saying that that dog saved Ruth's life?" Arthur asked slowly.

"Don't think there's any doubt. She got Jack Pentelow over – we know that. How she got out – well, I think we know that too now. And bless her, she never even touched the remains of the joint which was in there next to the jelly."

"Wow." It was noticeable that Ruth's eyes had misted over at the gratitude she felt for the dog.

"Did they say anything about the leg itself?" her father asked.

"Yes. Apparently it's going very well. Because of the infection they've cut back on the lengthening until it's cleared, but they've got to do a bit or the bones will fuse together and need separating again before I can start really lengthening it again." She shuddered. "I don't want that. So for the moment the nurses are turning the screws, but only one flat at a time they said – whatever that means – to make sure I don't make a mistake."

"And how long are you in here for?" Mary asked.

"Until the infection's gone. A few days, they say. Then it's back to normal."

"And you've only got six more weeks of treatment left," Owen told her.

"Have I? I hadn't been counting; at the start it seemed such a long time into the future."

"It's the last day of June today," Owen told her, having been anxiously counting down the days since the first operation. "Then it's just July, and twelve days of August, and you'll be in London having that lot taken out."

"It's still all over the summer holidays."

"One school summer holiday, and then a lifetime of *running* around," Mary reminded her.

She nodded. "I know, I know. But still, it's a lot to give up."

It was indeed just five days before she was allowed home, with admonitions from the hospital not to overdo it again. The first thing she did after hoisting herself from Max's car on two crutches was to sit down on an outside bench – an addition to the Mill House thoughtfully provided by Max "because it looks nice" but really for her benefit. Ada came up to her, wagging her tail, and Ruth almost cried again as she petted her and remembered what the dog had done for her. But now the story of her escapology and persistence had circulated the hamlet. Ada was held to be a heroine and received gifts of food from everyone until Ruth and Owen had to beg for it to be stopped as she was getting fat.

22 – Smuggling

Relief that the school term was over was tempered with the knowledge that in the following September he and Ruth, in their separate parts of the same school, would be in their GCE 'O' Level year. The year that would really decide their future – or so Owen had been told time and time again.

In all the excitement generated by the mill's being almost ready to open fully, by the incident of Ruth's leg, and by a busy life in general they had seen little of the Galleys, their son or Bee and Gerry. It came as something of a surprise to see the latter two, plus Freddie, cycling down the Drove towards them the Saturday after they had all broken up.

"We've got a house in West Street!" said Gerry as soon as there was someone to say it to. Ruth was sitting on the bench outside again, her leg supported.

"I saw they were building there," she said. "It's a good place. Near the shops and everything.

"Pardon me," said Owen, "but what's a West Street?"

Between them they explained that it was the west end of the street that led to the church and crossed Pelham Road, and that it was just round the corner from the cinema.

"So where is that compared to where you are now?" he asked, puzzled.

"In Seaford, silly!" Bee laughed. "We've moved so Dad is nearer his new work and we're in the same town as Gerry's school when he starts in September."

"Phew!" he said when he understood.

"Hallo, you two," said Max, appearing from the house and free from work for the day. "Social call? Or is something wrong?"

"Social, really, Mr Wilson. We wanted to tell you all that we're moving to Seaford – West Street."

"Really! Good for you? When do you move?"

"Well… today, really…"

"*Today?* Why didn't you tell us? We should be helping you – you helped us when we moved in here. Come on, let's pile in the car and hurry over there. Where are the Baker boys? Oh, sorry, Ruth, would you prefer Owen to stay with you?"

"Thanks, Mr Wilson, but at the moment there's nothing to do. The removals people have made a big mistake. All our stuff is on the lorry…"

"Pantechnicon," Gerry prompted.

"Yes, that. And is heading to a place called Sleaford. They can't stop them until they phone the depot."

"*Sleaford?*" Max was incredulous. "But that's miles away. It's in Lincolnshire. It's half way up the country. Whose fault is it? It can't be your father's. If they'd quoted for that distance he'd have had a heart attack."

"It's the dim driver's," said Gerry bluntly. "We thought he was a bit of a berk when he was loading our stuff, didn't we?"

His sister nodded. "He's going to get a shock when he makes that phone call," she said with a laugh. "He'll have to drive all the way back here and unload tomorrow. Actually the depot people say they'll stop in a guest house or something and come back down tomorrow. We shan't be able to unload until Monday."

"Oh good grief." Another voice had heard the comment. Alan was quoting from Peanuts. Bee smiled at him.

"Where will school be for you?" asked Ruth.

"Bee will go to Brighton, to the College there…"

"Not Brighton College?" asked Owen, shocked.

"No! The… what's it full title? Brighton, Hove and Sussex Grammar School," Bee told him. "We can't afford a place like Brighton College! That's just while I do my 'A' levels."

Ruth nodded. "How about you, Gerry?" She was careful not to assume.

"I'm the thicko of the family," he said with a grin. "I'll be at Seaford with Freddie."

"Oy!" exclaimed Alan, "I'm at Seaford! And I'm not thick!" He was genuinely aggrieved.

"And I never even got a chance at the exam," Freddie said bitterly.

"Sorry, Alan, Freddie. Didn't mean it that way. And Dad says that the whole eleven plus thing is a scandal anyway and the sooner they scrap it, the better."

"I'm doing mine this September, when we go back," offered Eric.

"Then don't worry about it. Just take it. You'll get a good job whatever you do, wherever you go." Max was certain of that.

"Why am I at Grammar School then, Dad?"

"Because you took the wretched thing and got through its ridiculous questions somehow. It doesn't mean you're better or worse, or more or less intelligent. It just means that you managed to find out what they were really asking about and played the question setters' game. If you'd gone to a secondary school in London – or if you were to go to Seaford's – your mother and I would make absolutely certain you were given a chance at GCE's. They're what really count, it seems."

They digested that.

"So would I be able to take GCE's?" asked Alan.

"Talk to your parents. I'm sure they would enquire if it's something you wanted. And that applies to Gerry and Freddie too. And Eric, if he goes to Seaford."

"Shan't know until October, Mum says," offered eleven year old Eric.

"Well, you have the same chance as the rest of us," Owen told him. "Seems stupid that if we fail an 'O' level we can take it again as many times as we want, but the eleven plus is a once-only chance. Something really wrong there, methinks."

"*Methinks*?" Alan chided. "Swallowed a dictionary?"

"No. Force-fed Shakespeare, more like!"

"So really," Barbara broke in to steer the conversation away from school choices, "you could do with our help on Monday. Can we manage that, do you think?"

"We can cycle over," said Eric proudly.

"Freddie's coming down too, said Bee.

He smiled at her. "I can cycle down too – if you tell me where it is!"

"Meet outside the Buckle, then we can go from there."

"And we'll bring the car in case you all need to go shopping for something," said Max.

"I know," Barbara exclaimed, "If Ruth can give me a hand I can do lunch here for everyone and save you cooking. How's that?"

Bee looked at her gratefully. "I was wondering what to do about food without involving Grandma and Grandad. They've offered to come, but really it's too much for Grandad's leg."

"They must come as well," said Barbara. "Will you ask them? And where are you staying now, seeing as you have no belongings?"

"We're with Grandma and Grandad," she told them. "And at least we have some clothes and some overnight things, even Gerry's teddy."

"Oy!" shouted that worthy. Eric looked thoughtful.

Further down the Drove Jack Barden was sitting outside his cottage. He heard the youthful voices along with the adults and knew that the time was approaching when he could engage that Owen to start helping him and his colleague. He wanted to give as little notice as possible so as to avoid long and awkward questioning and going to parents. He would catch him the next Sunday afternoon – should be easy enough – and tell him to be ready at midnight on the Monday.

Sunday at St Leonard's Church in town was the first appearance of Freddie in the choir. He'd been given two weeks of checks at choir practices by Mr Treadgold to ensure that his memory was up to holding musical arrangements. It was, and he was happy to take his place amongst his friends from Tide Mills and the other few youngsters in the choir. He had been given nothing special to sing, no solo, but enjoyed the blending of the voices around him.

Owen spent the day with Ruth, pottering gently about the place. She was starting to bear weight on her leg again, now with less of the pain which, she now realised, had been slowly increasing over the week before her 'incident'. Freddie was now back to full strength, "If you have frequent rests…" he was warned. He and the others went off on bicycles over the Downs, led as always by Alan.

It was when Ruth had disappeared home, before the return of the cyclists, that Jack Barden saw his chance. He walked purposefully up to where Owen was oiling his bike, wishing he could have gone with the others despite being happy to stay and talk to Ruth.

"You still up for helping me and a mate on a fishing trip? It's just that one of the regulars has gone sick, see, so we need someone with some muscle."

Looking back, the combination of a crewman going sick and a boat needing an inexperienced help should have rung bells. It didn't.

"Well, yes. But when?"

"Night after tomorrow. You'll need to be in Sleepers 'Ole by eleven, see."

"Sorry – where?"

"Sleepers 'Ole. Down west side. It's the bit that's a sort of big inlet. South side of that, where the shore of the 'Ole comes back to the river, there's a ladder down. Meet us there. Old clothes. Gloves. Hat. No lights as you cycle down there. It'll be dark, mind. No moon on Tuesday night."

"What time will we be back?"

"'Fore dawn. Don't take long. Fiver in it for you. First of many if you do all right. But no talk to any of the others, or parents. If talk gets back other's will be on the same area, fishing it out, and we don't want that."

"I'll try."

"No. If you want to come, you come. If you don't, say no. If you say yes and let us down your name will be mud, not just here, but round this bit of Sussex, see? You agree, you *got* to come."

"What would we be fishing for?"

"We're lobster potting. Hoisting pots to the surface, emptying them and chucking them back. You would be keeping the boat still while Andy and I hoist and empty."

"I've never steered a fishing boat. I could probably hoist the pots up, though."

"Nah... we want you to take the boat. We'll teach you, don't worry."

"Well..."

"Look, I'd like to, but why the secrecy?"

"Told you. We don't want the other fishermen finding out where our pots are."

"Why? They won't steal them, will they?"

"That's not the point. It's the area they're in, see. That's what we don't want to give away."

"Okay, but my Dad's not a fishermen. I can tell him."

"*No.* You tell no one. If they don't know, they can' tell."

Owen was keen to go. It was an adult-sized adventure and he knew, as a tall fifteen year old, that he was adult sized. But he still hesitated. There was the too-recent discussion about trust with his father and teachers, for one thing. And for another there was something in the back of his mind; something about a story that was not a story but fact. Fact that had seemed so impossible that it had taken a phone call and lots of talking to realise it was the truth.

The bell of memory finally rang.

"Where do these... do we unload these crabs?" he asked.

"Why d'you want to know?"

Owen, now in acting mode, shrugged his shoulders casually. "Seems that if it's so secret, landing them in Newhaven again would be seen by the other crabbers," he said as airily as he could. "Wouldn't make sense to go to all the cloak-and-dagger stuff and then get seen as they're unloaded."

Jack stared at him, calculating. Was this the equivalent of an agreement?

"Okay, boy. We unloads here and takes it up through the Mills on a trolley. That all you want to know?"

"Ye…es… Well, no. Who's the other person on board?"

"Why do you want to know?"

"If you've got one young local, you may have got another. It might be someone I know and don't like."

"It's not a youngster. It's someone who knows boats and the river better than me. His family's been fishermen and such for longer than any of us have been alive."

"Local family, then?"

"Was. 'Til about fifteen years back."

"Ah, so not local? But you say he still knows the river and such?"

"Yes, like the back of his hand. Look, his name's Andy. Andy Holden. That enough to calm your nerves?"

Owen hid the jolt he felt at the surname very well, he thought. How did he now let the man down without arousing suspicion?

"Okay," he said slowly. "I'll do it, but only if I can tell my father that I'm going."

Jack Barden shook his head. "Won't do. I told you. No one gets told."

"But I want to go. And I could do with that fiver. But dad's got to know where I am if anything happens."

"No one gets told. That's final."

"But he won't tell anyone."

"I said it's final. You either come, and promise no one has been told, or we forget the whole thing."

How much longer should he play the man along? Was he attracting too much danger? From either Barden or Holden?

"It's just that my Dad has… well… had words with me recently and…well, he's got into the habit of coming into my room to check I'm there and asleep." Not true. Well, perhaps a grain of truth, but convincing.

"You mean, you've been out at night recently?" Barden was horrified.

"Yes," Owen admitted, now wondering if he could enjoy himself. "I was up late once and thought I heard a noise, so I got dressed and came down to listen. Dad heard me and… well, you can guess the rest."

It had been fifteen years since Jack Barden's father had been around to beat his son for the many indiscretions his son had committed, but he guessed – wrongly of course – what Owen was hinting at.

"So you're saying that your Dad will be checking on you at times, and maybe even listening out?"

"Well, he'll be checking." Owen didn't want to think that anyone would be keeping a listening watch all night as it could stop the enterprise. "It was only when the wind blew the door shut that he woke that time. But now…" he shrugged again. "That's why I need to tell him."

"And I'm saying you can't. So that's that. You missed your chance there, boy."

"But…" Owen hoped he wouldn't be asked again. He wasn't.

"No. It's no good. If you can't do a little job, at your age, without asking Daddy's permission, you're better not doing it."

Owen longed to hit him, but just said: "It's not asking for permission, it's telling him I'll be out so he doesn't…well, you know."

Jack Barden shrugged unconcernedly.

"Not my problem. Or Mr Holden's. So that's it."

He turned away, as if expecting Owen to plead with him. Owen kept silent, a fact that should have disturbed the young man but didn't. When he was about to enter his home he looked round at Owen, only to find him gazing sadly at him.

"Your choice," he said as he went inside. Owen waited until he'd disappeared, smiled grimly and went home.

After the evening meal he cornered his father and asked for an interview in the study. Max looked worried.

"It's not trouble, is it?"

"Yes, Dad."

"What have you done?"

Owen was rather offended, but launched into the story and how it fitted in with the sightings of the van, particularly the most recent sightings when they had seen a boat bearing away whilst the cargo, whatever it was, was taken to a Morris Minor van parked the other side of the railway.

"So you believe there may be something other than fish being landed, do you?" his father asked.

"I don't know how to keep a boat still, yet Barden said that would be my job. I offered to hoist the lobster pots up, but he quickly said he didn't want that. I wondered if that meant he didn't want me to see what was being hauled up."

"Surely a boat will just keep still, if it's not being powered."

"She wouldn't be powered by an engine if it's the same one we saw that night. She was sailed."

"It does sound a bit underhand. But there might be a logical explanation for it like Barden says. Maybe they *have* found a lucrative crabbing area and he doesn't want the rest of the Newhaven fleet fishing it."

"And maybe it's a bit of smuggling going on, Dad. You know, 'Laces for a lady, letters for a spy' and all that. Remember that song old Archie sang at Christmas?"

"No. You have the advantage of me. What was that? And what's it got to do with this business?"

"It's a Kipling poem, set to music. *Smugglers' Song* I think it was called. The chorus went *'watch the wall my darling as the gentlemen ride by.'*"

"I remember the chorus. Do you think it's that?"

Owen shrugged his shoulders. "No idea. I just think it might be more than just crabs or lobsters. Look, what about the Police? Should we be telling them?"

Max thought for a moment.

"It's more of a Customs and Excise matter, really, I'd have thought. If they want to involve the Police it's up to them. But it'd be a good idea to get them down here and talk…"

"No, Dad! Barden would see, then that would be it. Nothing would happen."

"Isn't that what we want?"

"No! Holden – a new one – is involved in this. It's not just Jack Barden. If it's illegal, and a Holden is involved, it's got to be bad. If it's that bad, it needs to be stopped."

Max thought again.

"Perhaps you're right. But I hope it doesn't get any of us into trouble. And if they wanted you – when – tomorrow? – we need to get on with this. Where's the nearest Coastguard office? Newhaven?"

Owen hesitated. "If we go to Newhaven, will someone see us and suspect something? Should we go somewhere else?"

"Where *can* we go? The Coastguard are the people. Unless…" He paused. "I wonder if Isaac has any contacts."

"Of course! Isaac. He'd want to know about a Holden who's still involved in smuggling – or whatever it is. And we know we can trust him. Shall we go and see them? Now? Ruth would like to see Freddie, I'm sure."

"I suppose we'd better, seeing the timescale."

The Galleys were surprised and pleased to see the four of them, plus dog, at the door. It had been natural that Freddie should be a frequent visitor to Tide Mills and not that the others should come to Bishopstone. It was a matter of convenience that Edna and Isaac understood. So far as visits by villagers to the house were concerned, they were still newcomers. Incomers. Thus far they were neither on the visiting lists of the well-heeled, nor part of the casual drop-in habits of others. It had been a quiet period for them, apart from Freddie's presence, but one that enabled them to make those little adjustments to the house that really make a house a home.

Max and Owen told of the various sightings of the van and the rest of the story up to Owen's talk with Jack Barden. Ruth and Barbara had not heard the full saga until then. And sure enough at the mention of Andy Holden's name Isaac really sat up and took notice. When the two had completed their tale, he sat for a moment, staring at the wall opposite.

"I suppose, really, that I shouldn't blame this Andrew for the wrong his grandfather did to me. But I've been quietly obsessed by the name 'Holden' for so long… even some of my crew members over the years had the name – it's hardly uncommon – and I automatically viewed them with disfavour until I knew they had nothing to do with *that* family. And now…"

He snapped to alertness. In the space of a second he seemed to have donned the mantle of a decisive Captain, RN again.

"And you need help in getting to the right people, people who will be effective if necessary and merge into the background if not. And in doing so will ensure that your name and involvement is not noticed. Is that the correct reading of it?"

"Yes," said Max and Owen together. Because of the man's tone Owen added "...Sir." Isaac smiled at him for a second.

"Part of my command in London was to make sure a watch was kept on apparently innocent movements of small boats around the Port," he said. "Certain behaviour patterns made us sit up and take notice, and when we thought something was worthy of attention – like this – we had a special Navy service we woke up. We couldn't do it formally. We couldn't use the Police – even the River Police, although when we had evidence we called them in to act, of course.

"Now maybe, just maybe, some of that service's people would like a holiday by the sea. It's about time we had visitors here. Don't you think so, Edna? And I imagine the Mill House might welcome some friends they've never met before. And the Decks... do you think they would welcome a long-lost cousin? Or would that be too many sudden visitors? Perhaps it would. But then... Barden can't keep watch all the time. Max's two friends can come any time – if that's all right, Max and Barbara. All the others can rendezvous here and when Max tips us the wink that Barden's gone somewhere..."

"He always goes somewhere after work," Ruth interrupted.

"Does he now? Every day?"

"Yes. I... I watch."

She had become a student of the Mill staff's movements over her long, often boring, period of inactivity.

"So as soon as we hear from you that he's gone, and in which direction, your 'uncle' can come and visit. All these people will stay the night, and will make their own plans and take their own actions. That's how they operate. We shall know nothing until it's all over, just that relatives are visiting.

"Now, I need to make a long phone call."

"Should we go?" asked Barbara.

"Not on my account. Nor on Edna's, I imagine. We both enjoy your company. And I might need to ask Owen some questions while I'm on the phone."

In the middle of what indeed proved to be a long phone call he called Owen's name.

"Did they tell you the name of the boat?"

"No," said Owen. "And I didn't want to make them even more suspicious. But..." He thought a moment, imagining himself back on the beach with friends, watching a boat slip away into the darkness. "She's black. Or dark. With black or very dark sails. No, black sails. We saw the light of the lighthouse on them."

Isaac repeated this on the phone. Owen was still thinking, and after a minute put up his hand. Isaac paused the conversation.

"When we were in Newhaven, just before Christmas, we saw a boat come up the river," Owen said. "It was in really bad condition, but completely black. I think the name on the side was *Channel Pride* but it was part-covered by nets and stuff. Might be the same one."

"Black sails?"

Owen thought back again.

"Sorry. Can't remember. The only reason I remember the name was that it was such a bad name for such a scruffy boat."

Isaac nodded and continued his conversation. Owen, seeing he wasn't needed any more, rejoined the others.

Five minutes later Isaac returned, looking pleased and rubbing his hands.

"What is it Conan Doyle has Sherlock Holmes say at the start of a case? 'The game's afoot, Watson!' Well, the game should be now well and truly afoot. The River Thames Irregulars are swinging into action. There should be a telephone call within half an hour. My contact says that as far as he knows they'll all be happy to have a change from the Thames. Most of them are longing to get somewhere near the sea again.

"Now. How about some tea? I have no beer in the house I'm afraid, Max, Owen. But tea's what we need when we have to keep our heads clear, eh Max?"

Since Edna and Barbara had slipped off into the kitchen already, tea was quickly produced. They were still munching on sandwiches when the telephone rang. Isaac went to answer it.

Five minutes later the living room door opened.

"Any idea about somewhere near this Sleepers' Hole place a car could stay? And somewhere a bloke could be concealed?"

"There's the car park on the Esplanade, between the railway and the sea wall," Ruth told him. "And if he looks at all like a seaman he'd be at home in the Hope."

Isaac gave her a puzzled look.

"It's a pub right down the end of the harbour, before you get to the sea wall. I know you can park by the sea."

Isaac nodded again and returned to the phone. He gave the information, then laughed.

"They'll be intrigued, I should think... yes, that'll be fine. Seems to cover all eventualities we can see... Yes, I'll ask him."

He returned. "Owen, when you've seen the van go, which way did it turn?"

"Towards Newhaven."

"Every time?"

"Yes. Couldn't see it very far because the road bends, and it's always a moonless night when I see it."

"That occurred to me. When did you see it last?"

Owen thought. "The night after your wedding. Freddie, Gerry and I were sharing my room."

He returned to the phone to pass the information on. There was some muttering and the receiver was replaced.

"That's that," said Isaac with satisfaction. "Max's sister and brother-in-law are coming to visit on Tuesday, about midday. They are Christine and Simon Laws and they live in London. You'll find that Christine has laryngitis at the moment and can only speak in quite a low voice."

He waited. The grins came and went.

"I won't make up a double room for them then," said Barbara, cueing laughter.

"I think they'd prefer not," Isaac responded drily. "Once they've had a cup of tea or something, perhaps Max could take them to see the ferry leave, and have a good look round the harbour at the picturesque fishing fleet and the town. Maybe a look at the beach at the west end, too. Then they can come back. While you have your evening meal they'll eat in whatever rooms you've given them…"

"They will certainly not," said Barbara. "I will cook for them and they eat with us."

"There's no need…"

"There is for me, for my pride! And what if someone were to look in the window and just see the family at the table?"

Isaac smiled.

"Very well. Now, thanks to Barden we know he has to be at this boat at eleven at least. So one of your visitors will be missing from about an hour before that. The other one will be in the room.

"Once work is over and Barden has vanished into Newhaven, a man with a medical looking bag, looking like a doctor, will call on the Decks. He is a specialist who wants to observe how the leg is being used on a day-to-day basis so he can make judgements."

He paused. "Actually, Ruth, I'm afraid your leg is the last thing he's going to be interested in or indeed qualified to observe. But that's the story for everyone who asks."

Owen broke the silence. "So what's going to happen?"

"I can't tell you that, not least because I don't know. And nor must you. If you don't know, you can't say. And not a word of this – apart from the bit about your relatives and Ruth's doctor – who comes from Brighton, by the way, Ruth – must go anywhere outside this room. And that includes not to friends; not even the Baker brothers. In fact, nothing will happen tomorrow night. This is just to discover what happens where. Then next time – well, we shall see."

A very shamefaced pantechnicon driver appeared early the following morning in West Street. He was greeted by a very cold mannered Isaac junior and six youngsters ranging from eleven (Eric) to fifteen (Bee and Owen). Together they carefully moved the contents into the compact house over the course of the day. Little was said to the driver, but talked instead with his crew. It was an awkward time. Both parties were glad when the vehicle was empty and driving away.

Freddie, nursing an aching leg that still let him down from time to time, told them all they were expected back at Bishopstone that evening to rest and eat. Before anyone could protest or mention parents, he added that those authorities all knew and would be expecting their offspring back later.

The person answering the door of the Bishopstone house was Ruth, to Owen's surprise and delight. They crowded in and were fed almost immediately by a happy Edna.

The knock at the Mill House door was expected. Max gave a wide grin as he welcomed in a lady and gentleman and their cases. A Rover was parked nearby.

"I'll get the other cases, 'darling'," said the man, and received a grim look from the heavy-featured woman with him. 'She' was ushered in, and once out of sight of the door slipped off the heeled shoes she was wearing.

"Bloody hell, how anyone can wear those things beats me," said a strong, male voice.

"You should try stilettoes," said Max without thinking.

"Oh God, not you too? What have I landed in?"

Max chuckled. "No, not me. Wouldn't have looked good on the bridge of a destroyer, would it?"

"Are you Captain Wilson? The chap Isaac told us about?"

"The same."

He stopped himself saluting. "Not Navy now. Not this weekend. But it's good to meet you, Sir."

"You too… probably best if I don't know either. We'll wait 'til your colleague… er… husband… gets back, then I can show you the room."

"Thank you. I hear you're going to show us round a bit?"

"My son and I will, as soon as we've had a cup of tea. Ah, here's your… husband now."

The other man heard and allowed himself a smile.

"Captain Wilson," said the 'wife'. The two shook hands.

"You were saying your son would be with us. I don't think that's a good idea. He mustn't be put in danger, and I doubt he could add anything. Better he's left here to play as usual."

Max laughed and went to the living room door.

"Owen," he called. "Come and meet our visitors."

He watched, smiling, as the looks on the disguised couple's faces changed as he came to meet them.

"Owen Wilson," he said before Max could get a word in edgeways. "I'm glad you're going to investigate these people, and even more glad I didn't agree to go with them."

The two men exchanged glances. "When Isaac told us about your involvement we were a bit sceptical that a child could – or should – be one of the informants," said the 'man'. "He didn't say that the supposed child was about seventeen and well able to look after himself. I suppose you are?"

Owen smiled. "I'd hope so. Judo helps a little if I get into a scrape."

"Judo! The up and coming sport. Any good?"

"Black belt, first dan."

"Black… good heavens. That's excellent. What age were you when you got that?"

"A month after turning fifteen."

More surprise. "And how old are you now?"

Owen smiled. "Still fifteen."

"Nearly sixteen, surely."

"No, sir. Birthday was 13th May."

"Well, Owen, I'm impressed. And yes, of course you must come with us later. It's your experiences we need to know about in detail."

"So I'm better off playing in the car with Dad and you, than at home."

"Owen!"

"No, he's right. I jumped to conclusions and that's something I should never do. Apologies, Owen."

Owen nodded.

"You shouldn't have been listening, Owen."

"The door was open, Dad. Couldn't help it. But your relatives weren't to know, were you?"

They laughed. "Please, while we're here, we're Simon and Chris. Christine if we're out, Chris if we're in. I'll do my best with the laryngitis."

It was mid-afternoon before they set off in the car and Max drove them down East Quay "so you won't get lost when you catch the ferry," as he said loudly so as to be heard through the car's open windows as they paused to allow a horde of dock workers across the road. Further south, Beach Road petered out and the only way on was a footpath, one whose view of Sleepers' Hole was obscured by the Marine station, the hotel and warehouses.

"Okay," said Chris, "We know they won't be coming back this way. There's no way through."

"There is," said Owen. "We've done it."

This was news to Max as well.

"You have to climb one of the ladders up from the water, then walk through between the buildings to the level crossing. It's all unofficial but the workmen do it and if you're with them it can be done."

"But not in the middle of the night," Chris suggested.

"It depends when the ferry arrives, I suppose."

"But two men, or even one, carrying something they shouldn't – it'd be a bit of a risk."

"Probably," said Owen. "I've never been there at that time of night."

Access to the West Quay meant returning to the main road and waiting while, of all things, a locomotive trundled slowly past and over the swing bridge. Owen was amazed. He'd nearly got his cycle wheel stuck in the railway track once but had never imagined it was still used by trains.

"We'll avoid it and go down Chapel Street," said Max as the engine and its two vans took the first turning towards the quay. Indeed, it didn't have an option.

He took them all the way down to the coast, over more rails set in concrete until they were on the sea wall overlooking the harbour entrance.

"This is where Stan will be," said Chris quietly. "If they head west he'll still have a good line of sight."

Simon nodded.

They returned past the Hope Inn and parked, so as to explore the path to

Sleepers' Hole. There was an old boathouse there, with its slipway, and north of that a series of landing stages.

"He'll need to keep a watch on that to see when our boat comes down," Chris muttered.

Finally they drove the length of Riverside, passing the engine and vans – which seemed to be loading fish – and returned over the bridge. At Simon and Chris's request Max continued past the Mill Drove turning and continued towards Seaford.

"It looks open!" Owen exclaimed as they came in sight of the new cutting through Hawth Hill.

It proved still to have barriers across it, though there seemed to be no one working there now. There were direction signs in place already, directing traffic to Seaford along the expanse of new tarmac.. Max turned right as usual to delve under the railway bridge and pass the Buckle Inn. For the sake of completeness they drove up to the other end of the new bypass, only to find it also closed. There was a notice informing Seaford that it would open on Wednesday 15th July.

"That's this week!" said Owen. "Won't affect us much – it's still quicker to cycle along the seafront."

And with that they returned to the Mill house. Their 'relatives' elected to walk along to the East Pier "just to get another view," Chris explained. They were about to set off when Max mentioned Chris's deck shoes which he was wearing around the house.

"Damn," he said. "You're right. I'll have to struggle at least some of the way in those bloody heels or people will suspect."

23 – Opening

If the Wilsons expected any action that night they were disappointed. Before Owen and Ruth went to their bedrooms to sleep the two Navy men had made it very clear that no one was to venture outside, no matter what. No lights must come on in the house once they had gone off. Any sounds the two men made must be ignored.

Despite all this, Owen was sure he would hear one-sided conversations by radio, one of the men going out and returning, or at least something. As it was he was asleep within minutes of getting comfortable so as to listen.

Simon and Chris were still asleep when breakfast was ready the next morning. As usual Ruth went home for hers just to be at home with her parents for a while.

Once Jack Barden was safely in the Mill's warehouse where he now worked, Ruth's 'doctor' woke and had a cup of tea with her and her mother. He refused to be drawn over what had happened the previous night, despite Ruth's best efforts, saying only that "it will all come out in the open some time soon." He asked her and Mary to see him off, telling them in a clear voice that his next patient was in Lewes. Ruth went to visit Owen, finding that his visitors were now up and about, also having a cup of tea. Chris, who appeared to be the senior of the two, said that they had discovered quite a bit, knew how it worked and would be taking action. No other information was forthcoming from them either.

Freddie came down to Tide Mills to join them all, since all except Ruth had planned to cycle up the paths onto the Downs. Pressed for information he declared he knew nothing about the visitors' discoveries either. Isaac either knew nothing or would say nothing. Somewhat disgruntled, they cycled off, taking Ada with them.

A large packet arrived on Max's desk that morning. It had a London postmark. He read the letter and swore. Barbara, delivering tea, raised her eyebrows.

"Sorry, darling. We've been dumped into it by head office. They have no idea when the visitor centre will be ready but have told me that we should expect our first visitors in seven days' time. A week for it to be finished."

He started reading through the enclosures. Barbara waited.

"Well, at least they've gone to town on the publicity," he said. "Newspaper advertisements, leaflets for anyone who stocks our goods already, A mayoral visit on the Monday morning… you name it. Thanks so much for the tea, but I need to talk to Martin urgently."

Barbara put the cup down and realised that she could help by talking to Jack Pentelow. He was, after all, the man who would know the timescale. In his office she found Martin Killick.

"I was going to ask Jack, but you're actually the person Max needs to talk to," she told the two. "He's phoning your office now, Martin. The Board have set the date for the opening. It's a week today."

Eyebrows shot up.

"I'd better go and see him," said Martin when he'd recovered from the shock, and was about to do just that when Max appeared at the door.

"You found him. Thanks. Now then, Martin…"

The three returned to the comparative peace of the Mill House and Max's office where more tea magically arrived. Barbara left them alone.

It turned out to be mainly the visitor centre and the viewing areas that were the problem. Both were important; the first to offer a background to Tide Mills and its history, and the second because it was the key to viewing the workings properly. It was the main attraction.

"I'll talk to the steel people," said Martin. "If they can work hard at the remaining parts of the structure, we can get some extra people in and if necessary work overnight. It should be possible, but it depends on the materials."

"Use my phone," said Max. Martin did.

Mary and Ruth went for a walk. It was part of Ruth's routine now, and today she wanted to walk on the beach, an exercise recently recommended by the hospital. They had told her that she needed to be careful and slow, and avoid jarring the lengthening leg whilst still using it. The hated crutches would be hard work on pebbles, so Mary was there to provide moral and physical support.

Ruth found it painful and hard work, but recognised the benefits. Her balance had been put out, not just by a lack of use of the leg, but because of its increasing length. Indeed, it was by now almost level with the other one, a fact that was giving her great satisfaction. Another few weeks and she would be in hospital again, there to see the rods removed and to start a period of increasing strength.

They made slow progress, but Ruth had been determined to stand at the sea's edge, and even paddle in the – fortunately calm – warm summer water. She was quite glad to sit on the beach to replace socks and shoes, looking forward to a time in the near future when she could wear stockings on legs that were the same basic diameter once again.

Returning up the sloping beach to the concrete pathway was, again, a slow progress. Ruth's eyes were on the pebbles in front of her so she could judge where to place her feet. Near the top, by the line of seaweed, old netting and other flotsam and jetsam she paused and dug at something with her toe.

"What's that?" she asked her mother.

Mary bent and picked it up. It looked like an oilcloth bag, carefully sealed, designed to be waterproof.

"Don't know," she said. "Might be rubbish, might not."

During the lean years of World War II the inhabitants had relied heavily on beachcombing for all kinds of useful, money-saving items. Many a home had been kept warm by using scavenged wood, dried out, whose origins could only be guessed at. Other items had also been found which were not nearly so domestic and threatened to destroy the finder and damage the whole community. These were the mines which broke loose in harsh weather.

It was second nature, then, for something unexplained to be brought home and investigated, even nineteen years after the war's end.

Careful unwrapping of three layers of oilcloth revealed what looked like dried herbs, brownish green in colour. Mary sniffed it. There was a slightly sweet odour, a warm smell that was somehow intriguing. She looked at Ruth, puzzled.

"Not a clue," she said. "And I'm not going to try eating it – you never know if it's poison. And don't you, either."

"If it could be poison I'm hardly likely to, Mum! But what do we do with it?"

"Take it to your Dad? Or Max Wilson."

"What about Isaac?"

"The other two are here. See what they say."

But by this time Max, Arthur and all the staff of the Mill were in a meeting with Martin and his staff, formulating plans. The steel people said that their contributions could be ready by the following Thursday if they worked overtime – which would need to be paid for. Max agreed on the spot and Martin relayed the information.

This was all good, of course, but didn't solve Mary's and Ruth's problem. They left the package on a shelf above the Aga for opinions to be added by the others later.

The day had been overcast when they were walking. Now it had darkened further and rain started to fall, and gradually, over the next half hour it strengthened. Some forty-five minutes later there was the sound of wheels on gravel and Owen and Freddie appeared, wet through. Ruth saw them and opened the front door.

"Wet?" she asked. Owen looked to the ceiling.

"Never been drier," said Freddie cheerfully. "Got a towel?"

Mary had overheard and called to Ruth to invite them in.

"I'd better go home," said Owen. "But if you can lend him a towel that'd be helpful. I'll come back when I'm dry."

When he ran back to their house, dried and fully reclothed, it was to see Freddie looking belligerent with Ruth grinning broadly. Looking at Freddie, Owen was hardly surprised: he was wearing Ruth's pink, fluffy dressing gown and had been sat in the kitchen by the Aga. His clothes were on a clothes horse at the Aga's other side and steam was pouring off them.

Owen looked from one to the other, then at Mary, who was waiting for a comment. She was sure there would be one. Owen paused for effect.

"Which one is Ruth?" he asked, trying to sound innocent.

Two people launched themselves at him. He hugged one and fended off the other, and they subsided giggling onto chairs. Mary joined the laughter, almost hysterically.

He looked from one to the other. The joke hadn't been that funny. Why were they laughing so hard? And what was the strange smell in the kitchen? He asked the question.

"Is there one?" asked Mary.

"I thought I smelt something when I came in," said Freddie. "I didn't like to mention it."

Owen sniffed around like a dog and found the smell was strongest above the stove. He looked and found the open bag, picked it up and nearly sneezed when he smelt it.

Coughing, he put it back. "What is it?" he asked when he stopped coughing.

"We found it on the beach," Mary said between giggles at Owen's canine behaviour. "We don't know what it is and we want Max or someone to tell us."

Owen reached for it again. The package had been warmed by the stove. He took another sniff at it and coughed, holding it away from his nose.

"It stinks," he said, somehow feeling intrigue and a different sort of interest from his normal inquisitiveness, despite the odour.

Freddie, who hadn't seen the bundle, examined its contents and giggled. "It's cannabis," he said, smiling broadly. "Didn't know you were into that, Mrs Decks!"

Owen looked at him, snatched the oilskin and wrapped it up. He ran to the door and opened it wide. Despite the rain and his dry clothes the package was taken round the corner of the building and deposited under a blank wall, out of sight.

Back inside he marched to the front window and threw it open, allowing the rain in, and to the side window where the draught took away the fumes.

"You're under the influence of cannabis," he told them calmly. "Sit down and it should go away."

"My dresser..." muttered Mary, looking at the rain depositing itself generously on the polished surface. But she sat, anyway. Owen put the kettle on.

"I don't know if you should drink anything after that," he said, "but at least tea will take the smell away."

Freddie was the first to regain some normality. He had been in the fumes for a shorter period than the other two.

"Bloody hell," he said. "Cannabis! Where the hell did you get that from?"

"How do you know the smell?" asked Owen grimly.

"Lots goes on round the docks," said Freddie shortly. "You'd be surprised what you see and hear at times. No one sees boys round the place. They're all but invisible except when they do something wrong. Then there's hell to pay. And you never let on what you've seen or heard. And if you're there when some things are going on, you watch the wall."

"Watch the wall, my darling, while the gentlemen go by," said Mary, still giggling.

"Who's a darling?" asked Freddie indignantly.

"It's from a poem," she answered. "I wasn't calling you darling."

"Do you think..." Ruth started, trying to control her speech and her feelings "... that the packet was left from last night? You know – what our visitors were after?"

"I think it's more than likely," Owen said. "And we need to get it to Isaac as soon as possible."

"Can you, Owen? Please?" said Mary in a thick voice. "My goodness, I do feel odd."

"I'll go now," said Owen.

"I'm coming," said Ruth.

"Me too," said Freddie.

"No… best not, dressed as you are. Could you stay and look after Mrs Decks, please? I need Max to see what's happened to us and describe how we feel."

He looked resigned. "Okay."

Owen found that he was being hugged on the way over to the Mill House. He responded and received a kiss. There would have been more, but firstly it was raining hard still and secondly he was determined to get his father to act fast. The first comment he received when he appeared was short, to the point, and completely ignored the idea that he might need to speak first.

"Good. Glad you're here. Are you prepared to work for the Mill, or for Killicks, until Monday? And can you persuade Freddie to do the same?"

"Yes, Dad; but…"

"Good. That's all I've got time for now. I'll explain later."

Max swung away.

Given his father's mood, had this been a year previously Owen would have left any further comment or questions. Now, though, the goalpost positions had been subtly changed. He frowned in annoyance.

"Dad, this is important. I know you're busy, but this is really urgent."

"Owen, nothing's more important than the Mill opening to the public in a week and our not being ready. You know that."

"*This* is. Dad. And we have to talk to you privately. Now. Please."

Max looked at the two, frowning, and told Martin he'd be back in a second. He took them into Jack's office. He could see Ruth was struggling with something and immediately jumped to the wrong conclusion.

"Owen… Ruth…you haven't…?"

"What, Dad? Look, Ruth's found a packet of cannabis on the beach. It's been getting hot on a shelf above their Aga and they've been breathing the fumes, they're all right, but we need to get rid of the packet before someone else finds it. And no one must know, or when the others come to stop the smuggling they'll have nothing to stop. It'll all be out."

Max blinked. His mind swiftly moved from an assumed scenario to the correct one.

"Are they all right… are you all right?" This was to Ruth, who was starting to look more normal.

"I'm all right," she confirmed. "Just a bit… well, drunk, I suppose."

"And Mary?"

"Freddie's looking after her, but she's better than she was. Less giggly."

"Owen!"

"Just describing what they were like. But we need to get rid of the packet."

"Go to the Mill House, the pair of you. Phone Isaac from there – it's more private. Then come back. With Freddie if possible."

Owen nodded. "Okay, Dad."

They parted. The call was made. A suddenly very attentive and crisp Isaac promised to come down and collect Freddie. He had forgotten that there was a bicycle involved as well and that Freddie would hardly want to return home in the middle of the afternoon, rain or no rain, especially as his clothes were still drying out. Owen suggested that a spare set of clothes and Freddie's waterproofs would be a better excuse and was rewarded with a chuckle.

"You win," said Isaac.

Since Isaac brought Edna with him, Barbara ended up offering them tea, then a meal. The package had been surreptitiously collected, Freddie had thankfully given Ruth back her pink dressing gown having donned his spare clothes. The Decks, Wilsons and Galleys were all talking in the sitting room of the Mill House. Arthur Decks, trying to keep a straight face, wanted to know how it was that his wife had become 'high'.

"I've got to go back once we've eaten," he explained. "We're having to get ready for a formal opening in a week."

"Dad said something about it," Owen said. "Why so little time?"

"Blame Head Office," said Max tersely. "They've always thought that alterations could be done at the drop of a hat. Usually the Union's put them right, but down here we have everything to prove and a lot to lose. And we're going to give it our best shot. That's why I need all the manpower and, indeed, boy power, I can get."

"Count me in," said Owen.

"Me too," said Freddie, "if that's all right?" He looked at Edna and Isaac.

"All right by me," said Isaac. "Edna?"

She just nodded. "Look after your leg." Freddie nodded back.

"How about the Baker brothers?" asked Owen

"They're just kids…" Max started, and then thought back to some of the events of the last year.

"Alan's getting on for fourteen," said Owen. "That's how old I was when we first came here. And Eric's nearly twelve. He can run errands and so on, if nothing else."

"I'd better ask them too, then," said Max.

The only respite for Owen, Gerry, Freddie, Bee, Alan and Eric that week seemed to be for meals, sleeping and a very occasional rest. They were kept busy preparing, painting, hanging pictures and signs, running messages and generally rushing about doing what they were asked. Had there been any night time illicit activity, none of them would have heard it. They slept like logs and often woke in the morning with aching muscles.

The usual Boys' Brigade contingent came to camp on the nearby field. Through gritted teeth, hard at work painting, Alan had to watch his friends wander in their carefree, noisy way beside the camp with its lines of boys at drill. He could hear the scurrilous strains of "*The lads of Sussex-by-the-*Sea" ringing out over the Brigade campsite, no doubt to the disgust of their officers and the mirth of the boys. Alan was usually a part of the taunting and had been looking forward to introducing Eric to the fun. The Scouts vanished up onto the Downs, returning later covered with mud and smelling of the fire they'd started to boil their kettle. They visited the Mill and commiserated with the brothers, only to be told that they didn't mind as they were being paid for their troubles.

Choir members were let off to attend their practice. Work, all but complete, stopped for a while on Sunday morning to allow any who wanted to to attend the church service, at which choir members were needed as always. It was in the vestry afterwards that Mr Treadgold dropped his bombshell.

"Are you free for Evensong? I want Freddie, Ruth, Eric and Alan to sing the round Freddie sang – you all sang – the other week.

"Well, We'll need to ask," Freddie started.

"I have. All the families are happy about it – and yes, I know you've been working hard, and why. Mr Wilson says the work is just about ready. And he and all the other parents want to come."

"Mine too?" asked Freddie wistfully.

Mr Treadgold smiled at him. "Particularly yours, Freddie."

His smile lit up the church. Bee found her eyes moist on his behalf.

It was strange, that evening, for Mr Treadgold, Ruth, Alan and Eric. They had to leave the safety of the choirstalls and march up to the Chancel crossing just before the blessing. Freddie had to leave his seat immediately after it and stand facing the congregation. He was nervous, very, but managed to cast his mind back again to the times in the empty London church where he had first learnt to sing his heart out. The more he thought of it the more he relaxed.

The silence after the blessing reigned absolute for about ten seconds. The congregation's eyes started to lift. An adult choir member played the start note. Freddie, prompted beforehand, launched straight into it: *"Glory to Thee..."*

The rich, pure treble rang round the church, even with the congregation there acting as a baffle to the sound. More than one head snapped up from a hymn book to see who was creating this full, accurate sound. At the end of the first line Eric came in, automatically taking his lead from Freddie. Then in turn Ruth and Alan. It was only at the end of the verse that Mr Treadgold started to conduct the start of the next verse, sung the same way.

Freddie's job was to end it with a repeat of the first verse, but this time he sang whilst following the cross as it was carried to the vestry. They walked faster than normal as it would be quite a short piece of music. He was joined by the others at the Chancel crossing as the last verse ended.

In the vestry they all had to be shushed as pandemonium broke out, with congratulations from the entire choir. Freddie was pleased, being unused to being the centre of attention. He got the others involved in the congratulations as soon as he could, feeling embarrassed that they were in danger of being almost ignored.

Followed by the others he left the vestry and was immediately enveloped in a hug from Edna, much to his further embarrassment.

"You could make a record with a voice like that," she said, dabbing her eyes as surreptitiously as she could. Isaac was just smiling broadly; the Decks and Baker parents hugged their children too.

At the Mill House Barbara had somehow managed to arrange a buffet for all the staff with help from some of the other wives who had elected not to go to church. It was to acknowledge that the job was finished and to thank everyone. The Church contingent had returned, all the other staff crowded in and they set to in celebration. The one absentee was Jack Barden.

It was an early start on the Monday. Although there were no construction jobs needing completion, there was cleaning and tidying still to do. Steve and Annie Fuller, the couple who had been engaged as the baker and assistant, had been at work since the early hours, though in the gentle south-westerly breeze none of the wonderful smells of fresh-baked bread reached the Mill House from the new bakery in the old signalman's house near the crossing. They realised what a good idea it had been to install the bakery there. Visitors would be attracted by the smell of baking and could buy bread and cakes there without tangling with the Mill workings (unless they were paying for a visit, of course).

Dragged unwillingly from bed at six in the morning, the three boys and Bee in the Mill House and the Baker brothers in their cottage set to. The first thing that everyone saw and remarked on was a very quiet Jack Barden who was sporting a black eye and a limp. Max made a mental note to make sure he was out of sight at the opening ceremony and to talk to him after it was all over.

Everyone, staff and their spouses, together with the younger contingent, were tasked with jobs many were unused to; sweeping, washing surfaces, putting things away. Then there was the complication of installing bunting, craftily unearthed from St Leonard's Church where it had been still in storage after use for the Coronation celebrations eleven years previously.

Owen was putting the final touches to cleaning the Mill's Reception area when its door opened. He looked up. A suited man stood there. Remembering he was the only representative of the Wilson family currently available he stood and smiled at the visitor.

"Good morning, sir. Can I help? We're not open yet – the ceremony isn't until ten-thirty."

The man smiled back. "I realise that, young man. You're one of Mr Wilson's new staff are you?"

"No sir, his son."

"His son... but I thought his son was about thirteen."

"I was, sir, but two years ago."

"Really? How time flies... well, I can see that everyone is busy and that the place is looking very tidy indeed. Very tidy. Will it be ready for the Directors to open later on, do you think? Or would you like me to get busy with a mop and bucket somewhere?"

Owen smiled back. "I imagine, sir, that you are one of the Managers in

London."

"Nearly. I'm the Managing Director. I caught the earliest train I could so as to get down here first and have a look round before the others arrive. So, I ask again: will it all be ready?"

"It will be, sir. In fact it probably already is. But my Dad wants to present as tidy a ship to the world as he possibly can. That's why everyone who lives or works here has been up putting the finishing touches to everything."

Half way through this speech the door had opened and Alan had entered. He had been about to mention the presence of tea at the Mill house but had caught the word 'sir', seen the suit, and now just stood in respectful silence.

The suit nodded and turned to the lad, noting the water-stained clothing and the smudges of dirt on the face.

"And are you another of Mr Wilson's sons?" he asked.

Alan stood upright and would have saluted, but stopped himself. "No, sir. My Dad works here. I'm Alan Baker."

"Ah... and a great surname for someone who works at a mill. Well, young Baker, I'm the Managing Director."

He put out his hand. Alan wiped the water from his right hand on his trouser leg and damply performed a handshake.

"I'd better not ignore you, Wilson." The hand was extended again. It was Owen's turn to wipe his hands on his trousers and shake it.

"What happens now... oh, I'm Simpson. John Simpson. Is your father around, Wilson?"

"Yes, sir. He's working somewhere, but I'm not sure where. Perhaps if we go home... to the Mill House, that is... Mum will know where he is."

"There's tea being served there," said Alan helpfully. "That's what I came to tell you."

"Tea, did you say?" John Simpson exclaimed. "Then if a humble MD can beg a favour, it'd be to have a cup of tea."

"I'm sure Mum can manage that," said Owen with a smile. "Lead on, Alan. I'll dry my hands properly and follow."

As soon as they had vanished he was on the phone, which doubled, usefully, as an intercom – an intervention from the younger Isaac once he had seen the problems, and had quietly prioritised the Mill's new phone system. Ruth answered and he swiftly told her of the approaching dignitary.

"Okay," she said calmly. "He'll get a cup along with the others. They're gradually arriving. Are you coming?"

"Of course," he replied, "you're there. And I need a tea."

"Smoothy," she accused. "See you in a minute."

Alan, John Simpson and Max all but collided at the door. Max declined a handshake on the grounds that his hands were filthy.

"Everything inside is clean," he explained, "but some of the fronts of the buildings where we're attaching the bunting are far from it. We're all but there, so gradually we can relax and man the fort."

Simpson nodded. "You've done a good job," he said.

"It's everyone, sir. Without really, genuinely willing people we couldn't have done it. Not within the timescale. And if this were London, I imagine the Union would have had them out on strike by now."

He received a stare, a look that gradually softened.

"But when a man engages his son and his son's friends to help, and they do so willingly, it seems, there's more of a carnival atmosphere to it than a formal opening. Yes, Max, I'm very aware of the conditions in London. And can't comment, of course. But you – all of you – have done so well with this place. I'm genuinely impressed."

It was the first time his MD had ever used Max's Christian name and he was surprised – and pleased. He sensed a complete change in the man's attitude after the 'discussion' over the lack of publicity. It seemed to add a genuineness to the man's comments.

Max led them all in. True to style, the staff chatting inside fell silent as they saw a stranger, and a suited stranger at that. But to give him credit he realised what was happening and took advantage of the silence.

"Good morning to you all. I'm John Simpson and I'm your company's Managing Director. My words to Mr Wilson as we came into his home were that you have all done so well in getting Tide Mills up and running and ready for this morning's official opening. I'm really impressed with what I've seen so far, and that's just on the walk down from the station to here. My call at Reception was courteously dealt with. I only realised that I was talking to a volunteer rather than a staff member when a friend of the person concerned came in and it was clear that despite his name he was just under age to be on the staff. Thank you, Mr Wilson junior and Mr Baker junior."

There was a laugh. The atmosphere cleared.

"But there's one thing you haven't done. Two things, in fact. The first is the more important."

He paused. Max looked worried.

"You haven't shoved a cup of tea into my hands. I've been up since five this morning and I'm gasping."

This time there was a more heartfelt laugh, just in time to cue Ruth to come in and 'shove' a cup and saucer into his hands,

"Another volunteer, I see. Thank you so much. Miss...?"

"Ruth Decks," said Ruth. "Dad's the assistant manager."

"Then I should meet him and Mr Pentelow, the Manager, and ask them to put right the second thing you've not done."

Jack and Arthur edged their way forward.

"Don't look so worried, gentlemen. The other thing that needs doing is for everyone to congratulate everyone else on teamwork, application and above all getting everything done. I've been reliably informed by Owen Wilson that everything *is* ready, so I know it's true. So I'm going to put my money – well, the Company's money – where my mouth is, announce a bonus for everyone on the staff for next week or month or however it works here, and lead you in three hearty cheers for the staff and volunteers of the Sussex contingent.

"Hip, hip..."

They all joined in. When it was over he asked for a cloth, mopped up the spilt tea and was given another by Ruth. The ice had been broken.

At about nine-thirty he was to be seen up a ladder hanging the last of the bunting to an electricity pole at the side of the Drove. Grins from Alan and Owen greeted him once back on terra firma.

"Well done, sir," said Owen. "I never thought you'd volunteer to do that."

"It's hardly Scout pioneering, Owen. I used to be able to do that."

"You were in the Scouts, sir?"

" I still am. I'm a District Commissioner."

Owen extended his left hand. The man's face lit up.

"I should have asked," he said. The smile broadened further when Alan too offered his left hand.

"My brother too," said Alan, "and Freddie."

"You're almost a Troop here on your own, aren't you?"

"We're with the 1st Seaford," said Alan with some pride.

He nodded. "Good for you. Will you be in uniform for the opening?"

The three exchanged looks.

"Better than school uniform," said Alan.

"Can Freddie get his?" asked Owen.

"Edna and Isaac can bring it down. Will you phone them?"

It was soon after that that the remainder of the Directors arrived, followed shortly by Edna and Isaac. Freddie, the Baker brothers and Owen vanished briefly, to reappear in their uniforms. Alan received another handshake from the MD when he saw the Patrol Leader stripes.

"Not a PL yet?" he asked Owen quietly.

"I only joined when we moved down here, sir. And Alan's been in for years. So it's only right. He's good too. And anyway, I'll be going up to Senior Scouts in September.

"Good man. Enjoy it. Every success, not just to you but the other three and all your Troop. And now we'd better join your father and welcome the celebrities or he'll accuse us of being late."

The Mayor of Seaford turned out to be a short, balding man with a moustache. He looked like a character from a story book. Walking down from his car and over the level crossing he first saw the Scout uniform on Owen who was the tallest of the impromptu guard of honour posted there.

"What regiment, eh?" he barked.

Owen was confused for a moment. "No regiment, sir; Scouts."

"Ah. Scouts. Yes. Salt of the earth. Dyb dyb dyb and all that. Well done."

He continued to act like a fuddled old Colonel for the rest of the morning. Almost every sentence ended with a superfluous, barked 'What?!'

His colleague from Newhaven tuned out to be much more down to earth and viewed the old Colonel with an amused resignation.

They and their entourage toured the Mill and the new machinery in the old grain store, then were taken over the public viewing gallery whilst the sluices were reopened to start the mill going. They saw one of the improved cottages, the revitalised allotments and greenhouse, along with the bakery and shop. Max pointed out the building that would be used as a cafe once it had been renovated.

Introductions were made to the new staff, from the new head baker to a new, young cleaner and handyman, and at last they were taken back to the Mill House where Barbara, Ruth and a team of others had been hard at work loading the dining table with doorsteps of bread (Max's request), sandwiches and cakes, all labelled proudly to declare they had been made with Tide Mills flour or mixes, or both.

At Max's invitation all the staff were invited back too, to the pleasure of John Simpson and the confusion of some of the more staid Directors to whom such generosity of spirit was foreign. Once the samples had been eaten, John Simpson made a short speech, the kernel of which was how glad the company was to have opened a mill in Sussex, how grateful he was to Max for discovering it and how even more grateful he was to the staff for their unstinting support and enthusiasm.

The mood was then taken down by Seaford's Mayor, who laboured on the subject of history; then built up again by Newhaven's, who was glad to see a new enterprise which had the hallmarks of success and which would provide employment opportunities into the future.

Eventually the VIPs departed – except for John Simpson – and Max was left with his staff and helpers. He got their attention again.

"I'll second what they all said," he told them. "All I can say is 'thank you', and you'll know I mean it. Now we just wait for the orders to start coming in. For tonight, though, we are being catered for by The Buckle. All of us. Those who have laboured here today and have made cakes galore to help the bakery already know that, but to most it's a surprise. They're bringing food here and we're hosting the meal in every room we have on the ground floor. And no, there's no more work to do, as we've got a professional team in to do it all.

"I know a lot of you are still at work, because the mill keeps turning all the time it can, but come hell or high water please be here at six and we'll start the celebrations. All I ask is that we all go steady, because we know there is work tomorrow again. It'll be the first day of the rest of the Mill's life."

When they had all vanished back to work John Simpson buttonholed him and asked to speak privately. The two vanished into Max's office.

"I was wrong to take exception to your preferring your eventual contractor over the cheapest one, and even more wrong to think that the other directors and I knew better. I want to apologise for that. I also want to tell you that whenever the next vacancy on the Board occurs, you will be first in line to fill it. This business can do with people like you at its helm."

Max thought swiftly.

"I'm honoured by your trust, sir. You should know that the reason for the success down here is that the people are like the crew on a ship. They are all on-side. Also they have – many of them – become friends. Now, I know that's dangerous in a business but there are some people who you realise you can trust with your life. I should know; I've had to in the Navy on many occasions.

"As to your offer of a directorship, it seems churlish to ask for details. But my family and I are settled in Sussex and have grown to love it here. We have more genuine friends here and have a more genuinely happy life than ever we did in London. So if a directorship meant moving back, I'm afraid I would decline."

"But wouldn't you welcome the responsibility? Wouldn't the increase in rank attract you? Not to mention the financial advantages."

Max smiled. "For years I learnt about responsibility. It ended with my being responsible for a couple of hundred men's lives and many thousands of pounds worth of ship. Not to mention having a stake in the safety of my nation. So with respect, I've had my fill of the ultimate responsibility that a Captain in the Royal Navy has to wear on his shoulders.

"Helping to direct a company is a different responsibility. It's a slower process. It also involves directing staff who, because of misplaced union power, are suspicious of everything new. Because I can get excellent performances from enthusiastic staff here, it doesn't mean that I can with jaded staff elsewhere. In fact, being used to directing men whose lives depend on jumping to an order would mean that I would become a liability."

"Do you really think so? I think staff elsewhere would appreciate someone with a proven success record."

"If I was their manager, perhaps so. But not as a director."

"So is there a chance that if you were a director, based here but attending weekly meetings in London, we might be able to interest you?"

Max thought again. "It's a compliment that you're prepared to be flexible, sir..."

"John, please Max."

Max blinked, then smiled. "John... that will take some getting used to!"

John Simpson laughed. The atmosphere subtly altered.

"I need to talk it through with Barbara and Owen..."

"Impressive people, your wife and son. The catering that Mrs Wilson organised for us all leaves me staggered. And your son's calm efficiency when presented with a stranger in Reception... I'd imagine there's a job for him in the business if you wanted."

"It would be if Owen wanted, si... John. That's not a decision I would want to make for him. He has the intelligence and the character to make up his own mind about his life's direction. But thank you for the offer, which of course I'll pass on."

The man nodded. "Let's leave it at that for the moment, then. If anything happens on the Board, and I think it will soon, I will call you. Will you be in a position to say yes or no at that stage?"

"Yes, just as soon as I've spoken to the family and you've been able to confirm the conditions to me I'll give you an answer immediately."

At last the Managing Director was seen onto a train. Max walked with a spring in his step back to the Mill where he sought out the bruised and ill looking Jack Barden. The two went to Max's office in the Mill House. Max pointed to a chair and sat himself behind his desk.

"What happened?" he asked, peremptorily.

There was a silence. It was obvious the young man was thinking. Max let the silence hang until at last his interviewee looked up.

"I'm going to have to leave, sir."

"Why?"

"Because if I didn't you'd fire me anyway."

"That'd be my decision, not yours. Why do you think I'd fire you?

"Because... because you would."

"Not good enough. Try again."

"It's... it's too difficult."

"Facing death is difficult. I've had to do that and it's bloody. I've seen men die under my command. That's more than difficult and even more bloody. You're not in that position. You're nowhere near it. You have a bruise and you're limping. All you need to do is tell me what's happened. Compared with facing death at the hands of an enemy that's peanuts."

Another silence.

"I might be facing death, sir. And to avoid it I have to go away."

"Then it's a Police matter."

He shook his head violently, winced and held his head for a moment. Max was alarmed.

"No.... he'd still get back at me. Somehow."

"So this person is the one who might kill you. Yes?"

"No. It's the others who'd do that."

"The others."

He nodded again, and held his head again, looking white.

"A simple question: who gave you the bruise and made you limp? Local man?"

"I feel dreadful, sir. I don't know how I've lasted the day. But there's been so much to do..."

"If you're ill I'll get a doctor."

"I... I'll need one if there's trouble."

"Tell me who it is so I can protect you and the rest of us from him. Or them."

"The rest of... I'd never thought that he might... Oh God..."

The head vanished into the hands again. Max waited.

"Holden."

"I beg your pardon?"

"Andy Holden."

"He's the local man? Or the 'others'?"

"Local. He hit me for losing something."

"Must have been important."

"It was. It's... it's something the others want."

"Who are they?"

"I don't know."

"But Holden would. We can ask him."

"No! For God's sake don't ask him, or get involved."

"Why?"

"Because... because they'll come after you if you do."

"So what's Holden going to do next?"

"Dunno. That's why I've got to get away."

"You need to tell me what is going on, Jack. All of it. Not just the threats that have been made against you and might come our way. You've shown that you're concerned about my family and me and the rest of the people here, but we need to decide best how to protect us properly – you too, to get Holden and these 'others' under lock and key."

"You'll never do it, sir."

"I think we shall. But it has to start with you. I can see that you have no loyalty left for Holden, and that's hardly surprising if he's injured you so badly... hey..."

Jack felt he had to try and stand. He was swaying on his feet. He felt as if he was a child again, had been beaten once too many times by his father after a long day at school with work afterwards. He had to stop. He had no option. His legs crumpled under him and he fell to the floor in a dead faint.

Navy training kicked in. Max had him in the recovery position in a matter of seconds and in his best Captain RN voice shouted for help.

24 – Navy operation and its aftermath

When Jack Barden came round he found there was a nurse at one side of him and a large policeman at the other.

"Don't try to speak," said the nurse in a kind voice, reaching for his hand.

"Beg pardon, Miss, but he needs to talk. We need information, and quick."

"And I want him to get better quickly."

Jack found he couldn't cope with someone else's argument. His eyes closed and he slept again.

Waking later he found there was still a white uniform one side of him and a dark one the other. His eyes screwed up. Surely this uniform was Navy? It was. Why? Police he could understand; Navy he couldn't.

"Hallo, Jack," said the Navy type in a kind voice. "You've had a bit of a beating, they say. No, don't answer. All I want to do is to tell you that we are keeping you safe in here until you're better. You need to trust the nurses for when that will be. Although you'll probably feel better after a bit, what you went through – what they did to you – will take considerably longer to heal. Please don't say anything to anybody except me or anyone else I introduce as a safe person. Say nothing about what happened, not to the nurses, police or anyone else from Tide Mills or anywhere. Got that? You can trust me, Max Wilson or Isaac Galley. Only them at the moment. Good man. Sleep again now. One of us will come back when you're better."

"You've given us all one hell of a shock," said the same Navy man. It was later by many days and he was feeling that he might now be back to normal. Sitting in a chair in a private ward with a choice of radio or a book or, if he was lucky, a game of cards with one of the Navy people who came to see him, was a very acceptable way of passing the time. They had even told him that his family were being looked after and were safe. At least no one else knew where they were.

This had made Jack sit up and take notice. "You know about them? Are they all right? Maisie too?"

"We've been to see them, quietly, and they will be looked after. No one knows where they are, and we'll make sure that is still the case. If you do anything silly, of course, we'll have to divert more efforts to you and away from them, and that will put both mother and daughter at risk."

Jack took this in, amazed that the authorities knew so much about his secret family that not even his old grandmother was aware of.

"So we know about Holden," the officer continued matter-of-factly. "We've been very carefully watching him. We're just waiting for him to make his next move, and for that we'll have to wait for the next new moon. I'm afraid that you'll need to stay in here until after then. It wouldn't be safe for you to be anywhere near them when we get them."

Jack's mouth opened and closed, but no sound came out.

"I suppose you'd been helping them for some time," the officer mused.

"That boat of Holden's – Channel Pride – has been doing the rounds for years, hasn't she? I'm surprised she's still holding together. But then all she has to do is go fishing – so-called fishing – when Holden gets the signal and beaches off Tide Mills. But the shingle must pound her hull in bad weather. Doesn't that worry you?"

"Stronger than she looks," muttered Jack. "Look, how do you know all this? Has that Owen been talking?"

"Owen? Who's Owen? Is he one of the 'others'? It's not a name we've come across yet, but I'm sure we shall."

"No... no. He's just someone I tried to get to help out when someone went sick once."

"Oh. Well, we'll get Holden and the rest easy enough when they do the next run. If this Owen hasn't helped yet maybe he won't be one of them."

"How *did* you find out all this?"

"We watch, you know. You may think that no one sees what goes on, but we watch, for all that."

Jack was horrified.

"So what happens when... when you get Holden? Will I get into trouble?"

"What do you think? You've been involved in smuggling cannabis for the last – what – couple of years? You tried to get this 'Owen' to help, and presumably he's just an innocent person. So that's an attempt to encourage someone else into crime. We're doing our best to keep you out of any more trouble by keeping you here and letting it be known around the area that you have brain damage and it's serious. But it's not looking good for you.

"And of course the other problem is that if we manage to keep you out of it all, the French might want you as there's obviously a connection. Or is it the Dutch? I can say that neither French nor Dutch prisons are very nice places, especially if you're good looking, young and male.

"I imagine the only way you can keep out of jail there or in Britain, and out of trouble with the rest of them, is to tell us more about the London connection. We know quite a bit, of course, but the final bits and pieces would be useful."

Jack sat back in the chair and thought. All that night he tossed and turned, trying to come to a decision. This time he had no work, no family, no Holden there to distract him.

When the officer came to see him the following day, he started talking.

New moon was on Saturday 12th August, four days after Jack's latest interview. The Mill House top floor was occupied again, this time by a radar set and an operator. It and he had arrived with one or two 'medical personnel' who had visited to ensure Ruth would be in a fit condition to have the rods removed soon – or so it was put about. Three extra tents appeared in the Boys' Brigade camp. The Wilsons' new relatives reappeared. Edna and Isaac had two visitors in full Navy uniform – obviously Isaac would be expected to see his old colleagues.

A week previously two small Navy cutters had arrived in Shoreham harbour on a public relations mission. They were due to leave on Saturday 12th and did so, about midnight, heading out to sea to join the eastbound traffic, though at a slower than usual rate of knots. A very elderly car sat on Newhaven's deserted sea wall with a very new and impressive aerial extended from its roof.

The *Jean Baptiste* dropped her cargo into the water as usual. As usual each batch was weighted down to the sea bed and supplied with buoys on the surface for easy identification. They looked like lobster pot buoys; indeed there were lobster pots on the end of them. But these lobster pots would never attract any lobsters.

She was followed back into French waters at a distance by the two cutters. Radio messages flashed between the cutters and French Naval shore establishments. Once safely docked she was arrested, with her crew, at the port. Quietly and unofficially the crew was transferred to the two Royal Navy vessels and taken to Portsmouth.

In *Channel Pride* Holden, plus a friend of his and the friend's son who had been press-ganged into service to replace Jack Barden, dropped their cargo on Tide Mills beach in the early hours of the morning. They wheeled the bags up to the car park above the level crossing. Two from the London contingent stowed it quietly into the nondescript Morris Minor van that had been waiting there. *Channel Pride* was sailed back to Newhaven, cautiously navigating in the almost pitch dark, up the river to a mooring behind Denton Island. The three crew secured the boat and came ashore in an old praam dinghy. They started walking home. On their way off the Island using its only bridge, they were surprised to be stopped by six men in dark uniforms and flat caps. They were hustled into a van which had a Royal Navy driver and embarked on a long journey down to Portsmouth where they were held in a prison which, surprisingly to them, was guarded exclusively by Navy personnel.

Very carefully the nondescript van from London was shadowed on its long drive from Tide Mills' car park. It used the secondary road through Denton and Tarring Neville to join the main east-west road, then made its way through Lewes. All sorts of vehicles checked on its progress, from a fast and erratically driven sports car with two obviously inebriated young men who waved as they passed, a milk lorry, a Lambretta scooter and even a Police car with a blue flashing light – although the latter was going the wrong way. It unnerved the driver and passenger so much that they failed to check their rear-view mirror for some time, concentrating instead on other vehicles ahead that looked official. Another decrepit car, which they would probably have thought was safe, followed them at a distance.

At its destination in a row of mean-looking houses in east London, there was a short break as the driver and his passenger rested their nerves before starting to unload the vehicle. They heard a milk float approach from in front of them as they offloaded the first of the cargo. Whilst they were inside one of the houses the 'milkman' offloaded some bottles into a metal crate. Over the rattle of milk bottles they didn't hear a quiet, ramshackle van approach at speed. Had they done so they might have wondered why it stopped at the van's rear bumper. As they came for the rest of the cargo the milk float had moved to the front bumper.

Suddenly the Navy was everywhere. The two, plus others from the house, were bundled into what looked like newspaper wholesalers' vans, but which had locked cages in the back.

News percolated back to Bishopstone over the next day. In the morning Freddie told the others (surreptitiously, during the sermon) that the operation had been a success. Edna and Isaac appeared at the Mill after lunch to flesh out the details. All of 'the others' from the London end who had been dragged from the building had been taken to Naval cells in Portsmouth so as to remove them from any possible 'contamination'. It had been suspected that there had been leaks of information from inside the Metropolitan Police, so endangering the subsequent investigation.

As visitors came to the London house the next day they were let in, immediately arrested, and removed via a back door, also to endure the long journey to cells in Portsmouth.

Ruth had been told at a previous hospital appointment that she should stop turning the screws on her rods as the legs were by then at the same length. She was suddenly aware that she was near the end of the first part of her treatment, a fact that caused her heart to leap.

"We need you to come in at ten o'clock on Wednesday the twelfth," said her specialist. "I will be removing the rods myself so I can check to see that all is well. You will be in hospital for a week, then home with the thigh in plaster.

"About time too," she said to Owen as she emerged from the specialist's clinic. He had gone with her and Mary, unnecessarily, but he wanted to show his usual support and to be with her.

"You'll soon be leaping around the house like a five year old," he said.

"Hardly," she said, suddenly downhearted. "It'll take six months after the plaster's off for that to be anywhere near."

He swiftly backtracked. "I know," he lied, "but it'll be worth it in the end."

"I hope so."

Come the day, they had no option but to leave Ruth on her own at the hospital. She was to be given a sedative immediately, they were told, and the operation, under a general anaesthetic, would take place within two hours. Knowing the procedure by now, Mary phoned the hospital at lunch time. Arthur and Owen were standing by. Owen was wringing his hands as he had when the results of the original operation were awaited.

Mary was finally connected with the right person and asked the obvious questions. She was given the stock answer: Yes, she was out of the operation; yes, she was fine; no, she was still under the anaesthetic; no, there would be no point in their visiting her until the following morning.

And that was that. They had to be content with it. Owen didn't feel like cycling anywhere that afternoon, so the brothers went to collect Freddie and vanished over the Downs somewhere on their bikes. Owen moped about with Ada, seeing little and doing nothing apart from throwing pebbles for the dog to fetch.

The boys' eventual report of the ride, when they returned hours later with numerous scratches to their shins, had nothing about the beauty of the rolling, green hills, the skylarks' song, the hares they had spotted – rabbits were too common to mention – or anyone they had met. The topic they were most keen to talk about was returning through the new Buckle by-pass on the bikes, a first for any of them.

The brothers had been banished to bed an hour previously. Owen, unused to self-imposed inactivity, was feeling out of sorts. He took the dog out for a last walk, something that was by then his job. As usual he went up through the knapped flint and clapperboard hamlet, past the brick building that was now the new bakery and shop, and over the level crossing. He could see lights at the Boys' Brigade camp, and occasionally an adult figure would cross in front of one. Idly he wondered what Boys' Brigade was like. There seemed to be quite a lot of drill, but sometimes they could see games in progress. Perhaps he could arrange for the Scouts to take them on at football some time... although whether he could overcome the scorn that Alan and Eric would pour on the idea he had no idea.

As he smiled to himself there was a yelp from some way in front of him, where Ada was foraging in the bushes. He started forward but as he did so there was a report which sounded, even to his inexperienced ears, like a shot; a sound which echoed off the bush-hung cliff at the opposite side of the nearby road.

Feeling suddenly sick, he ran up toward the car park. Just before it he saw what in the dim light might have been a discarded roll of dark carpet. But something told him that this was no manufactured item. He ran to it, just as a car engine started in the car park. He paused at it and looked.

Ada.

Ada, her eyes open in death. A scrap of paper was attached to her collar but he ignored it. Enraged, beyond any anger he had ever felt, adrenalin gave him the impetus to sprint to where a car was waiting for a slow late bus and a few following cars to pass along the coast road. He ran as fast as he could to the driver's door and wrenched it open. The driver turned to him, astonished, then almost snarled. He jammed his foot on the accelerator and Owen's grip on the doorframe failed. He found himself rolling clear of the rear wheels.

Cars following the bus were still passing the turning. The driver's instinctive effort at ridding himself of an unwanted intruder propelled the car directly into one of the queue. There was a bang, a crumpling noise and a squeal of rubber on tarmac. The innocent car was pushed sideways across the road with its passenger door grossly misshapen.

The driver of the first car had been jerked forward with the impact and had hit his head on the windscreen. As the speed of the collision had not been great he was pushing himself backwards to regain the steering wheel. Owen, accustomed by Judo to breaking his fall safely, had recovered quickly. He was shortly at the driver's door, wrenching it open again. He reached for the keys, stopped the engine, withdrew them and threw them as far as he could into the bushes.

The fate of the driver of the innocent car flooded into his mind over the desire to inflict damage on the injured driver. He backed away and looked. The other car's door was open and a driver was emerging.

"Are you all right?" he asked.

"You bastard! Are you old enough to drive?"

It wasn't the answer he was expecting.

"No. But he is, and it's his fault. He just killed my dog. Shot her."

There was silence. The driver emerged fully. He appeared to be undamaged. Owen returned to the injured man. He was turned, groping for something on the back seat despite the blood that was dripping into his eyes from a cut on his forehead.

Owen, alarmed, guessed he was searching for the gun.

It was, fortunately, a four-door car. Hoping the rear doors were unlocked, Owen tried one. It wasn't. Instead he reached for the still open front door, then hesitated. This wasn't a scenario where judo would help. He was tall and lightly built, strong for his age maybe but still only fifteen. He didn't pause to think this through, but was aware that he stood little chance in this situation of subduing an adult.

Footsteps ran towards him. A man. Friend or foe?

"What happened?" The man was quite crisp. Owen recognised the style from his father.

"He shot my dog, then tried to drive away. I chucked the keys into the bushes so he can't drive. He's got a gun in the car."

A nod. A hand shot into the car and grabbed the man's collar, pulling.

"Grab his other arm when you can. I can deal with this one."

Again, it was the tone of command that Max would have used in days when Owen was a mischievous eleven-year-old. He complied, then noticed there was an evil looking pistol being held in the hand.

As they dragged the weakly struggling man from the car Owen found he could hold the forearm with his two hands. He brought it down hard against the steering wheel. There was a loud report from the weapon. A hole appeared in the windscreen, which shattered, fortunately without collapsing. On the second attempt there was another crack, quieter but somehow more sickening. This time it was from the arm, not the gun. A shout of pain, the fingers loosened and the gun clattered to the car floor. At last they freed the man from the car, but he was still struggling despite the injured arm and head.

In the distance was a boyish shout, followed by crashing through the bushes. Half a dozen useful-sized teenagers in various stages of night attire appeared. Boys' Brigade, thought Owen.

"Give us a hand, lads," said one of the older teenagers who was still in normal clothes. "Sit on him, hold arms, legs or anything else. He's killed a dog and he was about to threaten us with a gun until this chap disarmed him. His left arm's broken, I think, but don't let that worry you too much. Marshall, run down to the nearest house and get them to call the police, would you?"

"I'm getting the gun," said Owen now that there were several other boys his age sitting on the man, who was moaning. He was still coldly angry, the first time he had experienced such an emotion. He made his way to the car and looked, reached inside and was about to pick up the weapon.

Fingerprints.

Damn.

If he picked it up his fingerprints would be on it. He backed away, his anger ebbing away and the usual Owen-like common sense returning. Looking around he saw a stick. Wrapping a handkerchief round his hand and part of the stick he returned to where the man was lying.

The others parted when they saw him, out of what they imagined was the line of fire. A man who had appeared on the scene and who was presumably their leader, intervened.

"Put it down, son. Another shot fired won't help. And it would make you a murderer."

Owen turned so that the man on the ground couldn't see and showed the man the stick in his hand. Almost without a blink the man continued.

"All right, all right. But on your head be it."

Keeping well back, Owen levelled the stick at the man's head.

"Give me one reason why I shouldn't treat you as you treated my dog."

It was said in such a slow, grating voice, one that, had Owen realised it, caused the man's heartbeat to rise and doubts to form in his mind.

"No... please... it...it'd be murder," said a shaking voice.

"Like you murdered my dog, you mean? My dog who saved my friend's life? The dog's life was worth more to me than yours. Think again."

Silence.

"You wouldn't dare."

Owen laughed; a tight, humourless laugh. "Maybe not murder. But then I can cause you a lot of agony. In fact that might be more effective."

He slowly swept the stick down the man's front, but at a suitable distance away. First it was the chest, then the abdomen, then the fly zip.

"How about there? Do you think that would do the trick?"

To his satisfaction there was a flinch, a sound.

"Could you hold him down again, please? I promise you're in no danger. But I don't want him bolting. Thank you..."

The boys had resumed their positions at a nod from their officer.

"That would be a bit messy, I think. Perhaps in the thigh..."

Two boys hastily moved away.

"...Or maybe the knee. Yes. That's it. Difficult to repair that. Painful too, I shouldn't wonder."

To his relief he heard approaching sirens. A flashing blue light reflected from the cliff where it was bare of trees at the lay-by.

"Or shall we just leave it to the authorities? Perhaps that would be best, after all."

He unwrapped the handkerchief from around the 'gun' so they could all see it, then tossed the stick to the injured man. He turned his back and walked up to the road; anything rather than return to see the body of their shared, beloved dog.

Two people came running up from the main hamlet as the police cars turned in to the Drove. Wearily Owen waved the police officers down to the car park, then stood, taking in gulps of air. The adrenalin was leaving him and he felt sick and shaky. There were steps behind him and he turned swiftly, just in case.

Max.

Max who did something he'd not done for four or five years. He almost rushed to his son and held him in a tight embrace.

The voice, when it came, was as shaky as Owen still felt.

"Are you all right?"

Owen nodded.

"What?"

"Yes. Can't breathe."

"Why? What did he do to you?"

"Not him, you. You're holding me too tight."

The arms released him. Had there been a moon Owen would have been disturbed to see the tear tracks on his father's face. He did manage to see that the eyes shut tight for a moment.

"Thank Christ."

"He killed Ada, Dad."

"I found her as I came up when I heard shots."

Owen thought back. There had been the shot that... that... And then...

For the first time the tears found him.

"After she'd saved Ruth's life too," he sobbed.

The arms, the comforting arms of his father, were round him again, this time less tightly, but just as welcome.

A minute passed.

"Did you shoot him?"

"I wanted to. I really wanted to." He sniffed. "But that would have put fingerprints on the gun. I threatened him with a stick. Made it look like a gun."

"So that's why he fouled his clothes."

Owen pushed his way out of the embrace.

"He *what*?"

"He... er... let go. Lost control."

Owen's eyes, red though they may have been, widened.

"Are you feeling well enough to go and face some questions?"

"Police?"

"Yes."

Owen took a deep breath and calmed himself as best he could.

"Yes."

At the car park they found a surreal number of people. Six well-built teenaged boys – maybe junior officers of the Boys Brigade – in a mixture of pyjamas and outdoor clothes; one Boys' Brigade officer in ordinary clothes; Steve and Annie Fuller from the bakery; a dazed and now angry driver (of the innocent car); four uniformed police, including their friendly Jim; and a handcuffed, stocky man who was holding his injured arm and stank.

No wonder everyone was giving him a wide berth.

Jim looked at another policemen, a sergeant, who nodded permission to him.

"Hallo, Owen. Are you all right?"

Owen nodded.

"We need to ask some questions. Before we do, you should know that we will be charging this man with dangerous driving. Is there anything else we should be charging him with in your and your father's opinion?"

"Killing my dog," said Owen shortly. "trying to injure me as I was getting into the other side of the car to stop him. Trying to threaten me and... and this man... with a gun..."

"A gun?" asked Jim, all traces of the gentle tones of a moment previously gone. "What gun?"

"It's still in the car."

The sergeant nodded to another officer who went to look.

"It'll have his fingerprints all over it." The injured man spoke for the first time.

Owen's eyes fixed on his face, anger once again in them.

"The only thing that will have my fingerprints on it will be the stick I pointed at you. It seems to have scared you more than I thought possible. More than the gun scared me, in fact. Just goes to show what a coward you are. Kill a defenceless, trusting dog, then threaten... me. I'm fifteen, by the way. Just as well there are others of us here who can help each other."

There was shouting to the south of them. Two figures, also in pyjamas, scurried up. A man's voice followed them: "come back, you young varmints. It's not boys' work."

Alan and Eric, slightly bleary eyed, found themselves included in the circle. Any embarrassment they might have felt at their nightclothes vanished at the sight of even older boys in theirs.

Owen, despite the drama, smiled at them.

"You okay?" Alan asked.

He nodded.

"What was that policeman doing down there? Phew! What's that smell?"

Owen took a deep breath, then wished he hadn't.

"It's what it smells like. He's a coward. He killed Ada. That's what the policeman was looking at."

Alan's face was a picture. The look of horror gradually left his face and he a scornful look swept over the handcuffed man.

"You killed a dog? She was probably walking up to you to make friends,

313

wasn't she? She does that to everyone. *Did* that to everyone. And you just shot her? We heard. So you think that's manly, do you? You are nothing but a coward, like Owen says. And you're a lot of really horrible things beside. Well, you're going to prison. And when you come out we'll have grown up so there'll be a lot more adults down here who'll be waiting for you if *ever* you show your face here again. Or anywhere in Newhaven or Seaford. We'll get a picture and every Scout in the County will know you and what you are."

It was a long speech for Alan. He was upset and angry, feeling some of the rage that his friend had experienced. He turned away, finding his father who had his arms round Eric.

"And that goes for us, too," said one of the pyjama clad young men who had struggled through the hedge to help. "Get us that photograph and we'll get it published in our magazine. And we'll get prints made and make sure they're all over London."

The handcuffed man's face jerked up at the word and his jaw dropped.

"Ah, I wondered if you had anything to do with that," said the sergeant. "This will help prove it." He waved the scrap of paper that had been attached to Ada's collar and which had just been handed to him by his colleague. Everyone watched him expectantly. He continued, aware of being the centre of attention.

"It says this: 'This is just the beginning. You had better watch your backs if you think you can get away with telling the police and standing up in Court."

There was another silence.

"Is that what it was for?" asked Owen in a disbelieving voice that nevertheless demonstrated rekindled anger. "He thought that we had somehow told the police what we had seen? And he thought we could be scared off going to Court?

"Well, we had seen nothing. Nothing at all. We heard a van's doors slamming in the car park back there on one or two nights, and once seeing its lights vanish towards Newhaven. But what we had seen? Nothing.

"And then, believing that we had seen some evidence or something, he thought he could scare us, did he? He doesn't know much about what we have in Sussex, does he? More manpower to fight back with than ever he could muster in his gang. Most of the gang are in prison now, I should think, along with the bent cops they thought they had in their pockets."

Owen was surprised to hear his own words. It was mostly bluster, he knew, but the man had to realise that more was known about the London operation than he expected and that it had not come from Tide Mills. He had decided to say nothing about the discovery of the cannabis.

Max looked at him, an unfathomable look which he didn't notice, but there may have been pride in it.

A dark Rover estate pulled into the Drive and was driven down to them. To the surprise of everyone it was four Naval officers who jumped out. They were armed. One had a Captain's stripes on his uniform. Behind them in the car park another car door slammed and another figure limped down to join them. Once in the circle of torchlight he appeared white and drawn. Owen noticed the new arrivals, then looked back at him.

"Isaac!" he called. Isaac looked over and his face cleared.

"Thank God," he said, hurrying over. Owen thought he was in for another hug, but he had his hand, not just shaken, but pumped, by both of Isaac's.

The Captain from the Royal Navy Rover looked at the handcuffed man, then sniffed and recoiled in disgust.

"Is this him?" he asked the police sergeant.

"Yes. You have an interest in him too?"

"We have the rest of the gang in Portsmouth under lock and key. They're isolated from each other, and the Customs people we're helping want to keep it that way. Apparently there are one or two in the Metropolitan force who aren't as scrupulous as the local officers here and we need to keep them guessing too. It's a bit awkward.

"The thing is, we need to take over from here – as you know, since the Customs people are involved, that's our duty. So we need you people to forget all about this for the moment. Put it down as a false alarm, please. We'll take this one to Portsmouth..."

One of the others whispered to him.

"Yes... that's a thought. Anyone got a boiler suit they don't want? And a hose? Somewhere out of sight so that we don't cause offence with him?"

"Dad's got one," Alan volunteered before Ernie could say a word. "And a hose."

"He's got a cut to his head," said the police sergeant, "and a broken arm."

The Captain nodded.

"Excuse me," Owen interrupted. "Before you dispose of this... this *thing*, what are we going to do about Ada? We can't just leave her there." His voice grew higher at the end of the sentence and Max's arm went round his shoulders again. Despite his son's strength of character he recognised that fifteen year-old shoulders are not really designed to cope with the mental, physical and emotional stresses of the past hour.

"We'll get the prisoner to dig a grave before he's hosed down," suggested the sergeant. Although the answer was a suitable one in some respects Owen decided that it wasn't going to be possible given the state of the man's arm, and to him it seemed inappropriate.

"No," he said in a positive voice. "I don't want that scum of the earth to have anything to do with the dog, *our* dog. I will dig it. Tomorrow. Or when Ruth comes home. She saved Ruth's life, don't forget."

He had had enough. He had seen all he needed to see of the man who had fired the shot. Part of him still wanted to exact revenge on the killer, but he knew the only way that could happen was for an accurate account of the evening to be given to the police.

"When do you want my statement?" he asked the sergeant, surprising both the officer and Max.

"Tomorrow. We'll come and see you."

"Best left to us, if you don't mind, sergeant. Or to the Revenue men. The record of an interview by you would mean entries on Police files. We can't have that."

"Very well, sir." It seemed odd to hear a sergeant call anyone 'sir'.

"Not too early, please, gentlemen," said Max. "I need to sleep late tomorrow, and I imagine Owen will want the same."

"Speaking of sleeping late," the Boys' Brigade officer interjected, "We need to return to camp. I'm glad we were here and able to help."

Owen turned to him. "I owe you a debt of gratitude," he said, recalling a saying of his father's. "Without you I think I would have come off worse. A lot worse. Thank you for being there and for coming to help. More than I can say."

The officer cleared his throat, but it was one of the pyjama clad ones who answered.

"Least we could do. A bit of adventure. Pity you're Scouts, but still..."

A voice from the circle called out, still with the remnants of emotion in his voice. "We'll take you on at football any day, and win."

The Boys' Brigade lad wheeled round to see Alan, once more defiant, but this time smiling.

"Done. And..." he crossed to where the boys and Arthur were standing. "...you can teach us all that song, too. Win or lose."

Alan's grin broadened, but turned into a yawn.

"Done."

"Come on, lads," said their officer. Back to camp. We'll meet you again, I'm sure."

He saluted, and was immediately saluted back by Owen, Alan and Eric who had opened his eyes just in time. The others followed their officer back to camp. Alan and Eric were led away by their father, but all three stopped just to pay their respects by Ada's body as they passed.

"I think it's time I spoke, if I may..." said Isaac, walking further into the circle. "I will offer to represent the Navy in this, if my colleagues here don't mind. It will offer some continuity and help the local police in their efforts to gain the information that the Court will need. The local Force also need to be on their guard against efforts by other forces to muscle in, or try to take over the investigation. We still need to investigate where the spy or spies in London are, and who they are. I suggest that this should be recorded as an awkward false alarm in official notebooks, as has been suggested. That way no suspicion needs to be raised elsewhere.

"That means, of course, the Navy has to continue its investigation whilst the Sussex Force – officially – cannot. But my Irregulars are very efficient, very wide ranging and will eventually pass the credit back to the local Police. So it will not, in the long run, reflect on the Sussex force in any way except positively. After all, we want to keep our efforts very much under the radar. Unknown and unguessed. So not a word, please, any of you. I'm a thankfully retired Naval Captain. Nothing else. My colleagues know this too, of course."

The police nodded. Owen made a mental note to ask some questions of Isaac when the two were next alone. But all he said was: " What about Ada?"

The sergeant raised his eyebrows at their friendly policeman, who nodded.

"We've got a blanket in the car. We'll carry her down on that and put her wherever you want. I suggest that you leave it until tomorrow to bury her – you're all but done in tonight."

Owen nodded. "Thank you."

They loaded the body onto the blanket with as much respect as they could. Eventually the pall bearers were the policemen, with the Navy contingent guarding the silent prisoner. They separated near the glasshouses, where Arthur remembered there was a hose. He left them, and there were soon shouts as the man was hosed down, shouts that were silenced by threats from the officers. Arthur smiled, and fetched the old boiler suit which smelt strongly of oil. At least it would be a pleasant change.

The pall bearers took the body to the bike shed, where Owen made room. Swiftly, Max locked the door, thanked the police officers and ushered Owen in to a worried Barbara and, soon after, to bed.

Owen thought that he would never be able to sleep, but five minutes after his head hit the pillow, did so.

The burial the following morning was a sombre affair. Owen did most of the digging of the grave, but allowed his father to help, along with Alan and Eric, and Freddie – who appeared early on, having been told of the events by Isaac. Owen was monosyllabic. His main concern was telling Ruth, and what she would think, and how she would take it.

There was a showing from all the staff. Everyone had heard the news. Owen didn't know whether to be pleased or embarrassed. Ada was, after all, only a dog. But just a dog or not, this was like saying goodbye to a human friend, though without the religious ceremony. It was left to Jack Pentelow, a man who never put himself forward, to speak; Owen couldn't, Max didn't think any words he could say would be suitable and Barbara was as emotional as Owen.

Jack spoke simply. "To some people, a dog is just an animal. Maybe some dogs fit that description. Ada didn't. She had a charmed life and was rescued by some remarkable people. She was a remarkable dog, loved by everyone here, and the more so when her actions saved young Ruth's life.

"Her passing was cruel. We won't dwell on that. But who knows what her old age might have been like? Perhaps she would have been in pain and suffered greatly. We shan't know. We do know that she never suffered, that she will still be loved, and she will still be remembered by all of us. And human or canine: who can ask for more?

He nodded to the Wilsons, who were to let the body down. "We now bury her body, but not her spirit, with love and dignity, as she deserves."

There were moves to help with filling in the grave, but Owen shook his bowed head, wanting neither help nor the spectacle of his tears to be made public. He took the spade and started shovelling, still keeping his head down. As the level of earth rose, his spirits became more balanced. When it was complete he looked around. The brothers and Freddie were still there, looking down. He stopped.

They stood with him for a moment until he spoke.

"Thank you," he said. "Thank you for staying. But now I just need to be alone, please. Sorry."

Everybody else had dispersed to their various homes. He went to his. With neither Ruth nor Ada there the house seemed very empty.

He decided to escape on his own. A swift dash towards the sea was the best thing, he thought. He cycled swiftly along Marine Drive towards Seaford. Rather than join the road by the Buckle, as he should have, he continued all the way along the promenade until, near the Viking pub, he was shouted at by a policeman, who turned out to be their friend, Jim. He was sympathetic, and quiet when Owen described the burial.

"Doesn't stop my telling you to use the road, though," he said. "Have you had the Customs people round yet?"

Owen gasped. "I'd forgotten all about that! Damn. I'd better go back."

He did, feeling better. The house still felt empty despite the presence of his parents – who told him they were worried about him. His inquisitors arrived an hour later.

The interview went well. They were quite friendly. Owen wondered what to say about Jack Barden but was saved the worry as he wasn't asked. Max, when he faced them, was asked for more details of the young man, and gave them as much as he'd promised to Barden himself that he would.

The last paragraph of the conversation with each of them was that they must, at all costs, say nothing to anyone about the events, about the Navy involvement or anything about it. "Except Captain Galley," they qualified with a smile.

Mary and Arthur had already left for the hospital by the time the questioning was done, so Barbara told him. They had received a phone call saying that Ruth was awake and well, if still tired. Owen said some rude words when alone again. He told Max when he emerged and the questioners had left. A watch was consulted.

"Darling, when did the Decks' leave for Brighton, please?"

"About half an hour ago. Why?"

"Owen was going. If I take him, can you field any enquiries, please? I should only be just over the hour if I leave him there."

Owen's heart leapt.

318

25 – Toads, Barden and Mrs Fox

Ruth was pleased to see them all, smiling tiredly as she was.

"It feels strange not to have things coming out of my leg," she said. "They're waiting for the wounds to heal, then I can have a cast on, and gradually be able to *walk*! Without limping!"

Owen just held her hand and looked into her face. She looked so vulnerable, so happy, She still had that elfin look which had first attracted his attention and which had made him revisit the then unknown settlement to see her. His face softened, then he remembered that he had dreadful news to give, and his face dropped.

"What's the matter?" she asked.

Slowly, from the beginning, he told the story. Her face when she heard of the shot was enough to make Owen go to her and hug her, trying to sooth the tears away but knowing that his own were starting again too. Her parents just watched, powerless, as their emotions played out.

At last she took a deep breath.

"At least it was quick."

He had to agree. And wasn't that what Jack Pentelow had said?

The rest of the story came out. She gasped at Owen's actions and winced when he described the sound of the man's arm breaking. Then just said: "Good."

Despite what the Naval officers had said he told her the complete story. It seemed the right thing to do. But just as he'd been told not to say anything about it, he told Ruth and her parents not to.

"It would give the Police in London – the dodgy ones – warning if they get to hear that it's Customs or the Navy or whoever are investigating. And it could mean that they get away with it."

He didn't tell them that Isaac seemed to have a greater part in that investigation than they thought.

By the time the story of the burial was over Ruth's eyes were nearly closed again. It worried them that there would be no one with her to comfort her when she woke next and remembered, so Owen found a nurse and gave her the bare bones of the story, asking that she look after her if need be.

They returned to Tide Mills by bus.

Owen was relaxing that afternoon when something occurred to him. More than occurring, it hit him like a sledgehammer. He went downstairs.

"Mum – when does school start again?"

"Two weeks' time," Barbara said quietly.

"Two weeks? It can't be! We've only just broken up!"

"Well, if it isn't two weeks it's a fortnight," she said placidly. "Do you need any new uniform? Shoes? How about football stuff?"

It was the last thing he wanted to think about. "Don't think so," he said, retreating. "Going up to the Bakers place."

He did. The brothers were pleased to see him, though a little gentler in their treatment than usual. He persuaded them, without difficulty, to come with him to their usual place on the Downs, Home Bottom, to brew a kettle of tea over a fire and chat.

Ruth was less tired when they visited her that evening. Her scars were itching, she said, but she had been told that meant they were healing and that she mustn't scratch them. It was trying her patience,
"I can't get used to the idea that Ada's gone," she said. "I know she'd only been with us for a few weeks, but it seemed like we'd never not had her."
"Just over three months," said Mary. "I had a look at my day book just last night,"
Ruth smiled at the expression.
"Seems like forever," agreed Owen.

At last Owen tackled the issue of school uniform and sports equipment, finding that his football kit, last used in London, was too tight for comfort. The boots, too, seemed to have shrunk. He remembered the occasional foray into Seaford's shops for shoes of one type or another and the disliked comments about growing feet. It was good to know he was still getting bigger, but six feet tall at the age of fifteen was a bit much. Shopping for clothes was still a drudge even if, now, he could do it on his own.
There was less for him to do at Tide Mills now that the new machinery was doing its stuff, all the redecorating and repairs that had been hidden during the opening ceremony had finally been completed, and everything was working as it should. The donation to his personal funds – not to be called wages by him or the other under-sixteens at Max's insistence – had been welcome.
The mill was going well, even just a week after fully opening, with sales creeping up. Jumping up, as Owen said to his family after a particularly good review of their offering had appeared in the local papers.
The end of August it might have been, but the climate seemed to think it was already October, to judge by the variable weather. Despite it, the adults seldom saw the younger contingent. They were all making the best of any good weather when possible, or were to be found talking or messing about in one of the homes in Tide Mills or Bishopstone when it wasn't. Bee and Gerry would join them almost as a matter of course.
"Wouldn't you just believe it?" thought Owen to himself after a chance conversation with Mary Decks. He had been told that Ruth would be home from hospital the day before he started the new term. Freddie, Alan and Eric were due to start two days before.
With the Mill doing more or less what he had hoped it would, Max was conscious that his own role was subtly changing too. Gone were the frenetic days of builders, suppliers and engineers, deadlines, budgets and head scratching. Life was more serene. He found that he was almost Jack Pentelow's assistant. Only when there was a supply problem or something else to do with the new machinery was his involvement really necessary.
The Monday before term restarted was another Toad-in-the Hole match.

Jack Pentelow had invited Max – as usual – to help form a team.

"And there's another bit of entertainment seeing it's summer," Jack had said. "You'll have to come and watch, though, and for goodness sake don't be led into betting!"

Max was intrigued, and after consultation with Barbara, he accepted. Owen was listening to the exchange, listlessly, and Max suddenly felt sorry for him.

"Jack – how about Owen coming too, if he's a mind to? I know he's never played Toads before but we might get a game in before the match, don't you think?"

Jack looked searchingly at the boy, who knew he was being weighed up in some way.

"Max Wilson: if you get my son drunk, I shall never talk to you again. And the same applies to you, Jack Pentelow. He's not allowed to drink away from home, you know that." Barbara was indignant

"Nothing was further from our minds, was it, Jack? And Owen's got more sense than to get drunk."

Owen was startled by the invitation. Just eighteen months earlier, in London, he hadn't even been allowed out on his own at night, or to stay in the house on his own. And now, his father was inviting him to a match in a pub. Suddenly he felt different. Older. More responsible.

"I'd like to come," he said, trying not to let his eagerness show.

Barbara looked exasperated, but took pity on him.

"All right, then. But no alcohol."

"Mum! I promise I won't buy *any*."

"It's not you I'm worried about," she said with a wry smile. "go on, then. Enjoy yourself. You've had a pretty tough week and deserve something to lift the mood."

He told Ruth of the plans when visiting them that afternoon. "We don't go until about half past seven," he said. "The match doesn't start until half-eight. I hope you don't mind if I miss a visit?"

He asked, rather than just checked. She grinned.

"You go," she said. "You'll have plenty of time to be bothered by me when I get home."

"I won't, you know," he said. "School starts the morning after you get out."

"Well? After a week I shall be starting school too."

He hadn't heard about that, but nodded anyway.

"What do I dress in, Dad?" he asked later, thinking of ties, smart trousers, even a suit.

"Come as you are. It's fun, not formal."

"Isn't fun formal sometimes?"

"It can be. That depends what you make it – or what other people make it. This is just letting your hair down. No fuss, just be yourself."

"What about beer? It's Harveys, isn't it?"

"Your Mother said you mustn't buy any."

"She said I mustn't drink any."

"I think she meant that you shouldn't come home drunk. We can make sure of that between us, can't we?"

"After last time, yes!"

He received a sharp glance.

The old pub was full of holidaymakers enjoying a pre-dinner drink before returning to their hotels to eat. In one of the bars there was an argument in progress.

"Oi tell 'ee I *can*. Stands t'reason, dunnit? Oi'd not brag 'bout it if 'tweren't summink I could do..."

An old man, just about five feet tall and wearing a flat cap that seemed to have a life of its own, was standing and holding court by the dartboard. None of the people round him looked as if they believed what he had boasted. An ageing Jack Russell sat on the floor by him, looking bored.

Jack Pentelow and Martin Killick noticed Max and Owen pause as they entered and saw the scene unfolding.

"That's old Scobie," said Jack, laughing. "Gets all the visitors wound up, he does, then proves he can do what he boasts he can do. 'Course, by then they've bet with him that he can't do it. Sometimes he wins quite a bit of money."

"What can he do?" Owen asked. Martin did a double take as he noticed Owen for the first time, then grinned.

"Watch. He's about ready. Someone else is keeping the book, along with the money that's been placed. Here he goes."

Owen watched. The old man fished about in the pocket of his disreputable jacket and produced three six-inch nails. Ordinary nails. He crossed to the throwing line and paused.

With a jerk of his arm that was so fast and powerful that it couldn't be followed, the first of the nails left his hand and appeared in the dartboard.

There was a gasp from the watchers, who expected that it would fall out, or at the very least, droop.

It was followed in quick succession by the other two nails. Each buried itself in the board satisfactorily. True, as dart scores go it wasn't particularly high, but the fact that astonished all the visitors was that three ordinary nails had stuck in the board as if they were darts with sharp points and flights.

There was a round of applause from everyone except those who had made bets, though even they were impressed.

One or two of the onlookers asked to have a go. Scobie grinned, pulled the nails free and handed them over. One was a London docker who was built, as Martin described him afterwards, 'like a brick shit-house'. Even he couldn't make the nails stay in the elm dartboard. Money was handed to Scobie, who grinned and ordered a pint. The visitors gradually drifted away to their hotels.

"Useful things, emmets," said Scobie when the last of them had gone. "Allus good fer a point or three." The others laughed.

Martin brought three and a half pints back from the bar. They found a table. Each of the men reached for a pint glass. Owen didn't know what to do.

"Well, boy; either that half is yours or one of us uses it to top up their pint, see how. If old Jim comes in, it's mine, see, and you've just finished a ginger beer. Okay?"

"Thanks, Martin. Cheers."

Max watched his son being shown the rudiments of Toad-in-the-Hole and could understand the annoyance on his face as he discovered just how difficult it was to be accurate. He had gone through the same process himself.

The match itself was as raucous as usual, and Max was pleased to see that Owen joined in the banter – though without being rude. Once or twice a team member – side immaterial – was still in the toilet when it was his turn, so Owen would be told to take the shot. Gradually he improved; certainly he wasn't bad enough to be accused of favouring one side or the other.

Max kept an eye on his and Owen's beer intake, and ensured that they missed a number of rounds. Once the match had finished and the conversation became general he wondered if it was time to go. But Owen was in an animated conversation with a tall, thin man from Rodmell who seemed to be offering him something.

Max bought another round but omitted Owen.

"Who was that?" Max asked when eventually they left.

"He's from Rodmell. Said he'd heard about Ada having died – I didn't tell him she had been killed – and was sympathising. He said that his Labrador was pregnant, but he didn't know the father. He hasn't a clue what the puppies will be like but if I wanted one I should let him know."

"What did you say?"

"I was – well, surprised." He continued more thoughtfully: " I'm not sure I want another dog. Not yet, anyway. Ruth's not had the chance of being here without Ada. Perhaps she needs to get used to that. Perhaps the Bakers might like a dog. Anyway, I told him I didn't know, it was too soon, but I'd ask. He seemed to think that if no one wanted them he'd have to give them to the RSPCA."

Max was silent. He was unsure about taking on a puppy. Ada had been a very sedate, older dog, and she had been fine. But a puppy...

"You're right," he said. "Best to wait and see what Ruth and the rest of us think. And... I wonder... could it be that he's actually a breeder and that Ada was his dog?"

Owen was horrified. "We should tell the Police!"

"No proof, son. No proof. We could ask if anyone knows him, though."

Ruth returned to Tide Mills on the Wednesday before term restarted, as permitted by the hospital. Max drove Mary to collect her. As on her return from London there was room for only two in the car apart from the patient since her leg had once again to be supported for a few days. Ruth took up all the back seat.

There was a royal welcome from Owen, naturally, as there was from her father and all the staff at the Mill who saw her arrive. She was pleased and relieved to be in the open air again, with space around her, knowing that by November the plaster would be off and she would have two legs the same length. Mary and Arthur were just glad to have her home. So was Owen.

Term restarted for Owen without any unpleasantness. Botting, now in his last year at the school, gave him a wide berth. For Owen, 'O' level GCEs beckoned.

At the Seaford school Isaac made it very clear to the Headmistress that Freddie was to be prepared properly for GCEs. He mentioned his grandson too and made it plain that Gerry was to be given the same opportunity. Now in his stride he mentioned the Bakers, particularly Alan, who he knew deserved the same treatment.

"I hate the eleven-plus," admitted the Headmistress. "It's unfair and inequitable. I've been doing my best to persuade the powers that be that most of the pupils here need a chance at qualifying for the 'O' Level and maybe continuing to Advanced. It isn't as if there were enough technical school places anywhere to offer the middle tier that the tri-partite system was meant to provide...

Isaac interrupted. "I'm glad to hear that. If it will help I'll arrange some pressure from pupils and parents to ensure you have ammunition to shoot at those powers that be of yours to persuade them to provide those chances."

She looked shocked. "I don't think there's any need for that!"

Isaac smiled humourlessly. "I do."

All had gone quiet about the smuggling gang until one of the national newspapers eventually shouted a story about corrupt Police in London, and a successful 'sting' operation that had unearthed them.

Jack Barden returned quietly to Tide Mills one evening to talk to Max.

"Are you completely recovered now?" he asked his ex-employee.

"Yes, thanks sir. Holden must have hit me so hard that it did some damage. They called it concussion, or some such. It just took a long time to heal properly and even now I'm sometimes dizzy if I get too tired. But a lot of the time I was away it was to keep me safe and make it look like I was really ill, so that Holden would be scared about facing a murder charge."

"I'd come to the conclusion that might be what it was about."

"I... well, I'd told the Navy more about the scheme than was good for me. But they made it look as if they'd discovered it themselves, so they told me."

"That's good. So I imagine what you're going to tell me is that you're going to make an honest woman of your girlfriend and remove the stigma the baby would otherwise be under."

"Don't know about a stinger, sir. What's she under?"

"Not a stinger, Jack, a stigma. What other people will think about her. They'll call her a bastard. Not a nice thing when it's said other than as a swear word. And totally unfair, as the little lass is innocent of any wrongdoing. But marriage is the way to make sure she doesn't get any unpleasantness flung at her."

"That's what Jackie said, sir. I think I should go to London where I'm not known."

"I suggest not London, Jack. Too many temptations. Try looking in the country. Maybe think about the other end of milling; the farm. You're good with machinery. Yes, start at a farm, why don't you, and get a qualification for working on farm machinery. It'll be out of doors, and you're used to that. It'll be where there's lots of space, and you're used to that. And your Jackie can keep a better eye on you than when you were here.

"I hope, by the way, you had nothing to do with the thefts from the Buckle."

The statement took Jack by surprise. He shook his head. "Holden, sir, with other people. I haven't told anyone about that. I never told anyone about things arriving in my shed here, and my having to hide them at Mum's house, in her shed, for collection."

"So there *is* unfinished business. Right. From what you didn't say at the time and haven't said so far I guess that you were near to death after passing out that day we were last together in this study. You were unable to tell me."

He stopped and looked outside. Ruth and Owen were sitting on the bench, just visible from the office window. Two schoolboys, one now quite tall and almost serious looking and one, shorter, but with a good-natured grin on his face, stood talking to them.

"How old are you, Jack?"

Another surprise. Why lie?

"Twenty two, sir."

Max thought again. Seven years older than his own son. Probably during his life to date he would have gone without any of the benefits Owen had taken for granted. Benefits which had helped make him the steady lad that he was.

Max grinned, then looked back.

"You've made some pretty bad decisions over the last few years."

Jack didn't know what to say to that. As he thought there was more coming he kept quiet.

"Parents?"

"Mum's in Rodmell. That's where the shed is. Chap she's living with... I can't get on with him at all. She takes his side in everything."

"Your Dad?"

He hesitated. Oh, what the hell.

"In prison, sir. He attacked someone who tried to break in when he was living with Mum and just carried on beating him until he nearly died. Doesn't surprise me. Used to hit me about a bit too."

Fox and his son, and now this Barden and his son. Max hoped it wasn't some sort of by-product of Tide Mills. He sighed. Those seven years of difference. He came to a decision.

"Jack. Listen, and listen well. I am going to go to the Police with the story about Holden and the Buckle. As with the information you gave the Navy, this will not be traceable back to you but will be the result of fingerprint evidence, independently got. You take that girlfriend and baby and get into the country somewhere, on a farm or similar. I want to know where, and what you're doing. Tell me. Tell your mother or, if you prefer, I'll keep her informed how you are.

"Unfortunately, I have a hold over you now, and that's something neither of us enjoys – well, I don't, anyway. If I hear of you doing anything illegal in the area you go to I shall talk to the Police there. I'll also talk to the Police here. I'll get into trouble, but so will you; and your trouble will be far greater than mine.

"On the other hand, if there is anything I can do for you, for a reference upwards – but not loaning money – you should talk to me. First, before talking to anyone else apart from your wife."

Barden's eyes had been fixed to the surface of the desk in front of him. As Max finished speaking he looked straight at him.

"Are you serious, sir?"

"I don't joke about things like that."

Silence.

"No one's ever been that good to me before."

"Perhaps that's one of the reasons why I said what I said."

"How do I find a job on a farm somewhere?"

"Probably pick an area and get a local paper. W H Smiths will get it for you. Or ask at the labour exchange. They can give you addresses of other exchanges around the country. Then you could write to one of them, but maybe give them a telephone number to contact you on. Do you have a phone where your family is?"

"You mean Jackie and the baby?"

"Yes."

"No, sir; can't afford one."

"Ok. Give them this one. Mine. I'll tell the others. Check with me every few days – in the evening – and I'll give you news. If I hear anything I'll send a postcard by the first post. Okay?"

Barden nodded. "And you'll really do this for me?"

"For you, your Jackie and the baby, yes. I see no reason to add problems to an already troubled life. Now, go on. Get yourself to a labour exchange and start the ball rolling. And talk to Jackie too!"

Max found a hand being offered, and shook it. He took that as the sign of a bargain, and hoped that his trust wouldn't be wasted or misplaced.

When the young man had left he sighed, and made the promised phone call.

With great relief Ruth returned to school in late August and was welcomed by all her friends – and by some who had never been her friends. She found that, thanks to the work sent home over the months, she was not too behind in her new school year and was ahead in some respects. If there had been things she couldn't understand there had been plenty of adults to ask.

In September a very nervous Eric sat the eleven plus and came out of it looking perplexed. As Owen was walking from the Lewes train he bumped into the boy.

"Well?" he asked.

"I got so confused. They seem to make the questions as hard to understand as they can. And what questions? Who cares about how long it takes to fill a bath if you leave the plug out? Who would be so stupid? Anyone who'd do that doesn't deserve to pass the exam!"

Owen laughed. "Sounds typical of mine. Do you think you did all right?"

Eric shrugged his shoulders. "Search me!"

The results, given in mid-October verbally by the school as if they were of no importance, proved that he had done all right. He had passed.

His brother's school day now finished later so Eric cycled home alone. On the journey he was full of conflicting thoughts; part happy and part very anxious almost to the point of unhappiness.

Maud Baker saw his straight face as he came in the door. "Results day, wasn't it?"

He nodded. "Any tea in the pot?"

"Come on. How did you do?"

He lifted the pot, remembered that he had neither cup nor strainer and put it down again.

"Passed."

A hug was inevitable. He endured it.

"Your father *will* be pleased."

"What about Alan?"

"He will be, too."

"But it means I'll be in the Grammar and he'll still be in Seaford."

"But Seaford are starting to prepare kids for GCEs. Freddie's going to do that, and so's Gerry. And lots of others.

"Then why can't I stay in Seaford with them?"

She hesitated.

"Ruth and Owen are at Lewes."

It was Eric's turn to hesitate.

"But they're special."

"No they're not. They just passed the eleven-plus, that's all. Just like you have."

"I don't want to be special."

"You're not! Well, yes you are. You and Alan are both very special, to your Dad and me. I mean you're all the same. It's just whether you passed some silly exam, that's all."

"It wasn't silly. It was really hard."

"But it's only an exam. It's not more important than..."

She searched round for the words, but none came.

"Let's talk about it later, when your Dad and Alan are here. Perhaps we can ask Max And Barbara as well. And Ruth and Owen."

"And Alan?"

"Especially Alan."

They did talk about it later. Ideas floated around. No conclusions were reached. At last Max suggested that they should all sleep on it. Maybe it would be a good idea to talk to Bee and Gerry about what happened there, since Bee had passed and Gerry hadn't. Eric, yawning, decided it would be a good idea. Most of all, though, he wanted to talk to Alan about it alone, in the bedroom they shared.

They did so that night, and in the morning. Eric got the impression that Alan wasn't as worried about the idea as he expected him to be.

"If you were at Seaford, I'd hardly ever see you anyway. We're two years apart. Same as if we were both at a Grammar. And we're still brothers, and live in the same house."

That was some comfort to Eric. "So you really wouldn't mind if I went to the Grammar?"

"It's a good chance. You take it. If you don't like it you can come back to Seaford."

That was thought. "But..." Eric said slowly, "...if I went to Seaford I couldn't switch to the Grammar."

Alan nodded.

"You're still my brother, whatever happens, right?"

"Of course I am. Don't be silly. I'm also your Patrol Leader."

That produced a smile.

All the Bakers were sitting round the breakfast table the following morning.

"Alan and I have been talking," Eric started in a deliberate voice that made his parents prick up their ears. Alan just smiled. "I'd like to go to the Grammar School, please, if that's all right."

He was the embarrassed focus of three smiling faces, and squirmed.

"If you want," said his Dad, as if it didn't matter either way. But the smile never left his face.

It was later that week that the General Election resulted in a narrow win by Labour, ending thirteen years of Conservative government. Knowing their intentions about education, the Bakers wondered how long it would be before the eleven-plus was scrapped, and what would take its place.

In a house in West Street, Seaford, the doorbell rang. It was during the short period between Bee returning from College in Brighton and Isaac finishing work. Gerry, already at home for half an hour, was nearest and answered it. He looked, gasped, and stood, astonished.

His mother.

After almost six years of no contact whatsoever, his mother had decided to return and see them. She looked smart, but older.

"Gerald?" she asked with some doubt. "You're Gerald?"

"Yes," he said, his voice almost back to a youthful treble with the shock. "I'm Gerry."

"You know I hate you shortening your name. Are you going to invite me in?"

Silently, wondering why he was doing it, he stood aside. She seemed almost a stranger, this smart woman, despite her having been his mother once.

"Bee!" he shouted up the stairs. "Bee, you'd better come down."

328

There was something in his tone that got her rushing down as if to tend to an emergency.

"Gerald, please. I've told you before. "This family uses names, not nicknames."

The word 'sorry' was on his lips and he had to stop himself.

"We use nicknames. So does Dad."

Bee saw her mother and gave a short gulp.

"How did you find us?" were her first words.

"And why shouldn't I ask around our old neighbourhood and ask where my family was? It wasn't difficult. And you, Beatrice, have grown up a lot from the skinny little girl you were. Quite the young woman now, aren't we?"

"Where have you been?" asked Gerry suddenly, angrily. "Why did you just leave us all?"

"That's something between your father and me..." she started, when Bee interrupted with a word that made even Gerry jump.

"It bloody well isn't," she said in a loud, firm voice. "No mother leaves her husband and two children for absolutely *years* and then reappears and refuses to tell them why. No mother leaves her children at all, unless she's sick to her death or has gone mad. Oh, we get taught all sorts of things in school, not just science and languages and things. So don't look so shocked. What you did was unforgiveable. What Dad will say when he finds you here I hate to think."

"How dare you talk to me like that? Your own mother."

"Are you? You were once," said Gerry.

"He's right," Bee confirmed. "He was – what: nine years old when you vanished. Imagine how he felt. I wasn't much better at eleven. No. We've done without you for all the years since when you've made no contact at all. And as soon as you come in the door it isn't 'how have you been' or 'it's good to see you'. It's instructions about what we call each other. Some mother."

There was a silence, broken by Gerry.

"Why *have* you come back?"

"I can see that you have been very badly brought up whilst I've been away. And your attitude to me is horrible. Hurtful..."

Again, she was interrupted by Bee, who was now thoroughly roused.

"*Hurtful?* You called us *hurtful?* And you caused each of us to cry ourselves to sleep for *months?* What sort of person are you? What have you become?"

Bee stood in front of the woman, this near-stranger, and was prepared to slap her face. Her demeanour was so imposing that her mother took a step back.

"Now now, let's not do anything that we regret, shall we?"

"You already have," said Gerry, defusing a situation without realising it. "You've come back, and we regret it. So will Dad. He's discovered a few things about you..."

"Gerry!" Bee interrupted. "That's for Dad to say."

"What's for Dad to say?" said a cheerful voice at the front door. None of them had heard it being unlocked. "I don't mind saying it if... good God!"

"You and I need to talk, Isaac. Preferably without these two."

"Good God," said Isaac again.

"Dad, she muscled her way in here..."

"Sorry, Dad; I let her in..."

"How the hell did you find us? And why did you bother after six years?" Isaac had almost found some equilibrium and was chasing thoughts around his head.

He tested the idea of having her back in the family, but found it so intolerable that he had to shake his head to get rid of the notion. Not least of the reasons was that he felt no love for her any more.

"I could see that I was wrong to leave you," she said. "I've come back."

There were gasps from the two youngsters. Isaac held up his hand to stem any comments.

"You walk out on your growing children and your husband to go and live with another man. Or is it men, by now? And then you return as if nothing had happened. Worse, you expect to be welcomed back into the family you think is still yours.

"I'm appalled at your gall. As are Bee and Gerry, by their attitude just then." He held up his hand to stop them speaking again. To give them credit, they held their peace.

Josephine was about to speak again but he continued in a louder voice.

"You abandoned them against the laws of nature. You abandoned me against the vows of the wedding service. For six years.

"And..." Again he had to talk over her protestations.

"And you forbade me to have anything to do with my mother. When we married you refused to have her at the ceremony. When old Fox died you hid the notification of the funeral. You were never the mother you should have been to these two, and now they're older and you've made your sudden appearance I will say that in front of them with absolute conviction. Lastly, over the last few minutes I've tried to detect one iota of love for you in my soul that might remain after all these years. I have to say that I can find none."

He paused for breath. This time she was silent, as were Bee and Gerry who wondered how their father was going to finish.

"And lastly, Josephine Fox, I have discovered that your father is a crook. He's currently awaiting trial for smuggling drugs. Your grandfather was a crook. He nearly killed a young lad. My mother had to nurse him back to health, even though she'd just married Fox. She and the lad became close. I am not Fox's son. I am the son of my mother and that lad. His surname is Galley – does that mean anything? Ah, I can see it does.

"Yes, he is my father, is Isaac Galley, Captain, Royal Navy, retired. He has rescued my mother from abject poverty, a poverty that was largely your doing. And he is a far, far better man than the man whom I called my father ever was. So much so that when we got to know him last year, we decided to change our family name by deed poll to what it should have been from the start. Galley.

"You are not talking to the family you left. You are talking to Beatrice Galley, Gerald Galley and Isaac Galley.

"So, Mrs *Fox*... as none of us in this house wants you back... well, let me check on that. Come outside, would you, you two?"

"Anything you say should be said in front of me," Josephine snapped at him.

"Not when it involves you. And you should realise this is *our* house, Bee's Gerry's and mine..."

"I wish you would stop using those names for them. It really is most unbecoming."

"*Unbecoming*? From a woman who abandoned her family? I think we can ignore that comment, don't you? Come on, you two."

He swept out, seething. Bee and Gerry followed. They went into the main living room. Isaac shut the door and took a deep breath.

"Dad, you're not going to have her back, are you?" this was Bee answering his unspoken question. Gerry was quiet.

"How about you, Gerry? Do you want her back in our lives again?"

He thought for a moment.

"No," he said quietly. "I don't. Once, when she'd just left, I hoped she'd come back and be a Mum again. But what she's said today shows she'll never be that. It would be impossible for her, and impossible for us to live with that attitude."

"Wise words, I think. I certainly couldn't live with her. And there aren't enough bedrooms in this house for us to have one each. So no. I think we tell her to stay away. Are we agreed on that?"

They did, and returned to the kitchen where Josephine was sitting, drumming her fingers.

"We have had a very short family conference, we *Galleys*," said Isaac, now icily calm. "We all agree that you cannot just walk back into our lives as if nothing had happened. We agree that your attitude since you have been in this house shows that you have no remorse about what you have done to us. We agree that you have no place in our lives any more.

"So now you know that, you should also know this. I will be filing for a divorce, quoting desertion. That will release each of us to remarry – not that it has stopped you from committing adultery with the man you went to live with, I'm sure. Give me your address – or do we have to follow you and see where you go? And then we all want you to leave."

The look that she gave Isaac held pure venom. She paused, thinking. Then, before they could stop her she spat on the table they had been standing around, wheeled and marched to the door. Flinging it open so that it knocked a lump of plaster from the wall she marched out, turning right towards Pelham Road.

"Quick!" said Gerry, "after her! We've got to get that address for Dad."

But they had very little distance to run. She climbed into a large car, parked just along the road. As Gerry drew level with it the engine started and although he reached for the handle she swung into the street and accelerated away.

"4802 UF", said Bee calmly at Gerry's side.

"What?" he puffed.

"Her registration number. The police will be able to trace it and get an address. I think Dad needs to phone Grandad, don't you?"

Edna and Isaac were appalled at the woman's nerve, and came to visit. Although neither was happy about there being a divorce in the family it was Edna who was the more level-headed about it.

"If Isaac had been around when you were being mistreated, who knows whether I might have had the courage to divorce Fox. It would have stopped him mistreating you. And me. To stop this Josephine mistreating you all, I'm on your side."

Isaac sighed. "I'm old fashioned, but I can't fault the logic in that. Yes, you must go ahead. Use my solicitor – the firm which helped us with the gaining of this house. You say you have her car registration number but no address? As it's a civil matter I think the Police won't help get you the address, but I know some people who can. Leave that with me. What was the number?"

"4802 UF," said Gerry immediately.

"UF is Brighton," Edna said quietly.

"Is it? Is there no end to your knowledge? Thank you, darling, That's useful as it cuts down the search."

"How did you know that, Grandma?"

She laughed. "From that cottage of mine I watched vans and lorries come and go all day. I saw the new ones and where they came from, and their registrations. There had to be something apart from reading library books that I could do to keep my brain from melting from boredom."

Isaac touched her hand. "If there's anything you need me to do to give you problems to solve, just say the word."

"I don't need problems; I have Freddie."

Freddie looked up from the book he was pretending to read and put out his tongue. Edna returned it and they both grinned widely.

Isaac, both the adopted father and his son, were pleased to see it. It meant that Freddie was comfortable with these two – even if they were considerably older than parents might normally be.

"When you find out where she lives I could go and spy on her," he suggested cheekily.

"What? All day for a week? In school time? I don't think so," said his adopted Dad. "She'd soon get to see the same boy hanging around, and jump to conclusions. And we'd get into trouble from the education people for not sending you to school. No thanks!"

"Oh well. Just a thought," he said with another grin, this time in Bee's direction. She returned it, and his heart leapt again.

26 – New entrants and new beginnings

Mary and Arthur Decks readjusted their lives now that Ruth was – carefully – back at school. So did the Wilsons. It didn't stop their respective offspring from nipping over to visit the other one on a whim on a regular basis.

With an increasing number of sightseeing and customer visitors to the Mill, even in Autumn, Max had to recruit another member of the baking staff. From ingredients and kits supplied by the Mill, their home-made bread, cakes and scones were in considerable demand, not just from tourists but from local people too. He engaged a middle aged lady whose job in Eastbourne had vanished with the closing of a bakery "because it wasn't making enough money for the new owners," she said bitterly.

Max did some research and discovered that the bakery had been sold following the retirement of the original owner, and the purchaser was a high street 'name' which had never wanted to keep the place going. The same thing seemed to be happening all over the country.

Valerie Tilling offered to bring with her many of the recipes from her ex-employer's business "as the new lot aren't interested in them, sir," and gave details. Many of them Max immediately told her she should start making again as he was sure they would sell well.

"Does that mean you're offering me the job?" she asked.

"Well... er... yes, it does. Didn't I mention it?"

"No, sir, you didn't; and that's the truth. But if you're offering, I'm accepting. But..." She trailed off.

Max waited patiently.

"Baking starts early in the morning, sir."

"Yes."

"I rent a place in Eastbourne. My daughter lives with me. She's only twelve."

"Ah. So you're concerned about her getting to school."

"No, sir," she said patiently. "I don't know how I'd get here so early each morning."

"But wouldn't you be prepared to live here?"

"What, in Seaford? We couldn't afford that, sir."

"No. Here. In Tide Mills. We have some spare cottages. And there's the school in Seaford your daughter could go to, or Lewes Grammar if she's passed the eleven-plus. Are there just the three of you?"

"Two, sir; May and me. But are you sure? And what would the rent be?"

"Two? Well, that's no problem. There's no Mr Tilling, I gather?"

She looked uncomfortable. "He... he dumped me for a younger model when May was born. Said he married me for better or worse, but not for children."

"Then he's a fool," said Max, shocked. "Divorced, I suppose? Not that it makes any difference to the job. That still stands."

"Thank you, sir. Yes, sir, divorced; and thank you for not holding it against me."

"I know some firms do," said Max, "but I work on a more Christian principle."

"In Eastbourne it was the church people who criticised, damn their e... sorry, sir."

"For some, Christianity only goes as far as they want it to," said Max. "Two things: Firstly can you come back again with May on Saturday? We can take you round one or two cottages that might do, and see what you think. And you can both meet some of the families here and see how you get on with them."

"Thank you, sir. I'd like that. And she and I can go for a walk along the beach, too."

"You'll see plenty of beach if you live here!" Max told her.

She smiled, and the anxious look that she'd worn up to then vanished. She looks a peasant, comfortable woman, thought Max.

"What was the second thing, sir?"

Max laughed. "Very simple. Please stop calling me 'sir', would you? It makes me feel old and an ogre. And I'm really neither unless someone does something stupid or illegal. Then I get very old-fashioned."

She smiled again. "I'll do my best, sir. Oh, damn!"

With trying to increase the production in the bakery, together with an unexpected problem with telephones and one or two more minor issues, Max forgot to tell anyone about the Saturday visit. So Val and May appeared at the Mill's Reception and were immediately shown to the queue for the next tour around the machinery. Puzzled, but trusting, they paid their fee and took the tour, and found themselves amazed at the story of the improvements and additions and the new lines that were being both produced and packaged on site. What impressed Val even more was the happy, friendly manner of the tour leader. He'd introduced himself as Jack Pentelow; it was indeed Jack who had stepped in so as to allow the proper tour guide to help at the bakery. Indeed, everyone working at the machinery was friendly, chatty, and keen to answer questions.

When the group had emerged and questions had been answered, Val and May hung around instead of following the other visitors to the cafe and bakery.

Jack smiled at them. "Another question? Fire away."

"Not exactly," said Val. "You see, Mr Wilson asked us to come back today to visit so he could show us one or two of the cottages we might live in. He'd... he'd offered me the job of the second baker."

Jack laughed. "That Max! And you've allowed yourselves to be herded round the Mill like sheep. I'm going to make him squirm for that!"

"Oh, please don't... not on my account. I don't want to make any trouble."

He laughed again. "I'm the manager of the Mill here; Max is my boss. He looks after everything else. And me too, if it comes to that. But as well as that, we're friends. In fact all the people here are friends. If you two come and live here you'll discover that, unless you're the stand-offish type."

"Oh, we're not that, are we, May?"

The girl gave a smile like her mother's, but said nothing.

The door swung open and a young, slightly hoarse, slightly deepened voice asked "Have they all gone now, Mr P? It's just that... Oh, sorry."

"You've come at a good time, you two. This is... sorry, I never asked your name, Mrs...?"

"Val Tipping. This is May, my daughter."

"These two horrors... no, not any more. These two young gentlemen are Alan and Eric Baker, and they live here too with their parents. Mrs Tipping and May will be joining us soon; she's going to be the second baker. Val, that is, not May. You'd better come with me. We'll find that Max, and he and the brothers can take you to whatever cottages he's going to offer you. He can answer your questions and these two can answer May's."

Eric was grinning at May in his typical, welcoming fashion as if he knew her already. Alan was also looking, thinking what an attractive face May had. She looked fun, too.

Max was mortified at having forgotten to tell anyone of the visit. He invited them all in for a cup of tea, causing confusion for Val and pleasure for the brothers. Owen and Ruth were in a corner, discussing some problem with a practice 'O' level paper, and looked up as the strangers came in. Owen jumped up, followed, more slowly and with the aid of crutches, by Ruth.

In Max's temporary absence in the kitchen Owen introduced Ruth and himself, aware that something like amazement had dawned on May's face as he uncoiled his six feet two inches of height from the chair. He smiled at her.

"Have we met before?" he asked.

She shook her head, wonderingly, and blushed. "You're so tall," she said.

"May! That's not the right thing to say. You should apologise."

Owen laughed. "No apology, please. I'm six feet two, and nobody is more surprised than me, seeing that both Mum and Dad have to look up when we're talking. I suppose it's useful, because I can see more in crowds." He smiled, and Val could see that no offence was going to be taken by her new boss's twenty year old son, for so she assumed him to be.

Ruth took over. "Hallo, May, hallo Val, if I can call you that. My parents work at the Mill too. You'll meet them once you've moved in because we'll have a get together. Probably in here."

Val was speechless. Never before had she been accepted so readily by anyone, and by the boss's family, too. May had no such qualms.

"Are you two married?"

Val was about to tell her off again but Ruth just laughed.

"No. We're not old enough yet. We're only fifteen. But it depends what happens after that."

She was conscious that Owen's attention had switched from the newcomers to her, but determined not to meet his look.

"But... but I thought he was twenty, or something," said Val.

Ruth smiled again. "No. It's just that sometimes he thinks he is, or does something that a twenty-year-old would do."

"Oy!" Owen had found his voice at last, and was now looking at an innocent faced Ruth. "Was that a compliment or an insult? I can't decide."

Oddly, neither of the Baker brothers looked anything but serious.

"I was his Patrol Leader 'til he went into the Seniors in September," said Alan, some fifteen inches shorter than his friend. "He's a useful bloke to have around, but he's got a lot to learn still."

There was no answer that either Val or May could give to that, so they said nothing and just smiled faintly.

Tea arrived, conversation circulated, and gradually Val relaxed as she saw that there was none of the 'them and us' in this family; nor even, it seemed, in the Mill. It felt so much more relaxed than the attitudes she had encountered in her previous job.

At last Max and the brothers, now chatting animatedly to May, took them to look at some of the cottages that were available. They found one that Val particularly liked, quite near the Bakers' home, and she sighed with something like contentment.

"This is so like the place I grew up in. It's old, and it's comfortable, and it's quiet."

"And we're close if you need anything," said Alan to May before he could stop himself.

Val ignored him. "Can I talk to you alone, s... Mr Wilson?"

"Of course. If it's about rent, it'd be rent free. That's the way we're going, by agreement with everyone. It means that we don't have to pay salaries and then take some back. It also means you pay less tax, I think, and you don't lose out. It does mean, of course, that if you try to compare your salary here with somewhere else it needs a bit of guesswork. But that would be your business and I hope it doesn't ever come to that. I hope that if you're not happy you'd come to me first so we can talk it through."

There was the sound of a vehicle drawing up in the Drove outside; an unusual occurrence now as visitors were asked to park above the railway crossing. This was partly for safety's sake but mainly so as to ensure that The Drove was kept clear for trucks working from one part of the Mill to another. The fact that it also meant that visitors had to walk past the bakery with its smell of fresh bread was, of course, neither here nor there.

Max looked out. A green Post Office Telephones van was there. Isaac had decided to combine a social call with the last formal job of a rare Saturday morning working.

Max greeted him, and a thought struck him. "Isaac, while you're here, can you just come inside this cottage, please? I'm not sure if Val wants a phone when she moves in."

At the sound of her name Val made for the door. She and Isaac collided.

"*Oof!*" came from Val, and "Sorry," from Isaac. They saw each other properly.

"It's a heck of a way to meet someone," said Isaac as they separated. She was impressed by the distinguished looking face and the halo of whitening hair.

"Good morning," she said, as politely as she knew how.

"Good morning," he echoed, thinking what a pleasant, comfortable person she looked. "Max tells me you might want a telephone installed."

"Er... I really don't know. It's very early days for me to be making that sort of decision."

"I'd be grateful if you would," said Max. "You see, we provide the instrument and pay for the wiring to the internal system. That means that you can call anyone in the hamlet free of charge at any time. And if you were to order an external line it'd be at a much reduced rate if it's all done at the same time. You have to pay for your own calls outside Tide Mills, of course."

"Mum! Please?"

Val looked down into the pleading eyes. They'd never had a telephone before.

"Oh, go on, then."

Everything was moving very fast. Too fast, she thought.

"Where would you like it, Mrs... er..."

She looked at Isaac again. And suddenly, it seemed to her without reason, she smiled.

"Tipping. Val Tipping. And to be honest, I really don't know yet. We've only just seen the cottage. I don't know where furniture is going to go, or anything. At this stage I don't know how I'm going to be able to afford to move, or when."

Isaac thought, furiously.

"Max," he started in a wheedling voice, "you know that new van that the Mill bought for deliveries?"

"Yes... and I know what you're going to say. I'll provide some of the staff for it too. Owen will help. And how about you two? Would you help Mrs Tipping with a move?"

"Will Freddie come too?" asked Eric.

"I'll ask, but if Bee's there I'm sure wild horses won't keep him away. Val – how soon can you start?"

It was the next Saturday that a crew of young people shoehorned themselves into a new Tide Mills Bakery van, driven, appropriately, by Ernie Baker, followed by Freddie, Bee and Gerry in Isaac senior's car which was driven by his son.

They managed to complete the move in two shuttles, with Val trying to keep track of what was where, Isaac keeping track of her, Alan keeping track of May, and Freddie keeping track of an amused but increasingly intrigued Bee.

A last surprise for a completely flustered and exhausted Val was to have Max on her new doorstep telling her that there was a cup of tea at the Mill House now, and that she and May were expected for an evening meal later. Isaac was surprised to receive an invitation too, along with Bee, Freddie and Gerry.

That evening, over the meal, they would have told them both the full saga of the Wilsons and the Galleys, but they could see that their prospective listeners were too tired to take it in. The younger Galleys took them home – all of fifty feet – and she and May hurriedly made beds and slept.

The idea was to have been that Val should have a week to herself to allow time for sorting out a place for May at the Lewes Girls' Grammar. She had passed the eleven-plus and had started at one of Eastbourne's Grammar schools a few weeks previously. As it was, Val was introduced to Steve Fuller, the main baker, and his wife Annie; both fortunately liked her and respected her experience and abilities. Their chat was interrupted by the exodus from the Mill of the first of the day's coach parties. Val saw that the young girl in the shop, even helped by Steve, was inundated, and immediately went behind the counter to help.

It was a move that impressed Max and the baker more than any talking could have done. Max made a mental note to ensure that any future new staff were introduced to their prospective colleagues as part of the interview process, and give a chance to show their mettle at the coal face.

When they had bidden farewell to the crowd of visitors Steve tuned to her.

"I think you're in, lass. Thank you."

"You're welcome. That's what I'm here for, isn't it?"

"No," Max interrupted, "really you're here as a baker, but help in the shop in a situation like that is an occasional necessity too. So don't let Steve treat you like a shop assistant."

"Given her experience, there's no chance of that!" Steve exclaimed. "I need her to do what she does best. Not that she's not good behind a counter too."

Val glowed. The anxiety of the interview had vanished. She felt needed and, even after half an hour, a part of something important. Her thoughts unaccountably went to that GPO engineer she had met – what? Was it really only a week ago? – who had in the course of her house move become a friend. Would he be installing her phone soon?

May was taken to the Grammar school by Val. Ruth had asked if she could accompany them on the visit, an idea welcomed by them both. May met a lot of girls in advance, mainly Ruth's friends, which had been her plan. The newcomer liked the school and the people, as did Val, and both were reassured that as it was so close to the starting of the Autumn term, May would have no difficulty academically.

With more and more coach parties, usually arranged by Eastbourne and Brighton hotels who mainly hired the coaches from Southdown, Val found that her settling in time was being eroded by calls for help in the shop and, towards the end of the week, in the bakery. She sighed and accepted the situation with good humour. Work would start in earnest the following Monday.

Her early start was interrupted by a break to see May onto the train to school, along with Ruth and Owen. It pleased her that Ruth, although some three years older and in a different set of classes, would be there if needed.

338

May, with her short introduction to some of the girls in her year, was keen to get started. She reappeared from the train with the others in the late afternoon with a smile on her face, removing any lingering doubts about her settling in.

The promised Mill staff get-together helped them both, and once again Val and May were amazed at the generosity of the Wilsons in giving over their home, at the generosity of the Mill (and Barbara, with help from the Buckle) for providing food and drink, and the rest of the staff for their increasing friendliness.

The weather continued kind into the autumn, allowing the growing squad of young cyclists to spend time on Downland paths. They introduced May to the freedom of lighting a fire to make tea in their usual special place, and she loved it.

Ruth was asked if she felt she could stand for long enough to help with decorating cakes for sale in the shop.

"It's something May likes to do at times," said Val, "but your friends are taking her all over the place so she's hardly ever here!"

Ruth, glad to be of use, accepted, and found that she enjoyed it. It took her a little practice, but before long she could manage the basics quite easily. It took her an hour of concentration on what she was doing to realise that she was standing level.

Standing level. No built-up shoe. Oh, a plaster cast, yes. But no special shoe and standing level.

She experienced a sudden warm feeling of pleasure. Did she mind missing a whole summer's fun to get to this stage?

No. Absolutely not.

There was a little wobble on the cake she was icing. She told herself it was a happiness wobble, laughed, and put the cake on one side to buy later for herself. At the end of her spell Val heard the story. She told her to finish icing it with a message of celebration to herself and to take it home.

When the cyclists reappeared they were surprised to be ushered in to the Mill House and provided with tea. At the end of it the cake was brought in. In large, red, approximate, iced writing it said: 'My legs are the same length!'. Underneath was: 'Thanks to my friends for being there for me.'

"Oh, wow!" said Alan. "That's lovely. And we want you with us on a bike just as soon as you can." The rest made suitable noises. Owen just smiled with her. Ruth engineered it that they were alone for a moment.

"I'll say thank you properly to you later," she told him. The look of surprise she received made her smile. Owen, at fifteen and used to the *double entendre* from school, didn't quite know how to take the comment, but even then a tingle ran up his spine . He bent, but not now by very much, to kiss her. Freddie, noticing, found himself looking at Bee – who continued looking out of the window.

"What are we going to do for them at Christmas?" Barbara asked her husband when they were at last alone. Ruth and Owen had vanished upstairs to listen to Radio Caroline.

"Buy them engagement rings, I should think," Max answered.

"I just hope it doesn't have to be wedding rings. They're up there on their own at the moment, you know. And they're only children, when it comes to it."

"Technically speaking, yes. But they've also got sense and decency. And Ruth does have a leg in plaster."

"If you think that would stop them... well... going too far then you don't know men."

"But Owen can't be both a man and a child. We just said they were children."

"You know what I mean. And yes, he can. As you very well know."

"Should we go up and interrupt them, then?"

Barbara hesitated. "We could go and make a noise in the bathroom."

"Both of us?" Max mocked a shocked expression and Barbara had to laugh.

"You're as bad as he is."

"Worse. I imagine all he's doing is listening to the radio, lying next to Ruth who's probably wriggling and trying to get a bigger share of the single bed so she can get her leg comfortable. "

Which was exactly what was happening. Owen had planted himself on the bed and had patted the space beside him. The look he received was one that was difficult to read. She sat next to him.

"Rest your leg," he said.

"What on?"

"The bed."

"I can't. You're in the way."

"If I lie down I won't be."

"But that means I'll be lying by your side."

"Well?"

"What happens if your parents come in."

"They won't. If they want to come in, they knock."

"And what do we do if they knock?"

"You hop up and sit, I suppose."

"Owen, at the moment I don't hop anywhere."

"You know what I mean."

Three minutes later they were lying on the bed, side by side, looking at the ceiling and listening to the radio. Owen gave a deep, happy sigh.

"What was that for?" Ruth asked.

What should he say? How should he answer that?

"Just happy." It seemed the safest thing to say.

"Why?"

He looked back at her, and was surprised to find her eyes on his face. It made him smile.

"Do you not know?"

She smiled back.

"Perhaps. But tell me anyway."

He didn't want to sound soppy. He didn't want to say what he felt. But he

340

had to say something.

"Because…" A long pause. She waited. "Because you're by my side."

It was enough. Her head moved closer and kissed his nose.

Minutes afterwards there seemed to be more spare room on the bed. Arms were encircling, mouths together. And bodies were moving against each other. After what seemed a very short time of increasing movement Ruth pushed him away.

"Owen!"

He was suddenly ashamed of his body's reaction.

"Can't help it," he muttered. "It's you…"

"I haven't done anything!"

"You're here. That's enough."

"I'd better go, then."

"You can't do that… please?"

"I think I'd better." She looked down the bed. "Look at you!"

He moved toward her to hide his embarrassment. She swung her legs back to the floor.

"Awww…"

"Whining won't have any effect."

"That's not kind."

"Shh!"

There were sounds below them, cupboards being opened, voices, the door closing again noisily. It might not have taken long but it was a very effective come down for Owen. And, if truth be told, for Ruth. Equilibrium was regained and a look was shared. Smiles turned to embarrassed laughter. Owen lay back on the bed again. Once more he patted the space beside him. She sighed, and occupied it.

"This time we stay facing the ceiling," she commanded. Owen gave a whimper but complied. It was better than not having her close.

"What I *meant* was…" Barbara was continuing her original question after their noisy investigation of the bathroom together during which all they heard were the radio and one tenor and one soprano laugh. "… what are we going to do for the staff this Christmas?"

"Are you happy to do the same as last year? With help?"

"It was hard work last year, even with Ruth's help and a lot of the others," she admitted.

"If I go for this directorship…" he started, and let it hang.

They had discussed it before but had reached no conclusion. Each was worried lest his time away from Tide Mills should grow from one part-day a week to several. Responsibility and increased salary – or his remuneration package, as John Simpson called it – came with a price.

"You mean that we could add to whatever the Mill contributes?"

He nodded. "And that means that we could get outside caterers to do the hard work."

"But then it's less personal. It's just so nice when we know it's just us, with help from others."

"But which others? There are the wives, but some are cooking for their own families."

"And anyway there's only enough room in the kitchen for a certain number. Don't forget that Ruth can't stand for long. She'll have her plaster off by then and her muscles won't have recovered."

"There's young May…"

Barbara thought, and laughed. "If you invite her, you'll have Alan helping too, I think."

"That might not be too bad. He's got a good head on his shoulders."

"What about the Galleys? All of them?"

"For Christmas, yes. Not for the staff do."

"True. Let me start by asking Maud Pentelow, Jessie Baker and Mary Decks – and maybe May Tilling…"

"And Alan Baker!"

"Oh, good grief! And Alan Baker then. I suppose he has some experience from Scouts. And a few other adults. I would ask them to prepare a couple of dishes at their own homes for which we'll provide the ingredients. We can turn your office into the bar and a sitting area – we'll need to hire extra seats. Comfortable ones. And people can spread themselves out between this room, the dining room and the office."

"You've been thinking about this in advance, haven't you?"

"Yes, I have," Barbara told him. "I suppose what we could do with are some professional washers up – and more plates. Always more plates. And glasses. And, I suppose, some of your favourite Harveys from the Buckle."

"You deal with the supplies and getting people to make and provide things, and I'll deal with the beer and hiring side of it. Cutlery as well, I imagine."

"Of course! How could that have escaped me?"

They continued sorting out details and then turned to their own Christmas celebrations, and who was coming.

"Ruth will be here if Owen has anything to do with it. And if her, her parents too," Barbara mused.

"Of course they must come. How about the Galleys?"

"Why not. They're part of our story too."

Max's eyebrows shot up. "What a novel way of looking at it! Yes, they most certainly are. And if them, young Isaac, Bee and Gerry."

A smile from Barbara. "And if young Isaac is coming, should we ask Val and May? Have you seen how much more we're seeing of Isaac since Val started with us?"

"You know, I *thought* he'd been a more regular visitor. I wondered if it was so that his kids could play with the others. I'd also noticed that Alan's always around somewhere – even just on the allotment for a change – when May is here."

"You're not without your sensitivity to what's going on, are you, Max? But I think the Bakers should be left to their own devices, don't you? Maybe the youngsters can do the rounds of calling on each other later in the afternoon. But if we're inviting people without husbands or wives we'd better ask old

Archie again."

"Yes. I'm glad you mentioned him. He was good value, wasn't he? And we'll get the singers amongst us to get some songs ready, too."

Individually, and later conferring, they made arrangements and other plans. Val and May were asked, firstly to help with the buffet evening for staff. When May was asked if she could produce anything – her mother would be at work so it'd be unfair to ask her – she firstly went boggle-eyed and then smiled broadly.

"If I can have some help it would be good, though," she said.

"We're running out of adult help," Barbara told her gravely. "Would one of your friends do?"

"If they know what they're doing," she said doubtfully.

"I know one of them can cook for about six," Owen said. "I've been one of the six and it's not bad."

"Who's that?" she asked, intrigued.

"Alan Baker."

The reaction was almost comical.

The reaction in the Baker family was more normal. It produced a guffaw from Ernie, a look of resignation from Jessie and Eric, and a Cheshire cat grin and immediate affirmation from Alan. Had anyone been outside later they would have seen him jumping up and down as if he were still eight.

All the wives loved the idea of contributing something. Barbara wondered if between them they would be over-catering. The date set for it left enough time before Christmas itself so that any extra food could be redistributed and used, or revitalised for the Christmas lunches.

Isaac asked Val if she would come to have dinner with him at one of Seaford's restaurants. She accepted. He collected her, the two enjoyed each other's company and Val laughed more readily and for longer than she had for years. They discovered a common love of modern dancing and Isaac told her the two must go to the Regent Ballroom in Brighton's Queens Road soon. When he dropped her at her cottage she looked up at him and touched his arm when saying goodbye.

They did indeed go dancing. And she brought him back to Tide Mills where they talked in (mainly) low voices until two in the morning. May smiled to herself and went back to sleep. Bee, in Seaford, was worried, went to bed late and dozed. She was woken at two-thirty by the front door, went down to see a smiling Isaac and the piece of her mind she was going to give him stayed in her head. It was just good to see him happy.

He apologised. They both slept late, to Gerry's disgust. He left a note and went to Tide Mills.

Val and Isaac saw each other quite often after that, going to one or other of the dance halls. An easy-going relationship grew. Isaac started wondering if there was s future for them together. He asked her and May to come for a meal in West Street and then panicked about what to cook. The efficient Bee came to the rescue, and although it wasn't the show-off menu he would have liked the soup was good (from a tin), the pie was home made and the ice-cream easy.

He sat Bee and Gerry down in their living room the following day.

"You know Val and I have been going out together a lot recently?"

Bee nodded sweetly, half aware of what was coming.

Gerry just said: "Yes. We noticed. When are you going to get married?"

He let the exclamations die down. "It's pretty obvious you're sweet on each other. We like her – and May – so what are you going to do about it?"

"Gerry, you have the tact of a Sherman tank. To answer your question, there's nothing I can do until the divorce is finalised. But if you two are reasonably happy about having Val as a new Mum…"

"Well, we've not had one for years. So a Mum of almost any kind would be quite nice. And we like her. Don't we, Bee?"

Bee, also amazed at the blunt way her brother was dealing with this, nodded. "Yes. She's kind and smiley. And has good sense."

"There you are then, Dad. We agree. Now what are you going to do?"

Isaac sighed. "I need to ask what May thinks about the idea, and about having you two as brother and sister."

"Oh, she's happy about it," said Gerry triumphantly. "We asked her."

"You did *what?*"

"Well, we thought you'd be popping the question sometime, so we asked her what she thought. She likes you. And us, I think, because she said it'd be nice but that we'd need to live at Tide Mills so her mother could carry on working."

"But… Gerry, how do you know more about this than I do?"

He shrugged. "Bee and I talk. We're not as innocent as you think we are, you know. Or as stupid."

"I know you're not stupid. But can't a man have his private affairs kept private?"

"Nope. Not when he's got two children like us. We're special."

Two weeks later, on a Monday at the start of December, letters dropped through two doors. One was at a newly built house in West Street, Seaford. The other was at a two-hundred year old, knapped flint cottage in Tide Mills.

Isaac tore open his heavy envelope and read the subject of the letter from his solicitor: "In the matter of the Divorce Proceedings between Isaac James Galley (previously Fox) and Josephine Beatrice Fox (nee Holden)."

He read it carefully and heaved a sigh of relief. His wife's lover had taken her back. She wasn't contesting the proceedings. He had been hoping for that, almost beyond hope. But better, her current partner must have persuaded her that she should ensure the children weren't impoverished. She had decided not to pursue a claim against any shared property – the house being the obvious concern.

The other letter – at Tide Mills – was addressed to the Parents or Guardians of Miss Ruth Decks and started "Ruth Decks, d.o.b 12-03-49". It requested her to attend the Brighton Hove and Sussex Hospital, Outpatients' Department in Eastern Road, Brighton, on Tuesday 7th December to have the plaster cast removed.

"They've finally realised you're no longer a child, gel," said her father. "Now the hard work starts in getting that leg strong again."

Ruth was dropped back at home by Max, who had once again provided the taxi service. She hobbled in, followed by Mary and Max, still needing one crutch as her muscles were indeed almost non-existent on the treated leg. Max followed her in and found Arthur there.

"Hope you don't mind, Max. Just had to be here."

"I'd be sorry if you weren't, Arthur."

"Stand up, gel?"

Ruth stood, swaying slightly, and gradually transferred the weight off the crutch.

"I had to do this in the hospital," she said, gritting her teeth. She looked at her father for approval. He held out his arms. Cautiously she took a small step towards him with the weak leg, then once again, with teeth clenched and eyes closed, transferred her weight to it. The other leg hurriedly came to join it.

She repeated the performance, and found that her father's arms were holding her.

"That's my girl," he muttered, and repeated, this time with a catch in his voice: "that's my girl."

She looked him in the eyes, surprised to hear the catch, and saw a tear run down his cheek.

"Oh Dad...!"

"I'm the same," admitted her mother. "We've been looking forward to this day for months. Years, really."

Ruth had caught the mood. Her delight had been to see and hear the reaction from her parents, but more, to stand, unaided, with legs that were the same length. She felt as buoyed up as she had been when first realising she was standing level with the leg in plaster. But this time it was even more so. She was walking. Naturally. Maybe only two steps, but walking. She knew it was now just up to her to get her strength up again.

And she was looking forward to starting work on it. Not just now, though. Now all she wanted was to sit down. Sit down now. This instant. Her Dad held her weight and helped her to a chair.

"I'm an old fool," he said, impatiently wiping his face.

"No, you're not," she told him, looking up. "You're my Dad."

"And I'm your Mum," said Mary, softly, embracing her.

"And you're my Mum, and I love you both very much. And thank you for putting up with... with all this."

There were now two pairs of arms around her. She was looking forward to the third, but they and their owner were still at school.

"It's still very weak," she told him when, once again, she had performed her two steps into his arms.

"May I see?" he asked.

Gingerly she lifted the hem of her skirt to show the lower set of scars where the rods had come out. They had healed, but still looked raw.

"Do they hurt?" he asked.

"No. Not exactly. They're tender. I wouldn't want to have someone poke at them."

He nodded, awed by the marks and by the long period of having had the rods protruding from them.

"Is the leg much thinner than the other one?"

Daringly she lifted up the other side of the skirt.

"Wow!"

There was a marked difference between the two,

"How long before it's back to normal?"

"About six months more before I can start treating it as a normal leg, they say. I have to be careful not to jar it too much, especially to start with. They say the bone's good, and straight, but it's still quite thin. If it gets mistreated it might snap, and then I'm back on my back in traction, like Freddie was."

He winced. "You're still in cotton wool, then."

She smiled. "For the moment. Maybe I'll get some of the cotton wool off for my sixteenth birthday."

"Okay... I'll get you on your bike then. And on *my* sixteenth birthday you can get the rest off."

"Rest of what off?" she asked

"The cotton wool."

"I wondered what you meant."

His mind went into overdrive. And then: "Ruth Decks, what are you suggesting?"

The smile was innocent. More or less.

In the rest of the run-up to Christmas the Mill went into hectic mode, maybe nearly into chaos mode, despite the best efforts of Jack Pentelow and Max Wilson. Demand for cakes would have exceeded their ability to produce and decorate them had it not been for May and Ruth being drafted in to help.

Val Tipping played her trump card and unearthed a large number of pre-prepared Christmas cakes she had secretly made almost as soon as she had been appointed.

"These'll be even better," she said. "The mix was done when I was in Eastbourne, in my own kitchen, and I was hemmed if I was going to leave it to go to waste. It'll have matured nicely now. We can charge extra for these and tell people they were made with Harveys Old, because they were."

Max nearly kissed her. Steve Fuller did.

Sunday the 19th was the day of the staff get together. It was also the Carol Service in Seaford, so Ruth, Owen, Alan and Eric were taken to the church by Max – who was glad to get out of his wife's way – to sing. When they returned, with Freddie, it was nearly eight o'clock and people had started congregating.

As they drove down to the house Max called to them. "Don't forget now,

Eric and Freddie first at the front door, then at the second verse it's the rest of us too and we start walking."

He mustered them at the door, checked round, and then opened it. In a Captain-on-the-bridge-in-a-storm voice he yelled out.

"Crew! Attention! Muster call!"

The buzz of conversation from inside faltered, then stopped. He nodded to Eric.

In a voice that had matured over the previous year Eric started *"Once in Royal David's City..."* He had the first two lines. Then Freddie's voice, now capable of a rich alto joined in: *"Where a mother..."*

At the second verse the rest joined in, in harmony, as they walked into the hall where they paused for the rest of the carol so that it could be heard in each of the three rooms they were using.

When the last notes had faded into the darkness outside there was a pause, a roar of approval and a great deal of applause. The singers smiled, one or two of the listeners wiped their eyes, and Barbara came out to greet them all.

The evening was a resounding success. This time, Barbara had little to do except worry that the hired staff were doing what they should be doing. Max found her and made her sit down and leave it to them.

"They know your kitchen almost as well as you do," he told her. "If we need anything, all we have to do is ask and they'll get it. It's what they're here for."

There was more singing. Sometimes it was choral, with Alan leading the others; and sometimes they sang traditional songs with Archie taking centre stage. When the singers tired he would break into tunes which, he said, "were old when I were a lad."

At last people started drifting away, with only the following day's Mill late shift remaining. At last Ruth found that she couldn't keep her eyes open any more and told her parents she was either going home or would collapse on Owen's bed if she could get up the stairs. They received the message, Owen realised there was to be no miracle. The family made its way home; accompanied, as always, by him. He returned, found it wasn't the same without Ruth, excused himself and went to bed.

There were some bleary eyes and sore heads the next morning, but flour was milled, mixes were made and packed, and customers were served. Monday was an early night for many, not least Val and May, the latter having been left in bed by her mother when she left for work at 4.30 that morning. May woke late and missed the last day of school – to her mother's horror.

"We did knock at the door," Ruth told her that evening, "but guessed you had stayed on until late and overslept. It was only a lot of nonsense and the Service, so you didn't miss anything important. Some of the others were missing, too."

May had already made her peace with her mother using the same logic, so was pleased to have it confirmed.

The extended family's Christmas was at times raucous, at times quiet and pensive. Once again, because of the Church service, they were late eating and took the natural break of the Queen's speech as a resting period between main course and Christmas pudding – which was once again set alight by Max and sung in by Archie and the assembled company.

Once they'd eaten their fill and Barbara, Max and Owen had moved to clear the table, there was an interruption.

"One moment, if I may…"

The voice was Isaac's, the junior one. Chat stopped. Table clearing stopped. The Wilsons stood, surprised. Barbara put her pile of bowls back on the table. Isaac was standing, looking self-conscious and, it appeared, slightly nervous. It seemed he was having to make himself speak.

"I'm very glad to be able to be here amongst friends. I want to thank the Wilsons for their invitation and for their friendship. I want to thank my mother and father for being here. But most of all I want to thank Val Tilling for her friendship."

Here it comes, thought Bee, Gerry and May.

"We've only known each other a few months. But in that time we've found that we speak the same language, are very happy in each other's company and have shared interests. I am at last free of… well, I find myself able to…

"Oh damn. Val: I've sounded out my two, and they are happy. Unbeknown to me they've sounded out May, and she'd be happy. So, Val, I'm asking you: please, will you marry me?"

There was a gasp from the surrounding company. Val, though, was watching him with a smile on her face, a fact that registered with him, causing a look of puzzlement. She gave a laugh.

"Isaac, I have a daughter who's lived with me for all her twelve – nearly thirteen years. We have few secrets. She let on that you had sounded out your two and yes, they sounded her out. She also sounded me out. I just smiled and said "we'll see."

"And now it's time we did see. And my answer to you is 'yes'. I…"

She was drowned out by cheers and applause from a suddenly standing crowd around the table. Isaac crossed to her and hesitantly put his arms round her. The offered lips were kissed.

"You have made me a very happy man."

"And you have made me a very happy woman."

There seemed to be a long pause as the two looked into each other's eyes. It was broken by old Archie who started singing very quietly:

> "Come write me down, ye powers above
> The man that first created love…"

They applauded again when he was done, to the old man's delight.

"An' I wish you all health and happiness."

"So do we all," called Max. "And we'll drink a toast to these two."

They did. When it was over, Ruth found Owen's eyes on her and blushed. The table was cleared. The men went to wash up. Owen hung back a moment to corner Ruth.

The two looked at each other, smiling gently. At last Owen could hold himself back no longer.

"Is it our turn next?" he asked.

She continued to smile. "Do you think you'll still want to ask that in a few years' time?"

"I'll want to ask it for as long as you're around. And even if you're not."

"How are you going to do that?"

"Letter to you at University?"

"Maybe."

"Maybe what?"

"Maybe a letter would work."

"Only maybe?"

"Maybe a question would work."

"But what would the answer be?"

"That depends on you. It depends on me."

"It might depend on who else you meet," he said, suddenly bitterly.

"You might meet someone else too. I'm not much of a catch."

"Who's talking about catches? You're a friend, someone I can trust and talk to like I talk to no one else. And…"

He gulped. "And I love you."

Her smile brightened. "And I love you too, Owen Wilson. Very much. Now, you *are* a catch, and I'll be jealous if ever another girl gets her fingers on you."

"But for me you *are* a catch," he told her seriously. "You're a face I was immediately attracted to, from a train. Remember? And we've known and loved each other ever since. Not just for the face, but for… well, everything. And yes, I want to spend my life with you. Nothing's going to change that."

Silence. Her eyes seemed misty. He was about to say something else but she put her finger on his lips.

"I *really, really* hope it doesn't."

Later, they were all once again sitting round when there was a knock at the door. Max, expecting a Mill problem, answered it.

"Hallo, sir. Happy Christmas."

"*Jack*? Jack Barden? But you look completely different. Are you all right? Come in."

The young man, now with well-tended stubble on his face that spoke of a growing beard, looked happy and healthy. He was also smartly dressed. Max took him into the office.

"Well, Jack, how are you doing?"

"That's what I've come to say, sir. For once I was in the right place at the right time. They sent me a job near a place called Berkhampsted and I went for it. Farmer's a lovely guy, wanted someone to look after his new-fangled tractors, as he calls them, and the other machinery. I told him about my girl and daughter and immediately he wanted to see them. He met them, loved them, and – well, I've got a job. I've also got a little house. And a fair wage. And, just a fortnight ago, Jackie and I were married."

Max smiled. "I'm really, really pleased for you. And – I have to ask this, I suppose – are you keeping yourself out of trouble?"

Jack Barden grinned. "I reckon I'd still say 'yes' even if I wasn't! But yes, I am. I've got all I want now. But…"

Max thought he could smell trouble.

"I heard about Ada. What happened. Oh okay, I followed the case in the papers and learnt a lot more than I wanted to. I heard a dog had been shot but didn't connect it to you. To the Wilsons. But then – well – there's someone in Berko who…"

"Berko?" asked Max.

"Berkhampsted, sir. There's someone there I met when we were shopping. We popped into the Rising Sun and got chatting to this bloke who it turned out was just out of clink. I wanted to know…" He swallowed. "…what it was like in there. What… well, what I'd been saved from. Thanks to you.

"He talked about the bad times – to be honest there aren't too many good times inside. He told me about a man who came in when he was there and started throwing his weight about. Trouble was, there was a hard nut in there who was the *real* one to be scared of and he took an instant dislike to this chap.

"Turned out that the hard nut made it his business to find out about the bloke's case. It wasn't the drugs that he hated, or the violence that goes with them…" He smiled wryly at that recollection. "…it was that he was also done for threatening a child and killing his dog.

"Hard nut put it about and – well, newcomer isn't popular at all. They've had to segregate him because everyone gave him a hard time, then he threatened the wrong people with revenge. When he mentioned the dog I put two and two together."

He stopped for breath. Max wondered what was coming.

"On the farm, they train dogs to the gun. There was one, a black Labrador, who hated guns, would just sit down when there was a loud noise. They said eventually that she was no good and they'd have to give her away. I did some thinking. Said I knew a family who'd give her a good home. A really nice family." He swallowed.

"Look, sir. I've been lent the farmer's car so I could come down and try and see Mum, I've got the family in it as well as the dog. Can I bring her in? Would you look at her?"

"You've got Jackie and the baby in the car? Good heavens – bring them in. And the dog." He hesitated. "Shall we give them a shock in there? There's a few people you know…"

"I don't know if…"

"Come on, Jack. It's Christmas. They're mellow and full of bonhomie. And a thought – have you eaten? Any of you?"

He shook his head. "We called on Mum. She said it wouldn't be safe for me to go in. Her man was inside, he'd had a skinful and she wouldn't trust him with me. So I left. She still doesn't know about Jackie and Maisie."

"And you're famished."

"We're going straight back after this."

"Well, I think we should introduce the dog to them, and then you can come in, or be discovered out here. Then we'll give you a meal. Probably best in the kitchen as everyone else has eaten their fill. But let's get her introduced first."

Chat was still in progress in the living room. The door opened a crack. The next thing anyone knew was that a cautious, young black dog was finding her way around the room, sniffing at people and causing exclamations. Ruth was entranced.

"I'd better introduce her, hadn't I?" said Max who had quietly entered the room when they were engrossed with the dog. Jack, Jackie and Maisie were with him and attention switched to them.

Those who knew Jack gave him a sincere welcome. Soon they were amazed to hear that he had a wife and a two-year old daughter they knew nothing about. It took them at least a quarter of an hour to be told the story of the family. Then in his own, halting words, he told them about the dog.

There was a pause whilst the information was taken in.

"We've got to have her," said a quiet voice. Ruth. Owen just laid a hand on her shoulder, his way of showing agreement. He found he didn't trust himself to speak.

"It seems that settles that, then," said Max, quietly pleased that they would once again have a dog around the place. "And now, the Barden family haven't eaten today and the least we can do is to put that right. We'll be in the kitchen."

Barbara jumped up, as did Mary Decks. With Max, they vanished to help.

Owen looked back at Ruth. The dog was sitting with her head on her lap, looking up at her while she scratched the head gently, the eyes half closed in ecstasy.

"So the Mill has got a shared dog back again?" said Owen softly. "It's like having… having Ada's spirit back."

"She has the same look about her," said Ruth in a soothing voice. "I think she's a fixture now. If the Baker brothers don't mind."

"I'd take a guess that they won't," he said, sitting on the floor by her legs so that the dog was at his side.

To his surprise her other hand started stroking his hair, so he half closed his eyes too.

The end

Glossary

Included to explain some of the older or more obscure references made in the story for those who are not UK based or who weren't around in the 1960s. They are therefore unlucky enough not to have grown up with the music of the Beatles, to have to use common sense and self-preservation instead of relying on health and safety regulations, and to realise that not every incident can be legally blamed on someone else.

The Ark A pub on the west side of Newhaven harbour, in River Side, south of the swing bridge. It's still there.

The Coppers
A family of singers whose written and oral records of traditional songs reach back for centuries. They still live in Sussex and still sing the age-old songs in multi-part harmony.

The Downs
The South Downs are an enigma. Low, rolling and of no interest to a mountaineer, they worm their way into most people's affections without notice. To a Sussex man they say "home". They are the remnant of a massive dome of chalk dome which stretched from east Hampshire to mid-east Sussex, and from the south coast to Surrey (where their equivalent is, to state the obvious, the North Downs).

Dripping Pan
Lewes FC's ground since Victorian times, just west of the Boys' Grammar School (now Mid-Sussex College VIth Form). So called because of the raised banks that surround it.

Emmets Sussex for ants. Often applied to tourists in the bigger towns where they flocked in their dark-clad hundreds.

Flying Fish
A small pub at the south side of Denton Road at the foot of Mount Pleasant. It's still there.

Harveys The brewery building itself is often referred to as Lewes Cathedral. For details, refer to the Internet.

Hawth Hill (Buckle By-pass)
The hill between Seaford and Bishopstone. Before a direct road was cut through it in 1963-4 all traffic heading east turned right to the coast and passed the Buckle Inn to get to the town. When the sea broke over the road its landlord had to operate a switch to turn on a

'Road Closed' sign at the bottom of Hawth Hill. Buses were affected too: Pool Valley bus station in Brighton often had chalk boards saying "Buckle closed" and drivers knew what to do. All traffic had to turn left at the hill and use a narrow circuitous route into town.

Home Bottom unofficial tea brewing place

OS map reference 464040. With apologies to the Monningtons, whose land it is.

The Hope Inn

Now the southernmost building on Newhaven's West Side, The Hope is still a traditional, unspoilt pub.

King Alfred

Opened as a wartime Navy training centre as soon as built, it housed an indoor, salt-water, just-heated, swimming pool almost adjacent to the beach in Hove. There were two pools; the Major with its high diving board and the Minor used for beginners and groups. The AMF Ten Pin Bowling opened about 1960 and is still operating.

"Lads of Sussex-by-the-Sea"

Sung to the tune of *Old King Cole* this was a favourite in the 16th Hove Scouts – at least when the leaders weren't listening. Here's a sample verse –

Old King Cole was a merry old soul and a merry old soul was he.
He called for his wife in the middle of the night and he called for his butchers three.
"Wave your chopper in the air" sang the butchers.
Merry merry men are we,
There's none so fair as can compare with the lads of Sussex-by-the Sea.
How's tour father? All right. How's your mother? She's tight. How's your sister? She might.
Old King Cole...

It is a cumulative song, so by the end there was very little left to the imagination.

Lewes Grammar Schools

The Priory School was established in the mists of time, but well before the 1960s it had divided into the Lewes County Grammar Schools, one for boys and one for girls. On separate campuses, naturally. Nowadays the two are together as the Priory School, a normal, mixed Comprehensive.

Mac   Mackintosh coat, actually gabardine or something like it. It's a form of semi-waterproof, belted knee length coat usually dark blue in colour, the rain protector of choice for most schools in the 1950s – 1970s.

Money   £1 in 1963 was the equivalent of about £20.34 in 2018. The value of the 1914 sovereigns in 1963 would have been £600, or over £12,000 in 2018 values.
            The average weekly wage for men in 1966 was £23.50 and for women was £12.00 (equivalent to £433 and £221 respectively in 2018).
            A phone call from a phone box (there were no mobiles!) cost 4d, or 1.67 pence.
            An old penny was written 1d. The 'd' is the initial of 'denarius' a Latin coin from which the idea of the penny was derived.

Newhaven Marine Station
            Newhaven boasts three stations, not bad for a small town. Newhaven Town lies to the east of the river by the main road (A259). Newhaven Harbour is about half a mile south of it. Newhaven Marine was the station for the Ferry in a time when the majority of travellers chose rail. By 2018 it was all but derelict, yet still used once daily by an empty train to provide an excuse to keep it open.

Newhaven Swing Bridge
            To every local's dismay the town still has a swing bridge that carries the A259 over the river Ouse. It replaced the previous one in 1974. That one had railway tracks along it, taking goods from the East Quay to the West. Google "Our Newhaven" for photographs.

Nippy   Waitress in a Lyons Corner House. Lyons Corner houses were a chain of cafés around London, often with different styles of décor on each floor. They ran from 1909-1977.

Peanuts A cartoon by Charles Schultz which was a gentle comment on human attitudes Its characters were a group of 5-7 year old children, a dog and a bird. Found in the Daily Sketch which stopped publication in 1971.

Ritz Cinema and shops
            The cinema's doors were on the junction of Pelham Road and Dane Road. Small shop units occupied much of the rest of its exterior. It's since been demolished and a busy supermarket is in its place.

Royal Oak, Piddinghoe
            A large pub, quite well patronised. Suffered a major fire in 1992, was repaired, but is now a private house.

Scobie   There was indeed an old man, a dock worker who had a Jack Russell. And Scobie could indeed perform the trick of throwing 6" nails as if they were darts, into the dartboard, though it may not have happened in The Buckle. The recollection is from Joe Templeman (thanks!); Scobie's real name is not recorded.

Sleepers' Hole

A semi-circular bay on the west side of Newhaven Harbour where railway sleepers were soaked before preservation. It's now the site of the Marina, just down from the RNLI station.

Southdown

A large Sussex bus and coach company with depots as far flung as Portsmouth and Eastbourne. The author worked for them from 1968-85 on the coaching side, including a year in the hire department in Eastbourne in 1969.

'Sussex wunt be druv' (Sussex declines to be driven)

W. Victor Cook was a novelist and journalist in West Sussex. He wrote this poem in 1914 and it was soon adopted by his County:

Some folks as come to Sussex,
They reckons as they knows –
A durn sight better what to do
Than simple folks, like me and you,
Could possibly suppose.

But them as comes to Sussex,
They mustn't push and shove,
For Sussex will be Sussex,
An' Sussex wunt be druv!

Mus Wilfred come to Sussex,
Us heaved a stone at he,
Because he reckoned he could teach
Our Sussex fishers how to reach
The fishes in the sea.

But when he dwelt among us,
Us gave un land and luv,
For Sussex will be Sussex,
An' Sussex wunt be druv!

All folks as come to Sussex
Must follow Sussex ways –
And when they've larned to know us well,
There's no place else they'll wish to dwell

In all their blessed days –

There ent no place like Sussex,
Until ye goos above,
For Sussex will be Sussex,
An' Sussex wunt be druv.

Sweet Bells (carol)

Many links to the tune are available on the internet.

Sussex dialect

As far as I know it had only just started fading away in the 1960s as a result of the influence of incomers – like the Wilsons.. Because it can be very tedious to read your way through phonetic dialect spelling, I've used it as little as I could get away with whilst showing it was still around. If you're interested, try *Sussex As She Wus Spoke* by Tony Wales, or search Google for *Sussex dialect*.

TCP

A proprietary liquid antiseptic often used neat on minor wounds despite the makers' instruction that it should be diluted.

Thruppeny (threepenny) bit

A coin worth three old pence – 3d, or a quarter of a shilling, or $1/80^{th}$ of £1. It's worth 1.25p in decimal currency. It was distinctive in being twelve sided and was brass coloured (actually a mix of nickel and brass)

Tide Mills

The reality is that the Mill was first built shortly after 1761 when its enabling Act was passed. Sold to Messrs Barton and Catt in 1795, William Catt arrived there in 1801 aged 26. He developed the mill and surroundings so that around 1850 there was accommodation for around 100 people. At its zenith there were 16 pairs of millstones working there.

His son George Catt succeeded William in 1853. The devastating flood of 1875 demolished the windmill on top of the Mill and washed salt-tainted shingle into the mill ponds. Railways provided cheap transport to steam driven mills. Trade at Tide Mills diminished and ceased in 1883.

At various points there have been a WWI aircraft hangar, a holiday camp, a racehorse hospital, and a Chailey Heritage hospital nearby.

The cottages were occupied until the start of WWII and then demolished. The ruins are now part of a nature reserve.

More information from both Seaford and Newhaven Museums.

Toad-in-the-Hole

      Pub game of Sussex. Usually the 'table' is really an 18in square small cupboard with a drawer in it. Also usually it slopes forward slightly, is covered with lead sheet, and stands about 2ft 6in off the floor. In the centre of the lead is a hole. They are all different! Four 'toads' (brass coins) are thrown; if one goes in the hole the score is 2, if one lands on the table without touching the back up-stand it's 1. Scoring starts at 31 and the first player to reach zero wins that "leg".

Wavy Navy

      From WWI until 1952 the uniform sleeve rings worn by Royal Naval Volunteer Reserve officers had two interlocking stripes. They had a distinctive wavy pattern, so passing the name 'Wavy Navy' to the RNVR.

Wolseley A marque of car of the BMC group (by 1963). British Motor Corporation became British Leyland in 1969.

Talk!

Any author, apart from those who have achieved sales in the thousands, wants to know what readers think of their work. Sometimes they just want confirmation that what they have offered is good. Sometimes they want to hear comments about what works, what doesn't and where improvements can be made in future stories – or even in future editions of the current one.

I want the latter. Please.

Whether you contact me direct by email, on the blog, on Facebook, Instagram, or Twitter, or even by sending a pigeon, I really value your comments (You'll have to clean up after the pigeon, though).

Email: richard@rw2.co.uk
Facebook: Richard Wright
Instagram: harbroeuk
Twitter: @harbroeuk
Pigeon: Coo coooo, Coo. Coo coo.

By the same Author -

Loft Island

Set on the Salcombe (Devon) Estuary in the 1950s. Rescued from a flood, Mary (11) comes to live with the father and 13 year old son who saved her; her parents and brother were drowned. The land they farmed is now an island. Practical and emotional help comes sometimes from unlikely sources. They face a variety of attitudes from authorities and friends.

The long established friendship between the children develops slowly,, innocently, with neither of them realising. Gradually life becomes stable, only to be ripped apart again.

A continuation of the story will be published in 2020, to be called
The Island and The Town

The Suspects

A light-hearted story with spikes. Faced with little to do over the summer, six mid-teen mates camp illegally. Evicted back to their home town, they soon find they have to return to camp to keep out of the way. A dog, a Dutch recluse, a town gang of adults, parents, maps and a hospital all play their part. There are brambles, nettles, blackthorns, wild swimming, self-sufficiency, fires, friendships and of course the dog. And those truffles…

Printed in Poland
by Amazon Fulfillment
Poland Sp. z o.o., Wrocław

60628376R00208